# THE KANSAS RELAYS

## TRACK AND FIELD TRADITION IN THE HEARTLAND

Joe D. Schrag

ADINA PUBLISHING

ISBN-10: 0-9915086-0-2 (print)
ISBN-13: 978-0-9915086-0-0 (print)

The cover photograph is reprinted courtesy of Kansas Athletics, Inc. It shows University of Kansas athlete Jonathan Fuller high jumping at the 2012 Kansas Relays with the iconic Campanile Hill, and the beautiful KU campus and Memorial Stadium in the background.

The back cover photograph is reprinted courtesy of Spencer Research Library, University of Kansas Libraries. It is a ticket from the Saturday, April 22, 1967 competition at the Kansas Relays -- the day that Jim Ryun ran a 3:54.7 mile to set the meet record that still stands. Cost was only $3 to see that bit of history.

Permission notices for photographs reprinted in this book can be found on pages xxxiii-xxxv.

**Editor:** Myles Schrag
**Assistant Editor:** Nancy Schrag
**Graphic Designer/Graphic Artist/Cover Designer:** Nancy Rasmus

Proudly printed in the USA by The Covington Group, Kansas City, Mo.

10 9 8 7 6 5 4 3 2 1

**Publisher:** Adina Publishing
**Website:** www.AdinaPublishing.com

Address:
**Adina Publishing**
P.O. Box 791
Flagstaff, AZ 86002
928-679-5060
e-mail: Myles.Schrag@adinapublishing.com

# Praise for
# *The Kansas Relays*

" The Kansas Relays' significance as a historical account, the development of
its rich culture and its influence in developing track and field
as a dominant force in the world are all well-displayed. "

**Coach Joe Vigil**
Olympic Distance Coach, 1988, 2008
National and International Clinician

" For so many, the Kansas Relays was their first introduction to a university campus,
KU or elite track and field. This book is an important personal history for over
100,000 athletes who for almost a century through the Kansas Relays saw
the very best that our school and our sport have to offer. "

**Tim Weaver,**
KU Relays meet director, 2000-2006

" Joe takes me back and reminds me of the impact this great event has had on
track and field both nationally and internationally. Growing up in Kansas, I can
remember the fantastic stories my dad and his friend told about the Relays.
Joe brings all the moments back in vivid overwhelming color! "

**Tom Hays,**
KU vertical jumps coach, 2004-present

" If I miss the Kansas Relays, I have a broken leg or I'm dead. "

**Scott Huffman,**
KU alumnus and 1996 Olympic pole vaulter

" KU was my favorite relays to go to. If I was going to break any records, I wanted to be at KU or nationals. Joe captures many special moments in this book. It was an exciting time whether freezing cold or sunshine, truly a great event. Readers may be surprised at the number of quality athletes whose marks and stories are inside Joe's book. "

**Pinkie Suggs,**
Kansas State alumna, 12-time KU Relays discus and shot put champion in high school and open divisions

" When I vaulted, the Kansas Relays was always my favorite meet of the year! I broke my first high school outdoor record my junior year, vaulted my highest ever at the time in collegiate competition, and set one of my American records (19 feet, 4 ¾ inches), all at the Kansas Relays. Being inducted into the Hall of Fame was an amazing bonus. I have so many great memories from those Relays. It is wonderful that the history of this amazing event is being put into print! "

**Joe Dial,**
Three-time KU Relays Most Outstanding Performer,
KU Relays record holder in the pole vault for both high school and open divisions

" The Kansas Relays played a big part in my development as an athlete. This book provides an excellent opportunity to learn about the history of the Kansas Relays and its traditions. "

**Leo Manzano,**
Two-time 800m high school champ at KU Relays, 2012 Olympic silver medalist in the 1500m

" The Kansas Relays jump-started my professional career in 2003. I was a kid running in a big setting; when I won, it gave me confidence to believe I could do this. No matter how far I may go or how many championships or Olympic medals I may win, I will always remember where it began, and that's why I love coming to the Kansas Relays. The Kansas Relays is a great book. I'm impressed with the research and the way Joe has presented the information in an exciting way. "

**Bershawn "Batman" Jackson**
2008 Olympic bronze medalist, seven-time KU Relays 440m hurdle champion

" The Kansas Relays is an enduring perennial spring-time bloom in the otherwise shrinking track and field landscape. I'm grateful that such a tradition still exists in the sport that I love and that with Joe's book we all still have the opportunity to experience a taste of how track and field was in the past and could potentially be in the United States. "

**Amy Acuff,**
Five-time Olympian, high jump

# Table of Contents

## PART I    TRADITION

# PART II MOMENTS

# PART III ACTION

# Meet Director's Foreword

## Milan Donley

### *Athletics.*

This is what the rest of the world calls our sport of track and field: *athletics*. Since the first conversation between Dr. John Outland and Dr. Forrest C. "Phog" Allen laid the groundwork for the first Kansas Relays in 1923 all the way to the latest edition, the meet has been one of America's signature events in athletics.

Milan Donley

Every Relays takes on a life of its own. It runs on time; it runs late ... it rains; it's hot ... records are set; medals and trophies are won; new events – and occasionally a new venue -- are added ... All of this put in motion by a cast and crew of thousands, each with a story to tell. For any event to survive the test of time, its organizers must embrace change. Change is the constant of any major sporting event, and the Kansas Relays has seen its fair share of it over 86 years. Fortunately, the changes have been guided by some pretty creative guys. Phog Allen, Bill Easton, Bob Timmons and Tim Weaver, to name a few. Each brought his own individual ideas in shaping the meet to maintain an important role in the sport of athletics.

In this first-ever book devoted to the history of the Kansas Relays, Joe Schrag has chronicled those changes, as well as many memorable individuals, traditions and moments that have shaped the meet. He captures the excitement of track and field – of athletics – as someone who has experienced it first-hand every April in Lawrence for the past 60 years, and as a researcher who wants to ensure that the nation's third-oldest annual collegiate track spectacular is remembered.

The feature of any sporting event is the athletes, but an event like the Kansas Relays cannot operate without multitudes of officials and volunteers. Behind the scenes is a tremendous team of people who are committed to its success. These individuals take time off from work and home duties to spend endless hours in heat, rain and cold each year to be part of our event. These certified officials bring decades of experience working events ranging from youth meets to Olympic Trials, and even a few who have officiated at the highest pinnacle of athletics – the Olympic Games. Careful selection of these officials ensures all athletes will be provided honest and fair competition, a reputation the Kansas Relays has held for decades with coaches and contestants from the high school, collegiate and professional levels. Volunteers of all ages have been the backbone of the Relays for decades, coming from in town, across the state, and even farther away, to contribute their time and demonstrate their love for this event, and athletics in general.

The most important concept of the Kansas Relays has always been opportunity. The opportunity for fans to watch high school, collegiate and professional track and field athletes come together for four days to compete against the best in the sport. The opportunity to travel to Lawrence to compete at the Relays has developed into a ritual carried over from family generations. Parents and grandparents share stories and accounts of the excitement and anticipation felt in preparing to race, jump and throw in the same venue where the likes of Glenn Cunningham, Al Oerter, Harrison Dillard, Kenny Harrison, Allyson Felix and many others brought their best efforts. The Kansas Relays will continue to provide an opportunity to compete, watch and cheer great athletes in a great sport. If you have ever been in Memorial Stadium in April as an athlete, coach, official or spectator, then you too have a story.

As you read the tales, view the photos, and peruse the tables and appendixes in this book, you may recall memories you once experienced. Read about the moments, action and innovations through the years in Joe's words as he shares this athletics tradition in the heartland … the Kansas Relays.

**Milan Donley**
Kansas Relays Meet Director

# Foreword

## Scott Huffman

I first competed in the Kansas Relays as a high school senior in 1983, the year the Soviets came to town. It was the height of the Cold War, and only a month earlier President Ronald Reagan had given his "Star Wars" missile defense speech to the nation, which he claimed would protect the United States and allies from Soviet nuclear attack. The Soviets were greatly angered and stated that Reagan's speech would "open a new phase in the arms race." Against this backdrop Lawrence, Kan., residents Bob Swan and Mark Scott somehow diplomatically maneuvered to bring an entire team of Soviet athletes to town to compete in the Kansas Relays. The following year the USSR would repay the USA for its boycott of the 1980 Olympics in Moscow by boycotting the 1984 Los Angeles Olympics. This was no small deal that these athletes were coming to the Kansas Relays. And though athletics was far more important to me than politics at the time, I knew this was a very big deal.

My idol, American record holder Jeff Buckingham, was competing against the powerful Soviet pole vaulters. Jeff only stood 5 feet, 8 inches, but he was a great technician and an incredibly fierce competitor. I watched with awe as Americans Buckingham, Steve Stubblefield and Doug Lytle did battle, matching each height cleared by the Soviets. In the end, Russian vaulter Alexander Krupsky soared 18 feet, 4 inches for the win. Lytle

placed second, also clearing 18-4. It was the first time I'd seen an 18-foot clearance in the pole vault. I was astounded. I couldn't imagine ever jumping that high.

Two years later, as a redshirt freshman at KU, I competed in my second Kansas Relays. It was the first Relays in which I proudly wore the hot pink and baby blue KU track uniform. It was also the day I did the "Huffman Roll" for the first time. A beautiful sunlit day in Memorial Stadium, the bar rested at 18 feet, ½ inch, a height I'd never attempted in competition. And that's when it happened. Instead of peaking in the normal "pike" position while clearing the crossbar, I suddenly and inexplicably dropped one leg completely under the bar and shot the other leg up over it, straddling the bar much like an old western-roll high jumper. As my body began to clear the bar, I somehow executed a full 360-degree spin as my chest just barely brushed the bar off the pegs, my body and the bar falling towards the landing pit. It was a very close miss.

As I landed I laughed at the odd jump. So did my KU vault coach, Rick Attig. Never before had we seen a pole vaulter attempt to clear a bar with such a ridiculous technique.

**Scott Huffman, preparing his approach while a member of the Kansas track and field team.**

We had no idea that a few weeks later at the Big 8 Outdoor Championships the roll would reappear suddenly in a clearance over 18-5 ½", setting a new NCAA freshman record. From then on the roll became part of my vault. This strange, unique technique lives on in perpetuity on YouTube, where I can be seen clearing an American record of 19-7 in 1994, and clearing bars in the 1996 Olympics. Strangely enough, people still seem to remember me for the "roll." And it began at the Kansas Relays that day in 1985.

I grew up hearing stories about Wilt Chamberlain competing at the Relays from my dad, Galen Huffman, a former Missouri state record holder in the pole vault. One year Dad was jumping at the Relays when Wilt arrived to compete. Dad told of Wilt pulling up right next to the stadium in a red convertible and parking in a non-designated spot conveniently located very near to the track entrance. Of course nobody said anything about where Wilt parked his car. He was, after all, Wilt Chamberlain.

I'd also heard numerous stories of the days when Memorial Stadium was packed full of fans wanting to see the great Jim Ryun run the mile. But I never knew the details behind stories like this. The historical details in this book give me a far greater understanding of what it must have been like to see Chamberlain and Ryun, and other legends like Santee and Oerter, compete at the Relays. The pages of this book contain more than just the history of the Kansas Relays. They also provide a rich narrative on some important history of the evolution of track and field in America.

I was surprised to learn that football coach John Outland (of Outland Trophy fame) was the original visionary of the Kansas Relays. Nor did I know that in 1921, none other than Phog Allen, while serving as KU's athletic director, insisted that a track be included in the new football stadium that was under construction.

A little over three decades after the completion of Memorial Stadium, Joe Schrag competed in his first Kansas Relays in 1954 and has been there every year since in one capacity or another. He coached many outstanding athletes, like my good friend and KU teammate Sharrieff Hazim, who under Coach Schrag's tutelage cleared 7-2 in the high jump as a high schooler at perennial track and field power Topeka West.

Among the other many roles Joe has held over six decades, Joe is obviously also a fan. That is evident in the pages of this book. Joe says one of his most prized possessions is the Kansas Relays medal he won as a high school miler. With this book, Joe has given all of us another prized possession. This wonderful book captures the history, tradition and memories of 86 years of the Kansas Relays at Memorial Stadium.

So now we look forward to the next chapter of the Kansas Relays. To continue KU's rich athletic tradition, the reality is that to be economically competitive is to be athletically competitive. Nostalgia and tradition can't pay the bills for Olympic sports like track and field. It's a tremendous testament to the rich history of the Kansas Relays that Memorial Stadium was the last school in the Big 12 conference to keep a track inside its football stadium. Now it's time to give the track program its own dedicated facility with a modern venue more in line with the other elite track and field programs in America.

Last year we celebrated the 86th edition of the Kansas Relays. I wonder what the next 86 will be like. I know one thing: I'm going to be a part of as many of them as I can. I'm betting Joe Schrag will too.

## ROCK CHALK JAYHAWK!

**Scott Huffman**
1996 Olympian
Three-Time USA Champion
Former American Record holder, pole vault (19 feet, 7 inches)

# Preface

I spent most of July 2013 in the Spencer Research Library on the campus of the University of Kansas, where a very friendly and helpful staff assisted me in the pursuit of information pertinent to this book. To get there, I trekked up the Campanile Hill from my parking spot in the east lot of Memorial Stadium, lugging a computer and heavy briefcase up the foreboding hill. Aside from the joy of reliving the Kansas Relays through articles and photos, I was impressed anew every day as I emerged from the artificial light of the building's interior to the brilliant splendor of Memorial Stadium, basking in the sunshine and shadows of the late afternoon. No photo could adequately replicate that view, and I could not help but wish that that red oval would always circle the lush green of the football field. Alas, it will not. What is left are the memories of glories past and the hope of a glorious Relays rebirth in another place. Therein lies the essence of this book.

I have been involved with the Relays in various capacities for 60 years come April 2014. Let me give you a resumé of that involvement:

## Athlete

My love affair with the Kansas Relays began in 1954 when, as a skinny farm boy from Norwich, Kan., I came to Lawrence and KU for the first time in my life. I remember staying with my teammates and athletes from other schools in barracks underneath the east stadium. The next day I would run a mile on the very same six-lane cinder track that might possibly be the site where Wes Santee would run the first sub-four minute mile in human history, an ongoing drama that would play itself out in that and upcoming years. It captured my attention to the point that I have devoted a chapter in this book to it.

As a high school senior in 1957, I won the slow section of the small-school classification in the mile run. In my old age I forget a lot of things, but I distinctly remember my brother Myron and his Bethel (Kan.) College teammates cheering for me from about 12 rows up in the southeast corner of the stadium, urging me to step it up on the backstretch. The resultant victory provided me with one of my most prized possessions, a Kansas Relays medal. The following year big-school and little-school classes were combined, and rather than occurring only on Friday, high school events were interspersed with collegiate and open events on Saturday. If there had been only one division rather than Class A and Class B in 1957, I would not have my medal because I would have been far outclassed by emerging legends such as Billy Mills, Bill Dotson, and Archie San Romani, Jr., among others. As a Bethel College trackster, I competed at the Relays, but never with distinction.

## Spectator

In 1962, the year after my college graduation and the year before my involvement as a coach, I was merely a spectator. To those who may never have been to the Relays, I recommend it as a wonderful way to spend a week in April.

## Coach

My first year as a coach at the Relays came in 1963. I began as an assistant at Topeka West (Kan.) High School to Gene Smith, who put me in charge of the distance runners since I was head cross country coach. I took over as head track and field coach in 1972 and continued in that position until my retirement in 2003. Over the years, I experienced with my athletes the thrill of victory and the agony of defeat. I watched with pride the individual victories of Mark Pickens, Winston Tidwell, and Sharrieff and Harun Hazim. Tidwell and Sharrieff Hazim were both record holders for a time. Tidwell's 800-meter record was broken by future Olympian Leo Manzano. The back-to-back 1600-meter-relay victories in 1980 and 1981 and the back-to-back two-mile relays in 1993 and 1994 were especially satisfying.

But so were the near misses, like the distance medley relay in 1975 that broke the existing record only to lose the race to Shawnee Mission (Kan.) South. Or the time when Sharrieff Hazim thought he had the triple jump record only to discover, when the steel tape was brought out to verify, that the measuring rail was six inches off. Then there was the despondent Jeff Shelar, apologizing for not winning the mile run in 1984, not realizing his quality opponent was future Arkansas star Joe Falcon. There are dozens of stories to tell, but you get the idea.

Among the most rewarding features of my coaching years were the many coaching friendships I developed. Especially in the early years, great

high school coaches like Bob Timmons, Merlin Gish, Orlis Cox, Francis Swaim, and "Heavy" Irwin, among others, treated me like an equal when I wasn't. Over the years, I have been blessed with lifelong friends, compliments of the Kansas Relays. The Relays format fosters a wonderful atmosphere for coaches. There are no points to quibble over so there is no reason to wish for anything except good fortune for everyone, including your competitors. As a coach of many years, my advice for Relays coaches is to relax and enjoy. The value of the Relays experience is not tied to winning or losing nearly as much as the thrill of participating in one of the greatest sporting events in the Midwest.

This carved Jayhawk was a gift from my coaching mentor and friend, Merlin Gish.

## Referee

In 1977, I was chosen to be the honorary high school referee, a position coveted by every high school coach. What a thrill it was to share the referee duties with Mel Brodt of Bowling Green (Ohio), Fred Beile of Doane (Neb.) Colllege, Terry Masterson of Hutchinson (Kan.) Community College, and Chris Murray of Iowa State. In 2003 Chris Wintering wrote an article about the meet referees for *The University Daily Kansan.* "Honorary referees have been named since the first Kansas Relays in 1923. ... ," he wrote. "The Kansas Relays will be held April 16 to 19. Past referees include Knute Rockne, Glenn Cunningham, Bill Easton, Joe Schrag, Steve Miller, and Al Oerter."

I had to chuckle and ask myself, how did I come to be listed with that group of icons? At any rate, I would never have been able to win a watch as an athlete. Maybe that's why I cherish so much the watch I was given as a referee, even though it has never kept accurate time.

## Committee Number One

Because of increased participation in the Relays, it became necessary to establish standards to reduce the field to manageable numbers. I won't say it was commonplace, but more frequently than desired, athletes were admitted based on bogus times. On one such occasion when my runner was supplanted by another who was entered under a time I knew he had never run, I confronted the coach, whom I had always respected. His reply was, "I learned from [another coach I had respected] that there is an art to knowing how much to fudge to get a guy in." To me, "fudging" and "lying" were synonyms.

Perhaps because my protests were loudest, in 1986 KU coach Bob Timmons put me in charge of a committee of my peers from around the state to scrutinize entries and weed out the fabrications. In those early years of the committee, after a few phone calls questioning where such and such a mark was accomplished, the situation improved considerably. Nowadays, with electronic entries and internet access to meet results from virtually everywhere, such detailed scrutiny is no longer necessary, but the committee still exists to help verify entries.

## Committee Number Two

The Student Relays Committee has contributed mightily over the years. Another committee called the Greater Relays Committee, consisting of Relays management, coaches, starters, announcers, alumni and volunteers has also made significant contributions to the running of the Relays. Meet director Tim Weaver asked me to join this group in 2003. I was excited to do so.

## Volunteer

Prior to Milan Donley's first Relays as meet director in 2007, he called two retired coaches, Rich Ludwig and me, into his office to give us a volunteer opportunity. Our task would be to make the Relays run as smoothly as possible. In other words, do the little things that often get overlooked, such as making sure results boards are up, and that the competition sites are ready to go with chairs and indicator boards. We were to be available to run errands, check hurdles, and do any other task that improves the efficiency of the meet. I was flattered to be asked and eager to accept. What could be better than an all-access pass to the Relays, to be in the same general area as wide-eyed high schoolers and seasoned professionals? Rich has since gone on to be a Relays starter, and another retired coach, Steve Sell, has capably replaced him.

## Kansas Relays Hall of Fame

April 21, 2007, was a glorious day for me. I was inducted into the Kansas Relays Hall of Fame. Others to join me that night were Dr. Wayne Osness, Joe Dial and Dr. Forrest C. "Phog" Allen. The list of those preceding me and those inducted after me are shown in Appendix D of this book. It is a staggering display of accomplishment. All, except myself, are known not only nationally, but internationally, while I am basically unknown outside of Kansas or even Topeka. As the only high school coach in the Hall, I consider myself to be representative of the hundreds of dedicated high school coaches who have brought their charges to the Relays for one of the most exhilarating experiences of their young lives. I am under no illusion that I was more deserving than others who could have been chosen as that representative.

## Author

With the news that the Kansas Relays would leave Memorial Stadium after the 2013 Relays, my son Myles urged me to do what I had long considered but was reticent to act upon: write a book about the Relays. It seemed the perfect time to look both back and ahead in regard to the Relays experience. As an acquisitions editor for Human Kinetics Publishers and an experienced author of two books of his own, he had the expertise necessary to prepare a book for publication. Without that knowledge, this book had no chance for success.

My regret is that, as long as this book is, there is far more left out than included. Eighty-six years is a lot of material. Choosing what to include and what to leave out was agonizing. My other regret is that thousands of people who have made the Relays relevant are not included. Without them, the elites would not have had their day in the sun – or rain, as is often the case. For every elite athlete who has graced the Relays, there are dozens who have benefitted from participation with no pretense of greatness. Each has a story to tell and they, while not specifically named, are the real heroes of this book. The facilities staff, the media relations, volunteers and office staff are mentioned only here, but their contributions have been invaluable.

And so, another chapter of the Kansas Relays has come to a close. My research has led me down a nostalgic lane I will forever be grateful for, and it is no secret that I am saddened by the vacating of a venue which has given me such great pleasure. Still, I cannot deny the excitement presented by the challenges and opportunities of a new beginning. I say loud and clear,

### ROCK CHALK, JAYHAWK PARK!

**Joe Schrag**
Topeka, Kan.
February 2014

# Acknowledgments

Before becoming an aspiring author, I never knew how many people it would take to write a book, especially non-fiction. For sure, many have left their fingerprints on this one. The following are just a few who deserve to be thanked for it.

My thanks start with my family. When I was coaching, I always told my assistants and athletes that family should come first. Because of the demands of the profession, there was always an inherent hypocrisy in that statement, because I knew that I would be taking time away from those I most cared about. Thus it was that I approached this endeavor with a bit of trepidation, knowing that it would impact traveling, my wife Nancy's favorite hobby. Nevertheless, she encouraged me. Before either of us knew it, she immersed herself into the project with the same fervor I had. Her various skills, such as proofing my text and connecting with people, filled gaps left by my incompetence in certain areas. She was effusive in her praise, thus contributing to my motivation; and relentless in her criticism, thus assuring a greater accuracy. Her positive contribution to this book cannot be overstated.

The words, "I'll help you with it," uttered by my son Myles, were enough to make me undertake this project. As an acquisitions editor for Human Kinetics, he lives in a world of pdfs, fonts, ISBNs, bar codes and copyrights; and has himself been the author of a couple of books. Only the skills he possessed made it possible for this book to ripen to fruition. It is both humbling and exhilarating when the son becomes the mentor to the father.

Speaking of family, Myles' wife Shelley and daughters Zoe and Ava have supported this project throughout, even though it has been enormously time-consuming. Despite the fact that time used is irreplaceable, they have graciously and unselfishly yielded to the demands of the project.

Thanks to the encouragement from my daughter, Monica. As the distance coach for Topeka High School, Coach Schrag knows, like her dad, the anticipation of waiting for the Sunday night Kansas Relays entry lists and the joy of watching her runners compete on one of the Midwest's most prestigious stages.

After family, thanks are due, in no particular order, to all the other entities that have made this book possible. Thanks to Relays meet director Milan Donley. In the fragile moments when an idea begins to germinate and an unkind word could render it barren, he provided support and encouragement instead. Assistant Relays meet director Josh Williamson went out of his way on numerous occasions to provide services and information, and seemed to share our enthusiasm for this venture. Administrative Assistant Debbie Luman and coach Stanley Redwine and his staff never left a question unanswered.

Another great source of information and encouragement came from former Relays meet director Tim Weaver. He generously provided many constructive comments and unselfishly made materials from his personal collection available.

Thanks to the KU Athletic Department for allowing access to photos that complemented perfectly the Spencer Research Library photos.

The Spencer Research Library and those who staff it are a true campus treasure. Nancy, Myles and I were always treated with the utmost courtesy and respect, even though we might have been a pain in the neck. To our good fortune, our forays into the Marilyn Stokstad Reading Room allowed us to interact with this dedicated group of staffers: Rebecca Schulte, University archivist; Letha Johnson, assistant archivist; Kathy Lafferty, library reader services; as well as Toni Bressler, reader services operations manager; Karen Cook, special collections; Caitlin Donnelly, public services; Deborah Dandridge, field archivist; Elspeth Healey, special collections; Sheryl Williams, curator of collections; and very cooperative student assistants.

Thanks to Paul Vander Tuig, KU trademark licensing director, for being flexible and enthusiastic in helping us work through the details of intellectual property.

Thanks to Candace Dunback, Director of Traditions, for helping us make important contacts and for being an encyclopedia of KU athletic history knowledge. Careful readers will also notice her photo and name in Chapter 13, a testament to her multi-event athletic prowess. Abbi Huderle, manager of the Booth Family Hall of Athletics, helped facilitate these contacts and find photos.

We cannot be too effusive in our praise for Nancy Rasmus, our graphic designer and graphic artist who made this book visually appealing in a way we could never dream of, and was flexible enough to work through our constant requests for changes with a positive attitude and professional results.

Thanks should be extended to Mark McCombs and his crew at The Covington Group that printed the book and allowed us to reach a final product in the time frame we needed it.

To Lawrence photographer Mike Yoder, we express thanks for his willingness to meet with us, to offer advice and to allow us to be the benefactors of his photographic skills.

When I asked Scott Huffman to write a Foreword for this book, I was thrilled by his enthusiastic response. Given the diligence and energy he put into the effort, it's easy to see how he could become an Olympic pole vaulter and an American record holder.

Many thanks go to those who helped track down photos and helped identify people in them: Hilary Winter, University of Nebraska Assistant Media Relations Director; Anthony Meier, Kansas State University Athletics Communications Graduate Assistant; David Johnston, Director of Internet Services & Marketing at the KU Alumni Association; and Mark Lentz, Assistant Executive Director at the Kansas State High School Activities Association.

Many people were valuable sources in trying to locate specific bits of information, provide verification on facts and offer their time or content for no reason other than helping to make this a better project: Mark Dyreson, Penn State University sport historian, for sharing his insights and previous research on the Tarahumara experience and ultra-running craze of the 1920s; Jan Todd and members of her staff at the H.J. Lutcher Stark Center for Physical Culture and Sports at the University of Texas at Austin (home of another prominent Memorial Stadium); Gregg Ireland, publisher of the *Topeka Capital Journal* for generously letting us share for another generation of readers the late Pete Goering's column on Cliff Cushman's letter to his hometown. Being able to share that column in its entirety was a must for Chapter 6, and I am grateful that Gregg saw it the same way. Also, Dean

Brittenham and Bob Elwood for their attempts to track down an elusive Cornhusker athlete.

A special thanks goes to those who read portions of the book during the development stage and voiced support for the project and enthusiasm for the KU Relays: Bob Anderson, Joe Dial, Tom Hays, Bershawn Jackson, Leo Manzano, Jim Ryun, Pinkie Suggs, Joe Vigil. You can find some of their comments at the front of the book on pages iii-iv. Their praise is at first humbling, given their respective lifetimes worth of accomplishments on and off the track. But beyond that, their praise is affirming toward the project. I had no doubt that telling the history of the KU Relays was a worthy endeavor for a book. But for this varied group of track and field "lifers" to instantly recall Memorial Stadium memories and get excited about seeing the finished product was proof positive that my hunch was right.

I sincerely hope readers take away from this book my appreciation for the many volunteers and behind-the-scenes efforts that make the KU Relays happen each year. But just in case, I want to state here that those nameless but essential masses have my utmost respect.

To the anonymous policeman who gave me a parking ticket on the first day of my research at Spencer, thank you for giving me an opportunity to extol the competence you bring to your profession. Now, please go buy a book to mitigate the expense of the $25.00 fine.

And so, to all mentioned and to those who have inadvertently been omitted, I send a huge thank you for your contributions. It is customary for an author, despite the help of many others to complete the book and make it as accurate as possible, to take responsibility for any errors that may still have crept in. I will do the same.

**Joe D. Schrag**

To my wife, Nancy

# Photo Credits

**Kansas Athletics, Inc.**

**Front cover:** (high jumper). **Front matter:** pages ix, x, xi, xxxiv. **Chapter 1:** page 6 (Redwine). **Chapter 3:** pages 25, 30 (Quigley), 31 (Huske and Herring), 33, 34 (Johnston). **Chapter 5:** page 55. **Chapter 8:** pages 81, 83 (Hudson), 84 (Cox, Gruber), 95, 96. **Chapter 9:** pages 105, 107 (Hicks), 108, 109, 112, 113, 115, 120 (Wells, Williams, Cox, Moore). **Chapter 10:** pages 135, 137 (Wade), 141 (Goulbourne, DeLoach). **Chapter 11:** pages 145, 147 (Branson), 151, 152, 153, 154, 157, 158 (Acuff, Wentland). **Chapter 12:** pages 165, 167 (Mulabegovic), 172, 173, 178, 181, 184 (Welihozkiy, Agafonov), 186 (Tarasova, Krechyk). **Chapter 13:** pages 191, 200 (Burrell, Mason). **Chapter 14:** pages 202, 214. **Chapter 15:** pages 217, 219, 221, 223, 224 (Jones, Gatlin). **Chapter 16:** pages 227, 229, 231 (Campbell-Brown running, Campbell-Brown signing autographs), 232, 233, 234, 235, 236, 237, 238 (DeLoach outdoors, DeLoach indoors), 239 (arena, Roberts fans, Hoffa/Young, Hoffa smoke, Hoffa cartwheel). **Chapter 17:** pages 243, 245, 246, 247. **Back matter:** pages 249, 251 (Cantwell, Lee, Felix), 253, 254, 256, 260 (Cox), 261, 262, 263.

## Spencer Research Library, University of Kansas Libraries

**Front matter:** xiv, xxxvi. **Chapter 1:** pages 3, 5, 6 (Outland, Schlademan, Timmons, Schwartz), 7 (Hamilton, Hargiss, Kanehl, Easton/Mills), 8, 9, 10 (relay quartet, Rooney). **Chapter 2:** pages 13, 15 (mid-race, finish), 16, 17 (committee, Meyn), 18, 19 (Illinois, dignitaries), 20, 21 (1930 coach invitation, cover and interior; 1931 coach invitation, cover and interior; Nebraska interview) 22 (time schedule, floats on parade route), 23 (cartoon, sunflower girls float, car on parade route, queens reading). **Chapter 3:** pages 27 (cover and interior), 28, 29 (Topeka, Punahou), 30 (Ryun running), 34 (Buckingham). **Chapter 4:** pages 36, 39, 41, 42, 43, 44, 46 (marathon route, runners). **Chapter 5:** pages 49, 51, 52, 53, 54. **Chapter 6:** pages 59, 61 (signs, Matson), 63 (two vaulters, autograph), 64, 67. **Chapter 7:** 69, 71, 72 (wreath-laying, barn, Timmons speaking), 73, 74, 75, 76 (Kansan front page, Jayhawk/bear cartoon). **Chapter 8:** pages 78, 83 (steeplechase-black and white), 84 (Cunningham, Santee), 85 (Mills, Dotson, Ryun), 87, 88, 89, 91, 92, 93, 97. **Chapter 9:** pages 107

Jayhawk sprinter and jumper Crystal Manning at the KU Relays, 2008.

(hurdles-black and white), 114, 118. **Chapter 10:** pages 137 (Graham), 140, 141 (McKnight). **Chapter 11:** pages 147 (pole vault-black and white), 148, 149, 160. **Chapter 12:** pages 167 (shot put-black and white), 168, 169, 170, 171, 175, 179, 180, 183. **Chapter 13:** pages 193 (Bausch, Coffman), 195, 196 (Wilt in stands, Wilt high jump progression, #1-3), 197 (team photo, Wilt long jump, Wilt with shot put, Wilt high jump progression, #4-5), 198, 199. **Chapter 14:** pages 205, 207, 208, 210, 211, 212. **Back matter:** 250, 257, 260 (Outland, Osness, Greene, Elbel, Easton/Cushman, Dillard, Dial, Allen, Salb, Alley, Hershberger, Tidwell, Mulkey, Ryun, Nieder/Oerter, Timmons,

Mills, Cunningham, Santee). 264-290 (all KU Relays program covers). **Back cover:** (1967 ticket).

Photo of Jim and Anne Ryun on page 32 by Rich Clarkson and used courtesy of the photographer.

Photos of Merlene Ottey on pages 110 and 260 used courtesy of Nebraska Media Relations.

Photos of Kenny Harrison on pages 138 and 260 and Pinkie Suggs on page 34 used courtesy of K-State Athletics.

Photo of Pinkie Suggs on page 260 by Phil Bays used courtesy of K-State Athletics.

Photo of Kym Carter on page 34 used courtesy of the Kansas State High School Activities Association.

Photos on pages xviii (front and back views), xx (watch and carving), 208, and 291 all taken by Mike Yoder.

Photos on pages 248 and 260 (Schrag) taken by Nancy Schrag.

Kansas Jayhawk logos used in color and black and white by permission of the University of Kansas and conform to the specifications for use outlined by the University.

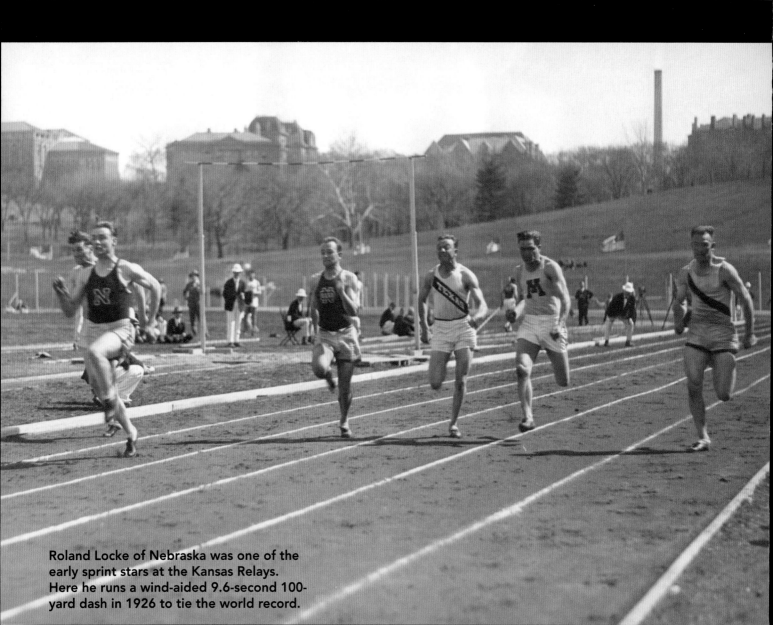

Roland Locke of Nebraska was one of the early sprint stars at the Kansas Relays. Here he runs a wind-aided 9.6-second 100-yard dash in 1926 to tie the world record.

The Kansas Relays began with a dream. One dream. By a football coach, no less. It was carried forth and nurtured by a basketball coach in a brand-new, state-of-the-art stadium. The athletic tradition at the University of Kansas is as rich as any intercollegiate program in the country, and the intradepartmental cooperation that the Relays represented in its formative years provides a fine example of why that tradition was able to blossom. In Part I of this book, you will read about John Outland's vision for a track and field meet in the American heartland (Chapter 1). Forrest C. "Phog" Allen, best known as "The Father of Basketball Coaching" for fine-tuning the invention of his KU colleague James Naismith, was also a formidable ambassador for Outland's Relays. Allen and others used entrepreneurship, humor and creativity to promote the meet in the critical early years (Chapter 2) – traits that would also prove valuable for future KU leaders in overcoming obstacles in the ensuing decades. The inclusion of high school athletes has changed through the years, but a major interscholastic meet actually predated the intercollegiate Relays on campus. The prep division has always been integral to what makes the Kansas Relays a unique track meet. Chapter 3 explains how the youngsters, on the same track and field as their elite elders, have helped to shape this great tradition.

# 1

# Dr. Outland's Dream Fulfilled
## The Tradition Begins

"From the sun-kissed slopes of Mount Oread, on the banks of the majestic Kaw, there was sent in the spring of 1923 a call to athletes of America inviting them to meet on the Kansas memorial stadium field in a major outdoor relay classic."

-- 1926 Kansas Relays meet program

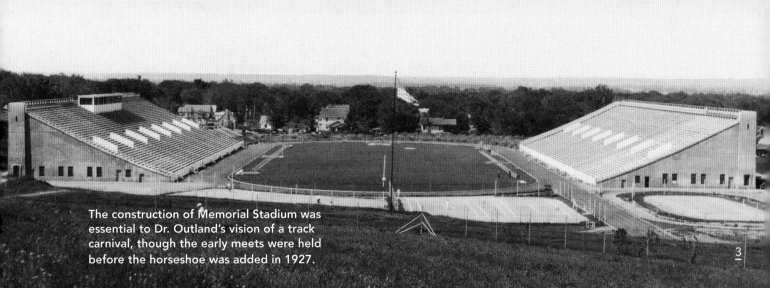

The construction of Memorial Stadium was essential to Dr. Outland's vision of a track carnival, though the early meets were held before the horseshoe was added in 1927.

3

When a University of Kansas multi-sport athlete named John Outland made the decision to attend medical school at the University of Pennsylvania, the Kansas Relays was conceived. Outland gained fame for his exploits on the gridiron as he was the first football player to be named All-American at two different positions. Most sports fans who know of him today don't think of track and field. They know Outland by the trophy he brainstormed that now bears his name. He believed tackles and guards deserved more credit, so the Outland Trophy was established in 1946 and awarded to the best interior lineman in college football.

Outland starred in baseball and football at Kansas in 1895 and 1896, after which he went to Philadelphia to pursue a medical degree at the University of Pennsylvania, where he continued to play football. Here he became enamored of the Penn Relays, which was established in 1895 and almost immediately was reputed to be the largest track and field meet in the world in terms of participation.

In 1900, Outland returned to Lawrence as Dr. Outland, established his medical practice and coached football at KU for a year. He then moved his practice to Topeka, Kan., and coached football at Washburn University for two years before joining the Trinity-Lutheran Hospital in Kansas City, Mo., as a surgeon. While practicing in Kansas City, he served on the KU athletic board with such notables as Dr. James Naismith and Dr. Forrest C. "Phog" Allen. Especially with Allen, Outland shared his vision of a large-scale track and field meet similar to the "carnival" at Penn. It would be, Outland said, a way to promote the university. As he said in a Relays "pep" convocation prior to the 1924 Relays, "The name of Kansas can go further through the Relays than any other form of athletics because of the numbers competing" (*University Daily Kansan*, April 15, 1924).

While KU's geographical location in the heartland of America was an advantage, there were no facilities adequate to hold such an extravaganza.

That all changed in 1921 when construction of Memorial Stadium, built to honor KU students who served and died in World War I, was completed. The venue is recognized as the first stadium built on a college campus west of the Mississippi, and KU claimed to be the eighth oldest collegiate stadium in the nation.[1] Allen, football coach for one year in 1920, coached in the last football game at old McCook Field. On Monday after that game, a 20-20 come-from-behind tie with Nebraska, exuberant students and faculty pledged over $200,000 toward the building of a new stadium. Construction of the facility began, under the watchful eye of Allen, who was also director of athletics. Allen envisioned a horseshoe-shaped, concrete stadium and insisted that a track be built inside. A "Stadium Day" on May 10, 1921 brought more than 4,000 students to demolish McCook Field in

**FOUNDING FATHER.** Kansas native John Outland (right) is shown here presenting the winner's cup to the Notre Dame 440-yard relay team in 1927, after the Irish tied a world record of 41.6 seconds. Dr. Outland championed the idea of a major track and field meet in his home state. He was inspired by the Penn Relays all the way back in the late 1890s.

what is considered the groundbreaking date for the new stadium. It was ready for football on Oct. 29, 1921, a 21-7 victory over the rival Kansas Aggies (Kansas State) in front of 5,160 fans.

With this edifice, Outland's dream of a large-scale track meet could become a reality (although the horseshoe didn't connect the east and west bleachers until 1927). The university's athletic board gave the go-ahead. Head coach Karl Schlademan, who in his first four years had built KU into something of a regional track power, was given the responsibility of putting it all together in time for the 1923 season. This job of directing the Relays became the responsibility of the head coach in the formative years.

## KU's Coaching Tree

The Kansas men's basketball program famously has had only eight head coaches since the game's inventor James Naismith coached the first team in 1898. But the KU men's track and field program has been nearly as stable with only 12 head coaches in 114 years (1901-2014). Three of those, which includes Naismith, served before the Relays era was begun by **John Outland** (upper left). Of the nine head coaches since the Relays began in 1923 are several significant names from the collegiate ranks. **Karl Schlademan** (above), shown here in 1923 flanked by four of his athletes, was KU coach at the inaugural Relays and from 1919-1926, followed by H.J. Huff for three years before **Brutus Hamilton** (opposite, upper left) took over from 1930-1932. Hamilton had a brilliant coaching career, but was only at KU for three years. Here he is shown in the middle of four Lawrence-based athletes who qualified for the 1932 Los

Angeles Olympics: (from left) KU miler Glenn Cunningham, Buster Charles (from Haskell Institute in Lawrence), and Jayhawk decathletes Jim Bausch and Clyde Coffman. **Bill Hargiss** (above) was known primarily as an innovative football coach, but he also coached four world-record holders. **Ray Kanehl** (right) was coach for four years, from 1944-47. **Bill Easton** (bottom right), shown here with KU alumnus and 1964 Olympic gold medalist Billy Mills, replaced Kanehl and in 18 years turned the Jayhawks into perennial national contenders. **Bob Timmons** (opposite, bottom), who like Kanehl arrived in Lawrence from Wichita East High School, continued KU's national-level tradition in an illustrious 24-year career. Here (middle, in blazer) he visits with meet officials while fans watch from Campanile Hill. **Gary Schwartz** (opposite, bottom left) followed Timmons in 1989, becoming the first coach of both the men's and women's programs, a post he held for 12 years before **Stanley Redwine** (opposite, center left) followed suit in 2001. Redwine led the Jayhawk women to their first national outdoor championship in 2013.

Once the decision was made to hold a relays carnival, the next order of business was to find a suitable date. Already in place was the State Inter-Scholastic Track Meet, which Chancellor Frank Strong established in 1904 as a ploy to get students on campus at a time when recruiting by athletic teams was illegal (see Chapter 3 for more on the origins of the high school meet). This one-day meet had been held successfully for 19 years on an April weekend at McCook Field, so it seemed logical to put the university relays, also conceived as a one-day meet, on the same weekend. Thus the two separate events were permanently linked as the Kansas Relays.

In the inaugural Kansas Relays, the Saturday schedule of collegiate and university events included two Kansas high school championship relays and three high school open relays, which made it possible to get non-Kansas students on campus. After the first year, the two Kansas relays were dropped and four open high school relays were contested on Saturday.

On April 21, 1923, people arrived by Model T, bus and train to attend the first Kansas Relays. Stadium capacity at this stage of construction was 22,000. Entered in the event were over 1,000 competitors (about 400 from high schools alone) from 23 universities, 19 colleges, four military academies and 35 high schools. The program consisted of 18 relay events and nine individual events. A downpour the day before left the track a muddy mess, and almost every

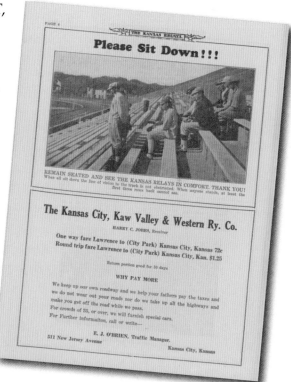

**THOUGHTFUL FANS.** Early fans took the train to Lawrence to watch the KU Relays (round-trip fare between Lawrence City Park and Kansas City, Kan., was $1.25). Once there, as this public-service announcement from the 1927 program shows, they were urged to observe proper track and field etiquette: "When all sit down, the line of vision to the track is not obstructed," it reads. "When anyone stands, at least the first three rows back cannot see."

event on competition day was run in a steady rain. Still, an estimated 7,000 fans endured the windy and cloudy conditions, paying 75 cents to $1.50 for the privilege of doing so.

The visions of Outland, the "Father of the Kansas Relays," and Allen, "The Founder of the Kansas Relays," had come to fruition. The Kansas Relays, which skeptics called "Phog's Folly," became, and continues to be, one of the premier track and field carnivals, not only in the Midwest but also in the nation.

Presaging future years, the inaugural KU Relays featured notable performances and star athletes. Despite a soggy track, the Kansas quarter-mile relay team ran 43.0 and missed the world record by one-fifth of a second.

Two Kansas athletes would become Olympians for the 1924 Paris Games. All-American Tom Poor won the high jump at 6 feet, 1¼ inches and defended

**EARLY OLYMPIAN.** Jayhawk Tom Poor represented the United States at the 1924 Olympics, a year after his victory in the high jump at the first Kansas Relays.

**EARLY RECORD-BREAKERS.** The KU Relays was the site of top-flight competition from the beginning. In 1925, the meet's third year, Kansas' 440-yard relay team (photo above, from left): Ray Fisher, Tin Luke Wongwai, George Powers and Howard Rooney set a world record, as anchorman Rooney crosses the finish line (photo on right) to complete the 42.0 performance.

that title the next two years. He placed fourth in the 1924 Olympics. Merwin "Marvin" Graham jumped 22 feet, 1½ inches in the broad jump. Graham placed ninth in the hop-step-jump in Paris.

Earle McKown of Kansas State Teachers College (now Emporia State) won the pole vault by clearing 12 feet, 9 inches. He also won the event the next two years. Milton Angier of Illinois won the javelin with a throw of 193 feet, 5 inches, not surprising since he was a former American record holder in the event and had placed seventh in the 1920 Olympics in Antwerp, Belgium.

[1] KU's claims about Memorial Stadium not withstanding, it should be noted that among stadiums built on college campuses west of the Mississippi, Husky Stadium in Seattle was constructed in 1920 and today sits on the southeastern corner of the University of Washington campus. Boone Pickens Stadium in Stillwater, Okla., was originally built as Lewis Field and hosted football games as early as 1913. A permanent grandstand was finished in 1920, giving it stadium status by our modern definition, and is near the eastern edge of today's Oklahoma State University campus. Let Huskie, Cowboy and Jayhawk fans quibble over the details. As for the claim of Memorial Stadium being the eighth oldest collegiate stadium in the United States, among NCAA Division I schools, that appears to hold true, with Neyland Stadium (originally Shields-Watkins Field) being finished earlier than Memorial Stadium in 1921 at the University of Tennessee in Knoxville to take the seventh-oldest spot.

# Results of the First Kansas Relays, 1923

| UNIVERSITY EVENTS | | | |
|---|---|---|---|
| Event | Mark [1] | Athlete [2] | School |
| Medley Relay | 7:45.5 | McNatt, Stinutt, Reese, Laaf | Texas |
| Four-Mile Relay | 18:46.3 | Hall, Scott, Marzolo, Wells | Illinois |
| Two-Mile Relay | 8:08.5 | Higgins, Allen, Coats, Gardner | Nebraska |
| Mile Relay | 3:22.6 | Morrow, Wilson, Brook-ins, Noll | Iowa |
| Half-Mile (880-Yard) Relay | 1:29.6 | Woestemeyer, Griffin, Firebaugh, Fisher | Kansas |
| Quarter-Mile (440-Yard ) Relay | 43.0 | Griffin, Woestemeyer, Firebaugh, Fisher | Kansas |
| UNIVERSITY CLASS SPECIAL EVENTS | | | |
| 100-Yard Dash | 10.1 | Lester Erwin | Kansas Aggies (Kansas State Univ.) |
| 120-Yard High Hurdles | 15.5 | Harold Crawford | Iowa |
| 220-Yard Low Hurdles | 25.5 | Riley | Kansas Aggies (Kansas State Univ.) |
| Broad Jump [3] | 22-1.5 | Merwin Graham | Kansas |
| High Jump | 6-1.25 | Tom Poor | Kansas |
| Pole Vault | 12-9 | Earle McKown | Kansas State Teachers College (Emporia State) |
| Discus | 132-10.38 | Francis Auge | Haskell (Lawrence, Kan.) |
| Shot Put | 41-7.13 | Charles Purma | Kansas State Teachers College of Pittsburg (Pittsburg State) |
| Javelin | 193-5 | Milton Angier | Illinois |

> continued

> continued

| Event | Mark [1] | Athlete [2] | School |
|---|---|---|---|
| **COLLEGE EVENTS** | | | |
| Medley Relay | 8:06.5 | Kleemeier, Kennedy, Barbour, Bond | Cornell (Iowa) |
| Two-Mile Relay | 8:31.4 | Meyer, Sumner, Tate, Talbot | Kansas State Teachers College (Emporia State) |
| Mile Relay | 3:32.8 | Northam, Huberton, Carancy, Gray | Butler (Ind.) |
| Half-Mile (880-Yard) Relay | 1:32.0 | Northam, Kilgore, Carraway, Gray | Butler (Ind.) |
| **MILITARY SCHOOLS** | | | |
| Medley Relay | 3:46.2 | Cusack, Spencer, Graves, Bloker | St. John's (Wis.) |
| Mile Relay | 3:47.4 | Cusack, Spencer, Clayton, Krogh | St. John's (Wis.) |
| Half-Mile (880-Yard) Relay | 1:36.3 | Tillotson. Sparks, George, Root | Kemper (Mo.) |
| **KANSAS HIGH SCHOOL CHAMPIONSHIP** | | | |
| Mile Relay | 3:39.5 | Brown, Fowler, Tarrant, Doornbos | El Dorado (Kan.) |
| Half-Mile (880-Yard) Relay | 1:37.2 | Brown, Shortess, Fowler, Tarrant | El Dorado (Kan.) |
| **HIGH SCHOOL OPEN** | | | |
| Two-Mile Relay | 8:33.9 | Yeisley, Tait, Healey, Murray | Cedar Rapids (Iowa) |
| Mile Relay | 3:39.8 | Knapp, Loftus, Cutel, Heath | Cedar Rapids (Iowa) |
| Half-Mile (880-Yard) Relay | 1:37.8 | Henley, B. Cooke, Stocker, Miller | Kansas City (Mo.)-Northeast |

[1] Measurements were made in one-eighth inch increments.
[2] Newspapers at the time did not provide first names.
[3] The long jump was called the broad jump.

## 2

# 'Asking Guests to One's Home'
## The Tradition Grows

"The wonderful response [in 1923] insures the future success of the Relays."

-- "Phog" Allen, quoted in the *Topeka Daily Capital*, 1924

Wisconsin star distance runner Don Gehrmann receives a kiss from Relays royalty just before Kansas legend Glenn Cunningham presents him with his trophy in 1949.

Even with John Outland's grand vision put neatly into place, with an impressive Memorial Stadium ready to host it, Forrest C. "Phog" Allen, the director of athletics at the time, did not take success for granted. He believed promotion was necessary to see that the Kansas Relays would be well established. Whether offering impressive athlete awards, securing community involvement, or having a knack for brainstorms that were able to generate buzz, Allen did just that.

"Twenty-one cups and special trophies will be given to relay teams that win firsts in the Kansas Relays here April 21,"announced Dean Boggs, trophy chairman of the Relays committee, before the inaugural Relays in 1923. To mitigate the cost of these incentives, organizations, clubs and businesses sponsored various events. Most were "challenge cups," meaning they required victories in two subsequent years to acquire permanent ownership. As an example of how this worked, Outland sponsored the half-mile relay, and thus provided the trophy for it. Various individuals, businesses and groups sponsored other events, such as the Associated Banks of Lawrence and the KU Alumni Association. Several of these trophies were valued at $100 each, a sizable sum in any age. In addition, 85 engraved white gold watches were awarded to the individual members of relay teams and winners of individual events. Silver and bronze medals were given to second and third-place finishers in both relays and individual events. Another innovative method of attracting participants involved an impressive act of generosity. The entire gate receipts were pro-rated back to the entering teams. That policy had a short life, but the precedent of event sponsorship and the awarding of watches to winners continues to this day.

Now that the athletes were enticed to come to the Relays, it was time to attend to the spectators. Curiosity would get some to attend, but Allen thought more incentive – pressure, actually – was needed to ensure success. He found an ally in the campus newspaper, *The University Daily Kansan*. In 1924, because it was Easter weekend, additional tactics were needed to ensure students stayed on campus to support the Relays. In fact,

PHOTO FINISH. KU's Charles Doornbos (center) was declared the winner in the 1927 high hurdles after Ray Dunson of Oklahoma and Charles McGinnis of Wisconsin were disqualified for knocking down too many hurdles.

the university administration didn't start vacation until after classes on Good Friday, late enough so students would not be tempted to go home before the Relays. Allen was quoted in the April 11 edition of the *Kansan* beseeching students to stay and support the Relays: "Inviting, as we have, a large number of athletes to compete in the Relays and then not having

**COVETED AWARDS.** Loving cups, such as these on display in the infield in 1938, were coveted awards to early athletes (that's Glenn Cunningham on the far right) posing with (from left) Queen's Attendant Betty Martin, Queen Elizabeth Short and Queen's Attendant Patti Payne.

a big crowd out to watch them would be as bad as asking guests to one's home and not being home to receive them. It is essential to the success of the Relays that everybody stay in town and attend. The change in Easter vacation date makes it possible for everyone to do it, so let's all fight, fight, fight for the Relays."

Two days later, in its Sunday edition, the editors scolded those students intending to leave early, and issued an impassioned challenge in the column's concluding paragraph: "Ninety-five [sic] institutions will be the judges of student conduct the 19th. One thousand athletes will carry away impressions of the University of Kansas and one thousand opinions will be broadcasted from one end of the United States to the other. Shall these visitors of Kansas spread the word at their respective institutions that the school of the famous Rock Chalk is dead? Shall they sneer at Kansas as an

**STUDENT LEADERS.** The student committee for the Relays has been a staple since the beginning of the meet. Committee members, like these shown in 1950 for the Relays' silver anniversary, ensure details and innovations for the meet are carried out.

institution that tried to put on a great athletic event and failed? Well, NO!" Outland, in speaking to a Relay "pep" convocation, said, "Students of the University will be hosts to about one thousand athletes Saturday, and it will be disastrous if they are found not at home." Allen also took to the airwaves, using KFKU, the KU radio station, to spread the word about the Relays.

**PUBLIC-ADDRESS SYSTEM.** Fritz Meyn used a megaphone to perform his duties as Memorial Stadium announcer in the early years of the KU Relays.

Dr. Ed Elbel, an athletic department fixture since coming to KU in 1928, was a friend of Allen and manager of the Relays for over 40 years. In a March 1973 article in *Kansas Alumni* magazine commemorating the Relays' 50th anniversary, he spoke of other early promotional events. "One year six people, including some from the Chamber of Commerce, flew around the state in a little airplane," he said. "They all had white coveralls with 'KU Relays' written on the back." According to "The First Fifty Years of Track Athletics at the University of Kansas," a master's thesis written in 1964 by 1955 graduate Art Dalzell, a prominent KU distance runner in his own right, the plane struck a tree when taking off in Abilene and tore five holes in its fuselage. The pilot had to take it to Ft. Riley for repairs. At a stop in Russell, Kan., the committee was welcomed by a 68-piece band, which escorted it through town.

**RELAYS STALWART.** Ed Elbel served as a professor in the KU Department of Physical Education and as a manager at the Relays for nearly four decades.

Allen also made it a practice to bring in famous personalities – not necessarily track people -- to serve as referees. A few notable examples include: Outland, in 1924; Knute Rockne (1925), Notre Dame football coach; Fielding Yost (1926), Michigan football coach for 25 years who had been KU coach in 1899; Avery Brundage (1930), AAU President, who would later serve 20 years as the fifth President of the International Olympic Committee; and Amos Alonzo Stagg (1931), nationally renowned coach of several sports at different institutions.

Another early Relays promotion occurred in 1931, turning the hillside overlooking Memorial Stadium into a golf course of sorts. The golf driving contest was open to both amateurs and professionals. Golfers teed off from the middle of the football field and drove toward the green sloping side of Mount Oread where a grid with point values was marked on the hillside.

In an April 24, 1955 interview with Dick Snider of the *Topeka Daily Capital*, Allen recounted some of his promotions in the early years of the Relays. One such caper in 1930 involved a rodeo in conjunction with the Relays. It was called "The Rodays" and was held on the football field on Friday night after the high school meet. The show was staged under flood lights borrowed from Haskell Institute, a Native American college on the south side of Lawrence, the same as were used for night football. A

FLYIN' ILLINI. Illinois set a new world record with a 1:27.0 clocking in the 880-yard relay at the 1925 KU Relays.

DIGNITARIES. The Relays was a prestigious place to be already in 1925. From left: KU director of athletics Phog Allen, Capt. Harold G. Archibald of the ROTC, meet referee and legendary Notre Dame football coach Knute Rockne, Kansas Gov. Ben S. Paulen, KU Chancellor E.H. Lindley and Relays visionary John Outland.

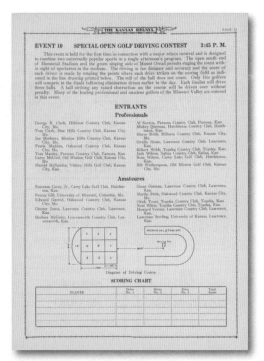

**DRIVING ON MT. OREAD.** The 1931 program listed the entrants from all over the region who took part in the golf driving contest. Note that the horseshoe portion of Memorial Stadium, in place since 1927, is part of the sketch.

buffalo was purchased and allowed to graze on the field. After the rodeo, the buffalo was slaughtered and barbecued as a meal for the coaches and meet officials. To make things more interesting, a contest was held whereby students could guess the buffalo's weight. The nearest guess received four tickets to the Relays, the second closest got three tickets, third place received two, and fourth received one. Elbel said of the barbecue, "I'm sure it was a dwarf buffalo because it was the toughest meat I've ever tasted."

Dalzell, in his master's thesis, details the events of the week leading up to the Relays:

"April 13 at 3 p.m. a great, new, ultra modern two motor and double control airplane will bring four rodeo performers and two of the most valuable horses to the Lawrence airport. They will load at Hays.

April 14 – Nine year old "Baby" Lorraine Graham will dash 28 miles from Lawrence to Topeka, using eight fast horses in pony express style, and carrying a message from the University to Governor Reed.

April 15 – Rodeo performers will work out in Robinson Gymnasium at the University.

April 16 – "Baby" Lorraine will stunt for the students.

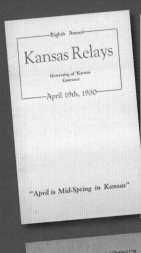

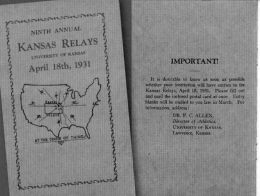

ALLEN'S INVITES. Phog Allen's subtle edits to the invitations to attend the Relays show his promotional skills at work. In 1930 (above), the director of athletics mentions the barbecue and night rodeo, in addition to the vague "climatic conditions." In 1931, with the stirrings of the Los Angeles Olympics still more than a year away, Allen fans the emotions with the challenge of US "supremacy" at stake. He also is slightly more honest about the fickle Kansas weather, saying it "almost without exception has been ideal" each year.

April 17 – Pottawattomi [sic] Indians will arrive.

April 18 – Egg rolling on Mt. Oread at 7 p.m.

April 19 – Final day of Relays. Several thousand feet of movie film will be ground out during the week by camera men operating for national news reels."

MEDIA DAYS. Even the visiting athletes, like this Nebraska Cornhusker in 1959, got the star treatment when the KU Relays commenced each year.

# Early Traditions

The pageantry that surrounds the Kansas Relays was particularly strong in the early years, from downtown floats promoting the Sunflower State (opposite, top right, in 1949) to parades featuring a Henry J car (opposite, bottom left, in 1950). The 1953 queen's program schedule (right) shows the extent of the planning of these activities, including the crowning and kissing of the queen and the Cunningham Mile awards being presented by none other than Glenn Cunningham. Queen candidates in 1957 pose to read the program (opposite, top left), though no one will find Lucky Strikes ads on the back cover anymore. *The Daily Kansan* takes a light-hearted look at a queen's duties on April 16, 1946: "She certainly takes this Queen business seriously," it reads.

Little Man On Campus — By Bibler

"She certainly takes this Queen business seriously."

# 3

# The Young Guns
## Establishing a High School Legacy

"If out of that crowd of 1,000 high school students we can capture a freshman class of 600 next year our inter-high school meet will not have been in vain."

-- *The University Daily Kansan,*
Staff Editorial, April 29, 1905

Future Olympian Leo Manzano of Marble Falls (Texas) won the high school boys 800-meter run in 2002 and 2003.

Dr. Frank Strong left the presidency of the University of Oregon in 1902 to become Chancellor of the University of Kansas. Strong was adamant that his new university needed to expand. During his 18-year tenure as chancellor, it did. Enrollment went from 1,300 to 4,000. He tried every way he could to get students on campus. Strong felt like athletic contests were a way to make that happen, so he had the KU Athletic Association sponsor the first Interscholastic Track and Field Meet to be held at McCook Field on April 29, 1904. The student newspaper, *The University Daily Kansan*, supported the effort and wrote in its April 23rd edition, "We wish them (athletes) to come here to continue their studies and the meet will offer them a fine chance to give them a good opinion of the university." On a beautiful April day, eight schools were represented. They were Kansas City (Kan.), Anthony, Carbondale, Beloit, Atchison, Lawrence, Osage City and Topeka.

The second year was even more successful than the first with more schools and greater participation. Prizes were about the same, with a silver loving cup provided by the Schmelzer Arms Co. to the winning team and gold medals to the individual first-place winners. An oratorical contest was held on the evening of the same day to get more high school students on campus. According to the April 29, 1905 *Daily Kansan*, a crowd of over 2,000 attended. As the paper described, "The track meet was like a three- ring circus, [sic] you couldn't see all of it at once."

The Interscholastic Track and Field Meet continued to grow in size and popularity. Usually it was paired with a debate competition, baseball game, basketball tournament, tennis tournament or some other activity to maximize the number of students coming to campus. Trains, the common form of transportation for most teams, often reduced fares for the trip to Lawrence. More cups and medals were provided as the numbers grew.

In 1907, in order to increase the number of in-state schools, Missouri schools were not allowed to come because in the previous year they had swept nearly all the cups and medals, and no Missouri athlete enrolled at Kansas. Preventing their participation was accomplished by some clever scheduling. By having the meet on May 4, the Kansas City, Mo., schools would not be able to send teams because they would be going to a Missouri interscholastic meet in Columbia. When the KU Relays came into existence, the practice of the meet being primarily for Kansas schools continued for decades.

By 1909, what was being billed as the greatest event of its kind in the state of Kansas had amassed at least 30 teams, so they were divided into four classes: A1, A2, B and C. Although the classifications changed frequently, this divisional format was a staple of the high school meet until 1958.

**THE BIG EVENT, PRE-RELAYS.** The Interscholastic Track and Field Meet preceded the KU Relays as the big athletic event on campus each spring. Here is the program from the 10th annual meet in 1913. Note how the classifications of schools were already in effect. The inclusion of national, meet, and KU school records for each event shows how the obsession with statistics that track and field fans are known for was already being satisfied at KU.

When the interscholastic meet shared the weekend with the first Kansas Relays in 1923 – the established high school events, primarily held on Friday, with the new intercollegiate offerings on Saturday – a new excitement was in the air. Some spectators and teams arrived in Lawrence as early as Thursday afternoon, but most arrived Friday morning. Off every

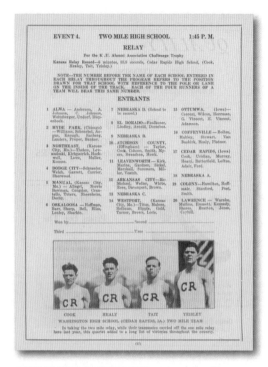

**RETURNING CHAMPS.** As with all KU Relays programs, the high school entrants and schedule are featured just like the collegians. In this 1924 program, the Cedar Rapids-Washington (Iowa) High School two-mile relay team came back to try to defend its title from the previous year.

passenger train, several teams disembarked. Most were quartered at fraternity houses and with families and students all over town. Girls were, of course, not yet allowed to participate in track and field endeavors. High school participants from the Friday meet, approximately 200 of them, were given free tickets to Saturday's collegiate action. Even though the Interscholastic Track and Field Meet continued to be a separate entity from the events in the College and University classes, everyone considered the high school events to be an integral part of the KU Relays. Thirty-five high schools attended in 1923. Most of the high school events were held on Friday, but the Kansas High School Championship mile relay and half-mile relay races were contested on Saturday. A high school open class consisting of a two-mile relay, a mile relay and a half-mile relay was created for Saturday's schedule to allow Missouri and Iowa schools to participate since they could not be included in the Kansas portion of the meet.

Despite a soggy beginning, the inaugural Kansas Relays was so successful that it continued in 1924 with some modifications in the high school meet. For example, the first Junior High Division was included. The junior high meet had a life span of five years. Also in 1924, the Kansas Championships were held entirely on Friday. The Kansas schools with student populations above 200 were designated as Class A, and schools with less than 200 were labeled Class B. Medley, half-mile, mile and two-mile relays for out-of-state schools were retained as part of the Saturday program.

These were considered to be high school opens and competing schools came from not only surrounding states, but from as far away as Illinois, Texas, West Virginia and Kentucky. Occasionally Kansas schools would participate, but not often. This format continued until 1931 when high school events were dropped out of the Saturday program entirely. However, in 1935, a Saturday afternoon medley relay was added solely to accommodate Kansas City schools from the Missouri side of the state line. In 1938, the medley relay for Missouri high schools was replaced with a half-mile relay for Missourians, a change which would last until 1958.

The Kansas Relays for colleges and universities was suspended in 1943, 1944 and 1945 because of World War II travel restrictions, but the high school portion continued to flourish. In fact, participation was so high that a third

NEAR AND FAR. The 1946 Punahou track squad (right) came all the way from Hawaii to participate in the Kansas Relays. Topeka High School (above) from just down the road has been a regular participant in Lawrence each spring from the first Interscholastic Meet in 1904, to these sprinters from the 1950s (from left to right, Jim Allen, Bill Peterson, Ray Drum, Coach D.L. "Heavy" Erwin, Alfred Goodwin, Dale Ridgeway), to the present.

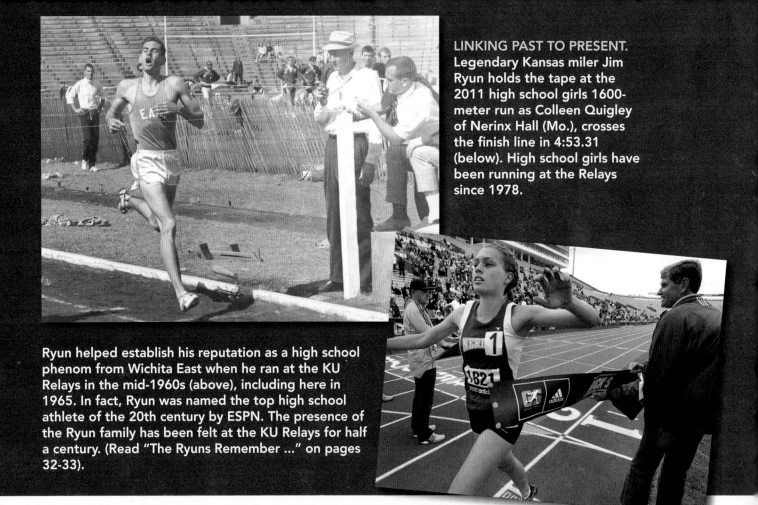

LINKING PAST TO PRESENT. Legendary Kansas miler Jim Ryun holds the tape at the 2011 high school girls 1600-meter run as Colleen Quigley of Nerinx Hall (Mo.), crosses the finish line in 4:53.31 (below). High school girls have been running at the Relays since 1978.

Ryun helped establish his reputation as a high school phenom from Wichita East when he ran at the KU Relays in the mid-1960s (above), including here in 1965. In fact, Ryun was named the top high school athlete of the 20th century by ESPN. The presence of the Ryun family has been felt at the KU Relays for half a century. (Read "The Ryuns Remember ..." on pages 32-33).

division was added in 1945. High schools with a student population of 476 or more were labeled AA, schools with 176-475 were A, and 175 or less were considered B. When the colleges returned to the Relays, the high school division returned to two classes, thus resulting in fewer races.

An interesting one-year addition to the Relays occurred in 1946. Punahou High School in Honolulu, Hawaii, entered the Relays. The private school has gained recognition in recent years as the alma mater of President Barack Obama, Class of 1979. The Kansas State High School Activities Association (KSHSAA) rules did not permit Kansas students to participate against schools that were not members of the National Federation of State High School

Associations (NFHS). Since Hawaii was not yet a state, Punahou had no such membership. Meet management solved the problem by adding two special events, a half-mile relay and a mile relay, to be run against junior colleges and military academies.

The Kansas high school mile relay was added to the Saturday program in 1948. The six teams with the fastest times, regardless of class, from Friday's meet were invited to participate in the Saturday mile relay.

The biggest change came in 1958 when the high schools were incorporated into a two-day meet with the colleges and universities. Furthermore, there would no longer be classes as in prior years, and invitations would be extended to high schools outside of Kansas. While a large number of coaches welcomed the opportunity to see their athletes compete against the best athletes from other states, these changes did not sit well with some Kansas high school coaches. The two-day format increased their expenses, particularly for schools coming from a long distance, because it necessitated staying an extra night and required more money for meals.

**INTENSITY.** Jared Huske of Topeka (Kan.)-Highland Park (left) and Gerron Herring of Park Hill (Mo.) were both double winners at the KU Relays in 2005 – Huske in the 110 high and 300 intermediate hurdles and Herring in the 100 and 400.

# The Ryuns Remember ...

" The Kansas Relays has long been a Ryun family tradition even prior to our having our own family. As an East High School sophomore, I ran in my first KU Relays. I won the mile and helped my two-mile relay team take first place. That early in my running career, Coach Timmons had instilled in me that running was a team effort.

I recall being housed in the WWII military barracks on the land that is now the west-side stadium parking lot.

There are several memorable Relays for me.

My second date with my wife-to-be, Anne, was at the 1967 Relays. She witnessed first-hand what it was like to sit in a ticketed seat among Kansans who absolutely were the very best supporters of the Relays. There is nothing in my memory that compares to running for my hometown supporters. I set the still-standing Glenn Cunningham Mile record at 3:54.7 to show Anne what a great guy she could get for a husband!

In 1972, I returned to the Relays to run the mile in preparation for, and in hopes of making, the USA team for the 1972 Munich Olympics. It was overwhelming for me to have such a crowd of "my" fellow Kansans cheering me on. It was a sellout crowd of 32,000-plus (the plus is due to the fact that they ran out of tickets to sell).

In 1980, we were living in Santa Barbara, Calif. We

Anne and Jim Ryun, after they announced their enagement in May 1968.

brought the family back to the Relays to witness the thrill of my jogging a lap with Wes Santee and Glenn Cunningham. It was an honor to be on home turf and in the company of those two world-class runners who had gone before me to begin the tradition of great middle-distance running at the University of Kansas.

In 1981, we moved back to Lawrence. Our children (Heather, Ned, Drew and Catharine) all began running for the Lawrence Track Club and eventually Lawrence High School, where they set many records as members of relay teams. Ned recalls his junior year of high school when Lawrence High swept all four of the boys high school relays. Ned led off both the 4x800 and distance medley, both times handing off to his twin brother Drew, who ran the second leg on both relays and if memory serves correctly, both times handed off in the lead. Lawrence High never looked back, beating neighboring state powerhouses Lee's Summit (Mo.) and Jenks (Okla).

Jim Ryun enjoyed his 2004 KU Relays induction with daughters Catharine (left) and Heather.

Heather's distance medley relay team took first in 1988, her junior year. They ran a record time that remained on the books for several years.

All four children made their parents proud, yes, for their physical abilities but more importantly for the character of good sportsmanship and humility with which they conducted their lives.

Running is still an integral part of our family life, physically, mentally and spiritually (www.ryunrunning.com).

The Kansas Relays will always hold fond memories for the Ryun family. Here's to many more years of great competition and memory-making at the Kansas Relays for all families involved with the meet. **"**

IN-STATE PREP STARS. Prep athletes from the Sunflower State have starred at the KU Interscholastic Meet and the Relays since 1904. They come from all over the state, and go on to attend college in a variety of places. Wichitan Kym Carter (above left) left her home state to compete at LSU. David Johnston (middle), a high school mile champion while at Lawrence High School, stayed close to home. Here he helps the KU distance medley relay team win at the 1994 Relays. Jeff Buckingham of Gardner (upper right) became one of a long line of Jayhawk pole vaulting greats. Pinkie Suggs (lower right) stayed in her hometown of Manhattan to throw for K-State.

The admission of out-of-state athletes reduced the possibility of Kansas athletes winning awards. Also, with the elimination of classes along with the admission of athletes from other states, it became more difficult for athletes to have the requisite marks necessary to be admitted into the Relays.[1]

The last major change to the high school portion of the Relays came in 1978 when high school girls were added. This move coincided with the Relays being moved to five different sites due to renovations at Memorial Stadium. The high schoolers competed at Shawnee Mission (Kan.) Northwest High School. When the Relays were cancelled in 1998 and 1999, once again for stadium renovation, Olathe (Kan.) East High School, under the direction of Mike Wallace, hosted the young guns.

Outstanding performances in the high school events are legion. Many are mentioned in Part III of this book, but many more deserve to be. A measure of the quality of performances can be seen in the number of high school athletes who competed at the KU Relays and later became interscholastic, intercollegiate, national, and even world-record holders. At least 25 high school performers at the Kansas Relays went on to become Olympians.

[1] In this writer's opinion, as a future high school coach at the Relays for 41 years and a member of the high school committee for 28 of those, the changes made in 1958 were some of the wisest decisions that meet management has ever made. Overnight the quality of the meet was richly enhanced, and the prestige of winning a high school event at the Kansas Relays was vastly more significant to the athletes and their schools. It was good for the University of Kansas as well, because recruiting was greatly improved by getting a significant number of out-of-state students on campus who had not previously been familiar with the university.

## Results of the first Interscholastic High School Track and Field Meet, April 29, 1904, McCook Field

| Event | Mark[1] | Athlete[2] | School (All Kansas) |
|---|---|---|---|
| 100-Yard Dash | 10.6 | Commons | Lawrence |
| 120-Yard Hurdles | 20.8 | McGrath | Carbondale |
| 220-Yard Dash | 24.0 | Commons | Lawrence |
| Mile Run | 5:21 | Madston | Beloit |
| 220-Yard Hurdles | 29.6 | Miller | Osage City |
| Quarter-Mile (440-Yard) Run | 56.8 | Cook | Beloit |
| Half-Mile (880-Yard) Run | 2:19 | W. Ferguson | Kansas City, Kan. |
| Shot Put | 38-1 | Rouse | Beloit |
| Hammer Throw | 91-9 | Foster | Carbondale |
| Discus Throw | 90-4 | Hunt | Lawrence |
| Pole Vault | 9-0 | Mayberry | Lawrence |
| High Jump | 5-2 | McGrath | Carbondale |
| Broad Jump[3] | 19-7.5 | McGrath | Carbondale |

[1] In races 880 yards and up, tenths of a second were not always considered.
[2] Newspapers at the time did not provide first names.
[3] The long jump was called the broad jump.

Running for Mexico, José Torres ran the 50.7 miles from Kansas City, Mo., to Lawrence, Kan., in less than seven hours.

MENTS # MOMENTS MOME

The Kansas Relays is made up of moments. Millions of them. In Part II, discover the stories of two days and two years that were highly anticipated and put Memorial Stadium in sharp focus around the country and world: the invitation of several of the famed Tarahumara Indians from Mexico to run in Kansas in 1927 (Chapter 4); Wes Santee's valiant effort to run the first recorded four-minute mile in the history of the world (Chapter 5); a Vietnam War protest clashing with a huge crowd primed to watch the sensational Jim Ryun (Chapter 6); and an ambitious, optimistic, and ultimately successful, effort by Bob Swan and Mark Scott to bring Soviet athletes to KU in an era between two Olympic boycotts for détente on the track (Chapter 7). These were distinctively major moments, made possible by superior athletic talent and leadership, all branded with the spirit of their respective times. These and many, many more moments have helped to construct the KU Relays' legacy. There are many more to come...

# 4

# A Footrace from Kansas City to Lawrence
## Inviting the Tarahumara, 1927

The finest Marathon runners
   in the world,
nourished on the bitter flesh
   of deer,
they will be the first with the
   triumphant news
the day we leap the wall
   of the five senses.

-- Mexican poet Alfonso Reyes,
   "Yerbas del Tarahumara," 1934

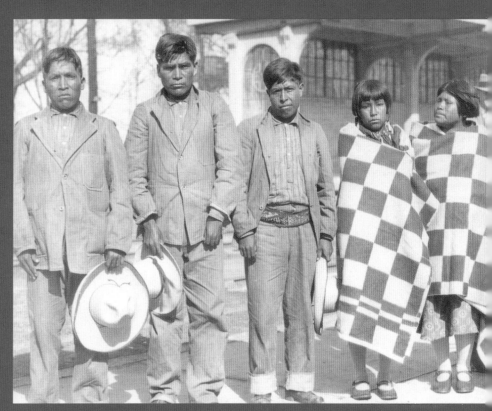

A contingent of five
Tarahumara arrive from
Mexico before the 1927
Kansas Relays.

" At 7:25 on a Saturday morning, April 23, 1927, three Tarahumara, a Navajo, and an Apache set off on an ultramarathon. Under a leaden sky, facing an unseasonably cool spring wind, they ran through the streets of downtown Kansas City, Missouri. Thousands of spectators lined the streets of the Midwestern metropolis while police held traffic at bay to make way for the foot runners' procession. Silver bells jangled on the runners' belts, mingling rhythmically with the crowd's claps and cheers. A crowd of Kansas schoolboys chased the foot runners out of town. A gaggle of automobiles followed them onto a dirt road that led toward the hilly grasslands of eastern Kansas. The foot runners were bound for Lawrence, Kansas, a bit more than fifty miles of rolling prairie west of Kansas City. Nearly two hours after the first group of foot runners left Kansas City, two female Tarahumara runners ran through the streets of Topeka, Kansas. More than a thousand spectators lined the boulevards of Kansas' state capital to cheer the women as they began their journey. People stood on the running boards of their automobiles to get a glimpse of the female foot runners. Hundreds of little boys ran behind the two racers as they glided through Topeka. Thus began the third installment of long distance races involving the Tarahumara tribe of northwestern Mexico. They first garnered international attention in a world-record setting 100-kilometer race from Pachuca to Mexico City in November of 1926. In March of 1927 they ran 89 miles from San Antonio to Austin. Heavy spectator traffic prevented them from capturing another world record, but they certainly seized American and Mexican imaginations during their Texas run. At the same time, a Tarahumara woman ran 27 miles from Kyle to Austin, Texas, staking the claim that Tarahumara women as well as men were the world's greatest endurance athletes. The Tarahumara's Kansas races reveal the intensity of Mexican and U.S. sporting nationalisms, the strange dimensions of early twentieth-century anthropological science, the strong patterns of commodification in 'golden age' sport spectacles, modern conceptions of primitivism, and popular fascination with the limits of human endurance.[1] "

By far the most ambitious Kansas Relays promotion of all occurred in 1927. The University Athletic commission arranged with the Mexican government and the U.S. consul in Mexico to import runners of the Tarahumara tribe from the High Sierras of Old Mexico to KU for the meet, which was then just five years old.

The fragile post-revolutionary government of Mexico was looking for a way to enhance patriotism among its citizens and improve its image with foreign countries, particularly the United States. The government was eager to send runners north for gold, glory and respect. Already, in conjunction with the Texas Relays, which preceded the KU Relays by a month, the Tarahumara had raced from San Antonio to Austin, a distance of 89 miles. Forrest C. "Phog" Allen, always on the lookout for ways to promote the KU Relays, thought that the Tarahumara would bring an exotic flavor to the meet and pique the interest of fans. He was right.

In an April 24, 1955, interview with Dick Snider of the *Topeka Daily Capital*, Allen explained how it came about. KU agreed to pay all expenses for the trip to Lawrence and back. Three men and two women would make the trip. According to Allen, when the president of Mexico demanded that the runners go, they

**MESSENGERS.** Lawrence Mayor R.C. Rankin (left) and Phog Allen (right) congratulate José Torres on his victory. As part of the spectacle of the race, the Tarahumara men carried a letter from Kansas City Mayor Albert I. Beach to Rankin, while the women brought him a note from Topeka signed by Kansas Governor Ben S. Paulen.

41

were apprehensive and feared they were going to die. In fact one man agreed to go only after the chief threatened to put him to death if he didn't. This exchange, of course, could not be corroborated. In keeping with the trend from primary newspaper sources and later re-tellings about this venture, it included some embellishment and a penchant for focusing on the American fascination with the supposed primitivism of the isolated culture. An article in the April 23, 1927, *Kansas City Times* even claimed that while in Kansas City the Tarahumara labeled the Midwestern metropolis the "city of the mysterious devils."

The Tarahumara refer to themselves as Rarámuri, which has been interpreted as "runners on foot" or "those who run fast." These short, muscular residents who live in mountainside caves or huts in the Copper Canyon are renowned for their ability to run long distances, purportedly running deer, birds and other game to exhaustion to provide food.

The three Tarahumara were challenged by two runners from Haskell Institute, a Native American college on the south side of Lawrence that also provided accommodations for the Mexican visitors during their stay. The five ultramarathoners ran from Kansas City to Memorial Stadium, a distance of 50.7

**RUNNER-UP.** Purcell Kane carries the American flag into the stadium to complete his second-place finish.

miles, culminating in a lap around the track at the end. The winner was José Torres, whose elapsed time was 6 hours, 46 minutes, and 41 seconds. Purcell Kane, an Apache from Haskell, came in 15 minutes later with an official time of 7 hours, 1 minute, and 34 seconds. He had never run farther than 20 miles at a time before this race.

Each Tarahumara ran carrying a short stick and occasionally stopped to apply a bit of grease to irritated areas. This grease was carried in a pouch in their shorts. Their shoes were huarache sandals, made from tires and leather straps. The crowd in the stadium received progress updates, and excitement built as their entrance into the stadium was imminent.

**RELAY, INTERRUPTED.** This photo from the 1928 program shows the scene from one year earlier, when Tomás Zafiro (front) sped up to keep Philip Osif of Haskell Institute (right) and the rest of the two-mile relay field from passing him after 50-plus miles on the roads.

As luck would have it, Tomás Zafiro, the Tarahumara who finished third, happened to enter the stadium shortly after the anchors of the two-mile relay, led by Philip Osif, a Haskell student and member of the Pima tribe, had gotten their batons. Thinking he was about to be passed, Zafiro, even after 50 miles, accelerated to the finish, much to the delight of the crowd. As Allen described the moment to Snider, referring to Zafiro in the plural: "They came into the stadium while one of the relay races was being run, and even after running as far as they had, those Indians just joined the race and finished alongside the college runners. We had a big crowd, and they [the crowd] went wild when it happened."

The lone woman finisher of the 30.6-mile run from Topeka to Lawrence was 20-year-old Lola Cuzarare, with a time of 5 hours, 37 minutes, and 45 seconds. Cuzarare, who was now being called Lolita as the Tarahumara phenomenon gained more attention, was credited with a world record for the distance, since there were few examples of women being timed at that distance. Her sister Juanita dropped out before reaching Lawrence.

Seeking to build on this long-distance venture, an all-Native Kansas Relays international marathon from just east of Topeka to Lawrence was scheduled for 1928, the very next year. Art Dalzell describes the planning of the race in considerable detail in his 1964 master's thesis, "The First Fifty Years of

**ENDURANCE WOMAN.** Lolita Cuzarare (center) showed women's endurance capabilities at a time when there were no women's events at most track meets.

Track Athletics at the University of Kansas." In the original plan, Mexico, Canada and the United States would hold tryouts to find two indigenous representatives from each country to run the marathon. It would be an attempt to "uncover Olympic material." In the United States, runners were chosen from Indian schools and reservations from around the country and brought to Haskell to train. Two from those finalists would then represent the Americans. Ultimately, Canada picked two Iroquois runners, and the United States chose two Hopi runners from Riverside, Calif. The Tarahumara from Mexico chose not to come, claiming the distance was too short. They wanted to run only if the race was set between 80 and 300 miles. Rather than have only four runners, the number of entrants was expanded to allow eight from each country, which the United States elected to do. The Canadians stood pat with two entrants. The winner was Harold Buchanan, a Winnebago from Mississippi, who represented Haskell. His time was 3 hours, 4 minutes and 26 seconds.

The feats of the Tarahumara in Texas and Kansas in the spring of 1927 did not go unnoticed. While the KU Relays tried to capitalize on the fascination with marathons and native running the following year, there was much speculation about the potential for Tarahumara marathoners to win medals at the Amsterdam Olympics. The Mexican government unsuccessfully petitioned the International Olympic Committee to include a 100-kilometer men's race and a women's marathon at the 1928 Games. The Tarahumara runners and the Mexican representatives were already looking ahead to that possibility. At KU they refused to accept money beyond their expenses in order to ensure they retained their amateur standing to be eligible for the Olympics.

Torres, the winner of the Kansas City to Lawrence race, finished 21st out of 75 entrants at the 1928 Olympics. Cuzarare was ranked number one in the World Marathon Rankings for 1927, although there were few women marathoners in that period. The Amsterdam Games were the first Olympics with track and field events held for women, and 800 meters was the longest distance for them.

KU Track  Campanile

Jayhawk Drive

24  2

19th St.

High
School

23rd St.

23  3

22  4

Wakarusa River

Lawrence
Baldwin
Road

21  5

O'Leary
Road

6

20  19  7

Louisiana St.

8

18  17  9

10

16

15  11

14  12

13
Vinland

MARATHON REVIVAL.
These runners turn the
corner on Lawrence
streets in 1986. The
marathon route is
shown in this pamphlet
from 1974.

Interest in the marathon as an annual event waned, but was reinvigorated at KU when an open marathon was added to the Relays schedule in
1970, during the national running boom. The marathon continued until
1988.

[1] This passage opens Mark Dyreson's paper titled "The Great Battle of Tribal Feet": Spectacles, Borders, and
Nationalism in the Golden Age of Sport. It was presented at the 2006 North American Society for Sport History
Conference.

# Kansas Relays Marathon Winners, 1970-1988

| Year | Name | City/Club | Time |
|---|---|---|---|
| | | **Men** | |
| 1970 | Chuck Ceronsky | St. John's, Minn. | 2:29.04 |
| 1971 | Chuck Ceronsky | Twin Cities Track Club | 2:32.08 |
| 1972 | Terry Ziegler | Oklahoma | 2:23.07 |
| 1973 | Terry Ziegler | Oklahoma | 2:21.15 |
| 1974 | Terry Ziegler | Tulsa Running Club | 2:21.58 |
| 1975 | Bob Busby | Warrensburg, Mo. | 2:22.38 |
| 1976 | Michael Bordell | Pikes Peak Track Club | 2:30.14 |
| 1977 | Bob Busby | Club Midwest | 2:23.01 |
| 1978 | Bob Busby | Club Midwest | 2:20.01 (Course Record) |
| 1979 | Anthony Radiez | Unattached | 2:24.33 |
| 1980 | Tony Conroy | Unattached | 2:26.52 |
| 1981 | S. Baker | St. Louis Track Club | 2:39.35 |
| 1982 | Dan Owens | Kansas | 2:27.32 |
| 1983 | Jim Brady | Colorado Springs, Colo. | 2:29.24 |
| 1984 | Ken Rader | | 2:25.28 |
| 1985 | Dan Schleicher | Mission, Kan. | 2:29.21 |
| 1986 | Mike DesRosiers | Lawrence, Kan. | 2:27.52 |
| 1987 | Mike DesRosiers | Lawrence, Kan. | 2:29.35 |
| 1988 | David Matthews | | 2:32.16 |
| | | **Women** | |
| 1983 | Durhane Wong-Reiger | Stillwater, Okla. | 3:06.13 |
| 1984 | Gabrielle Thompson | Wichita Running Club | 3:22.42 |
| 1985 | Joy Meyen | Mad Dogs, Lawrence, Kan. | 2:55.21 (Course Record) |
| 1986 | Jane Getto | Lawrence, Kan. | 4:08.04 |
| 1987 | Suyoung Jerrette | | 3:07.39 |
| 1988 | Marla (Rutter) Rhoden | Topeka Striders | 3:15.47 |

# 5

# The Race to Four Minutes

## April 17, 1954

"There was a time when running the mile in four minutes was believed to be beyond the limits of human foot speed. And in all of sport it was the elusive holy grail."

-- From *The Perfect Mile,*
by Neal Bascomb

Wes Santee captivated KU Relays crowds for many years.

On Saturday, April 17, 1954, the 29th running of the Kansas Relays was center stage for track and field's international assault on the record books. Wes Santee was poised to attempt the elusive four-minute mile. There was a sense of urgency because two other superb milers had the same goal. The great Australian John Landy had already made a concerted effort in Melbourne to break the barrier, but failed, claiming he could not hear his splits because of crowd noise. His time of 4:02.4 was considered a "magnificent failure" in newspaper headlines. Finnish ace Denis Johansson, however, was in attendance and impressed enough that he predicted that on a good cinder track, pushed by solid competition, Landy could run 3:55 and he would help him do it.

In London, Roger Bannister, under the watchful eye of Austrian coach Franz Stampfl was orchestrating an all-out effort at the four-minute mark. Known for a furious finishing kick, he came to the conclusion that he needed pacers to see him through the early going of the race. Those pacers, steeplechaser Chris Brasher and three-miler Chris Chataway, were accomplished runners in their own right and trained with Bannister. Bannister was gearing up for a paced attempt at four minutes in early May. Thus the KU Relays was Santee's stage to be the first man under four minutes.

He was running out of time because he was to report for Marine officer training in July. Another problem besides the shortness of time was that Santee had angered Amateur Athletic Union officials in Germany and was banned for a year from competing internationally. This eliminated the possibility of first-rate competition. No American miler at that time was capable of pushing Santee toward his four-minute goal. With his typical bravado, the Ashland, Kan., native said he could do it anyway if the conditions and track were right.

Kansas coach Bill Easton had reduced Santee's team obligations for the KU Relays, but Wes had run four quality races in the Texas Relays just two weeks earlier, including an anchor carry on a world-record sprint medley.

Reporters from major publications like *Time*, *Newsweek* and *The Saturday Evening Post* were in attendance. New York newspapers called him "Super Sonic Santee," "The Mile King" and the "Kansas Tornado." Bob Hurt, a Topeka, Kan., sportswriter, called him the "Ashland Antelope."

Despite the physiological doomsayers who thought four minutes was simply not humanly possible, many famous milers thought Santee was the man to be the first and it was just a matter of time to reach the mark. A decade earlier, two Swedes, Arne Anderson (4:01.6 in 1944) and Gunder Haegg (4:01.4 in 1945, a record that held until Bannister's famous run) had come close. Haegg wrote to Santee from Sweden: "I think you can be the first man under four minutes, but you must hurry on. I even will be very glad if you will be the first man under four minutes." Gil Dodds, accomplished American miler (4:05.3 in the Wanamaker Mile in Madison Square Garden in 1948) and coach at Wheaton College at the time, said, "Yes, of all the fellows I have analyzed, Wes Santee has the best chance of running the mile in four minutes." Landy himself is quoted as saying, "If anyone does it this season, I think it may be someone faster than I, possibly

**THE ASHLAND ANTELOPE. Wes Santee works out at Memorial Stadium in 1954.**

American Wes Santee will do it if he works up to it." Two years prior to 1954, Santee went on record saying he would run 3:58.3.

Relays weekend was to be a big weekend for Santee in more ways than one. He planned to be the first person in the world to run a four-minute mile, then marry his fiancée Danna Denning, also of Ashland, on Sunday. The campus was abuzz with the peripheral activities surrounding the Relays, including the traditional parade.

Unfortunately, shortly after the parade concluded, somewhere around 2 p.m., one of those April thunderstorms Kansas is famous for struck with a vengeance and sent 16,000 fans scurrying for cover. The storm didn't last long and the sun soon reappeared, but the track was a quagmire. Easton did his best to rectify the damage. He had track squad members scoop the water off the track and used a propane-fueled flamethrower to help dry it. Louis Stroup, a freshman trackster from Pittsburg, Kan., used a heavy roller on the entire track. He rolled the entire first lane twice and the east side four times. The concerted effort did not restore the track to its original condition, but it was at least runnable.

Santee's opponent that day was the clock. The other runners in the field were good, but not capable of pushing him to four minutes.

**EASTON EXPRESS AND SANTEE SPECIAL.** Wes Santee and his coach Bill Easton were celebrities at mid-century KU Relays, including being the subject of this float: "Easton is Easton, Wes is Wes, and finally the twain have met."

**SLOPPY CINDERS. A muddy track, such as this one in 1947 or during Wes Santee's attempt at a four-minute mile in 1954, was commonplace during Memorial Stadium's cinder days.**

The group included Bruce "Bulldog" Drummond, an Oklahoma graduate student who was the defending champion of the Glenn Cunningham Mile; Ray McConnell, who was the winner of the Drake Relays mile the previous spring; and Bjorn Bogerud, the freshman from Oklahoma A&M who had placed third in that spring's Texas Relays and would be runner-up to Santee. The race strategy concocted by Easton and Santee was simple. Run the first lap in 59 seconds, the second in 60, the third in 61, then gut it to the finish. The track was soft and wet and there was a bit of a crosswind, but Santee was determined to make the effort and was lustily cheered by the 16,000 in attendance – the largest crowd in Relays history to that date.

The first lap was 59.5, nearly on pace. However, the second lap was 61.7 and his 880 time was 2:01.2. His third lap slowed to 63.3. There was still a chance because he had run 55 seconds for a final lap before, but not under these conditions. His valiant try resulted in a 58.6 final lap. The effort was commendable, but the crowd groaned when the result shown on the scoreboard as 4:03.1. There were three official watches. Marion Miller had 4:03.0, Reeves Peters had 4:03.1, and Louis House had 4:03.3. The high and low clockings were thrown out in the days before electronic timing, leaving the middle figure as the official time.

Coach Bill Easton

The next day, Easter Sunday, Santee and Denning were married, with Easton and his wife standing in for the groom's parents. Eighteen days later, on Thursday, May 6, 1954, news began to spread around the world: "Bannister runs 3:59.4." Mother Nature had possibly deprived 16,000 Relays fans the opportunity to see an historic run. Only 1,200 witnessed Bannister's run at Iffley Road in Oxford, England.

The next year at the KU Relays, despite the fact that Bannister had already broken four minutes, Santee was determined to make another attempt at his own milestone. Three weeks earlier he had run 4:00.5 at the Texas Relays, and he had just recently run a 2:59 three-quarter mile on a training run at the Haskell Institute track. This was to be a paced attempt with Dick Wilson running the first half in 1:59 and Art Dalzell running a 60-second third quarter. But nature in the form of wind, rain and hail rendered such a run impossible. Santee settled for a 4:11.4, remarkable under the circumstances but not the record 13,000 fans had hoped to see.

Santee never achieved his 4:00 goal despite running under 4:10 a total of 22 times (counting relay carries). Santee appeared somewhat bitter about the various reasons the four-minute mile eluded him. Some feel that the "Cocky Cowboy", as he was sometimes called, never believed that either Bannister or Landy were superior runners to him. Josy Barthel of Luxembourg, the Olympic 1500-meter champion who had defeated both Bannister and Landy in 1952 said, "I believe Santee can beat them both. Santee has not yet been pushed." Santee's point exactly. The Kansan, who was fond of speaking of himself in the third person, stated rather hyperbolically, "If you locked Bannister onto the Twentieth Century Limited he couldn't beat Santee."

**SUB-FOUR PAIR.**
Alan Webb (left) and Peter van der Westhuizen battle it out in 2009 on their way to two sub-four-minute marks, one of four years that multiple milers have broken four minutes in the same race at the KU Relays.

The Glenn Cunningham Mile Run continues to be called that, in honor of the early Jayhawk star. The 1500 is now known as the Wes Santee 1500-Meter Run. At the Kansas Relays, the elusive four-minute-mile barrier has been eclipsed 18 times, not counting relay carries. It took a dozen years after Santee's Easter weekend effort for the Relays fans to finally see it happen the first time … by another Kansas native who had captured the track world's imagination. See the list on page 57, in chronological order of achievement, from Jim Ryun to Cory Leslie.[1]

[1] A more complete description of the assault on four minutes by Bannister, Landy and Santee is beyond the scope of this book. However, an informative and entertaining account is the outstanding book *The Perfect Mile: Three Athletes, One Goal, and Less Than Four Minutes to Achieve It*, written by Neal Bascomb and published by Houghton Mifflin Company.

# Four-Minute Milers at the Kansas Relays

| Year | Name | Affiliation | Time |
|------|------|-------------|------|
| 1966 | Jim Ryun | Kansas Freshman | 3:55.8 |
| 1967 | Jim Ryun | Kansas Sophomore | 3:54.7 (Meet Record) |
| 1971 | Jim Ryun | Ex-Kansas | 3:55.8 |
| 1971 | Tom Von Ruden | Ex-Oklahoma State | 3:57.2 |
| 1971 | John Mason | Ex-Ft. Hays State (Kan.) | 3:57.9 |
| 1971 | Larry Rose | Oklahoma State | 3:59.5 |
| 1972 | Jim Ryun | Ex-Kansas | 3:57.1 |
| 1972 | Tom Von Ruden | Pacific Coast Club, Ex-Oklahoma State | 3:57.9 |
| 1972 | Larry Rose | Pacific Coast Club, Ex-Oklahoma State | 3:59.6 |
| *1981 | Tom Byers | Unattached, Ex-Ohio State | 3:59.11 |
| 1996 | Michael Cox | Nike Track Club, Ex-KU | 3:59.20 |
| 1997 | Paul McMullen | ASICS, Ex-Eastern Michigan | 3:59.88 |
| 2009 | Alan Webb | Nike Track Club, Ex-Michigan | 3:58.90 |
| 2009 | Peter van der Westhuizen | Team Nebraska Brooks, Ex-Nebraska | 3:59.54 |
| 2012 | Peter van der Westhuizen | Unattached, Ex-Nebraska | 3:56.90 |
| 2012 | A.J. Acosta | Nike Track Club, Ex-Oregon | 3:57.08 |
| 2012 | David Adams | Lincoln Track Club, Ex-Nebraska | 3:58.44 |
| 2013 | Cory Leslie | Ex-Ohio State | 3:58.18 |

*This was the only Glenn Cunningham Invitational Mile held between 1979 and 1993.

# 6

## Protest and Promise
### April 22, 1972

"In a split second all the many years of training, pain, sweat, blisters, and agony of running were simply and irrevocably wiped out. But I tried! I would much rather fail knowing I had put forth an honest effort than never to have tried at all."

-- KU Olympian Cliff Cushman
"An Open Letter to Youth"

Kansas hurdler, Olympian, and MIA pilot Cliff Cushman

College campuses were fertile ground for the burgeoning number of Vietnam protests that were springing up around the country like mushrooms. The University of Kansas in 1972 was no exception. The Student Senate passed, by a vote of 49-19 with eight abstentions, to request of Chancellor E. Laurence Chalmers, Jr., permission to rally at the 47th annual Kansas Relays. The request was granted on the condition that the demonstration would be peaceful. David Dillon, student body president from Hutchinson, was asked to use his influence to keep it that way. "The idea was not to disrupt the Relays," Dillon said.

A mass march into the stadium was planned between events. At 11 a.m., with about 10,000 people in the stands, several hundred demonstrators marched silently into the stadium carrying banners opposing the war. Dillon then made a brief statement about the Student Senate resolution in opposition to the war before introducing John Musgrave, a member of the Vietnam Veterans Against the War. Musgrave, an ex-Marine who had been wounded three times during his tour in Vietnam, then proceeded to give some harrowing, but hardly verifiable, facts about the war. Among them:

- Over 300 Indochinese civilians have been killed in the war each day.
- Over one ton of bombs have been dropped for every minute the Nixon administration has been in office.
- More bombs have been dropped in Vietnam than in either World War II or Korea.

When he asked the spectators to stand up and join hands to show their support for the demonstration, the response was mostly favorable.

With 70-degree temperatures and defending champion Jim Ryun gearing up for the 1972 Olympics, perhaps seeking to break his own mile record, the stands filled up quickly. By the opening ceremony, approximately 25,000 were already in their seats. The 4,000 programs business manager John Novotny had ordered had long since been gobbled up. "We were

War Protestors Demonstrate Outside Memorial Stadium
*Demonstrators remained peaceful despite unfriendly crowd*

**SIGNS OF THE TIME.** This photo from the April 24, 1972 *University Daily Kansan* captured the sentiments of thousands of protestors on Campanile Hill.

setting up shop for about 22,000 people," Novotny said. The Campanile hillside was also full of spectators, as always. But this year they were not just freeloaders; they were part of the Vietnam protest that had been going on all week.

As 2:40 p.m., the scheduled time for the Glenn Cunningham Mile, approached, the crowd began to swell. Lines were so long at the ticket booths that KU officials eventually just waved the latecomers in. The orderly, but noisy, Campanile Hill protesters began to saunter down the hill and crowded the south fence, singing and shouting anti-war slogans. In 1972, the shot put area was at the base of Campanile Hill, and two shot putters who had both thrown farther than 70 feet before

**SHOT AT THE PROTEST.** 1968 Olympian Randy Matson and his shot put competitors threw just below the commotion of the 1972 protests.

were dueling it out. Neither Al Feuerbach, the winner with a toss of 69 feet, 1 inch, nor Randy Matson, blamed their sub-par performances on the distractions. Matson, the Olympic gold medalist in 1968 and the world-record holder at 71-5, only managed 68-3.75, a respectable throw for anyone else, but disappointing to him.

The pole vault was also affected by the protestors. An impromptu demonstration inside the stadium around noon delayed the vault for half an hour, critical because there were over 40 entrants, which included five open competitors who agreed to jump in conjunction with the university/ college competitors. Because of the size of the field, the collegians were to stop at 16 feet while the open competitors continued. For some reason, that did not happen. Among the open competitors was Bob Seagren, Olympic champion in 1968 and runner-up in 1972. He had to settle for third behind eventual winner Kjell Isaksson, world record holder at 18 feet, 2 inches, and his Swedish countryman Hans Lagerqvist. Both Swedes jumped 17-5, but Isaksson won with fewer misses. Isaksson didn't even take his first jump until 4½ hours after the competition started. He took three attempts at 17-10, but anxiousness may have cost him any realistic attempt to clear the height; he and Lagerqvist needed to make an 8 p.m. flight out of Kansas City for the west coast. They didn't make it and had to wait another four hours for a midnight flight. Isaksson was later to say in response to a question about the large field, "Twelve is enough and maybe that's a little too much, too. When you have to wait, it all disappears. The darkness made it difficult too."

By the time the Cunningham Mile was scheduled to begin, the crowd had grown to an estimated 32,000, still the largest crowd to ever attend the Relays. The drawing card was, of course, Ryun, who was set to run against an elite field that included another well-known Kansan, Ken Swenson. Swenson had run collegiately at Kansas State and was now running for the US Army. The competitors were warmed up, primed and ready to toe the line. At that moment of greatest exposure, the microphone was

SWEDISH VAULTERS. Hans Lagerqvist and Kjell Isaksson had plenty of down time during their 1972 visit to the Relays, whether resting between vaults (left) or signing autographs, as the winner Isaksson does here.

given to Mona Hamman, assistant instructor in Western Civilization, to read the second allowed statement about the demonstration. She was not so well received as Musgrave had been earlier in the day and the reading of the statement was drowned out several times by boos, even when she requested a moment of silent prayer for the men who had died in Vietnam. Musgrave was upset by the lack of respect for his fallen comrades. "Those people who booed and jeered are worse animals than I was when I was forced to do their killing," Musgrave said. Ryun's comment about the delay was, "I felt good after my warm-up, but there was a delay before the race and I lost some of it."

When the race finally started, the record crowd was not disappointed. The milers stayed tightly bunched throughout the first three laps. Ryun was the early leader, then drifted back into the pack. At the start of the final lap, Swenson surged to the front but was soon overtaken by Tom Von Ruden, and then Ryun. The duel was on. Ryun ran a devastating 53.8 for the last quarter and finished in 3:57.1 to Von Ruden's 3:57.9. Larry Rose was not far behind in 3:59.6. Swenson faded, but not much, finishing fourth in 4:00.5, closely followed by Peter Kaal in 4:00.8. When the race was over, thousands began to exit the stadium despite many top-notch events still on the schedule.

This is how it was in Lawrence, Kan., on April 22, 1972. Half a globe away near the hamlet of An Loc, South Vietnam, 65 miles northwest of Saigon, a beleaguered and outnumbered coalition of American

**STAR ATTRACTION.** Jim Ryun always brought big crowds to the Relays while he was on campus as a student, as shown here, and afterward when he returned, as he did in the chaotic 1972 meet.

and South Vietnamese staunchly defended the city against an attack by the Viet Cong. It was just another day in a battle that lasted 66 days, a part of North Vietnam's "Easter Offensive of 1972." Estimated casualties for the Viet Cong in that endeavor were 10,000 killed, 15,000 wounded and 27 tanks destroyed. American losses were estimated at 8,000 killed or missing (2,300 in An Loc) and 30 tanks destroyed.*

# Other Facts Related to April 22, 1972

- Herb Washington of Michigan ran a Relays record 9.2 for 100 yards to defeat Ivory Crockett of Southern Illinois, who also clocked a 9.2. Cliff Branch of Colorado edged former Nebraska star Charlie Greene for third. Greene and Branch had shared the previous record at 9.3 with Olympian John Carlos.

- The coordinating committee for anti-war activities planned a series of events, including a demonstration to be held at a Robert Dole speech and a demonstration at Forbes Air Force Base in Topeka.

- According to the Vietnam Conflict Extract Data File, 58,220 were killed in military-related incidents, 759 of which were killed in 1972. Civilian casualties, of course, were much greater.

- No protestors were arrested or injured.

- KU sophomore Barry Schur became the first Jayhawk high jumper to clear seven feet. His leap of 7 feet, 1 inch was a Relays record.

- Vietnam was never officially declared a war; only a "conflict" or a "police action."

- Jim Hershberger, on the track that bears his name, lunged at the tape to narrowly defeat Loren Schnell, who also recorded a 2:03.5 in the Master's 800. It was an interesting battle between 40-year-old, neatly groomed and attired Hershberger, a Wichita oil millionaire; and 41-year-old Schnell, a self-avowed hippie, with long, black hair and full beard wearing a non-descript white T-shirt. He had been running only three years "to get some exercise." Schnell had walked away from being a successful businessman in Boulder, Colo., for 16 years and now described his profession as "dishwasher." His description of the two lifestyles was, "The difference now is that I'm living. Before, I was just existing." His transportation to Lawrence? Hitchhiking.

- American involvement in Vietnam finally concluded on April 30, 1975, with a massive and hectic withdrawal of American assistance to South Vietnam. The South was soon overrun by the Viet Cong amidst much carnage and devastation.

* Casualty estimates varied greatly, depending on the source.

# Cushman's words still hold true

On Nov. 6, 1975, three years after the protests at KU and nine years after his plane was shot down, the 400 hurdles silver medalist at the 1960 Rome Olympics was officially declared dead. Cliff Cushman joined the U.S. Air Force after graduating from KU. On Sept. 25, 1966, the F-105D plane he was piloting on a combat mission over Vietnam was shot down. He was listed as Missing in Action until after the war. He was survived by his wife Carolyn and son Colin. One of the most moving and inspirational letters ever written in sport was the letter he wrote to the youth of his Grand Forks, Neb., hometown. It was written on his flight home from Los Angeles after he had tripped on the fifth hurdle in the 1964 Olympic Trials and failed to qualify. In it he urged the youth not to feel sorry for him but to set goals for themselves instead.

This column was written by Pete Goering and ran in the *Topeka Capital-Journal* on June 8, 1999. It is reprinted here, with the permission of that publication.

By PETE GOERING
*The Capital-Journal*

Thirty-five years ago, the late Kansas track star Cliff Cushman wrote "An Open Letter to Youth" after he stumbled and fell in the 1964 Olympic Trials and failed to qualify in the 400-meter hurdles.

Cushman's letter, which should be posted in every high school and college locker room in the country, has appeared previously in the *Capital-Journal*, most recently in 1977.

A yellowed copy of that letter arrived last week from Topeka reader Wilmer Piper, who included a brief note.

"I ran across this old clipping and I thought it was so good that it should be published again," he wrote. "I hope that you'll agree with me."

I do. Here is Cushman's letter, as timely and thought-provoking today as it was in the mid-Sixties:

"Don't feel sorry for me. I feel sorry for some of you! You may have seen the U.S. Olympic Trials on television Sept. 13. If so, you watched me hit the fifth hurdle, fall and lie on the track in an inglorious heap of skinned elbows, bruised hips, torn knees and injured pride, unsuccessful in my attempt to make the Olympic team for the second time.

"In a split second all the many years of training, pain, sweat, blisters and agony of running were simply and irrevocably wiped out. But I tried! I would much rather fail knowing I had to put forth an honest effort than never to have tried at all.

**Cliff Cushman with his KU ring and suit as a 1960 Olympic team member.**

"This is not to say that everybody is capable of making the Olympic team. However, each of you is capable of trying to make your own personal Olympic team, whether it be the high school football team, the glee club, the honor roll, or whatever your goal may be.

"Unless your reach exceeds your grasp, how can you be sure what you can attain? And don't you think there are things better than cigarettes, hot rod cars, school dropouts, excessive make-up and ducktail grease cuts?

"Over 15 years ago I saw a star -- first place in the Olympic Games. I literally started to run after it. In 1960, I came within three yards of grabbing it; this year I stumbled, fell and watched it recede four more years away.

"Certainly, I was very disappointed in falling flat on my face. However, there is nothing I can do about it now but get up, pick the cinders from my wounds and take one more step followed by one more and one more, until the steps turn into the miles and the miles of success.

"I know I may never make it. The odds are against me, but I have something in my favor – desire and faith. Romans 5: 3-5 has always had an inspiration to me in this regard: "… we rejoice in our sufferings, knowing that suffering produces endurance, and endurance produces character, and character produces hope, and hope does not disappoint us.' At least I am going to try.

"How about you? Would a little extra effort on your part bring up your grade average? Would you have a better chance to make the football team if you stayed an extra 15 minutes after practice and worked on your blocking?

"Let me tell you something about yourselves. You are taller and heavier than any past generation in this country. You are spending more money, enjoying more freedom and driving more cars than ever before, yet many of you have never known the satisfaction of doing your best in sports, the joy of excelling the class, the wonderful feeling of completing a job, any job, and looking back on it knowing that you have done your best.

"I dare you to have your hair cut and not wilt under the comments of your so-called friends. I dare you to clean up your language. I dare you to honor your father and mother. I dare you to go to church without having to be compelled to go by your parents.

"I dare you to unselfishly help someone less fortunate than yourself and enjoy the wonderful feeling that goes with it. I dare you to to become physically fit. I dare you to read a book that is not required in school. I dare you to look up at the stars, not down at the mud, and set your sights on one of them that, up to now, you thought was unattainable. There is plenty of room at the top, but no room for anyone to sit down.

"Who knows? You may be surprised at what you can achieve with sincere effort. So get up, pick the cinders out of your wounds and take one more step.

"I dare you."

-- Clifton E. Cushman

# 7

# Détente on the Track
## Inviting the Soviets, 1983

"I can't think of anyone who thought or said that this project would work. I think everyone in Washington was dumbfounded when they heard the news."

--Bob Swan, founder of Athletes United for Peace (AUP)

Alexander Krupsky set a new Relays record during his stay.

David Austin Walsh, editor of the History News Network, called 1983 the most dangerous year of the Cold War. Granted, the time of greatest tension during that year came about in the latter part of the year, but the countries of Ronald Reagan and Mikhael Gorbachev existed in a world of spies and paranoia, with each fearing a preemptive nuclear strike against the other. President Jimmy Carter's boycott of the 1980 Moscow Olympics was recent history.

Into this milieu of distrust and acrimony entered Lawrence insurance executive Bob Swan. Despite this backdrop, Swan decided to strive for peace. In November 1982, he founded an organization called Athletes United for Peace (AUP). The National Advisory Board included such notables as Jo Jo White, Kansas assistant basketball coach at the time; KU women's basketball coach Marian Washington; Norman Cousins, editor of the *Saturday Review* and an avowed world peace advocate; and Dr. Karl Menninger, who with his father founded the Menninger Psychiatric Clinic in Topeka, Kan. Swan wisely chose Mark Scott, a 1980 KU graduate, to be his executive director. Scott had spent several years in Russia on a work studies program and spoke the language fluently. Furthermore, he had also been a Soviet analyst for the CIA. As Swan said, "You can not believe how well he knows the Soviet mind."

Scott sent KU coach Bob Timmons a letter asking if he would consider letting the Soviets be a part of the Kansas Relays. Timmons was excited at the prospect, but not optimistic. "Quite frankly," Timmons remarked, "I thought he was crazy." Given the go-ahead, on January 13, AUP sent a formal request to Soviet Ambassador Anatoly Dobrynin, asking that the Soviets send a team of 20 world-class athletes to the Kansas Relays. The request was accompanied by letters from Kansas Governor John Carlin, Chancellor Gene A. Budig, Athletic Director Monte Johnson, Timmons, and world-renowned alumnus Jim Ryun.

In addition, and perhaps most importantly, thousands of letters from local grade-school children imploring the Russians to come to the Relays were forwarded.

"We are getting bags and bags of letters from your children," Dobrynin said later.

"I think those letters were very persuasive," Swan said.

The initial response to the AUP's invitation, as expected, was not encouraging. On March 1, Scott received word that the Soviet Sports Commission

**WELCOMING PARTY.** Lawrence school children with sunflowers and wheat bouquets await the arrival of Soviet athletes at Kansas City International airport. Letters from Lawrence children were part of the attempt to encourage the Soviet Union to participate in the 1983 Relays.

declined the invitation, citing their "very tight schedule of training and competitions." Scott and Swan were about to give up when a glimmer of hope appeared. Sergei Guskov, New York correspondent of the influential Soviet periodical *Sovietskiy Sport*, said he would be in Moscow on March 10 and would talk to Marat Gramov, the head of the Soviet Sports Commission, about reconsidering. In the meantime, Scott and Swan went to Washington to solicit help from Kansas Senator Bob Dole and Massachusetts Senator Edward Kennedy, a member of the Senate Foreign Relations Committee. Despite these efforts and support from Kansas Representative Jim Slattery, Kansas Senator Nancy Kassebaum, and Menninger, disappointment came again on March 14 in the form of a second letter of refusal from the Soviet Sports Commission. The media was advised that there would be no Soviets at the Relays in 1983. This announcement put the Relays in jeopardy for subsequent years, because a lack of star power and a waning of interest presaged a meager crowd, which would further exacerbate the bleak financial cloud hanging over the future of the Relays.

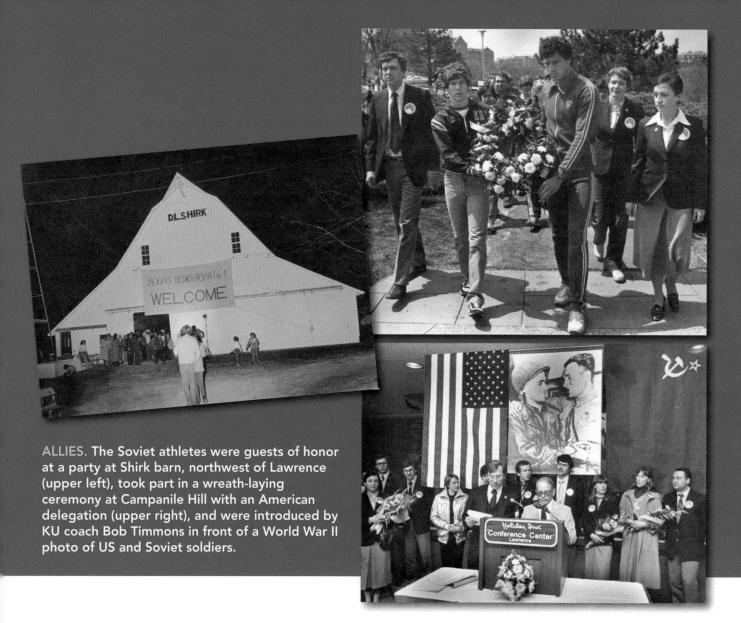

ALLIES. The Soviet athletes were guests of honor at a party at Shirk barn, northwest of Lawrence (upper left), took part in a wreath-laying ceremony at Campanile Hill with an American delegation (upper right), and were introduced by KU coach Bob Timmons in front of a World War II photo of US and Soviet soldiers.

Totally unexpected, an announcement came on March 22. Anatoly Dyuzhev and Sergei Skachko of the Soviet embassy called Scott and said they would be able to come to the Relays after all. They would send a contingent of 20, including coaches and a physician, and as many as 15 quality athletes to Lawrence via Montreal. The Soviets were to pay for the

trans-Atlantic flight to Montreal and the AUP would pay all expenses from Montreal to Lawrence and back to Montreal. This meant raising in the neighborhood of $10,000 to $15,000. "The quality of our accommodations will depend upon the size of our fund," Scott said. They were determined not to dip into the already strapped Relays budget.

Timmons was pleased, yet "terribly surprised" that the Soviets would come. Regrettably, these world-class athletes would not have a lot of competition from American collegians as there would be no open category for the second straight year because of the burgeoning costs of acquiring elite athletes. Still, the decathlon and the pole vault, with three American athletes having gone higher than 18 feet, appeared to be competitive. The Russians came with the disclaimer that this was not their competitive season, that they were here for fun competition, to relax a bit, and to use the good training facilities. "This is our preparational season," said the men's coach, Igor Ter-Ovanesyan.

**FLAG-BEARER.** After the pre-meet hoopla, hosts and guests got down to business on the track. Shot putter Janis Bojars carried the flag at the opening ceremonies. In deference to the Soviet visitors, no rockets were launched as they customarily were at the "bombs bursting in air" phrase in the national anthem.

Ter-Ovanesyan was well known in track and field circles. He was a five-time Olympian from 1956-1972 and well known for his long jump duals with U. S. Olympic champion Ralph Boston. He spoke fluent English, and was looking forward to seeing both Boston and Bob Beamon, who were expected to be in attendance at the Relays Saturday afternoon. The Soviet women were coached by Nikolai Malyshev.

RECORD-BREAKERS. Seven KU Relays records were broken by Soviet athletes, including Latvian Janis Bojars, who extended the shot put mark to 68-7.75. Bojars was silver medalist at the European Championships one year earlier.

CCCP. These ominous Cold War initials meant only friendship inside Memorial Stadium in 1983.

On a windy day in April, 14 Soviet athletes dominated the "Friendship Relays," and were heartily cheered by 19,200 American spectators. They recorded nine victories (every event they entered) and set seven meet records despite less than ideal conditions. As predicted, the pole vault was the most hotly contested event. Alexander Krupsky went 18 feet, 4 inches to win. Doug Lytle also cleared 18-4, but missed his first attempt at that height, thereby relegating himself to second. The Soviet athletes were given commemorative Relays watches, separate from those given to collegiate winners. Elena Petushkova, vice chair of the National Olympic Council of the Soviet Union, was complimentary in an account published in the May 14 issue of *Sovietskiy Sport*, one of the most widely read magazines in the world in 1983 with distribution in over 100 countries and a circulation of over 4,000,000: "With our very first steps on Kansas soil, we understood

FRIENDSHIP. *The University Daily Kansan* played up the cooperation between the school and the visiting Soviets in its special edition and its regular coverage.

that they really were waiting for us here. They were waiting with anticipation and with feelings of friendship." She went on to say that sport performance was only part of why the spectators came out to support the event. As she put it, "The American people want friendship with the Soviet people; our peoples must live in peace and harmony – this was the basic idea of all those with whom we spoke."

The efforts of Bob Swan, Mark Scott, the AUP, and the many advocates, both American and Soviet, illustrated the power of sport to bring people together and promote peace. Only three years earlier, the American boycott of the Olympics in Moscow refused to let that happen. Sadly, less than 18 months later, the Soviet boycott of the Los Angeles Games also snuffed out the power of sport. The diplomacy of the Lawrence contingent had succeeded where other international leaders could not.

# Soviet Performances at the 1983 Kansas Relays

| Name | Event | Mark | Of Note ... |
|---|---|---|---|
| Grigory Degtyarev | Men's Decathlon | 8,202 points | New KU Relays Record |
| Alexander Nevsky | Men's Decathlon | 8,178 points | |
| Yuri Tamm | Men's Hammer | 244-2 | New KU Relays Record |
| Janis Bojars | Men's Shot Put | 68-7.75 | New KU Relays Record |
| Nikolai Musyenko | Men's Triple Jump | 55-9.25 | New KU Relays Record |
| Gennadiy Valyukevich | Men's Triple Jump | 53-11 | |
| Alexander Krupsky | Men's Pole Vault | 18-4 | New KU Relays Record |
| Sergei Kulibaba | Men's Pole Vault | 16-6 | Only Soviet to lose to any American. Doug Lytle, Jeff Buckingham and Joe Dial all had higher jumps. |
| Svetlana Ulmasova | Women's 3000 | 9:13.50 | New KU Relays Record |
| Nadezhda Raldugina | Women's 1500 | 4:08.94 | New KU Relays Record |
| Nadezhda Olizarenko | Women's 800 | 2:06.87 | Was world record holder at 1:53.43. |
| Lyudmila Veselkova | Women's 800 | 2:09.9 | |
| Olga Mineyeva | Women's 800 | 2:10.5 | |
| Lyudmila Veselkova, Nadezhda Raldugina, Olga Mineyeva, Nadezhda Olizarenko | Women's 2-Mile Relay | 8:49.06 | |

# PART III

Jim Ryun anchors KU's distance
medley world record in 1969.

ACTION ACTION ACTION

T he Kansas Relays has hosted many athletes. Tens of thousands of them. They have competed to the best of their abilities, and to be sure, the Relays is not only about great marks and great athletes. But some have stood out more than the rest through their actions. The meet has always attracted elite performers in all events, from year one to the present. They arrived on the KU campus for many reasons, whether they were home-grown or from overseas. Some come in high school, and return as collegiate stars and even Olympians. The best are lured to the challenge of facing other comparable foes. Race directors have always relished the challenge of bringing the world's best athletes to Lawrence, Kan. In Part III, you will read about the best of the best, from distance runners (Chapter 8) and sprinters and hurdlers (Chapter 9) on the track, to horizontal (Chapter 10) and vertical (Chapter 11) jumpers in the pits, to the throwers (Chapter 12) and versatile decathletes and heptathletes (Chapter 13). A table of Olympians who have competed at the KU Relays ends each of these chapters. Those who won medals are listed first and chronologically by gold, silver, and then bronze. The non-medalists follow in chronological order, though this organization cannot be entirely precise because of overlapping Olympic appearances, and because some athletes naturally have different performances in different events.

# Like Pearls on a Necklace

## Distance Runners

"People can't understand why a man runs. They don't see any sport in it. Argue it lacks the sight and thrill of body contact. Yet, the conflict is there, more raw and challenging than any man vs. man competition. For in running it is man against himself, the cruelest of opponents. The other runners are not the real enemies. His adversary lies within him, in his ability, with brain and heart to master himself and his emotions."

--"What Makes A Man Run?"
By Glenn Cunningham

Charlie Gruber held off Alan Webb in a 2003 mile dual at the Relays.

Runners who have competed in distances of 800 meters or longer at the Kansas Relays have been in every Olympics since the inception of the meet. The University of Kansas has had its share of these competitors. Like pearls on a necklace, they have followed one after the other to form a circle of excellence unparalleled in collegiate history.

Glenn Cunningham started the legacy in 1932 by winning the first 1500 meters ever contested at the KU Relays. He would compete later that year in the Los Angeles Olympics and place fourth. Few stories in sport are as inspiring as the determination of an 8-year-old boy from the tiny southwest Kansas town of Elkhart, who was expected to possibly die and certainly never walk again, but grew into an Olympian and was at one time the world's fastest miler. The young Cunningham's job was to light the schoolhouse stove to warm it up before others arrived, but someone had mistakenly put gasoline rather than kerosene in the fuel can. The resulting explosion took the life of his 13-year-old brother Floyd and left Glenn's lower body badly burned. The doctor recommended amputation of his legs because the likelihood of him ever walking again was remote, but Glenn put up such resistance that it was not done. After years of therapy and stubborn determination, he gradually regained the use of his legs, attended KU and became a world-class runner. He followed up his victory in the 1932 Relays with another win in 1933. He also won the mile run in 1934 in the first running of the race that has since become the Glenn Cunningham Mile. Cunningham would win the 1500 again in 1936, the year he placed second in the Berlin Olympics in the same event. He also won the mile at KU in 1939. Until 1976, the 1500 was typically run in Olympic years and the mile run in non-Olympic years. Starting in 1977, the Wes Santee 1500-Meter Run has been run every year of the Relays except for 1994. The mile, on the other hand, was run only in 1981 between the years 1979 and 1993. Since 1995, both the Cunningham Mile and the Santee 1500 have been run each year.

**FROM VINES TO SHARKS.** The steeplechase looked much different when it was first contested in 1936 at the KU Relays (left) compared to 2011, when Meagan Hudson of Missouri Baptist, leaping over a "shark", won the second of three consecutive women's titles. Tom Deckard of Indiana took the 1936 men's race, when vines crept through the hurdle. The first women's race was held in 1997, when Melissa Teemant was victorious.

Cunningham ran the mile or its metric equivalent each year at the Relays between 1932 and 1940, winning five of those years. However the competition was fierce, and there were no easy wins. In 1933, he ran 3:53.3 in the 1500 to defeat a formidable opponent in Glenn Dawson, an Oklahoma runner who had won the Relays 3000 in 1931 and would defeat Cunningham in a special mile competition in 1935. Dawson was Cunningham's Olympic teammate in both 1932 and 1936 as a steeplechaser. Cunningham had to run 4:12.7 to best Penn's Gene Venzke in 1934, one of their many

Glenn
Cunningham

Wes
Santee

## KU's Distance Legends:
## From Cunningham to Gruber

Starting in the 1930s, Kansas track and field has been blessed by a nearly unending string of great distance runners. From Glenn Cunningham in the upper left, going clockwise through the years, are the Jayhawk distance-running pearls on a necklace, finishing with Charlie Gruber in the 2000s.

Charlie
Gruber

Michael
Cox

Billy
Mills

Bill
Dotson

Jim
Ryun

heralded battles. In 1932, Venzke broke the 1500 world record with a time of 3:53.4 while he was still in high school. However, he was already 24 years old, having dropped out of high school for a few years. Cunningham beat him out for the third spot in the 1932 Olympic Trials. Venzke was expected to qualify but had pulled a muscle in training and lost some conditioning, so he had to settle for fourth. He did make the Olympic team in 1936, finishing behind Cunningham and Archie San Romani of Kansas State Teachers College (now Emporia State) in the 1500 at the Olympic Trials. Cunningham would go on to place second in Berlin and San Romani fourth.

San Romani's career in many ways was similar to Cunningham's. He grew up as a coal miner's son in the small southeast Kansas community of Frontenac. At age eight, Archie was run over by a truck, which damaged his right leg so badly that doctors initially thought his life would be threatened if he did not have it amputated. Fortunately, it was not amputated and he began to run as a form of rehabilitation. In 1936, the same year that he, Cunningham and Venzke would run in the 1500 in Berlin, San Romani ran a 4:12 anchor carry to propel Kansas State Teachers College (now Emporia State) to a world record in the distance medley. San Romani went on to win the Relays mile in 1937 and 1938, beating Cunningham both years. The 1938 field also included Venzke. San Romani, like Cunningham and Venzke, was a world-record holder, running the 2000 meters in 5:16.8. The three of them, with the addition of Chuck Hornbostel (himself a two-time Olympian in the 800 meters) set a world record of 17:17.2 in a four-mile relay in London 11 days after Hornbostel's 800 run in the 1936 Olympics (On the same day, Hornbostel was also a member of a two-mile relay team that set a world record.). Cunningham and San Romani, who was two years younger than Cunningham, would race each other 28 times with each winning 14. Both had sons who were accomplished runners and state high school mile champions at the Kansas State High School Track and Field Meet. They were Glenn Cunningham, Jr. and Archie San Romani, Jr. A future pearl on the Kansas distance-running necklace, Jim Ryun, also had a son, Ned, who became a state high school mile champion.

In 1940, 12,000 fans watched Cunningham finish last in his final race at the Relays. The winner was Blaine Rideout of North Texas State, whose 4:10.1 mile was among the best in the nation that year. With no Cunningham or San Romani or other Kansan to cheer, there would be no favorite son for more than a decade. With the onset of World War II, track meets seemed a frivolous exercise. The Olympics were cancelled in 1940 and 1944, and the Kansas Relays were cancelled in 1943, 1944 and 1945. When they resumed, Olympians made their mark, but this time they were not from Kansas. Don Gehrmann, a 1948 Olympian from Wisconsin, won the mile in both 1949 and 1950, equaling Rideout's 4:10.1 from 1940. Gehrmann's 1950 win was over another Olympian-to-be, Javier Montez of Texas Western. The next year, Fred Wilt, formerly of Indiana, barely beat Gehrmann to keep him from a three-peat. Wilt was a U.S. entrant in the 10,000 meters in both the 1948 London Olympics and the 1952 Helsinki Games. Since 1952 was an Olympic year, the 1500 was run at KU instead of the mile. Montez was defeated by future Olympian Ted Wheeler of Iowa. Montez would run the 1500 in Helsinki in 1952, and Wheeler would run the 1500 in Melbourne in 1956. Wheeler and fellow Hawkeye Deacon Jones were the first black American distance runners in the Olympic Games. Wheeler had quit school in Rossville, Ga., at the age of 15 to get a job. One day he took a break from

**KU'S FOUR HORSEMEN.** Dick Wilson hands off to Lloyd Koby at the 1953 KU Relays. Those two with Art Dalzell and Wes Santee headlined the Jayhawks' distance relay dominance in the early 1950s.

work to go visit his father in Evanston, Ga., and happened to see some local high school runners go past. He joined them and ran along. When he got to the high school with the other boys, the coach inquired as to who he was and convinced him to enroll in school and become a member of the track team. Wheeler did so and not only became an elite runner at Iowa, he later became head coach at his alma mater. As a runner it was his avowed purpose to shatter the prevailing stereotype that black men could not be successful in distance races.

With the advent of the 1950s and the appearance of Wes Santee, Kansans again had someone to rally behind. His unsuccessful quest at the four-minute mile is chronicled in Chapter 5. Just as Cunningham and San Romani had plenty of competition before the war, there were plenty of good runners besides Santee in the '50s, and several of them ran for the University of Kansas. Herb Semper won the individual NCAA cross country championship in both 1950 and 1951. Santee was the winner in 1953 and with his "Four Horsemen" friends, Art Dalzell, Lloyd Koby, and Dick Wilson, won the NCAA cross-country title in 1953. They were called the Four Horsemen because they came to KU together, ran together and graduated together. Allen Frame, a member of that championship team, would be the NCAA individual cross country champion the following year.

UPENDED. Ron Eeles of Wichita University (now Wichita State) found the steeplechase barrier more than he bargained for during the 1957 Kansas Relays.

Clearly, Coach Bill Easton had plenty of firepower with which to fill relay teams for the prestigious Texas-Kansas-Drake Triple Crown series, and fill them he did. At the Kansas Relays, KU won 10 of 11 four-mile relays between 1949 and 1959. Only Oklahoma State in 1955, with Swedish Olympian Sture Landqvist on the team, was able to break the Jayhawk dominance. Kansas was also able to capture four of five distance medley crowns between 1951 and 1955. In 1952, Santee's sophomore year, he anchored in 4:11.6 to help the Four Horsemen set a meet record of 17:18.3. He then ran a 3:02.0 three-quarters to help his team win the distance medley. For his efforts, he was chosen Most Outstanding Performer.

The steeplechase in 1956 featured Iowa Olympian Deacon Jones. Unfortunately, the race started five minutes early and he heard the gun go off as he was entering the infield. He ran across the infield tearing off his sweat shirt as he ran. He never had time to take off his sweat pants. Not only did he start about 100 yards behind everyone else, he also ran the race with water-logged sweats. Needless to say, he did not win. Despite losing to Texas in the distance medley, 1957 was a good meet for the Jayhawks. KU, with Jerry McNeal running a 4:12.7 anchor, was the first intercollegiate team to dip below 17:00 in the four-mile relay at 16:57.8. Tom Skutka then doubled back from the four-mile relay to help the two-mile relay team set a new standard at 7:32.3. Billy Tidwell of Kansas State Teachers College (now Emporia State) was voted Most Outstanding Performer in 1957 for his anchor

SUB-17 MINUTES. In 1957, KU's quartet of (from left) Harold Long, Tom Skutka, Jan Howell, and Jerry McNeal became the first four-mile relay team to break the 17-minute mark.

carries in both the sprint medley and mile relays. In 1958, an all-sophomore team from Oklahoma set a world record in the sprint medley. South African Gail Hodgson anchored with a 1:48 half mile. He would return the next day with a 4:07.4 anchor to beat Texas in the distance medley and erase the Longhorns' year-old record by 13 seconds. Another South African, Ernst Kleynhans, clocked a 3:02 three-quarters. Hi Gernert and Bob Ringo were the other sophs on the team.

The 1960s opened with an exciting race as sophomore Bill Dotson of KU narrowly defeated Archie San Romani, Jr., then a Wichita State freshman. The time, 4:00.4, was impressive and 16,000 fans saw it. Crowds over 10,000 became the norm, thanks in large measure to the emergence of yet another Kansas miler sensation, Jim Ryun, who dominated the '60s as Santee had the '50s. Ryun began to make his mark at the Relays as a junior at Wichita East, the high school where Bob Timmons had also coached San Romani, Jr. Ryun ran 4:11 and broke San Romani's record by six and a half seconds. He followed that up as a senior with a 4:04.8 mile on Friday and a 1:47.7 half mile on Saturday to help East set a national record of 7:42.9 in the two-mile relay. Fortunately, the events were scheduled on successive days, because at that time high school rules forbade running more than one race of a quarter mile or more in a single day. Ryun's exploits only got better in 1966. Freshmen could not compete on varsity relays at that time, so he ran 3:55.8 in the Cunningham Mile, the second fastest time in the world that year. For an encore, Ryun came back a few hours later with a 46.9 quarter mile and anchored the Frosh-Juco mile relay to a Relays record of 3:15.5, all on a soggy track in front of 15,000 fans who braved less than favorable weather conditions.

The following year, 1967, brought not only a record crowd of 23,700, but also another mile record by Ryun. He ran 3:54.7 to not only better his time of the previous year, but also his national collegiate record. That record still stands as the stadium record. With 1968 being an Olympic year, the mile was replaced by the 1500. Despite foul weather, 20,000 showed up to see Ryun win. Olympic gold-medal winner and 10,000-meter Olympic-record holder Billy Mills was upset by Jim Murphy of Air Force when Mills misjudged the finish line and didn't start his kick soon enough. The 10,000 is now named the Billy Mills 10,000-Meter Run. In 1969, Ryun's last in the pink and blue of Kansas, he ran a 3:57.6 anchor carry to lead the team of Jim Neihouse (1:50.4), Randy Julian (47.1), and Thorn Bigley (2:57.9) to a world record time of 9:33.0 in the distance medley. This broke the former world record of 9:33.8, which was set by a KU contingent of Curt Grindal, Dwight

**WORLD RECORD QUARTET.** Front to back, in order of carry, is KU's 1969 distance-medley world-record relay team: Jim Neihouse, Randy Julian, Thorn Bigley and Jim Ryun.

Peck, Tom Yergovich and Ryun at the Drake Relays two years earlier. Kansas State Olympian Ken Swenson led the Wildcats to a very fast two-mile relay time of 7:22.60.

Ryun bypassed the Relays in 1970, but came back in 1971 with 11 other world and national record holders. He thrilled the crowd with a 3:55.8 mile time. Another Olympian, Florida law student Frank Shorter, lopped 30 seconds off the three-mile run in 13:08.6. 1971 also marked the 11th consecutive year of competition at the KU Relays by Kansas State's Conrad Nightingale, the last seven being in the steeplechase, which is what he ran in Mexico City in 1968. The largest crowd in Relays history, 32,000, came out in 1972 hoping to see Ryun run a world record. It was also the year of the Vietnam Protest, which is chronicled in Chapter 6. Ryun's time of 3:57.1 was certainly a quality performance, but disappointing to many. No one will ever know what effect the distractions of the protest had on the Cunningham Mile and other competitions.

The 1960s had many other outstanding performances besides Ryun's. In 1961, Jim Grelle, who ran the 1500 in the 1960 Rome Olympics, defeated Ernie Cunliffe, who ran the 800 in Rome, with a 4:07.4 mile. In 1962, Dotson anchored the KU four-mile relay with a 4:05.2 mile to help set a meet record of 16:53.1. Also in 1961, Howard Payne University from Brownwood, Texas, won its sixth consecutive two-mile relay. In 1963 Olympian Tom O'Hara's 4:06.6 closing mile led Loyola of Chicago to a collegiate distance medley record of 9:54.2. In the same year, Missouri ace Robin Lingle ran 4:04.8 to best John Camien of Emporia State in the Cunningham Mile. The following year, Lingle's 4:02 anchor led the Tigers to a meet record of 16:41.6 over KU in the four-mile relay, and Camien ran 4:03.2 to lower the college distance medley time to 9:48.4. Hylke van der Wal hitchhiked from Canada to set a record in the steeplechase at 8:56.3. He would go on to win the next two years in the steeplechase. George Scott of Oklahoma City pulled off a rare double in 1965. On Friday he won the three-mile and returned Saturday to win the mile in a close race over KU freshman Gene McClain and

**FASTER SHORTER: Former Yale star Frank Shorter ran for Florida Track Club when he won the three-mile race at KU in 1971, the year before he gave the burgeoning American running boom a major boost with his gold in the Olympic marathon.**

Kansas State sophomore Charlie Harper. Chris McCubbins, a Canadian 10,000-meter Olympian attending Oklahoma State, ran 8:46.6 to win the steeplechase in 1967. It was no surprise when Larbi Oukada was voted Most Outstanding Performer in 1970. All he did was win the six-mile in 28:45.5, anchor Fort Hays State to victory in the college distance medley, and place third in the steeplechase.

After Ryun's Munich 1500-meter appearance in 1972, KU would not have another Olympic distance runner until Charlie Gruber ran the 1500 in Athens in 2004, but there were plenty of Olympians from other schools performing at the Relays in between. Particularly impressive was 1973 when Dave Wottle of Bowling Green led his team to a four-mile relay record of 16:24.0. Kenyan Philip Ndoo of Eastern New Mexico won both the steeplechase and the six-mile run. As good as these performances were, the Most Outstanding Performer award went to his ENMU teammate, Mike Boit, a fellow Kenyan, who anchored the winning sprint medley and distance medley relays as well as the runner-up mile relay.

Ndoo got his Most Outstanding Performer award the following year when he set a record in the six-mile run, won the three-mile, and was part of the winning two-mile relay. He missed a fourth Relays watch when he failed to defend his steeplechase title. Also in 1974, Olympian Mike Durkin won the mile in 4:01.0. Since 1976 was an Olympic year, Rick Wohlhuter, a Notre Dame alum running for the Chicago Track Club, had to defend his mile championship

**WOTTLE AT FULL THROTTLE.**
Dave Wottle led Bowling Green to a meet record in the 1973 four-mile relay.

by winning the 1500 in a record time of 3:38.62. This was the first year for fully automatic timing (FAT) at the Relays. Randy Smith of Wichita State improved the steeplechase to the current 8:33.68. It was also the first year for metric distances, so the three-mile became the 5,000 meters and Shorter won in 14:17.20. The record lasted only a year, but that was still far longer than Bob McLeod of Pittsburg (Kan.) State held it in 1977. McLeod broke Shorter's record only to see Olympian Gary Bjorklund, formerly from Minnesota, lower it to 13:55.70 in the second heat. Bjorklund had made the 1976 Olympic team in the 10,000 despite losing a shoe at the Olympic Trials on the 14th lap of a 24½-lap race. While Shorter and Craig Virgin battled for first, Bjorklund made up a large deficit to edge Bill Rodgers for the coveted third spot. In 1977 at KU, Arkansas won its third consecutive distance-medley relay with Irish Olympian Niall O'Shaughnessy on the anchor carry. It was one of six Arkansas distance medley victories between 1975 and 1981.

The next sub-four-minute miler to attend KU after Ryun and Dotson was Michael Cox from Hannibal, Mo. Despite not being a native Kansan like the other KU greats already mentioned, he endeared himself to the Jayhawk faithful in 1991 as a freshman when he anchored both the distance medley and four-mile relays to championships. In 1992 he anchored the victorious four-mile relay victory and was awarded Most Outstanding Performer. As a KU senior, Cox narrowly missed the four-minute barrier when he ran 4:00.93 to win the Cunningham Mile. Cox had run a strong mile the previous day to help the Jayhawks win the four-mile relay. However, the next year, while running for the Nike Track Club, he ran 3:59.20. It was the 71st running of the Relays. Seven Jayhawk Olympians, were being honored, and Cox received inspiration from talking to them. As Cox said, "Yesterday I talked to Billy Mills, Jim Ryun and Wes Santee. All had great advice for me." So, with Ryun cheering from the sidelines, and Ryun's twin sons Ned and Drew serving as "rabbits," Cox battled a strong wind to become the third KU runner to break the magic barrier. It also garnered him his third Most Outstanding Performer award at the Relays.

With the turn of the century, yet another KU runner would join the four-minute club. Charlie Gruber from Denver won the Cunningham Mile

in 2000, and repeated in 2001. He also won in 2003; Gruber's mile time of 4:05.21 was just enough to defeat Alan Webb, then the American record holder in the mile. The 2002 race was cancelled due to inclement weather, though Gruber did anchor the distance medley to victory earlier in the meet that year. In 2004, both Gruber and Webb represented the United States in the 1500 meters in the Athens Olympics. Webb returned to the Relays in 2009 to win the Cunningham Mile in 3:58.9, the first sub-four mile since Paul McMullen ran 3:59.88 in 1997. The runner-up to Webb was Peter van der Westhuizen,

**DEAD HEAT.** Olympians Leo Manzano (foreground) and Nick Symmonds clocked an impressive and identical time of 4:00.13 in the 2013 KU Relays mile, but they still finished behind Cory Leslie's 3:58.18, the 18th sub-four-minute mile in meet history.

who also broke four minutes. Westhuizen, a Nebraska alum and something of a regular at the Relays, ran 3:56.9 in 2012 to defeat A. J. Acosta (3:57.08) and David Adams (3:58.44), who had also attended Nebraska. In 2013 Cory Leslie, formerly of Ohio State, broke the four-minute barrier in 3:58.18 with Leo Manzano (4:00.13), Nick Symmonds (4:00.13), Lee Emanuel (4:01.98) and van der Westhuizen (4:02.10) in hot pursuit.

Women athletes competed in the Relays in only a limited way until 1975, when a more complete program was added. One of the early highlights came in 1977 when Teri Anderson, who ran for Kansas State and later coached at KU, ran 16.06.8 and set an American record in the 5,000 that would hold up at the Relays until Patty Murray of Western Illinois broke it in 1986. Murray's record of 16:02.27 still exists. The 800-meter record for women was set by Olympian Leann Warren of Oregon in 1981. Her record of 2:01.3 survives despite the efforts of other Olympians to improve it. In the 34-year history of the event, Olympians other than Warren were Nadezhda Olizarenko of the USSR in 1983, Julie (Jenkins) Donley of Adams (Colo.) State in 1984, Maria Akraka of Iowa in 1987 and 1988, Inez Turner of Barton County (Kan.) Community College in 1992 and 1993, and Katya Kostetskaya of Russia in 2003.

The 1500 record is 4:08.94, set by Nadezhda Raldugina of the USSR in 1983. No other runner bettered 4:15 until 2013, when Nicole Sifuentes ran 4:14.54. Sifuentes ran collegiately at Michigan and competed in the London Olympics for Canada. She also won the Relays 800 in 2013 with a time of 2:04.17. The 3,000 record is still held by a member of the

**GRIT.** Amy Mortimer, formerly of Riley County High School and Kansas State, returned to her home state in 2006 as a Reebok-sponsored runner to gut out a 5000-meter victory at the KU Relays.

Russian invasion in 1983, Svetlana Ulmasova. The only runner to come close to her 9:13.50 is Jacque Struckhoff of Kansas State, who ran 9:14.2 in 1986. Kansas State runner Korene Hinds, who ran the steeplechase representing Jamaica in both the Beijing and London Olympics, won the 2004 KU steeplechase in 10:34.43. Trina Cox, who ran for Abilene Christian, set the current record of 10:07.3 in 2007. Meagan Hudson of Missouri Baptist, while not a record setter, did win three steeplechase races between 2010-2012. The two-mile relay record was taken in 1984 from the Soviets when Villanova ran 8:46.62. No other team has come within six sec-

COVER GIRLS. Women didn't compete in distance races at the KU Relays until the 1970s. Members of the Texas Track Club (from left) Paula Walter, Janice Rinehart, coach Margaret Ellison, Sue Schexnayder and Carvelynne Leonard competed in 1964, when the only women's events were the 100 and 4x100 relay. That same week, the Texas Track Club was on the cover of *Sports Illustrated*. "The Texas Track Club is celebrated on two counts," the April 20, 1964 article said. "Its athletic achievements and the uncommon beauty of its girls, who compete in dazzling uniforms, elaborate makeup and majestic hairdos."

onds of that time. The four-mile relay for women has only been run the last 10 years with Wichita State winning five of those, including four in a row between 2005-2008. The Shockers set the record of 20:06.04 in 2006. The distance medley record was set by Michigan at 11:32.61 in 1993. Kansas won three in a row between 2002-2004 and again in 2010-2012.

The first high schooler to break 1:54 in the 800 was Winston Tidwell of Topeka West in 1993. He ran 1:53.04 on a windy Friday to edge out Mark Cravens of Union, who ran 1:53.91. On Saturday, Tidwell anchored the two-mile relay to victory with a 1:53.8 carry. Those marks plus two sub-50-second quarters on mile-relay carries earned him Most Outstanding Performer honors. Tidwell ran 1:53.18 in 1994 in the open 800 to fend off a challenge from Ben Pitman of Putnam City, Okla., who ran 1:53.95 for second. Tidwell again anchored the two-mile relay to victory, this time in 1:54.2. Tidwell's record lasted until 2003 when Leo Manzano of Marble Falls, Texas, ran 1:51.54, his second win at KU.

This was a harbinger of things to come as Manzano, who ran collegiately at Texas, would go to the Beijing Olympics in 2008 and bring home silver in the 1500 from London in 2012.

High school boys ran the mile until 1997 when the switch was made to 1600 meters. Many of the runners went on to distinguished collegiate and post-collegiate careers and have already been written about in this chapter, including Bill Dotson from Concordia, who won at the Relays in 1958 and later became KU's second sub-four miler; Archie San Romani, Jr. of Wichita East, the winner in 1959; and, of course, the incomparable Jim Ryun of Wichita East, who won every year of his high school career and set the Relays mile mark of 4:04.8, the year after an Olympic appearance in Tokyo. A year later, in 1966, Glenn Cunningham, Jr. of Leon, Kan., was the champion followed by a two-year run from Bob Barratti of Wichita North. Other notable runs under 4:15 were made by Randy Smith of Wichita East (4:09.4) in 1971, and Joe Falcon of Belton, Mo., on a cold, rainy day in 1984 (4:14.40). After the changeover to 1600 meters, sub-4:15 runs were made by Juan Cardenas of Lockhart, Texas (4:13.96), Scott Loftin of Blue Valley (Kan.) North (4:13.97), Colby Wissel of Kearney, Neb. (4:13.88), Muhammud Ige of Denver South (4:14.21) and Daniel Everett of Westminster Christian Academy in St. Louis, Mo., in 2011 (4:12.58). The 1600 record is held by Spencer Haik of Glendale, Mo. In 2013, he narrowly edged out Amos Bartelsmeyer of Mary Institute of St. Louis 4:11.76 to 4:12.56. Both marks were under the previous record. Haik also won the 800.

Boys ran the two-mile until 2000, when the distance was changed to 3200 meters. Perhaps the most exciting high school two-mile race ever at the Relays happened in 1969. Jon Callen, another Wichita East sensation, took over the Kansas all-time two-mile record with a 9:03.4 in a race so close that runner-up Dave Anderson of Shawnee Mission (Kan.) South was given the same time. Joe Falcon of Belton, Mo., who won the mile in 1984, also won the two mile in 9:09.8. Others who won both the mile and two-mile were Reed Eichner of Shawnee Mission South in 1976, Steve Smith of Shawnee Mission South in 1980, John McClure of Stafford in 1983, and Alex Hallock of Shawnee Mission West in 1986. After the change to 3200 in

2000, Olympian-to-be Matt Tegenkamp of Lee's Summit, Mo., ran 9:03.38, a record which was broken by Kevin Williams of D'Evelyn, Colo., at 9:02.29 in 2008.

In two-mile relay action, no team has come close to the national record of 7:42.9 set by Wichita East in 1965 with Ryun anchoring a team of Doug Boyle, Bob Mark and Mike Petterson. No other team has dipped below 7:50. The four-mile record of 18:02.2 was set by Kearney, Neb., in 2012, and the sprint medley of 3:30.60 by Wichita North in 1965. In 1979 Shawnee Mission South ran the distance-medley relay in 10:19.93.

In the girls 800, the standout was Trisa Nickoley of Tecumseh-Shawnee Heights. She won all four years of her high school career with her best time being 2:06.67 in 2004. No other athlete has gone sub-2:10. The girls ran the mile until the changeover to 1600 in 1997. The first sub-5:00 miler was Anne Stadler of Shawnee Mission East with a 4:57.22 in 1983. Christy Swartz of Andover, Kan., was a three-time winner from 1993 to 1995. Shawnee Mission West standout Ali Cash ran 4:50.71 in 2012. Hannah Long, of Eureka, Mo., erased that mark in 2013 with a 4:49.95. Long also won the 800.

The girls two-mile began in 1982. Alyson Deckert of Salina (Kan.) South won the first three years. While Christy Swartz was winning the mile three years (1993-95), her sister Charity was winning the two-mile in 1993-94. Emily Sisson of Millard North in Omaha, Neb., won the 3200 in 2007, 2008, and 2009 to go with her 1600 victories in 2008 and 2009. Her time of 10:25.42 still stands. In the two-mile relay, Topeka-Seaman had three consecutive wins between 1985-1987. The record of 9:21.9 was set in 2011 by Ladue (Mo.) Horton Watkins. The sprint-medley relay record with Nickoley on the anchor was set by Shawnee Heights at 4:04.56 in 2004. In the distance medley, Jenks, Okla., had a four-year run between 2000 and 2003, with their 2002 time of 12:23.32 setting a record. Lee's Summit West, which has won five of the past six years, ran 12:23.78 in 2013. The four-mile relay has been run 10 years. Lee's Summit North won in 2005-07, and Lee's Summit West has won the last five with the 2011 time of 21:17.74 being the record.

# Runners Who Competed in the Kansas Relays and Olympics in Events of 800m and Longer

| Men | | | | |
|-----|-----|-----|-----|-----|
| **Name** | **School/Country (if not USA)** | **Olympics (Year)** | **Event** | **Result** |
| *Billy Mills | Kansas | Tokyo (1964) | 10,000m<br>Marathon | Gold<br>Did not medal |
| Frank Shorter | Yale | Munich (1972)<br>Montreal (1976) | Marathon<br>10,000m<br>Marathon | Gold<br>Did not medal<br>Silver |
| Dave Wottle | Bowling Green | Munich (1972) | 800m<br>1500m | Gold<br>Did not medal |
| Bronislaw Malinowski | Poland | Munich (1972)<br>Montreal (1976)<br>Moscow (1980) | Steeplechase<br>Steeplechase<br>Steeplechase | Did not medal<br>Silver<br>Gold |
| *Glenn Cunningham | Kansas | Los Angeles (1932)<br>Berlin (1936) | 1500m<br>1500m | Did not medal<br>Silver |
| *Jim Ryun | Kansas | Tokyo (1964)<br>Mexico City (1968)<br>Munich (1972) | 1500m<br>1500m<br>1500m | Did not medal<br>Silver<br>Did not medal |
| *Leo Manzano | Texas | Beijing (2008)<br>London (2012) | 1500m<br>1500m | Did not medal<br>Silver |
| Mike Boit | Eastern New Mexico/ Kenya | Munich (1972) | 800m<br>1500m | Bronze<br>Did not medal |
| Rick Wolhuter | Notre Dame | Munich (1972)<br>Montreal (1976) | 800m<br>800m<br>1500m | Did not medal<br>Bronze<br>Did not medal |
| Brian Diemer | Michigan | Los Angeles (1984)<br>Seoul (1988)<br>Barcelona (1992) | Steeplechase<br>Steeplechase<br>Steeplechase | Bronze<br>Did not medal<br>Did not medal |
| Earl Jones | Eastern Michigan | Los Angeles (1984) | 800m | Bronze |
| Adriaan Paulen | Netherlands | Antwerp (1920)<br>Paris (1924)<br>Amsterdam (1928) | 800m<br>800m<br>800m | Did not medal<br>Did not medal<br>Did not medal |
| Charles Hoff | Norway | Paris (1924) | 800m<br>400m | Did not medal<br>Did not medal |
| Ray Conger | Iowa State | Amsterdam (1928) | 1500m | Did not medal |

| Men | | | | |
|---|---|---|---|---|
| Name | School/Country (if not USA) | Olympics (Year) | Event | Result |
| Dave Abbott | Illinois | Amsterdam (1928) | 5,000m | Did not medal |
| José Torres | Mexico | Amsterdam (1928) | Marathon | Did not medal |
| Glenn Dawson | Oklahoma | Los Angeles (1932) Berlin (1936) | Steeplechase Steeplechase | Did not medal Did not medal |
| *Archie San Romani | Kansas State Teachers College (Emporia State) | Berlin (1936) | 1500m | Did not medal |
| Gene Venske | Pennsylvania | Berlin (1936) | 1500m | Did not medal |
| Don Lash | Indiana | Berlin (1936) | 5,000m 10,000m | Did not medal Did not medal |
| Don Gehrmann | Wisconsin | London (1948) | 1500m | Did not medal |
| Fred Wilt | Indiana | London (1948) Helsinki (1952) | 10,000m 10,000m | Did not medal Did not medal |
| Javier Montez | UTEP | Helsinki (1952) | 1500m | Did not medal |
| Sture Landqvist | Sweden | Helsinki (1952) | 1500m | Did not medal |
| *Wes Santee | Kansas | Helsinki (1952) | 5,000m | Did not medal |
| Ted Wheeler | Iowa | Melbourne (1956) | 1500m | Did not medal |
| Deacon Jones | Iowa | Melbourne (1956) Rome (1960) | Steeplechase Steeplechase | Did not medal Did not medal |
| Joe Mullins | Nebraska/Canada | Rome (1960) | 800m 1500m 4 x 400m relay | Did not medal Did not medal Did not medal |
| Jim Grelle | Oregon | Rome (1960) | 1500m | Did not medal |
| Ernie Cunliffe | Stanford | Rome (1960) | 800m | Did not medal |
| Tom O'Hara | Loyola-Chicago | Tokyo (1964) | 1500m | Did not medal |
| Oscar Moore | Southern Illinois | Tokyo (1964) | 5,000m | Did not medal |
| Tom von Ruden | Oklahoma State | Mexico City (1968) | 1500m | Did not medal |
| *Conrad Nightingale | Kansas State | Mexico City (1968) | Steeplechase | Did not medal |
| Rex Maddaford | Eastern New Mexico/ New Zealand | Mexico City (1968) | 5,000m 10,000m | Did not medal Did not medal |

> continued

> continued

| | | **Men** | | |
|---|---|---|---|---|
| **Name** | **School/Country (if not USA)** | **Olympics (Year)** | **Event** | **Result** |
| *Ken Swenson | Kansas State | Munich (1972) | 800m | Did not medal |
| Leonard Hilton | Houston | Munich (1972) | 5,000m | Did not medal |
| Mike Durkin | Illinois | Montreal (1976) Moscow (1980) | 1500m 1500m | Did not medal U.S. Boycott |
| Naill O'Shaughnessy | Arkansas/Ireland | Montreal (1976) | 800m 1500m | Did not medal Did not medal |
| Gary Bjorklund | Minnesota | Montreal (1976) | 10,000m | Did not medal |
| Rodolpho Gomez | Mexico | Montreal (1976) Moscow (1980) | Marathon Marathon | Did not medal Did not medal |
| Bobby Gaseitsiwe | Barton County (Kan.) CC/Botswana | Seoul (1988) Barcelona (1992) | 800m 4 x 400m relay 1500m | Did not medal Did not medal Did not medal |
| Einars Tuperitis | Wichita State/Latvia | Atlanta (1996) | 800m | Did not medal |
| Brandon Rock | Nevada/Arkansas | Atlanta (1996) | 800m | Did not medal |
| Paul McMullen | Eastern Michigan | Atlanta (1996) | 1500m | Did not medal |
| Rod DeHaven | South Dakota State | Sydney (2000) | Marathon | Did not medal |
| Kevin Sullivan | Michigan/Canada | Sydney (2000) Athens (2004) Beijing (2008) | 1500m 1500m 1500m | Did not medal Did not medal Did not medal |
| Charlie Gruber | Kansas | Athens (2004) | 1500m | Did not medal |
| Alan Webb | Michigan | Athens (2004) | 1500m | Did not medal |
| Dmitrijs Milkevics | Nebraska/Latvia | Athens (2004) | 800m | Did not medal |
| Derrick Peterson | Missouri | Athens (2004) | 800m | Did not medal |
| *Christian Smith | Kansas State | Beijing (2008) | 800m | Did not medal |
| Nick Symmonds | Willamette | Beijing (2008) London (2012) | 800m 800m | Did not medal Did not medal |
| *Matt Tegenkamp | Wisconsin | Beijing (2008) London (2012) | 5,000m 10,000m | Did not medal Did not medal |

| Women | | | | |
|---|---|---|---|---|
| Name | School/Country (if not USA) | Olympics (Year) | Event | Result |
| Madeline Manning | Tennessee State | Mexico City (1968) Munich (1972) <br><br> Montreal (1976) Moscow (1980) | 800m 4x400m relay 800m 800m 800m | Gold Silver Did not medal Did not medal U.S. Boycott |
| Nadezhda Olizarenko | USSR | Moscow (1980) | 800m 1500m | Gold Bronze |
| Olga Mineyeva | USSR | Moscow (1980) | 800m | Silver |
| Leann Warren | Oregon | Moscow (1980) | 1500m | U.S. Boycott |
| Julie (Jenkins) Donley | Adams (Colo.) State/ BYU | Barcelona (1992) | 800m | Did not medal |
| Maria Akraka | Iowa State/Sweden | Barcelona (1992) | 800m | Did not medal |
| Inez Turner | Barton County CC/ So. Texas/Jamaica | Atlanta (1996) | 800m | Did not medal |
| *Sarah (Heeb) Wilborn | Kansas | Atlanta (1996) | Steeplechase | Qualified at Olympic Trials, but the event was not held in Olympics. |
| Diane Nukuri-Johnson | Butler County (Kan.) CC/Iowa/Burundi | Sydney (2000) London (2012) | 5,000m Marathon | Did not medal Did not medal |
| Katya Kostetskaya | USSR | Beijing (2008) | 800m | Did not medal |
| Korene Hinds | Kansas State/ Jamaica | Beijing (2008) London (2012) | Steeplechase Steeplechase | Did not medal Did not medal |
| Nicole (Edwards) Sifuentes | Michigan/Canada | London (2012) | 1500m | Did not medal |

* Denotes that athlete competed at KU Relays while in high school.

# 9

# Bones, Batman, Diamond ... and other Speedsters
## Sprinters and Hurdlers

"It's my goal to be a fan favorite. I love to compete here."

--Bershawn "Batman" Jackson

"Batman" Jackson at KU, 2007.

The University of Kansas – and by extension the Kansas Relays – is synonymous with legendary milers, as we saw in Chapter 8. But many of the greatest sprinters in history have also graced the track at Memorial Stadium each April. More than 150 sprinters and hurdlers have competed at both the Relays and at the Olympics. Some outstanding sprint performances in the 1920s were instrumental in getting the fledgling track meet off to a good start (Chapter 2). Chapter 15 will explain how the introduction of the Gold Zone reinvigorated the meet in the past decade, with sprinters often providing marquee names for that successful innovation.

There are simply too many stories to tell of elite sprinters and hurdlers at the Relays. In no particular order, six have been chosen here who have had a significant impact on the meet. They represent different eras, different genders and different styles. See the table at the end of this chapter for a look at even more of the raw speed that Relays' fans have witnessed. Note that this chapter includes both sprinters and hurdlers because there are a large number who did both, especially hurdlers who ran on relay teams.

## DIAMOND DIXON

Diamond Dixon came to the University of Kansas campus from Houston Westside High School in the 2010-11 school year. While not exactly looking like an intimidating runner at 5 feet, 6 inches and 112 pounds, she nevertheless arrived with solid credentials: two-time 400-meter champion in sprint-rich Texas and a #1 ranking in the nation.

She made an immediate impact on the Jayhawk track program by becoming the NCAA Indoor runner-up in the 400 meters. At the Kansas Relays, her record-breaking performances in the 400 and 4x400 relay made her the recipient of the Outstanding Female Athlete award. Her sophomore

**EAST TO WEST.** From 1936, when the 110-meter hurdles went south to north along the east side of Memorial Stadium (left), to the 2009 competition that went north to south along the west side (right), there have been many great hurdlers at the KU Relays. Sam Allen of Oklahoma Baptist won his third straight Relays hurdles title in 1936 with a time of 14.8 seconds. Antwon Hicks (foreground) won his second in a row in 2009 with a time of 13.37.

year was magical. At the Big 12 Conference Indoor, she was victorious in both the 400 and 4x400. At the Relays, the team of Denesha Morris, Paris Daniels, Shayla Wilson and Dixon set the 4x400 record at 3:31.87. In the Big 12 Outdoor, she again won the 400 and anchored the 4x400 to victory.

Then on June 24, 2012, just five days short of her 20th birthday, at historic Hayward Field in Eugene, Ore., Dixon ran a school record 50.88 and placed fifth in the 400 at the Olympic Trials, thus earning a spot in the relay pool for the London Olympics. She was the youngest member of Team USA and the only NCAA athlete to win gold in 2012. In London, she ran the third leg of the qualifying 4x400 semifinal on a team that included Keshia Baker, Francena McCorory and DeeDee Trotter. Dixon's unofficial split was 50.15, second only to Trotter's 50.12. Despite her performance, which left the USA in the lead after her carry, Dixon and Baker were replaced for the finals by the more experienced Allyson Felix and Sanya Richards-Ross. Considering that Felix ran a 47.8 and Richards-Ross ran a 49.10, one could hardly question the decision. Those two, with Trotter leading off with a 50.5 and McCorory chipping in a 49.39, allowed the USA to win comfortably over

**DIAMOND TOUGH.** Diamond Dixon is shown here during her first KU Relays as a freshman in 2011. Since then, she has earned Olympic gold and headlined the Jayhawks' NCAA national championship team.

runner-up Russia with a time of 3:16.78. According to *Track and Field News*, it was the third-best time ever and fastest in the last 19 years. Coincidentally, the gentleman who sat next to me, high above the first turn in Olympic Stadium, just happened to be the grandfather of Diamond Dixon, John Moore, of El Paso, Texas. He was a proud man. Why wouldn't he be?

In the fabulous history of KU track and field, 27 Jayhawk athletes have become Olympians, but only two have been women. Dixon is the first woman to win gold, and the first Jayhawk to achieve gold since Al Oerter did so in Mexico City in 1968. Coach Stanley Redwine's signing of Dixon was not his only recruiting coup. He assembled a talented group of women that won the 2013 Big 12 Indoor and Outdoor team titles, and placed second in the NCAA Indoor. For good measure, the Jayhawks captured the ultimate prize for any college team, an NCAA Outdoor team championship in 2013. They did it at the same Hayward Field venue in which Dixon earlier did her Olympic qualifying.

**OLYMPIC TEAMMATE.** DeeDee Trotter set the KU Relays' 400-meter record in 2012, just four months before joining Diamond Dixon on the USA gold medal-winning 4×400-meter relay team.

# MERLENE OTTEY

Arguably no sprinter in track has been so good for so long as Merlene Ottey. She is a member of the Relays Hall of Fame for a reason. Her 100-meter dash time of 11.18 in 1982 was not broken until Muna Lee ran 11.10 in 2005. Allyson Felix ran 11.04 in 2006 and currently holds the record.

Ottey ran 22.11 in 1983, the fastest 200 ever run at KU but it was wind-aided. Her legal time of 22.61 run in 1981 was not bested until Aleen Bailey ran 22.59 in 2001. Veronica Campbell-Brown is the current record holder thanks to a 22.32 run in 2010. Ottey was a Jamaican who attended college at KU's Big 8 Conference rival Nebraska, so she was a regular at the Relays for many years. Amazingly, her Olympic career began at the age of 20 in Moscow in 1980; it ended after seven Olympics when she was 44, at Athens in 2004. She made the Slovenian team in the 4x400 in 2012, but could not run in London because Slovenia was not in the top 16 team qualifiers. She did, however, run in the European Championships that same year at the age of 52. She has won nine Olympic medals, more than any other woman in track and field history, but surprisingly, none of them were gold. The closest she came was 1996, a photo finish with Gail Devers when both were credited with 10.94 in the 100, but it was determined that Ottey was five thousandths of a second slower. Three years earlier in the World Championships, Ottey had lost to Devers 10.812

**JAMAICAN HUSKER.** Merlene Ottey was just beginning her career when she ran at Nebraska. Seven Olympics representing two countries resulted in nine medals and a spot in the Kansas Relays Hall of Fame.

to 10.811. As for Ottey's Olympic medals, three were silver and six were bronze, thus giving her the nickname of "The Bronze Queen."

In the World Outdoor Championships, she has amassed three golds, four silvers and seven bronzes; in the World Indoor Championships, the count is three golds, two silvers and one bronze. At the writing of this book, her world record of 21.87 for the indoor 200 meters, run in 1993, still stands; and she is in the top six all-time list of any race of 200 meters or less. Ottey moved to Slovenia in 1998 and began to train with Slovene coach Srdan Dordevic. She continued to run under the Jamaican flag until she became a Slovenian citizen in 2002. Thus she represented Slovenia in Athens. She missed qualifying for Beijing in 2008 by 0.28 of a second. Ottey holds every master's world record in both the 100 and 200 for age groups 35, 40, 45 and 50.

# BERSHAWN "BATMAN" JACKSON

Bershawn Jackson has had a long and distinguished career as a 400-meter hurdler and 400-meter sprinter. *Track and Field News* has ranked him among the world's top 10 in the 400 hurdles every year from 2003 to 2013, including a #1 ranking in 2005 after running a career-best 47.30 in Helsinki. In virtually all of those years, he has graced the Relays with his presence, and he soon became a fan favorite because of his performance, his exuberant personality and his passion for the meet.

Recruiters knew of Jackson because of his stellar career at Miami Central High School. His 300-meter hurdles record of 36.01 is still the high school standard in Florida. Instead of competing for a track and field powerhouse, he chose to join the roster of St. Augustine's College in Raleigh, N.C. His first appearance in Lawrence came in 2003 when he won his first of seven Relays watches with a time of 49.54. Only in 2013 did he run a slower time than that. All the rest of his Relays runs were under 49 seconds. Jackson returned to win again in 2005-08 and 2011-12. There was no 400 invitational hurdle race held in 2010. Notable wins in that span were the 48.34 run in 2006 (third best in the world that year), and 48.75, the fastest time in the world in 2007.

In 2008 he ran 48.32, which was again the fastest time in the world that year and earned Jackson the Male Most Outstanding Performer award. It was his fourth consecutive win and fifth in the last six years at the Relays. Later that year he won the bronze medal at the Beijing Olympics. Jackson broke his own Relays record with a world-leading time of 48.20 in 2012, thereby claiming his seventh Relays title.

**RELAYS' SUPERHERO.** "Batman" has been a Relays regular for more than a decade, including here in 2012.

Where did the nickname "Batman" come from? Bershawn says he was given the name because he had big ears when he was a boy and the name stuck. It has become one of the most recognizable nicknames in all of sport and is more descriptive of the gracefulness of his hurdling than the size of his ears.

# THE GREENES (CHARLIE AND MAURICE)

Two of the most charismatic and flamboyant runners to ever compete at the Relays were both named Greene. There was Charlie, who ran 100 yards in 9.5 for O'Dea High School in Seattle; and Maurice, a winner of three consecutive 100-200 doubles at the Kansas State High School Track and Field Championships while running for Schlagle High School in Kansas City. Both were world-record holders and have Olympic gold in their possession.

As a member of Nebraska's team, Charlie made several appearances at the Relays. He was easily recognizable wearing his headband and sunglasses, regardless of weather conditions. He joked that his sunglasses were his "re-entry shields."

**GREENE GREETS GREENE.** Two KU Relays legends, Maurice (left) and Charlie Greene, say hello at the 2006 meet.

Freshmen were not eligible for varsity competition in 1964, but in his varsity years from 1965-67, he won all three NCAA Indoor 60s and Outdoor 100s as well as equaled the world record with a 9.1 in the 100-yard dash. At the AAU Championships in 1968, he tied the world record twice. In the qualifying heats, he equaled the 100-meter dash record at 10.0. In the subsequent semi-final he ran 9.9 to equal the marks run by Jim Hines and Ronnie Ray Smith in the previous heats. The year 1968 was significant for Charlie in another way. At the Kansas Relays, which preceded the aforementioned AAU competition, he tied the existing world record for 100 yards, a record he shared with eight others. A major disappointment for fans came when Hines, one of the eight record holders, was disqualified for two false starts.

Charlie would go on to compete in the 100 meters in Mexico City in 1968, where he was considered a favorite for gold. However, he pulled a hamstring muscle prior to competition and with a heavily taped leg had to settle for

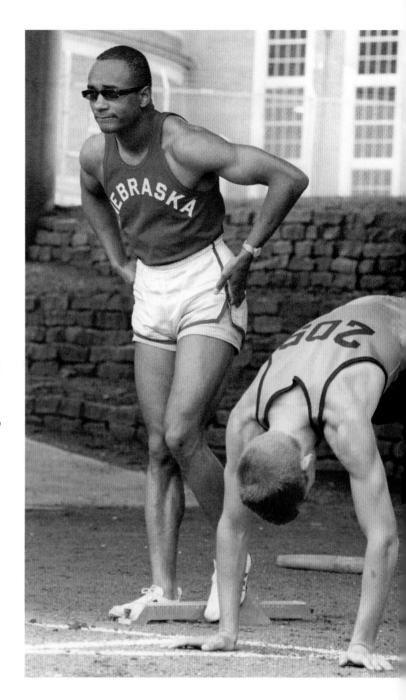

**'RE-ENTRY SHIELDS'. Charlie Greene was hard to miss on any track, with both his speed and sunglasses.**

bronze. Despite the injury, he won gold by leading off the 4x100 for a team that set the world record at 38.19. After his athletic career, Charlie became an Army officer and served as a track coach. After leaving the Army, he became a director for Special Olympics International.

The early years of Maurice's fabulous career were filled with frustration. After failing to make the 1996 Olympic team and a stagnation seeming to have set in, he left his AAU coach, mentor and friend Al Hobson, who coached sprinters at Kansas City Kansas Community College with considerable success.

In September 1996, Maurice cut ties with the Kansas City area and drove with his father to California to seek the coaching of John Smith. There he met a training partner and competitor, Ato Bolden, and

**STAR FOR A NEW CENTURY.** Maurice Greene was a local favorite who helped launch the Relays into a new era in 2000 after the meet returned from a two-year absence.

the two of them became principal players in a loosely knit group of elite athletes called HSI (Hudson Smith International. Hudson was sports agent and attorney Emanuel Hudson; Smith was former UCLA coach and 440-yard world record holder John Smith). After a somewhat rocky start, Maurice began to improve dramatically and won gold in the World Championships in 1997, 1999 and 2001.

In 1999 at the World Championships in Athens, he stunned the sprint world by running 9.79, the same mark run by Ben Johnson but later disallowed because of Johnson's drug infraction. Maurice broke the old record by five–hundredths of a second, the largest margin by which the record had ever been reduced. As far as the KU Relays are concerned, Maurice won the high school division 100 in 1993, the same year his older brother Ernest would win the college division 100. Maurice won the Invitational 100 in 1994 also.

Just two weeks after a win over Carl Lewis at the Texas Relays in 1995, he ran first leg to help Nike Central win the 4x100 relay at KU. In 1996 he won the Invitational 100. After a two-year hiatus for stadium repairs in 1998 and 1999, the Relays needed a star attraction to start off the new century. Maurice was one of them. With the help of Curtis Johnson, Bolden and Brian Howard, the quartet set a new stadium and meet record with a 38.45 in the 4x100 relay. Later in the season, Maurice won gold in both the 100 and the 4x100 in the Sydney Olympics.

In 2005, the year after winning a silver medal in the 4x100 and a bronze in the 100 at the Athens Olympics, Maurice would be one of the featured athletes for Gold Zone I (see Chapter 15). He placed third in the 100 behind John Capel (10.10) and Mark Jelks (10.15) in a very close race in which Maurice was also credited with 10.15. His HSI team won the 4x100 relay. The feature race in Gold Zone II in 2006 was between Greene's HSI team and Justin Gatlin's Sprint Capitol foursome. Gatlin's team won with an incredible 38.16, the fastest in the world in 2006 and the best in Relays history. The second-largest crowd in Relays history numbered 26,211, a large percentage of them coming to see their local hero in action, win or lose. Considering the consistent excellence of his long and storied career, the tattoo on Maurice's shoulder titled GOAT (Greatest of All Time), may truly be credible.

# HARRISON DILLARD

What is the likelihood of two sprinters from the same high school winning the 100 meters in consecutive Olympics? It happened. Both Jesse Owens, winner of four golds in Berlin in 1936, and Harrison Dillard, winner of two golds in London in 1948 and two more in Helsinki in 1952, both attended East Technical High School in Cleveland, Ohio. There were no Olympic games in 1940 and 1944 because of World War II.

When "Bones," a nickname given to Dillard because of his scrawny physique as a youngster, was 13, a parade was given to honor Owens for his Olympic exploits. During the parade Owens spoke a casual, "Hey kids, how ya doin'?" to Dillard and his friends from the open car in which he was riding. From that point forward, Owens became a source of inspiration and encouragement for Dillard. In fact, at the high school state meet in Columbus, Owens saw that Dillard's shoes were a bit worn, so he gave Dillard a new pair of track spikes, which Dillard used to win the state championship. Contrary to popular myth, they were not the spikes Owens had worn in Berlin.

Owens' alma mater, Ohio State, recruited Dillard, but he decided to stay closer to home and attended Baldwin-Wallace, where he ran for the highly regarded coach Eddie Finnigan. After a couple of years in college, Dillard was drafted into the Army and served combat duty with the famed Buffalo Soldiers, an all-black 92nd Infantry Division that performed courageously in Italy. He returned to college in 1946, the same year he first competed at

**WORLD-RECORD HURDLER.** Harrison Dillard is shown (second from left) hurdling at the 1948 KU Relays, which he won in a world-record time of 13.6.

the Relays, which had been put on hold from 1943-45. He won the high hurdles with a time of 14.2, but a tailwind of seven mph nullified it as a record. Dillard returned in 1948 to win in a world-record time of 13.6 with a narrow victory over Clyde Scott from Arkansas. Scott, who would later play professional football, took silver in the 1948 London Olympics, a race for which Dillard did not qualify. Heading into the Olympic Trials, Dillard had a string of 82 consecutive high-hurdles wins that had been broken shortly before the Trials by Bill Porter, the man who edged Scott for the gold medal in London. Even with the high quality of the competition,

Dillard seemed a shoo-in to qualify in the hurdles. Unfortunately, he clipped the first hurdle, cleared the second, and as he tells it, "bang, bang, bang, bang, I just hit a string of them."

Fortunately, he was destined for London because he had qualified third in the 100 the day before. The competition in the Olympic 100 finals was formidable. It consisted of Barney Ewell, who won the Trials in a world-record time at 100 meters; Mel Patton, who held the world record for 100 yards; and UCLA sprinter Lloyd LaBeach, the only athlete from Panama in the games. Patton was in lane one, Ewell in two, LaBeach in three, and Dillard in the dreaded lane six of a six-lane track, where runners could sometimes be overlooked by judges. This year was different, however, because a photoelectrical timing system supplied by Omega was being used for the first time.

The race was close, but Ewell assumed he had won because LaBeach blocked his view of Dillard four lanes away. He was in the midst of his victory celebration when LaBeach broke the news and said, "No mon, you don't win. Bones win." Omega timing confirmed the victory and Dillard was credited with equaling the Olympic record of 10.3. Owens was there to see it. Ewell and LaBeach were both credited with 10.4. Four years later Dillard did qualify for the 110-meter hurdles in Helsinki and managed to win in a narrow victory (both clocked in 13.7) over Jack Davis, thus making him the only male athlete to win Olympic gold in both the 110 hurdles and the 100 meters. He also won gold medals in both London and Helsinki for his contributions to the 4x100 relays.

Dillard tried but failed to make the Olympic team in 1956. He did, however, return to London in 2012 as a guest of the Omega watch company, still the official timekeeper for the Olympic Games. "Bones" was honored as the oldest living 100-meter Olympic champion at the age of 89, the ceremony taking place at Britain's Foreign Office where the 1948 torch was on display. When asked how he would like to be remembered, Dillard simply said he'd like for people to say, "He was a good guy."

ANNUAL OLYMPIANS. Pick a year in recent memory and there is probably an Olympic woman sprinting at KU, including (clockwise from top left) Kelly Wells (2010), Lauryn Williams (2011), Chrystal Cox (2006) and LaShauntea Moore (2012). Williams accomplished a rare double when she won a silver medal in bobsled at the 2014 Sochi Games to go with her silver in the 100 at the 2004 Athens Games and gold in the 4x100 relay at the 2012 London Games. That made her only the second American, and first American woman, to medal in both the Summer and Winter Olympics.

# Sprinters and Hurdlers Who Ran in the Kansas Relays and Olympics

| Men | | | | |
|---|---|---|---|---|
| Name | School/Country (if not USA) | Olympics (Year) | Event | Result |
| George Baird | Iowa | Amsterdam (1928) | 4 x 400 M Relay | Gold |
| George Saling | Iowa | Los Angeles (1932) | 110 Hurdles | Gold |
| Eddie Tolan | Michigan | Los Angeles (1932) | 100<br>200 | Gold<br>Gold |
| Art Harnden | Texas A&M | London (1948) | 4 x 400 M Relay | Gold |
| Harrison Dillard | Baldwin-Wallace (Ohio) | London (1948)<br><br>Helsinki (1952) | 100<br>4 x 100 M Relay<br>110 Hurdles<br>4 x 100 M Relay | Gold<br>Gold<br>Gold<br>Gold |
| Dean Smith | Texas | Helsinki (1952) | 4 x 100 M Relay<br>100 | Gold<br>Did not medal |
| Thane Baker | Kansas State | Helsinki (1952)<br>Melbourne (1956) | 200<br>4 x 100 M Relay<br>100<br>200 | Silver<br>Gold<br>Silver<br>Bronze |
| J. W. Mashburn | Oklahoma A&M (Oklahoma State) | Helsinki (1952)<br>Melbourne (1956) | 4 x 400 M Relay<br>4 x 400 M Relay | Did not medal<br>Gold |
| Jim Hines | Texas Southern | Mexico City (1968) | 100<br>4 x 100 M Relay | Gold<br>Gold |
| Charlie Greene | Nebraska | Mexico City (1968) | 4 x 100 M Relay<br>100 | Gold<br>Bronze |
| Maxie Parks | UCLA | Montreal (1976) | 4 x 400 M Relay<br>400 | Gold<br>Did not medal |
| Mel Lattany | Georgia | Moscow (1980)<br><br>Los Angeles (1984) | 100<br>4x100 M Relay<br>4 x 100 M Relay | U.S. Boycott<br>U.S. Boycott<br>Gold |
| Emmit King | Alabama | Los Angeles (1984)<br>Seoul (1988) | 4 x 100 M Relay<br>4 x 100 M Relay | Gold<br>Did not medal |

> continued

| Men | | | | |
|-----|-----|-----|-----|-----|
| Name | School/Country (if not USA) | Olympics (Year) | Event | Result |
| James Davis | Colorado | Atlanta (1996) | 4 x 400 M Relay | Gold |
| Allen Johnson | North Carolina | Atlanta (1996)<br>Sydney (2000)<br>Athens (2004) | 110 Hurdles<br>110 Hurdles<br>110 Hurdles | Gold<br>Did not medal<br>Did not medal |
| Clement Chukwu | Eastern Michigan/ Nigeria | Atlanta (1996)<br>Sydney (2000) | 400<br>4 x 400 M Relay | Did not medal<br>Silver |
| Jon Drummond | Odessa (Tx.) CC/ Texas Christian | Atlanta (1996)<br><br>Sydney (2000) | 4 x 100 M Relay<br>100<br>4 x 100 M Relay<br>100 | Silver<br>Did not medal<br>Gold<br>Did not medal |
| *Maurice Greene | Kansas City Kansas CC | Sydney (2000)<br><br>Athens (2004) | 100<br>4 x 100 M Relay<br>4 x 100 M Relay<br>100 | Gold<br>Gold<br>Silver<br>Bronze |
| Ken Brokenburr | Wayland Baptist (Tx.)/St. Augustine's (N.C.) | Sydney (2000) | 4 x 100 M Relay | Gold |
| Brian Lewis | Blinn (Tx.) CC/ Norfolk (Va.) State | Sydney (2000) | 4 x 100 M Relay | Gold |
| Dwight Thomas | Clemson/Florida/ Jamaica | Sydney (2000)<br>Athens (2004)<br><br>Beijing (2008) | 200<br>100<br>4 x 100 M Relay<br>4 x 100 M Relay | Did not medal<br>Did not medal<br>Did not medal<br>Gold |
| Jerome Young | Wallace State (Ala.) CC | Sydney (2000) | 4 x 400 M Relay | Gold-DQ |
| Otis Harris | South Carolina | Athens (2004) | 4 x 400 M Relay<br>400 | Gold<br>Silver |

| Men | | | | |
| --- | --- | --- | --- | --- |
| Name | School/Country (if not USA) | Olympics (Year) | Event | Result |
| Shawn Crawford | Clemson | Athens (2004) | 200 | Gold |
| | | | 4 x 100 M Relay | Silver |
| | | | 100 | Did not medal |
| | | Beijing (2008) | 200 | Silver |
| Justin Gatlin | Tennessee | Athens (2004) | 100 | Gold |
| | | | 200 | Bronze |
| | | | 4 x 100 M Relay | Silver |
| | | London (2012) | 100 | Bronze |
| | | | 4 x 100 M Relay | Silver |
| Clyde Scott | Arkansas | London (1948) | 110 Hurdles | Silver |
| Eddie Southern | Texas | Melbourne (1956) | 400 Hurdles | Silver |
| Cliff Cushman | Kansas | Rome (1960) | 400 Hurdles | Silver |
| Devon Morris | Wayland Baptist (Tx.)/Jamaica | Seoul (1988) | 4 x 400 M Relay | Silver |
| Ato Bolden | UCLA/Trinidad and Tobago | Barcelona (1992) | 100 | Did not medal |
| | | | 200 | Did not medal |
| | | Atlanta (1996) | 100 | Bronze |
| | | | 200 | Bronze |
| | | Sydney (2000) | 100 | Silver |
| | | | 200 | Bronze |
| | | Athens (2004) | 100 | Did not medal |
| | | | 200 | Did not medal |
| Tim Harden | Kentucky | Atlanta (1996) | 4 x 100 M Relay | Silver |
| Danny McFarlane | Jamaica | Sydney (2000) | 4 x 400 M Relay | Bronze |
| | | Athens (2004) | 400 Hurdles | Silver |
| | | Beijing (2008) | 400 Hurdles | Did not medal |
| Terrence Trammell | South Carolina | Sydney (2000) | 110 Hurdles | Silver |
| | | Athens (2004) | 110 Hurdles | Silver |
| | | Beijing (2008) | 110 Hurdles | Did not medal |

> continued

> continued

| Men | | | | |
|---|---|---|---|---|
| Name | School/Country (if not USA) | Olympics (Year) | Event | Result |
| Doc Patton | Garden City (Kan.) CC/Texas Christian | Athens (2004) Beijing (2008)<br><br>London (2012) | 4 x 100 M Relay 100 4 x 100 M Relay 4 x 100 M Relay | Silver Did not medal Did not medal Silver |
| David Payne | Cincinnati | Beijing (2008) | 110 Hurdles | Silver |
| Trell Kimmons | Hinds (Miss.) CC | London (2012) | 4 x 100 M Relay | Silver |
| Michael Tinsley | Jackson State (Miss.) | London (2012) | 400 Hurdles | Silver |
| Blake Leeper | Tennessee | London Paralympics (2012) | 400 200 | Silver Bronze |
| Andretti Bain | Oral Roberts/ Bahamas | Beijing (2008) | 4 x 400 M Relay | Silver |
| Dick Howard | New Mexico | Rome (1960) | 400 Hurdles | Bronze |
| John Carlos | San Jose State | Mexico City (1968) | 200 | Bronze |
| Sunday Uti | Iowa State/Nigeria | Moscow (1980) Los Angeles (1984)<br>Seoul (1988) | 4 x 400 M Relay 4 x 400 M Relay 400 4 x 400 M Relay 400 | Did not medal Bronze Did not medal Did not medal Did not medal |
| Calvin Davis | Wallace State (Ala.)/ Arkansas | Atlanta (1996) | 400 Hurdles | Bronze |
| Javier Culson | American Univ. (D.C.)/Puerto Rico | Beijing (2008) London (2012) | 400 Hurdles 400 Hurdles | Did not medal Bronze |
| Bershawn Jackson | St. Augustine's (N.C.) | Beijing (2008) | 400 Hurdles | Bronze |
| Claude Bracey | Rice | Amsterdam (1928) | 100 | Did not medal |
| David Bolen | Colorado | London (1948) | 400 | Did not medal |
| Lee Yoder | Arkansas | Helsinki (1952) | 400 Hurdles | Did not medal |
| Lynn Headley | Nebraska/Jamaica | Toyko (1964) | 100 | Did not medal |
| Godfrey Murray | Michigan/Jamaica | Munich (1972) | 110 Hurdles | Did not medal |
| Fatwell Kimaiyo | New Mexico/Kenya | Munich (1972) | 400 Hurdles | Did not medal |

| Men | | | | |
|-----|-----|-----|-----|-----|
| Name | School/Country (if not USA) | Olympics (Year) | Event | Result |
| Mark Lutz | Kansas | Montreal (1976) | 200 | Did not medal |
| Joseph Coombs | Alabama/Trinidad and Tobago | Montreal (1976) Moscow (1980) | 4 x 400 M Relay 400 4 x 400 M Relay | Did not medal Did not medal Did not medal |
| Cliff Wiley | Kansas | Moscow (1980) | 200 | U.S. Boycott |
| David Lee | Southern Illinois | Moscow (1980) | 400 Hurdles | U.S. Boycott |
| Andrew Bruce | Michigan/Trinidad and Tobago | Moscow (1980) | 200 4 x 100 M Relay | Did not medal Did not medal |
| Henry Amike | Missouri/Nigeria | Los Angeles (1984) Seoul (1988) | 400 Hurdles 4 x 400 M Relay | Did not medal Did not medal |
| Dawda Jallow | Barton County (Kan.)CC/Georgia/ Gambia | Seoul (1988) Barcelona (1992) Atlanta (1996) | 400 400 400 | Did not medal Did not medal Did not medal |
| Garth Robinson | Jamaica | Atlanta (1996) | 4 x 400 M Relay | Did not medal |
| Frank Waota | Arkansas State/ Cote d'Ivoire | Atlanta (1996) | 100 | Did not medal |
| Pierre Lisk | Kansas/Sierra Leone | Atlanta (1996) | 200 4 x 100 M Relay | Did not medal Did not medal |
| Dinsdale Morgan | Kansas City Kansas CC/Pittsburg (Kan.) State/Jamaica | Atlanta (1996) Sydney (2000) | 400 Hurdles 400 Hurdles | Did not medal Did not medal |
| Neil Gardner | Michigan/Jamaica | Atlanta (1996) | 400 Hurdles | Did not medal |
| Aime Issa Nthepe | France | Atlanta (1996) | 100 4 x 100 M Relay | Did not medal Did not medal |
| Claude Toukene-Guebogo | Cameroon | Atlanta (1996) | 4 x 100 M Relay | Did not medal |
| Paul Tucker | Guyana | Sydney (2000) | 400 Hurdles | Did not medal |
| Fabian Rollins | Eastern Michigan/ Barbados | Sydney (2000) | 400 4 x 100 M Relay | Did not medal Did not medal |

> continued

> continued

| Men | | | | |
|---|---|---|---|---|
| **Name** | **School/Country (if not USA)** | **Olympics (Year)** | **Event** | **Result** |
| Damion Barry | Trinidad and Tobago | Sydney (2000) | 4 x 400 M Relay | Did not medal |
| Eric Thomas | Blinn (Tx.) CC/ Abilene Christian | Sydney (2000) | 400 Hurdles | Did not medal |
| Ato Modibo | Clemson/Trinidad and Tobago | Sydney (2000)<br><br>Athens (2004)<br>Beijing (2008) | 4 x 400 M Relay<br>400<br>400<br>4 x 400 M Relay<br>400 | Did not medal<br>Did not medal<br>Did not medal<br>Did not medal<br>Did not medal |
| Benjamin Youla | Republic of the Congo | Sydney (2000) | 400 | Did not medal |
| Pierre Browne | Mississippi State/ Canada | Sydney (2000)<br><br><br>Athens (2004)<br><br>Beijing (2008) | 100<br>200<br>4 x 100 M Relay<br>100<br>4 x 100 M Relay<br>100<br>4 x 100 M Relay | Did not medal<br>Did not medal<br>Did not medal<br>Did not medal<br>Did not medal<br>Did not medal<br>Did not medal |
| John Capel | Florida | Sydney (2000) | 200 | Did not medal |
| Curtis Johnson | North Carolina | Sydney (2000) | 100 | Did not medal |
| Dudley Dorival | Connecticut/Haiti | Sydney (2000)<br>Athens (2004)<br>Beijing (2008) | 110 Hurdles<br>110 Hurdles<br>110 Hurdles | Did not medal<br>Did not medal<br>Did not medal |
| Ian Weakley | Jamaica | Sydney (2000) | 400 Hurdles | Did not medal |
| Patrick Jarrett | St. Johns (NY)/ Jamaica | Sydney (2000)<br>Athens (2004) | 100<br>4 x 100 M Relay | Did not medal<br>Did not medal |
| Aaron Cleare | Dickinson State (No. Dak.)/Bahamas | Athens (2004) | 4 x 400 M Relay | Did not medal |
| Gary Kikaya | Tennessee/Republic of the Congo | Athens (2004)<br>Beijing (2008) | 400<br>400 | Did not medal<br>Did not medal |

| Men | | | | |
|-----|-----|-----|-----|-----|
| Name | School/Country (if not USA) | Olympics (Year) | Event | Result |
| Brendan Christian | Antigua and Barbuda | Athens (2004)<br>Beijing (2008) | 100<br>200 | Did not medal<br>Did not medal |
| Ladji Coucoure' | France | Athens (2004)<br>Beijing (2008)<br>London (2012) | 110 Hurdles<br>110 Hurdles<br>110 Hurdles | Did not medal<br>Did not medal<br>Did not medal |
| Chris Lloyd | Dominica | Athens (2004)<br>Beijing (2008) | 200<br>200 | Did not medal<br>Did not medal |
| Adam Harris | Michigan/Guyana | Beijing (2008) | 200 | Did not medal |
| Rodney Martin | Kansas City Kansas CC/South Carolina | Beijing (2008) | 4 x 100 M Relay | Did not medal |
| Renny Quow | South Plains Coll. (Tx.)/Trinidad and Tobago | Beijing (2008) | 400 | Did not medal |
| Tabarie Henry | Texas A&M/Virgin Islands | Beijing (2008)<br>London (2012) | 400<br>400 | Did not medal<br>Did not medal |
| *Maurice Mitchell | Florida State | London (2012) | 200 | Did not medal |
| Jeremy Julmis | Cloud County (Kan.) CC/Kansas State/ Haiti | London (2012) | 110 Hurdles | Did not medal |
| Lehann Fourie | Nebraska/South Africa | London (2012) | 110 Hurdles | Did not medal |
| Eric Alejandro | Eastern Michigan/ Puerto Rico | London (2012) | 400 Hurdles | Did not medal |
| Roxroy Cato | Lincoln (Mo.)/ Jamaica | London (2012) | 400 Hurdles | Did not medal |
| Jarryd Wallace | Georgia | London Paralympics (2012) | 4 x 100 M Relay | Did not medal |
| Jeff Porter | Michigan | London (2012) | 110 Hurdles | Did not medal |

> continued

> continued

| Women | | | | |
|---|---|---|---|---|
| Name | School/Country (if not USA) | Olympics (Year) | Event | Result |
| Nawal El Moutawakel | Iowa State/Morocco | Los Angeles (1984) | 400 Hurdles | Gold |
| Esther Jones | LSU | Barcelona (1992) | 4 x 100 M Relay | Gold |
| Jearl Miles-Clark | Alabama A&M | Barcelona (1992) | 4 x 400 M Relay 400 | Silver Did not medal |
| | | Atlanta (1996) | 4 x 400 M Relay 400 | Gold Did not medal |
| | | Sydney (2000) | 4 x 400 M Relay 800 | Gold Did not medal |
| | | Athens (2004) | 800 | Did not medal |
| Inger Miller | USC | Atlanta (1996) | 4 x 100 M Relay | Gold |
| Beverly McDonald | Barton County (Kan.)CC/Jamaica | Sydney (2000) | 4 x 100 M Relay 200 | Silver Bronze |
| | | Athens (2004) | 4 x 100 M Relay | Gold |
| LaTasha Colander-Richardson | North Carolina | Sydney (2000) | 4 x 400 M Relay 400 | Gold Did not medal |
| | | Athens (2004) | 100 4 x 400 M Relay | Did not medal Gold |
| Veronica Campbell-Brown | Barton County (Kan.)CC/Arkansas/Jamaica | Sydney (2000) | 4 x 100 M Relay | Silver |
| | | Athens (2004) | 200 4 x 100 M Relay 100 | Gold Gold Bronze |
| | | Beijing (2008) | 200 4 x 100 M Relay | Gold Did not medal |
| | | London (2012) | 4 x 100 M Relay 100 200 | Silver Bronze Did not medal |
| Marion Jones | North Carolina | Sydney (2000) | 100 200 4 x 400 M Relay Long Jump 4 x 100 M Relay | Gold-DQ Gold-DQ Gold-DQ Bronze-DQ Bronze-DQ |
| | | Athens (2004) | Long Jump 4 x 100 M Relay | Did not medal Did not medal |

| Women | | | | |
|---|---|---|---|---|
| Name | School/Country (if not USA) | Olympics (Year) | Event | Result |
| Chrystal Cox | North Carolina | Athens (2004) | 4 x 400 M Relay | Gold-DQ |
| Joanna Hayes | UCLA | Athens (2004) | 100 Hurdles | Gold |
| Moushaumi Robinson | Texas | Athens (2004) | 4 x 400 M Relay | Gold |
| Aleen Bailey | Barton County (Kan.) CC/South Carolina/Jamaica | Athens (2004)<br><br><br>Beijing (2008) | 4 x 100 M Relay<br>100<br>200<br>4 x 100 M Relay | Gold<br>Did not medal<br>Did not medal<br>Did not medal |
| Allyson Felix | (ran professionally) | Athens (2004)<br>Beijing (2008)<br><br>London (2012) | 200<br>4 x 400 M Relay<br>200<br>200<br>4 x 100 M Relay<br>4 x 400 M Relay<br>100 | Silver<br>Gold<br>Silver<br>Gold<br>Gold<br>Gold<br>Did not medal |
| Mary Danner Wineberg | Cincinnati | Beijing (2008) | 4 x 400 M Relay<br>400 | Gold<br>Did not medal |
| Lauryn Williams | Miami | Athens (2004)<br><br>Beijing (2008)<br><br>London (2012)<br>Sochi (2014) | 100<br>4 x 100 M Relay<br>100<br>4 x 100 M Relay<br>4 x 100 M Relay<br>Two-person bobsled | Silver<br>Did not medal<br>Did not medal<br>Did not medal<br>Gold<br>Silver |
| DeeDee Trotter | Tennessee | Athens (2004)<br><br>Beijing (2008)<br>London (2012) | 4 x 400 M Relay<br>400<br>400<br>4 x 400 M Relay<br>400 | Gold<br>Did not medal<br>Did not medal<br>Gold<br>Bronze |
| Diamond Dixon | Kansas | London (2012) | 4 x 400 M Relay | Gold |
| Bianca Knight | Texas | London (2012) | 4 x 100 M Relay | Gold |

> continued

> continued

| Women | | | | |
|-------|---|---|---|---|
| **Name** | **School/Country (if not USA)** | **Olympics (Year)** | **Event** | **Result** |
| Merlene Ottey | Nebraska/Jamaica | Moscow (1980) | 200 | Bronze |
| | | | 4 x 100 M Relay | Did not medal |
| | | | 4 x 400 M Relay | Did not medal |
| | | Los Angeles (1984) | 100 | Bronze |
| | | | 200 | Bronze |
| | | Seoul (1988) | 4 x 100 M Relay | Did not medal |
| | | | 100 | Did not medal |
| | | | 200 | Did not medal |
| | | Barcelona (1992) | 4 x 100 M Relay | Did not medal |
| | | | 200 | Bronze |
| | | | 100 | Did not medal |
| | | Atlanta (1996) | 4 x 100 M Relay | Did not medal |
| | | | 100 | Silver |
| | | | 200 | Silver |
| | | Sydney (2000) | 4 x 100 M Relay | Bronze |
| | | | 100 | Bronze (Moved up when Marion Jones was stripped of gold.) |
| | Slovenia | Athens (2004) | 4 x 100 M Relay | Bronze |
| | | | 100 | Did not medal |
| | | | 200 | Did not medal |
| Sandra Farmer-Patrick | Arizona/Cal State/Jamaica | Los Angeles (1984) | 400 Hurdles | Did not medal |
| | | Barcelona (1992) | 400 Hurdles | Silver |
| | USA | Atlanta (1996) | 400 Hurdles | Did not medal |
| Michelle Burgher | George Mason/Clemson/Jamaica | Sydney (2000) | 4 x 400 M Relay | Silver |
| | | Athens (2004) | 4 x 400 M Relay | Bronze |
| Lyudmila Litvinova | Russia | Beijing (2008) | 4 x 400 M Relay | Silver |
| LaShinda Demus | South Carolina | Athens (2004) | 400 Hurdles | Did not medal |
| | | London (2012) | 400 Hurdles | Silver |

| | | Women | | |
|---|---|---|---|---|
| Name | School/Country (if not USA) | Olympics (Year) | Event | Result |
| Tonja Buford-Bailey | Illinois | Barcelona (1992) Atlanta (1996) Sydney (2000) | 400 Hurdles 400 Hurdles 400 Hurdles | Did not medal Did not medal Did not medal |
| Torri Edwards | USC | Sydney (2000) Beijing (2008) | 4 x 100 M Relay 4 x 100 M Relay | Bronze Did not medal |
| Passion Richardson | Kentucky | Sydney (2000) | 4 x 100 M Relay | Bronze |
| Natasha Danvers | USC/Great Britain | Sydney (2000) Beijing (2008) | 400 Hurdles 4 x 400 M Relay 400 Hurdles | Did not medal Did not medal Bronze |
| Halimat Ismaila | UTEP/Nigeria | Athens (2004) Beijing (2008) | 4 x 400 M Relay 4 x 100 M Relay 100 | Did not medal Bronze Did not medal |
| Shereefa Lloyd | Texas Tech/Jamaica | Beijing (2008) London (2012) | 4 x 400 M Relay 4 x 400 M Relay | Bronze Bronze |
| Priscilla Lopes-Schliep | Nebraska/Canada | Beijing (2008) | 100 Hurdles | Bronze |
| Rosemarie Whyte | Garden City (Kan.) CC/Foster/Jamaica | Beijing (2008) London (2012) | 4 x 400 M Relay 400 4 x 400 M Relay 400 | Bronze Did not medal Bronze Did not medal |
| Novlene Williams-Mills | Florida/Jamaica | Athens (2004) Beijing (2008) London (2012) | 4 x 400 M Relay 4 x 400 M Relay 4 x 400 M Relay 400 | Bronze Bronze Bronze Did not medal |
| Kellie Wells | Hampton (Virg.) | London (2012) | 100 Hurdles | Bronze |
| Janell (Smith) Carson | Unattached | Tokyo (1964) | 400 | Did not medal |
| * Judy Dyer | Topeka (ran unattached)/Texas Southern | Mexico City (1968) | 80 m hurdles | Did not medal |
| Pam Page | Missouri | Los Angeles (1984) | 100 Hurdles | Did not medal |

> continued

> continued

| Women | | | | |
|---|---|---|---|---|
| Name | School/Country (if not USA) | Olympics (Year) | Event | Result |
| Michelle Baptiste | Missouri State/St. Lucia | Atlanta (1996) | 100 | Did not medal |
| Juliet Campbell | Barton County (Kan.)CC/Jamaica | Atlanta (1996) | 4 x 100 M Relay | Did not medal |
| Michelle Collins | (ran professionally) | Sydney (2000) | 400 | Did not medal |
| Vernetta Lesforis | Missouri Valley/St. Lucia | Sydney (2000) | 100 Hurdles | Did not medal |
| Nadine Faustin-Parker | North Carolina/Haiti | Sydney (2000) Athens (2004) Beijing (2008) | 100 Hurdles 100 Hurdles 100 Hurdles | Did not medal Did not medal Did not medal |
| LaShauntea Moore | Barton County (Kan.)CC/Arkansas | Athens (2004) | 200 | Did not medal |
| Egle Uljas | Nebraska/Estonia | Athens (2004) | 400 | Did not medal |
| Laverne Jones-Ferrettte | Barton County (Kan.)CC/ Oklahoma/Virgin Islands | Athens (2004) Beijing (2008) London (2012) | 100 200 100 100 200 | Did not medal Did not medal Did not medal Did not medal Did not medal |
| Shandria Brown | Lincoln (Mo.)/ Bahamas | Athens (2004) | 4 x 100 M Relay | Did not medal |
| Allison Beckford | Rice/Jamaica | Athens (2004) | 400 | Did not medal |
| Myriam Mani | Cameroon | Athens (2004) | 100 | Did not medal |
| Damu Cherry | South Florida | Beijing (2008) | 100 Hurdles | Did not medal |
| Muna Lee | LSU | Athens (2004) Beijing (2008) | 100 100 4 x 100 M Relay | Did not medal Did not medal Did not medal |
| Angela Williams | Southern Cal | Athens (2004) Beijing (2008) | 4 x 100 M Relay 4 x 100 M Relay | Did not medal Did not medal |
| Nickiesha Wilson | Louisiana State/ Jamaica | Beijing (2008) | 400 Hurdles | Did not medal |

| Women | | | | |
|---|---|---|---|---|
| Name | School/Country (if not USA) | Olympics (Year) | Event | Result |
| Nickesha Anderson | Kansas/Jamaica | Beijing (2008) | 4 x 100 M Relay | Did not medal |
| Semey Hackett | Lincoln (Mo.)/ Trinidad and Tobago | Beijing (2008) | 100<br>4 x 100 M Relay | Did not medal<br>Did not medal |
| Tiandra Ponteen | Florida/St. Kitts and Nevis | Beijing (2008)<br>London (2012) | 400<br>400 | Did not medal<br>Did not medal |
| Kineke Alexander | Iowa/St. Vincent and the Grenadines | Beijing (2008)<br>London (2012) | 400<br>400 | Did not medal<br>Did not medal |
| Ajoke Odumosu | South Alabama/ Nigeria | Beijing (2008)<br><br>London (2012) | 400<br>4 x 400 M Relay<br>400 Hurdles | Did not medal<br>Did not medal<br>Did not medal |
| Queen Harrison | Virginia Tech | Beijing (2008) | 400 Hurdles | Did not medal |
| Aleesha Barber | Penn State/Trinidad and Tobago | Beijing (2008) | 100 Hurdles | Did not medal |
| Gloria Asumnu | Tulane/Nigeria | London (2012) | 100<br>200<br>4 x 100 M Relay | Did not medal<br>Did not medal<br>Did not medal |

* Denotes that athlete competed at KU Relays while in high school.

# 10

# Landing in the Sand
## Horizontal Jumpers

"The medals don't mean anything and the glory doesn't last. It's all about your happiness. The rewards are going to come, but my happiness is just loving the sport and having fun performing."

-- Jackie Joyner-Kersee, Olympic long-jump gold medalist, sister of triple jumper Al Joyner

Three-time Relays triple-jump champion Crystal Manning keeps her eyes on the prize. She owns the second-best women's mark in the event's history.

Given the oft-forgotten status of the long jump and triple jump, fans may have their heads in the sand and not realize that the Kansas Relays has hosted four horizontal jumpers who have won Olympic gold. Only die-hard track buffs would know that Ed Gordon (1936), a contemporary of Glenn Cunningham, and Jerome Biffle (1952), a contemporary of Wes Santee, stood atop the podium in USA uniforms. Triple jump gold medalist Al Joyner (1984), brother of Jackie Joyner-Kersee and husband of Florence Griffith-Joyner (Flo Jo), is much better known. However, he did not triple jump at the Relays in 1986. Instead he set a record in his favorite event, the 110-meter hurdles. As he eloquently phrased it, "The hurdles are my first love, and the triple jump is my mistress that came and took me away. But you always go back to your first love." Had he competed in the triple jump that year, he would have been matched up against up-and-coming Kenny Harrison, still a student at Kansas State and a decade away from his own gold medal in the triple jump. At the Relays, Harrison was a double winner in both 1986 and 1987. His 26-feet, 8.5-inch long jump and 57-feet, 2-inch triple jump in 1987 as a Wildcat senior are still meet records.

Aside from faster runways, better shoes and more sophisticated measuring devices, the long jump (the event formerly known as the broad jump) has not changed substantially in 86 years at the KU Relays. Unlike the pole vault, there have been no major technological breakthroughs. Drastic technique advancements, like the Parry O'Brien glide in the shot put or the Fosbury Flop in the high jump, have not materialized, though a gymnastic front flip from the toe board was a brief experiment before it became illegal. As a result, performance comparisons between the past and present in the horizontal jumps have more validity than comparisons for the vertical jumps.

The first Relays champion in the long jump in 1923 was Merwin Graham of Kansas with a leap of 22-1.5, not a quality jump by modern standards.

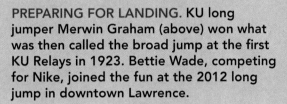

PREPARING FOR LANDING. KU long jumper Merwin Graham (above) won what was then called the broad jump at the first KU Relays in 1923. Bettie Wade, competing for Nike, joined the fun at the 2012 long jump in downtown Lawrence.

His forte was the triple jump, in which he placed ninth at the 1924 Paris Olympics. (The triple jump, formerly called the hop-step-jump, was not contested at the Relays until 1936.) The first big long jumps at the Relays came from another Olympian, Gordon, who competed for Iowa. In 1930, Gordon was the first Relays competitor to jump farther than 24 feet, and a year later the first to jump over 25. By the time Gordon competed at KU, he had already been to the 1928 Amsterdam Olympics. In 1932, after his KU

appearances, he won the gold medal in Los Angeles.

Gordon's mark of 25-4.75 in 1931 would not be beaten until Jim Baird of East Texas State did so in 1960 with a jump of 25-5.25, only a quarter of an inch better than Noel Certain of Emporia State that same year. In the interim between Gordon and Baird, three Olympians competed at the KU Relays. Biffle, competing for Denver in 1950, was the second Relays competitor to jump 25 feet before going on to win gold in Helsinki two years later. Another Olympian was Neville Price of Oklahoma, who represented South Africa in Helsinki in 1952, and in Melbourne in 1956. The third, John Bennett of Marquette, would miss Gordon's 1931 record by ¾ of an inch in 1953. However, he did defeat both Price and Texas A&M's Bobby Ragsdale at KU that year, and would defeat Price again in the Melbourne Games in taking home the silver medal.

**WILDCAT OLYMPIAN.** K-State's Kenny Harrison had some of his best early-career performances at the KU Relays before going on to win Olympic gold.

Baird's record lasted only two years before Bill Miller of McMurry (Texas) University sailed 25-6 in 1962. Miller was the first three-time long jump winner at the Relays. The first jumper to jump over 26 feet at KU was Clarence Robinson of New Mexico in 1965. The long jump was on Friday, and Robinson came back on Saturday to set a record in the triple jump at 50-6.5 as well, winning the Most Outstanding Performer award for his efforts. Three-time winner Danny Brabham of Baylor equaled Robinson's record of 26-2.5 in 1971. That record stood until Veryl Switzer, Jr., of Kansas State extended it to 26-3.5 in 1982. Then fellow Wildcat Harrison had his stellar Relays stretch that included:

- Breaking Switzer's mark and then extending the long jump record, to its current 26-8.5.
- Two long jump wins.
- Three triple jump wins, including breaking and then extending the record, to its current 57-2.
- A Most Outstanding Performer award. Although he broke both the long and triple jump marks in both 1986 and 1987, he only took MOP honors that first year, 1986, when he first penciled his name into the record books.

Other jumps – both triple and long – over the years have been longer than Harrison's, but they were wind-aided. For example, KU's Danny Seay long-jumped 26-9 in 1974. Olympian Charlton Ehizuelen of Illinois, who would represent Nigeria in the 1976 Montreal Games, had a wind-aided 27-4 in 1975, the only 27-foot jump in Relays history. Moses Kiyai from Iowa State jumped a wind-aided 26-11 in 1985, a year after he competed for Kenya in the Los Angeles Olympics in both the long and triple jumps.

Ehizuelen notched a wind-aided 54-6.5 triple jump that would be bested in 1980 by the wind-aided 55-3.5 of Kansas State star Vince Parette. His mark was then exceeded by Southern Methodist's Keith Connor in 1982. Connor's jump of 55-4.5 was then surpassed the very next year when Nikolai Musyenko of the USSR jumped 55-9.25; the record that stood until Harrison's prodigious 57-2 in 1987.

One of the stirring duals in the horizontal jumps came in 2001 between two Arkansas Razorbacks, Robert Howard and Melvin Lister. Howard had already competed in two Olympics, Atlanta in 1996 and Sydney in 2000. Lister had already competed in Sydney and would go on to compete in Athens in 2004. Howard eked out a Relays victory in the long jump 26-7 to 26-6.25. Having won the triple jump on Friday at 54-6.75, he was named Male Outstanding Performer in a weekend when eight meet records were set and 21 Olympians were performing.

**JAYHAWK OLYMPIAN.** KU's Kent Floerke, who first competed at the KU Relays as a high schooler from Kansas City, reached the 1964 Tokyo Games in the triple jump.

Women did not begin long jumping at the Relays until 1975. The first jump over 20 feet came the next year when Willye White, formerly of Tennessee State, jumped 20-9.5. By 1976, White was 36 years old and had already become the first American to compete in five Olympics, having won silver in Melbourne in 1956 as a 16-year-old high school sophomore. She was the first American woman to medal in the long jump.

The next great jumper was KU's Halcyon McKnight, who won four straight long jump titles spanning 1980-1983. Her best jump during that time was 21-10.25 in her junior year. That record stood until surpassed by Elva Goulbourne with a 21-11 in 2008. That mark was bested when London Olympian Janay DeLoach-Soukup jumped 22-4.5 in the 2013 long jump competition, which was held at the Douglas County Fairgrounds. The field of jumpers included Olympian Jimoh Funmi.

Other noted Olympians have competed in the horizontal jumps at the Relays. Angela Thacker of Nebraska long jumped at Los Angeles, and another Cornhusker, Karen Kruger, did so in Atlanta under the South African flag. Heptathletes Shelia Burrell (2000-2001) and Austra Skujyte (2004-2005) also long-jumped at the Relays. Two-time Olympian Trecia Smith, a Jamaican who had attended Pittsburgh, won three consecutive

HALCYON'S DAYS. KU's Halcyon McKnight won four consecutive long jump titles at the Relays, and held the meet record for 26 years until ...

JAMAICAN JUMPER ... Elva Goulbourne broke McKnight's record in 2008. Goulbourne held the mark for five years until ...

PLAYING INDOORS ... Janay DeLoach-Soukup extended it to 22-4.5 in 2013, when weather forced the competition indoors to the livestock arena at the Douglas County Fairgrounds.

Relays triple jumps from 2001-2003. Smith was fourth in the triple jump at the 2004 Athens Games, and also competed in Beijing. Her Relays mark of 48-10, set in 2001, is over four feet farther than any other woman has ever triple-jumped at KU. The next best jump went to Crystal Manning, a three-time winner from Kansas, who had a jump of 44-7 in 2009.

In boys high school competition, the first 23-foot jump (23-1.25) came from Larry Irwin of Topeka-Washburn Rural in 1961. That would be the best mark until Sherman Harold of Topeka-Hayden jumped 23-5.75 in 1973. Bill Campbell of Derby, Kan., improved it to 23-8.25 the very next year and Kevin Sloan of Topeka-Hayden would add a half inch to that the following year. Sam Jenkins of Topeka High School jumped 23-10.5 in 1977. The first 24-foot jump (24-1) was by Manhattan's Switzer, Jr., in 1980, a mark that would stand until Lister, then at Leavenworth (Kan.) High, jumped 24-9.25 in 1996 to set the current standard.

In the triple jump, Vince Parette of Shawnee Mission (Kan.) South had the first 47 and 48-foot jumps in the high school division. His record jump of 48-3.25 in 1976 was broken by Switzer, Jr., who jumped 48-4.5 in 1980. That mark would not be broken until Demetrius Phillips of Bishop Ward (Kan.) High jumped 49-7 in 1991. Martin Lewis of Liberal (Kan.), also a two-time winner in the long jump, tripled 49-6.25 in 1993. No one else jumped over 49 until Lister, double-winner in both the long jump and triple jump in 1995-96, jumped 50-0.75 in 1996 to give him the current high school record in both jumps.

The outstanding performance among girl horizontal jumpers at the Relays belongs to Leah Kirkland of John Marshall (Okla.) High School. In 1988, she long-jumped 19-4.25 and triple-jumped 41-1. The triple jump record still stands; the long jump record was tied in 2013 by Alexa Harmon-Thomas of Lawrence-Free State (Kan.). Two high school girls were noteworthy for their three-peats: Angela Graves of Lawrence in 1984-86, with all jumps being 18-2.25 or better; and Le'Tristan Pledger of Kansas City-Washington (Kan.) in 2009-11, with all jumps being at least 18-6. Megan Frausto of Royse City (Texas) High School jumped 19-3.5 in 2008. In the triple jump, Ashane Johnson of Moberly (Mo.) High School jumped 39-3, the only jump other than Kirkland's to surpass 39 feet.

The long jump and triple jump are rarely the featured events at the Relays. For most people, the horizontal jumps do not bring a crowd to its feet like two racers running down a track elbow to elbow, the looming danger in the pole vault and hurdles, or the suspense of seeing where an implement in flight will land. However, the speed and athleticism required of good jumpers are something to marvel at, and the Relays has enjoyed an astonishing number of Olympians who have competed in these events. The table on the following pages attests to that.

# Horizontal Jumpers Who Competed in the Kansas Relays and Olympics

| Men | | | | |
|---|---|---|---|---|
| Name | School/Country (if not USA) | Olympics (Year) | Event | Result |
| Ed Gordon | Iowa | Amsterdam (1928) Los Angeles (1932) | Long Jump Long Jump | Did not medal Gold |
| Jerome Biffle | Denver | Helsinki (1952) | Long Jump | Gold |
| Al Joyner | Arkansas State | Los Angeles (1984) | Triple Jump | Gold |
| Kenny Harrison | Kansas State | Atlanta (1996) | Triple Jump | Gold |
| John Bennett | Marquette | Melbourne (1956) | Long Jump | Silver |
| Keith Conner | SMU/Great Britain | Los Angeles (1984) | Triple Jump | Bronze |
| Merwin Graham | Kansas | Paris (1924) | Triple Jump | Did not medal |
| Neville Price | Oklahoma/ South Africa | Helsinki (1952) Melbourne (1956) | Long Jump Long Jump | Did not medal Did not medal |
| Jim Gerhardt | Rice | Helsinki (1952) | Triple Jump | Did not medal |
| Anthony Watson | Oklahoma | Rome (1960) | Long Jump | Did not medal |
| *Kent Floerke | Kansas | Tokyo (1964) | Triple Jump | Did not medal |
| Lennox Burgher | Nebraska/Jamaica | Mexico City (1968) | Triple Jump | Did not medal |
| *Preston Carrington | Wichita State | Munich (1972) | Long Jump | Did not medal |
| Charlton Ehizuelen | Illinois/Nigeria | Montreal (1976) | Long Jump | Did not medal |
| Phil Robins | Southern Illinois/ Bahamas | Montreal (1976) | Triple Jump | Did not medal |
| Ajiyi Agbebaku | New Mexico JC/ Nigeria | Los Angeles (1984) | Triple Jump | Did not medal |
| Moses Kiyai | Iowa State/Kenya | Los Angeles (1984) | Triple Jump Long Jump | Did not medal Did not medal |
| Ndabazinhle Mdhlongwa | Zimbabwe | Barcelona (1992) Atlanta (1996) | Triple Jump Triple Jump | Did not medal Did not medal |
| Brian Wellman | Arkansas/Bermuda | Barcelona (1992) Atlanta (1996) | Triple Jump Triple Jump | Did not medal Did not medal |
| Robert Howard | Arkansas | Atlanta (1996) Sydney (2000) | Triple Jump Triple Jump | Did not medal Did not medal |

> continued

> continued

| Men | | | | |
|-----|-----|-----|-----|-----|
| Name | School/Country (if not USA) | Olympics (Year) | Event | Result |
| *Melvin Lister | Arkansas | Sydney (2000) Athens (2004) | Long Jump Triple Jump | Did not medal Did not medal |
| Walter Davis | LSU | Athens (2004) London (2012) | Triple Jump Triple Jump | Did not medal Did not medal |
| Randy Lewis | Wichita/Grenada | Athens (2004) Beijing (2008) | Triple Jump Triple Jump | Did not medal Did not medal |
| Aarik Wilson | Indiana | Beijing (2008) | Triple Jump | Did not medal |
| Jeremy Campbell | Central Oklahoma | Beijing (2008) | Paralympic Long Jump | Did not medal |
| **Women** | | | | |
| Willye White | Tennessee State | Melbourne (1956) Rome (1960) Tokyo (1964) Mexico City (1968) Munich (1972) | Long Jump Long Jump Long Jump 4x100 Relay Long Jump Long Jump | Silver Did not medal Did not medal Silver Did not medal Did not medal |
| Janay DeLoach-Soukup | Colorado State | London (2012) | Long Jump | Bronze |
| Angela Thacker | Nebraska | Los Angeles (1984) | Long Jump | Did not medal |
| Karen Kruger | Nebraska/South Africa | Atlanta (1996) | Long Jump | Did not medal |
| Michelle Baptiste | Missouri State/ St. Lucia | Atlanta (1996) | Long Jump | Did not medal |
| Elva Goulbourne | Auburn/Jamaica | Sydney (2000) | Long Jump | Did not medal |
| Trecia Smith | Pittsburgh/Jamaica | Athens (2004) Beijing (2008) | Triple Jump Triple Jump | Did not medal Did not medal |
| Grace Upshaw | California | Beijing (2008) | Long Jump | Did not medal |
| Jimoh Funmi | Rice | Beijing (2008) | Triple Jump | Did not medal |
| Arantxa King | Stanford/Bermuda | Beijing (2008) London (2012) | Long Jump Long Jump | Did not medal Did not medal |
| Amanda Smock | North Dakota State | London (2012) | Triple Jump | Did not medal |

* Denotes that athlete competed at KU Relays while in high school.

# 11

# Flops, Rolls, and High Fliers
## Vertical Jumpers

"I love the pole vault because it is a professor's sport. One must not only run and jump, but one must think. Which pole to use, which height to jump, which strategy to use. I love it because the results are immediate and the strongest is the winner."

-- Ukrainian Sergey Bubka, world-record holder at 20-1.75, quoted in *Sports Illustrated*, Sept. 14, 1988, by writer Gary Smith

The pages of this book are filled with dozens of Olympians, but many elite athletes, especially Americans, did not have that opportunity even though they were world-record holders. On April 22, 1961, a duel at the Kansas Relays had 13,500 fans drooling. The faceoff pitted one pole vaulter who had been a world-record holder with another who would become one by season's end. What made this particular dual so intriguing was that the pole vault was at a crossroads. There was much controversy about whether the new fiberglass pole that some vaulters were beginning to use should be legal or not.

Representing the old was J. D. Martin of Oklahoma. Using an aluminum alloy pole, he was coming off a sensational 1960 season which saw him sweep the Texas-Kansas-Drake Triple Crown, win the NCAA championship and sail to a world record 15 feet, 9 ¾ inches, though the record was never allowed because the bar had to be turned around to keep the wind from blowing it off. (Officially, the record was held by Olympic champion Don Bragg at 15-9.5, the highest official height ever cleared using an aluminum pole.) Martin's opponent on this day was Oklahoma State sophomore sensation George Davies, who would become the first to break the world record using a fiberglass pole by soaring 15-10 at the Big Eight Conference Championships in Boulder, Colo., later that year.

However, at the Relays in 1961, the crowd was disappointed because neither Martin nor Davies could muster the 15-foot vault the fans anticipated. Instead, they shared the win at 14-10, which somehow seemed fitting given the clash between aluminum and glass. The 1951 jump of 15-0.13 by Don Cooper of Nebraska remained the Relays standard. After 1961, fiberglass became the pole of choice, much to the chagrin of Bragg, whose "straight" pole record Davies had broken. Bragg led the assault on the new technology, to no avail. His bitter comment: "What do they want, a circus or an athletic event?"

**NEW TECHNOLOGIES.** KU's Andrea Branson (right) flew 13 feet, 10 inches in winning the meet in 2000. Back in 1936, when the photo on the left was taken at the Relays, aluminum alloy poles were used for launching. Wayne Lion of Iowa State and Sherman Cosgrove of Nebraska both shared the victory. Each went 13-0.

What was the Relays pole vault like before the circus came to town? The first vaulter of note was Earle McKown of Kansas State Teachers College (now Emporia State), who won the first three years. His vault in 1925 of 13-2.88 was an intercollegiate record. In 1926, Frank Potts of Oklahoma, Frank Wirsig of Nebraska and J. C. Carter of Kansas State tied for first at 12-11.88. [1]

In 1928, the same year that Bill Droegemuller of Northwestern won the silver medal in the Amsterdam Olympics, he tied with three others at the Relays: Evert Brewer of Colorado State, Bruce Drake of Oklahoma and

**EARLY FLIER.** Tom Warne shared or held the Relays pole vault record for 10 years, from 1929-38.

Johnny Bryce of Oklahoma. In 1929, both Tom Warne of Northwestern and George Otterness of Minnesota cleared 13-4.75 to break McKown's four-year-old record. Warne raised that to 13-9.75 the following year. All winners between then and 1940 jumped between 13 and 14 feet.

The Relays saw its first over-14 vault in 1940 when Beefus Bryan of Texas sailed 14-2 in one of his three championships. Two-time winner Bill Carroll of Oklahoma broke that record in 1950 with a 14-5 jump. Jim Graham from Oklahoma A&M (now Oklahoma State) leaped 14-7 at the Relays in 1956. The same year, he qualified for the Melbourne Olympics, but in a display of sportsmanship, willingly gave up his spot to Bob Gutkowski of Occidental (Calif.) College, citing an injured ankle as the reason. Gutkowski subsequently won a silver medal and the 22-year-old Graham was awarded the first-ever Ted Husing Award for sportsmanship.

In 1962, the year after the Martin-Davies duel, another vault confrontation took place at the Relays. Fred Hanson of Rice was just learning his craft, but two years later he became the first vaulter to clear 17 feet. He also won Olympic gold in Tokyo to continue the American streak of never losing an Olympic vault. The overwhelming favorite at KU was John Uelses, the first to ever clear 16 feet, which was considered at the time to be nearly as unattainable as the four-minute mile. In fact, when Uelses cleared

16-0.25 at the Millrose Games on Feb. 2, 1962, the record was disallowed because in the pandemonium around the pit, a photographer accidently bumped the standards and knocked the bar off. Hence the height could not be measured both before and after the jump as record rules required. It didn't matter, because a week later he went 16-0.75 at the Boston Indoor. Since indoor marks were not accepted as world records at the time, Uelses took his fiberglass pole to Santa Barbara, Calif., where he duplicated his Boston jump.

With a resume as impressive as this, fans were geared up to see a 16-foot jump from Uelses. It didn't happen. Instead Hansen won the event at 15-6.5, nearly five inches higher than Uelses. Like Martin and Davies, world-record holder Uelses never competed in the Olympics.[2]

The pole vault is the most frequently broken world record in track and field history. The first world record recognized by the International Association of Athletics Federations (IAAF) was in 1912. Between American Marc Wright's 13-2.25 jump on June 8, 1912, and Ukrainian Sergey Bubka's 20-1.75 on July 31, 1994, the IAAF has ratified 71 world records broken by 33 different vaulters. (The fact that Bubka's record has lasted two decades would indicate that the vaulters have caught up with the technology.) With the advent of fiberglass technology, Kansas Relays records, like the world records, began to climb in small increments almost yearly. As an example:

DIAL UP. Joe Dial, shown here as a collegian jumping for Oklahoma State at the Relays, was also a high school champion while with Marlow (Okla.) High, and a meet champion while with Athletics West in 1987.

# Progression of Pole Vault Record at Kansas Relays, 1963-1987

| Year | Athlete | Affiliation | Height |
|------|---------|-------------|--------|
| 1963 | Fred Hansen | Rice | 16-0.75 |
| 1967 | Fred Burton | Wichita | 16-7 |
| 1968 | Chad Rogers | Colorado | 17-0.5 |
| 1972 | Kjell Isaksson | Sweden | 17-5 |
| 1975 | Vic Dias | Beverly Hills Striders | 17-6.25 |
| 1980 | Brad Pursley | Abilene Christian | 17-8 |
| 1982 | Joe Dial | Oklahoma State | 17-10 |
| 1983 | Alexander Krupsky | USSR | 18-4 |
| 1984 | Steve Stubblefield | Arkansas State | 18-4.5 |
| 1985 | Joe Dial | Oklahoma State | 18-8 |
| 1986 | Doug Lytle | Bud Light | 18-9.25 |
| 1987 | Joe Dial | Athletics West | 19-4.75* |

*Dial's 1987 jump remains the current KU Relays record. His record-breaking leap earned him his third Most Outstanding Performer award. He also received the award when he cleared 17-5.25 while competing for Marlow (Okla.) High School in 1980, and as a collegian in 1985 when he topped 18-8.

Already a crowd-pleasing event, several circumstances conspired to make the pole vault even more appealing in recent years. Landing mats had to get larger for safety reasons as vaulters jumped higher, but the vaulting boxes and runways were simply too close to the track to accommodate them. Also the chance of an errant crossbar striking an unsuspecting runner was always imminent. Therefore, in 2000, the vault was moved to the center of the infield with a raised portable runway platform. This made the vault visible to spectators from any area of the stadium.

A second reason for increased fan attention was a rash of talented high school performers who continued to return to the Relays collegiately and beyond as national and international caliber vaulters. Names like Tad Scales of Lawrence, Kan., the first high school 16-footer at the Relays; and Jeff Buckingham of Gardner, Kan., who won the high school division in 1978 and the collegiate division for KU in 1979. Perhaps the most spectacular example of all came in 1980, when future Olympian Doug Lytle of Shawnee Mission (Kan.) North was relegated to third while Steve Stubblefield of Wyandotte, Kan., and Joe Dial of Marlow, Okla., dueled for the top spot. Stubblefield jumped 17-1.25, but had to settle for second behind Dial's 17-5.25, which continues to be the high school record.

Lytle, who later competed for Kansas State, won a Relays watch in 1986 with a jump of 18-9.25. Stubblefield, competing for Arkansas State, won in 1984 at 18-4.5. And Dial, who had

**RELAYS REGULAR.** Olympian Scott Huffman, shown here in 2003, competed often at the KU Relays for two decades. He also promoted the event heavily to other elite vaulters, who themselves then came to Lawrence to compete.

taken his talents to Oklahoma State, would win in 1982, 1985 and 1987. Still another Kansas vaulter who had an enormous impact on the Relays vault was Scott Huffman of Quinter, Kan., who continued his career at KU. Like Lytle, he was not a high school champion at the Relays, but went on to become an Olympian and a collegiate champion at the Relays in 1988 and in open competition in 1991 and 1993. The event is now called the Scott Huffman Pole Vault.

His bar clearance method, "The Huffman Roll," whereby he cleared the bar with a straddle roll like a high jumper, made him a fan favorite around the world. He became, for a time, the American record holder at 19-7. Local interest was

**TWO-TIME OLYMPIAN.** Jeff Hartwig competed in two Olympics 12 years apart, and he vaulted at KU in 2007.

kept at a high level by Huffman's many appearances at the Relays and a series of All-American KU vaulters like Scales, Huffman, Bob Steinhoff, Jan Johnson, Terry Porter, Buckingham, Chris Bohanan, Pat Manson, Cam Miller, John Bazzoni, Vadim Gvozdetskiy and Jordan Scott. Still, perhaps Huffman's greatest contribution to the Relays could be attributed to his passion for the Relays and his ability to gather his friends for the Invitational Pole Vault. He once said, "Even though I compete all over the world, it's (KU) absolutely my favorite meet." In 1997, Huffman organized a pole vault field of eight, seven of whom had cleared 18 feet, including Pat Manson, who had a 19-2.25 to his credit. Bill Deering, formerly of Miami, won the event at 18-10.25 with Manson second at 18-6.5. The next year, a similar group of elite vaulters intended to make an assault on Dial's 1987 record of 19-4.75. Dean Starkey was victorious, but his leap of 18-8.25 fell short of the mark.

The women's pole vault was not contested until 1996, but what a debut it was. Stacy Dragila, a 1995 graduate of

ALWAYS APRIL. 2008 Olympian April Steiner won three titles in visits to KU during her namesake month.

Idaho State, was lured to the Relays and cleared 13-6.5, which was an American record at the time and secured her the Most Outstanding Performer Award. Dragila went on to have an illustrious career with many national and international achievements. She won the gold medal in the first ever women's Olympic pole vault competition in Sydney in 2000. She also qualified in 2004 for Athens, but an injury was a factor in her not making the finals. Dragila's mark was broken when KU's Andrea Branson cleared 13-10 in 2000, a record which lasted until Andrea Dutoit, formerly of Arizona, cleared 13-10.5. The following year, Dutoit upped the mark to 14-3.25. That record would last only a year as three-time Relays champion and 2008 Olympian April Steiner, formerly competing for Arkansas, raised the bar to 14-7.25 in 2006. That meet record would prevail until 2011 when Kylie Hutson, who had competed at Indiana State, vaulted 14-9, a mark which would be tied by Mary Saxer, formerly of Notre Dame, in 2013.

**GOING UP.** KU's Jordan Scott is known as much for his wild hair (see page 256 for one example) as his quality vaulting, but he had a tame look when he won his first of two Relays titles in 2009.

The first high school girls pole vault competition occurred in 2000. The first champion was Christi Lehman of Hesston, Kan., who jumped 11-0. Lindsey Bourne of Joplin, Mo., increased the record to 11-11.75 the following year. That record was broken by Natalie Willer of Elkhorn, Neb., in 2007 with a jump of 12-4, a record which stood until Emily Brigham of Mill Valley, Kan., went 12-5.5 in 2013.

# HIGH JUMPERS

The first three years of the Kansas Relays high jump went to KU's Tom Poor, who competed for the United States in the 1924 Paris Olympics.. His Western Roll of 6-5.13 in 1925 would not be topped until Ted Shaw of Wisconsin went 6-6.13 in 1930. Charles McGinnis of Wisconsin tied Floyd Short at just 6-2 in 1927. A year later, McGinnis would represent the USA in Amsterdam.

In 1938, Gil Cruter of Colorado jumped 6-7.5, a record that lasted until Robert Walters of Texas jumped 6-8.19 in 1949, despite the fact that three Olympians had a crack at it in the interim. Vern McGrew from Rice, who competed in London in 1948, won the Relays high jump at 6-6.75 in 1950. Walter Davis of Texas A&M and Arnold Betton of Drake tied at 6-7.25 in 1952. Both men competed in Helsinki in 1952 with Davis garnering the gold. The next advancement of the record came from Olympian Charlie Dumas of Compton (Calif.) College with a jump of 6-8.75 in 1956, a mark tied by Jackie Upton of Texas Christian in 1963.

Three time champion Steve Herndon of Missouri jumped 6-9.25 in 1966 before becoming the first Relays seven-footer a year later. The record was extended to 7-0.25 in 1969 by Fernando Abugattas, who represented Northwest Iowa at the Relays and Peru in the 1968 Olympics in Mexico City. From the 1970s to the present, the Relays were seldom won with jumps under seven feet.

One of the reasons seven-foot high jumps were becoming commonplace at the Relays can be traced to experimentation by a high school student in Medford, Ore. A 16-year-old student named Dick Fosbury was having no success with either the scissors style of jumping or the straddle roll. His experiments eventually resulted in his going over the bar backwards, which he could do while staying within the rule of taking off on one foot. This method, called the "Fosbury Flop," would not have been possible a few years earlier because jumpers had been landing in sand and sawdust pits that were rather unforgiving if they landed wrong. Fosbury went on to compete for Oregon State and not only won Olympic gold in Mexico City in 1968, but also set the Olympic and American record at 7-4.25. It is worth mentioning that Randy Smith of KU was the Relays champion as late as 1974 and 1975 while still using the straddle style of jumping.

New records for the high jump came in small increments as they often do in vertical jumps. For example:

## Progression of High Jump Record at Kansas Relays, 1972-1987

| Year | Athlete | Affiliation | Height |
|------|---------|-------------|--------|
| 1972 | Barry Schur | Kansas | 7-1 |
| 1976 | Bill Knoedel | Iowa | 7-1.25 |
| 1977 | Paul Allard | Drake | 7-2.25 |
| 1981 | Greg Shaper | Arkansas State | 7-3.5 |
| 1982 | Tyke Peacock | Kansas | 7-4.75 |
| 1987 | Hollis Conway | Unattached | 7-7* |

*Current KU Relays record. Conway set the American record at 7-8.75 while winning silver in Seoul in 1988. He won bronze in Barcelona at 7-8.5. His best jump was an American record 7-10.25, quite remarkable since he was only slightly taller than six feet. This meant his best jump was 22.25 inches over his head.

Since Hollis Conway leaped 7-7 in 1987, three Olympians have unsuccessfully tried to surpass it. Cameron Wright of Southern Illinois had jumps of 7-4.25, 7-5.25 and 7-4.5 in his three victories. He represented the USA in

Atlanta in 1996. Nathan Leeper of Kansas State, also a three-time winner at the Relays, had jumps of 7-5.75, 7-3.75, and 7-5.75. He competed in Sydney in 2000. Trevor Barry of Dickinson State (N.D.) University, represented the Bahamas in London in 2012. His winning effort in 2009 was 7-2.5. He had been the long jump champion in 2006. Also noteworthy was Dusty Jonas of Nebraska jumping 7-5.75 in 2006. Kansas State's Erik Kynard, silver medalist in London, did not high jump at the Relays, but he did long jump 23-6 in the 2010 Relays.

HIGH-JUMPING HUSKER.
Dusty Jonas won the KU
Relays in 2006.

By the time the women's high jump was first contested at the Relays in 1978, the Fosbury Flop was well established as the technique to use. In 1980, Mary Cragoe of Missouri jumped 5-11 to set the standard that would survive until Jan Chesbro jumped 6-2 in 1985. The Relays record that still stands was set by Julieanne Broughton of Arizona in 1990 at 6-2.25. Quite a few others have cleared 6-0. Rita Graves of Kansas State did so in 1988, and MaryBeth Labosky topped 6-1.75 twice out of her three championships. Hattie Anderson of Missouri jumped 6-0.5 in 1994, and two-time winner Kaylene Wagner of Kansas State soared 6-plus in her championship years.

Three Olympians have won Relays watches in the high jump. Connie Teaberry of Kansas State, who would compete in Atlanta in 1996, won in 1989.

LONG-TENURED HIGH JUMPERS. Five-time Olympian Amy Acuff (top) was runner-up at her 2005 KU Relays appearance to new mom Gwen Wentland, who also competed at an elite level for well over a decade.

Wanita Dykstra of Kansas State won in 1995 and 1996 and competed for Canada in the Athens Olympics in 2004. Karol Damon of Colorado won at the Relays in 2000 and also competed in Sydney later that year. She has since married Kansas State head track and field coach Cliff Rovelto, mentor to several international-caliber high jumpers.

Still another famous high jumper to compete at the Relays was five-time Olympian Amy Acuff, who competed collegiately at UCLA. She finished second to Gwen Wentland of Kansas State in 2005, a year after the birth of Wentland's daughter. Acuff has had an amazing career encompassing five Olympics from Atlanta in 1996 to London in 2012. She has won numerous national and international championships and has a lifetime best of 6-7. Her highest Olympic finish was fourth at Athens in 2004.

Wentland, who competed for Rovelto at Kansas State, had an equally illustrious career, which is not over yet as she continues to compete at a high level in master's competitions. She has competed in every Olympic Trials from 1992 to 2008, and despite a personal best of 6-5 and numerous national championships, was never able to finish in the top three on Trials day. However, she was paid the ultimate respect by being chosen to coach the women jumpers in London, most of whom she had competed against in the 2008 Trials, so she became an integral part of the 2012 U.S. Olympic team, just not as a competitor.

High school jumpers have also made significant contributions to Relays high jumping. In the pre-Fosbury years, two-time champion Steve Straight of Shawnee Mission North jumped 6-5.5 in 1962. Preston Carrington of Topeka (Kan.) High won in 1967 and he would go on to be an Olympian in the long jump. Randy Smith of McPherson, Kan., was a three time-winner in 1969-71 before going on to win two championships in the collegiate division as a Jayhawk. After 1972, only one year had a winning jump of less than 6-8, and that was 6-6 in 1979. The Fosbury Flop had indeed revolutionized high jumping.

Keith Guinn of Shawnee Mission North, set a new record of 6-10.75 in 1973. That record stood until Sharrieff Hazim of Topeka West recorded back-to-back wins of 6-11 and 6-10.5 in 1982 and 1983. Another Topekan, R. D.

Cogswell of Seaman, jumped 7-1 and 7-0 in 1987 and 1988. Sheldon Carpenter of Shawnee Mission East added ¼ inch to the record height in 1992. The next big jump would come from Jason Archibald of Garden City, Kan., when he cleared 7-3 in 1995. That record stood until three-time champion James White of Grandview, Colo., jumped 7-3.25 in 2009, which remains the standard. Nathan Leeper of Protection, Kan., jumped 6-10 in 1996 before going on to his success at K-State and as an Olympian.

The high school girls began competing in 1978. Sharon Logan of Wichita (Kan.) West won the first two years. The prevailing record came as early as 1982 when two-time winner Kym Carter of Wichita East jumped 6-2. Her high school jump of 6-2.25 was a national high school record. She later competed as a heptathlete in the 1992 Barcelona Olympics. No other high school girl has jumped six feet at the Relays, so her record is now over 30 years old. The second best jump of 5-10 belongs to Chris Hall of Chanute, Kan., who won three consecutive years between 1986 and 1988. Other notable performances include three championships by Allison Mayfield of St. Thomas (Kan.) Aquinas in 2005, 2006 and 2008; and two by Alexa Harmon-Thomas of Lawrence-Free State in 2012 and 2013.

**LAST OF THE STRADDLERS.**
Randy Smith eschewed the Fosbury Flop to win three high school titles and two college titles at the Relays. He would be the last to win without flopping.

[1] In the early years of the pole vault, measurements were taken in eighths, and ties for first were not broken. Ties were not unusual until a tie-breaking mechanism for vertical jumps was implemented in the 1960s. In fact, on a rain-drenched day in 1947, six men tied at the lowly height of 11-6.

[2] The birth name for German-born John Uelses was Hans Feigenbaum. During World War II, his father was sent to the Russian front where he was killed. Hans' mother, unable to provide for him and to protect him from the turmoil in Germany, sent him to Miami at the age of 12 to live with a German aunt and uncle, who adopted him. Thus, he became an American citizen with his adopted name Uelses. He anglicized Hans to John and, because he did not speak English, entered the Miami public schools as a fourth-grader, a couple of years behind children his own age. In 1962, the year he was making his record jumps and competing at the Relays, he was a corporal in the U.S. Marine Corps. Eighteen days after his 16-foot jump at Madison Square Garden, John Glenn became the first American to orbit the Earth. Uelses' comment about the two historic occasions was, "He was the second Marine astronaut to go into space. I was the first."

# Vertical Jumpers Who Competed in the Kansas Relays and Olympics

| Pole Vault | | | |
|---|---|---|---|
| Name | School/Country (if not USA) | Olympics (Year) | Result |
| **Men** | | | |
| Fred Hansen | Rice | Tokyo (1964) | Gold |
| Bob Seagren | Southern Cal | Mexico City (1968) Munich (1972) | Gold Silver |
| Nick Hysong | Arizona State | Sydney (2000) | Gold |
| Bill Droegemuller | Northwestern | Amsterdam (1928) | Silver |
| Charles McGinnis | Wisconsin | Amsterdam (1928) | Bronze |
| Jan Johnson | Kansas/Alabama | Munich (1972) | Bronze |
| Earl Bell | Arkansas State | Los Angeles (1984) Seoul (1988) | Bronze Did not medal |
| Jim Graham | Oklahoma A&M | Melbourne (1956) | Did not complete (Gave up Olympic spot to teammate) |
| Kjell Isaksson | Sweden | Mexico City (1968) Munich (1972) Montreal (1976) | Did not medal Did not medal Did not medal |
| Hans Lagerqvist | Sweden | Munich (1972) | Did not medal |
| Terry Porter | Kansas | Montreal (1976) | Did not medal |
| Sergei Kulibaba | USSR | Moscow (1980) | Did not medal |
| *Doug Lytle | Kansas State | Los Angeles (1984) | Did not medal |
| David Volz | Indiana | Barcelona (1992) | Did not medal |
| *Scott Huffman | Kansas | Atlanta (1996) | Did not medal |
| Jeff Hartwig | Arkansas State | Atlanta (1996) Beijing (2008) | Did not medal Did not medal |

> continued

> continued

| Pole Vault | | | |
|---|---|---|---|
| Name | School/Country (if not USA) | Olympics (Year) | Result |
| Women | | | |
| Stacy Dragila | Idaho State | Sydney (2000) Athens (2004) | Gold Did not medal |
| Dana Ellis | Univ. of Waterloo/ Canada | Athens (2004) | Did not medal |
| April (Steiner) Bennett | Paradise Valley (Ariz.) Community College/Arkansas | Beijing (2008) | Did not medal |
| Kelsie Hendry | Saskatchewan Univ./ Canada | Beijing (2008) | Did not medal |
| Tori Pena | UCLA/Ireland | London (2012) | Did not medal |
| Becky Holliday | Clackamas (Ore.) Community College/Oregon | London (2012) | Did not medal |
| Lacy Janson | Florida State | London (2012) | Did not medal |

| High Jump | | | |
|---|---|---|---|
| Name | School/Country (if not USA) | Olympics (Year) | Result |
| **Men** | | | |
| Walter Davis | Texas A&M | Helsinki (1952) | Gold |
| Charles Dumas | Compton (Calif.) College | Melbourne (1956) | Gold |
| Hollis Conway | Southwest Louisiana | Seoul (1988) Barcelona (1992) | Silver Bronze |
| Erik Kynard | Kansas State | London (2012) | Silver |
| Tom Poor | Kansas | Paris (1924) | Did not medal |
| Charles McGinnis | Wisconsin | Amsterdam (1928) | Did not medal |
| Vern McGrew | Rice | London (1948) | Did not medal |
| Arnold Betton | Drake | Helsinki (1952) | Did not medal |
| Fernando Abugattas | Northwest Iowa/ Peru | Mexico City (1968) | Did not medal |
| Cameron Wright | Southern Illinois | Atlanta (1996) | Did not medal |
| *Nathan Leeper | Kansas State | Sydney (2000) | Did not medal |
| Trevor Barry | Dickinson State (N.D.)/Bahamas | London (2012) | Did not medal |
| **Women** | | | |
| Connie Teaberry-Lindsey | Kansas State | Atlanta (1996) | Did not medal |
| Amy (Acuff) Harvey | UCLA | Atlanta (1996) Sydney (2000) Athens (2004) Beijing (2008) London (2012) | Did not medal Did not medal Did not medal Did not medal Did not medal |
| Karol (Damon) Rovelto | Colorado | Sydney (2000) | Did not medal |
| Wanita Dykstra | Kansas State/ Canada | Athens (2004) | Did not medal |

* Denotes that athlete competed at KU Relays while in high school.

# 12

# The Pachyderms and Other Behemoths
## Throwers

"The University of Kansas is blessed with three mighty shotputters, and they usually finish one-two-three, but not necessarily in the same order."

From "The Top Three By A Long Shot," by Joe Jares, *Sports Illustrated*, May 5, 1969

Scott Russell has dominated the 21st century javelin competitions at KU. Here he throws in 2009.

Despite a distance-running tradition that includes some of the biggest names in the history of track and field (see Chapter 8) and well over 100 Olympic sprinters (see Chapter 9), the Kansas Relays' legacy in the throwing competitions is illustrious in its own right. In this chapter, you will meet Pachyderms, a Paralympian and Pinkie, as well as the indomitable Al Oerter, while tracing the changes in technique and technology that have kept records rising. Here are the shot putters and the discus, javelin and hammer throwers who have left their mark inside Memorial Stadium, on the grassy knolls around it, and in recent years, downtown (see Chapter 16).

## SHOT PUT

April 19, 1969, 1:15 p.m. The university/college shot put event was scheduled to start. Among the contestants were three Kansas shot putters clad in the powder blue jerseys and fluorescent pink shorts that constituted the Jayhawks' uniform at the time. All three had previously surpassed 60 feet. Kansas was the first university that could make that claim.

This fun-loving trio was affectionately known as The Pachyderms, an obvious reference to nearly 800 pounds of muscle and bone: Karl Salb out of Crossett, Ark.; Steve Wilhelm from Los Altos, Calif.; and Doug Knop from Olathe, Kan. They usually, but not always, finished in that order. Their 1-2-3 finish at the 1969 NCAA Indoor was instrumental in propelling KU to a national championship. Indeed, 1-2-3 finishes were not unusual and they were destined to finish that way on the Texas-Kansas-Drake Triple Crown circuit in 1969.

The three were also accomplished discus throwers. In fact, at the Texas Relays, Knop broke Oerter's school record with a throw of 189 feet,

HEAVY METAL. Competitors in 1936 (left) were considerably lighter compared to 2012, when Croatian Olympian Nedzad Mulabegovic and other shot putters threw in downtown Lawrence, Kan. The victorious throws in those respective years show how much stronger and technically sound today's throwers are: Sam Francis of Nebraska tossed 49 feet, 2 inches in 1936, while KU's Mason Finley threw 65-3.25 to win in 2012.

8 inches. Of the three, Knop was considered the best discus thrower, Salb the best shot putter, and Wilhelm, while usually in the middle as a thrower, was the best weight-lifter and grunter.

By the time Salb, Wilhelm, and Knop completed their shot competition that afternoon with yet another 1-2-3 finish, in that order, their sweep was largely ignored. The reason? Around that same time their leaner teammates set a world record in the distance relay. KU's Jim Neihouse (880), Randy Julian (440), Thorn Bigley (1320) and Jim Ryun, with a 3:57.6 mile anchor, set a world record for KU in the distance medley relay.

Despite being overlooked on that occasion, The Pachyderms have secured their place in KU track and field lore. But they are only three of dozens of accomplished shot putters through the years at the Relays. The first noteworthy thrower was Herb Schwarze from Wisconsin, who threw 49 feet, 10.13 inches in 1925, a Relays record that stood for nine years. In those days, measurements were in one-eighth rather than one-quarter inch increments. Schwarze had a world record throw to his credit, but not at KU.

John Kuck from the tiny farming community of Wilson, Kan., fell just short of that record in 1926 when he threw 49-2.5. He was a student at Kansas State Teachers College (now Emporia State), and would go on to win a gold medal in the shot put at the 1928 Amsterdam Olympics

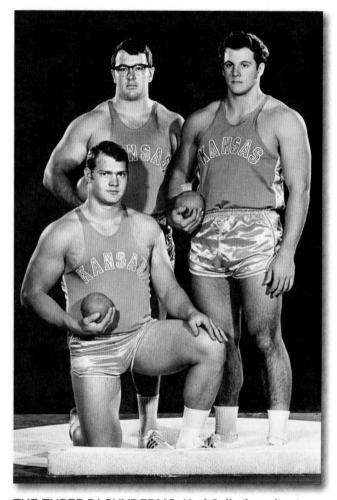

**THE THREE PACHYDERMS.** Karl Salb (kneeling), Steve Wilhelm (left) and Doug Knop were constant companions in the shot put and discus rings – and often on the podium – during their Jayhawk years.

with a world-record toss of 52-0.75. Hugh Rhea of Nebraska was a three-time winner in 1930-1932, but Schwarze's record was not broken until B. M. Erwin of Texas A&M threw 50-3.5 in 1934, with KU's Elwyn Dees an inch and a half behind. Dees surpassed that mark the following year by tossing 51-3.38. In 1937 Sam Francis of Nebraska improved the record to 51-6. Three-time shot winner Elmer Hackney of Kansas State threw 52-1.5 two years later.

The next big breakthrough came in 1948. Charles Fonville of Michigan threw a prodigious 58-0.38, which was 5 ½ feet further than Hackney's mark and nearly a foot farther than the long-standing world record held by Louisiana State's Jack Torrance since 1934. Fonville was considered a lock for Olympic gold in 1948, but a back injury kept him from qualifying. Darrow Hooper, one of

BIG BADGER. Herb Schwarze of Wisconsin won the 1925 shot put crown at the Relays.

a long line of Texas A&M throwers, was a three-time champion in both the shot and discus at the Relays, but no throws came close to Fonville's record. The distinction of breaking that record came in 1956 and belonged to Bill Nieder, a Lawrence resident and KU athlete, who earlier at the Texas

Relays became the first collegian to surpass 60 feet. His throw of 59-7.88 became a new Relays record.

Competing in that same year on an exhibition basis, Parry O'Brien, the first man to reach 59, 60, 61, 62 and 63 feet, threw 60-2.5. Many shot putters were beginning to emulate the glide technique made famous by O'Brien whereby the putter began his glide across the seven-foot ring by starting with his back, rather than his side, to the toe board. Nieder used the O'Brien technique to win silver behind O'Brien in Melbourne in 1956 and gold ahead of O'Brien in Rome in 1960.

Nieder hurt his knee water skiing prior to the 1960 Olympic Trials and did not finish as one of the three qualifers. The coaches, however, kept him on the team as an alternate. He did so well in the three meets between the Trials and the Olympics, including a world-record throw of 65-10, that he was picked ahead of Dave Davis, who had bested him in the Trials, for the coveted third spot. Davis relinquished his spot because of a sore wrist. Nieder then went on to win the gold with an Olympic-record toss of 64-6.75.

**JAYHAWK THROWER. 1935 KU Relays shot put champion, Elwyn Dees.**

O'Brien, who began experimenting with the new style in the early 1950s, participated in four Olympics between 1952 and 1964 and garnered gold in Helsinki and Melbourne, a silver behind Nieder in Rome, and a fourth-place finish in Tokyo. In another exhibition at the Relays, in 1957, Nieder beat O'Brien with the world's longest put of the year at 62-2. Three years later, in another Relays exhibition, Nieder had a 66-1.25 in warm-up, but had to settle for a new stadium record of 63-10.25 when the throws counted.

**BALANCED ATTACK.** Two-time Relays champ Bill Nieder was the first collegiate athlete to throw the shot more than 60 feet.

In 1965, on the heels of a silver medal at the 1964 Tokyo Olympics, Randy Matson of Texas A&M, in one of several memorable appearances at the Relays, extended the meet record in the shot to 65-10.75. Matson, despite his 6-foot, 7-inch frame, abandoned the O'Brien style of a 180-degree turn for the newest fad made popular by Brian Oldfield – the rotational technique, which involved a 360-degree turn. Matson was the first man to throw over 70 feet. He returned to the Relays in 1970, having won gold in Mexico City in 1968, and threw 67-9.5 to Salb's 66-4, which was a university division record. Future Olympian Al Feuerbach was third, slightly ahead of Salb's Pachyderm teammate, Wilhelm. Matson defended his championship in 1971 with a Relays record toss of 68-3.5, but was upended in 1972 when Feuerbach threw 69-1 to get both the record and the win. Feuerbach, an Olympian in 1972 and 1976, added an inch and a half to the record in 1973.

In the next decade, the most noteworthy achievements in the shot came from Michael Carter and Pinkie Suggs. Both would go on to have illustrious careers. Carter, a Southern Methodist University freshman in 1980, was already famous for his monstrous high school record throw of 81-3.5,

TOTH'S TOSS. Kevin Toth, shown here in 2002, won three KU shot put titles.

but threw only 62-6.5 to win the event at KU. (The college shot was four pounds heavier.) The high school boys record was set by Clint Johnson of Shawnee (Kan.) Mission South at 67-9 in 1980. Johnson would later become a winner of the Relays shot as a Kansas Jayhawk in 1984 and again for The American Big Guys in 1991.

Suggs won the shot as a Kansas State freshman in 1983, the first of four wins in the collegiate/open division. The other three wins came in a row, 1986-88. The longest throw in those four wins was 55-4.5 in 1987, which surpassed the record of 53-8 that she herself set the year before, and the

53-4 toss by Elaine Sobansky of Penn State in 1984. Suggs' record was finally broken in 2001 when Rebekah Green, another K-Stater, threw 56-0. In her illustrious career, Suggs had 12 total wins at the Relays – three shot put and two discus titles in high school, and four shot put and three discus wins after high school.

The dominant thrower in the 1990s was Kevin Toth with wins in 1993, 1994 and a huge throw of 71-2.5 in 1997 that broke a 24-year-old stadium record and made him the year's world leader. It also earned him the meet's Outstanding Performer award. He surprised everyone by throwing a whopping 74-4.5 in 2003, the best throw in the world since Randy Barnes, another Texas A&M shot putter, set the world record with a heave of 75-10 all the way back in 1990. Unfortunately, Toth's potential record was disallowed because of a violation of doping rules.

On the women's side in the first decade of the 21st century, Kansas State's Austra Skujyte, took center stage. Skujyte represented Lithuania in four Olympics

**SKUJYTE'S THE LIMIT.** Lithuanian heptathlete Austra Skujyte won four shot put titles at KU, including here in 2006.

between 2000 and 2012 as a heptathlete, and was Relays shot put champion in 2004-2006 and 2008.

# DISCUS

Mention Kansas and discus and the first name that comes to mind for most folks is Al Oerter. For good reason. This thrower came to Kansas from New York, and became the first man to capture gold in four consecutive Olympics. Carl Lewis later duplicated the feat in the long jump. As a Jayhawk, Oerter won the university division discus in 1956 (170-2), 1957 (178-1) and 1958 (175-2). He was the only athlete in history to win nine titles in the same event on the Triple Crown relays circuit of Texas-Kansas-Drake. Remarkably, as a 44-year-old he won again at KU in 1981 with a throw of 204-9 – his best-ever throw at the Relays and 12 years after his initial retirement.

Despite Oerter's undeniable success, it's a tribute to KU's throwing dominance that according to the 2012-2013 Kansas Track and Field Media Guide, Oerter is not even listed in the top seven Jayhawk discus throws ever, having never surpassed 190 feet as a collegian. The man at the top of the list is Knop, one of The Pachyderms. His collegiate record is 203-10. The two met at the Relays in 1969, Knop's junior year at KU, with Knop throwing 189-8 to beat Oerter by one-half inch. In 1977, Oerter attracted a crowd of about 1,000 fans to watch him throw 190-5.

The first discus toss over 150 feet at the Relays was achieved by KU's Melvin Thornhill with a throw of 153-7.25 in 1930. (In those days, the measurements were not rounded down to the nearest inch.) Jeff Petty of Rice extended that record to 154-0 in 1935, a record that would stand until 1941 when Archie Harris of Indiana unleashed a throw of 171-6.75. Oerter finally eclipsed the record with a throw of 178-1 in 1957. In between, Olympians

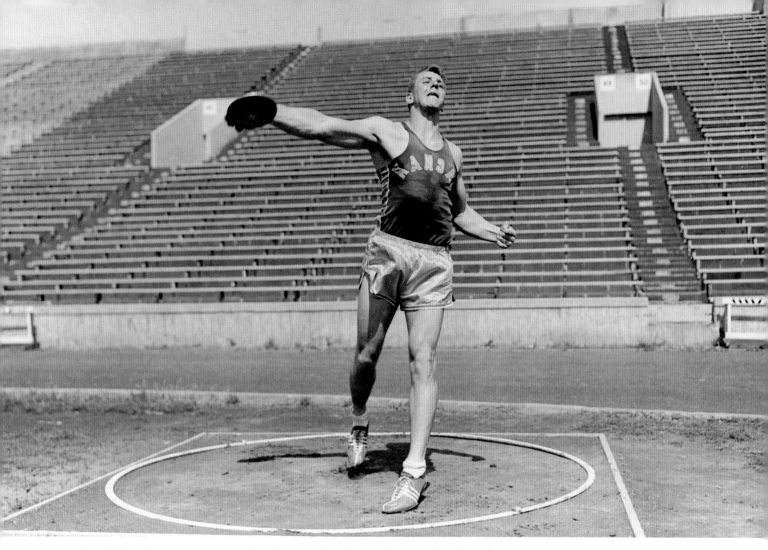

**AGELESS.** Al Oerter managed to be an elite discus thrower for four decades, including KU Relays wins 23 years apart and gold medals at four different Olympics.

Fortune Gordien of Minnesota and Darrow Hooper of Texas A&M could not beat Harris's mark despite the fact that Gordien won the discus event twice and Hooper three times during that span. Hooper had the rare distinction of winning both the shot and discus at the Relays all three years of his collegiate career. The next three-year discus champ and breaker of Oerter's record was Knop. His mark of 189-8 in 1969 only lasted until 1973 when Marshall Smith of Colorado State threw 194-10, which he increased by an inch the following year.

In 1976, Jim McGoldrick of Texas established the Relays record that still stands at 208-9. Just because the record has not been broken in nearly 40 years does not mean the event was sub-standard. Throws over 190 feet were commonplace. Jared Finley of the Wyoming Track Club threw 190-7 in 1980. His son Mason, competing for KU, was a two-time discus champion in 2010 and 2011 and threw 193-1 in 2011.

Other notables from the 1980s include:

- Scott Lofquist, former Shawnee Mission South star and Arkansas Razorback, who won in 1984 and 1985. His 1985 throw sailed 198-6.
- Rob James threw 191-11 in 1986.
- Four-time Olympian John Powell threw 194-0 three years after winning bronze in the Los Angeles Olympics.
- Ken Stadell from tiny Quenemo, Kan., and ex-Rice Owl, threw 199-0 in 1988.
- Marty Kobza, throwing for The American Big Guys, hit 196-6 a year later, in 1989.

The second-best throw behind McGoldrick's record came from Doug Reynolds in 2001, his first year as a KU assistant for coach Stanley Redwine. He threw 207-3 and beat Olympian Andy Bloom. Reynolds won again with a 197-2 in 2004. Other notables in the 2000s include:

- Another two- time winner, Sheldon Battle of KU, threw 191-6 in 2007.
- Vikas Gowda, a member of India's Olympic team in Beijing and London, threw 193-7 in 2008. He attended college at North Carolina.
- Jason Morgan threw 202-3 in 2012.

- Jeremy Campbell threw 200-9 in 2013. Campbell was a gold medalist in the discus in both the Beijing and London Paralympic games. He had his left leg amputated as a toddler and competes on a carbon-fiber prosthetic leg. He is planning to compete against able-bodied athletes and hopes to earn a spot in the Rio de Janeiro Olympics in 2016.

In the women's discus, the first throw beyond 160 feet was the 167-10 by Karen McDonald of Oregon in 1981. That record lasted until Los Angeles Olympian Laura Desnoo of the San Diego Track Club threw 183-10 in 1987 to deprive Pinkie Suggs from winning four years in a row. Penny Neer, formerly of Michigan, won her second title in 1991 with a record toss of 199-11, a record which still exists. Neer made the Olympic team the following year.

Other notables to compete since then include Dana Ruskule of Nebraska, who threw for Latvia in Athens in 2004, and Gia Lewis, who competed in London in 2012. Ruskule threw 186-11 in 2006 and Lewis threw 185-2 in 2008 at KU. Jessica Maroszek of Kansas claimed the title in both 2011 and 2012.

In high school boys competition, five Shawnee Mission South throwers won seven of eight competitions between 1973-1980. Gary Buchanan of Kingman, Kan., broke the string in 1975. The South throwers and their best Relays marks were Scott Calder (166-9), Floyd Dorsey (164-3), Mark Sutherland (183-3), Scott Lofquist (192-6) and Clint Johnson (196-5). No one bested Johnson's mark until Luke Bryant of Clearwater, Kan., threw 198-0 in 2007. In 2008, John Talbert of Kansas City (Kan.) East Christian threw 200-7, the current record.

In high school girls competition, the first big throw came in 1982 from a familiar face. Suggs threw 164-9, the same year she set the girls shot record. Sarah Stevens, of Fort Collins, Colo., performed a similar discus-shot double in 2004 when she threw the discus 156-6 and broke Suggs' shot standard.

# JAVELIN

The javelin competition in the 2000s pretty much belonged to Scott Russell. The Canadian won his first Relays title as a Jayhawk in 2000 with a throw of 239 feet, 0 inches. The throw itself was not as remarkable as what followed. In the span of 14 years, he won the event nine times to go with two hammer throw titles. His throws got progressively better with each season and his 2011 throw of 268-11 stands as a stadium record. He retired from competition in late 2012. His last throw at the Relays in 2012 was 264-5.

Russell was not the only Olympian among Relays javelin throwers. In fact, three of the first four winners were Olympians. Milton Angier of Illinois was the inaugural champion with a 1923 throw of 193-5. He had been seventh in the Antwerp Olympics in 1920. Gene Oberst of Notre Dame was the second champion with a throw of 197-6; he earned a bronze medal in the Paris

**JAYHAWK JAVELIN THROWER.** Canadian Olympian Scott Russell, shown here in 2008, holds the Memorial Stadium record in the javelin.

Games later in 1924. In the fourth year of competition, Kuck threw a Relays record of 206-6.5. He became a gold-medal winner in Amsterdam in 1928, but in the shot rather than the javelin. Kuck's javelin record held until 1937, when Alton Terry of Hardin-Simmons threw 229-2.25 for both a Relays and an American record. Terry had placed sixth in the javelin a year earlier in Berlin.

Terry's mark held up for two decades, until 1958 when Bruce Parker of Texas eclipsed it with a throw of 232-8.5. The new record lasted only a year thanks to KU thrower Bill Alley's toss of 254-9. Alley won again in 1960, the same year he threw the javelin in the Rome Olympics.

From Alley's record throw in 1959, new records came with considerable frequency. Ed Red of Rice, the man who has the distinction of having the shortest full name in Olympic history, threw 256-1.5 in 1963. Bill Floerke of Kansas State threw 266-5.5 in 1965, the first of six Wildcat titles in the next 10 years, along with Roger Collins, Mike Ross, Ed Morland (twice) and Bob Obee. Morland had the best of those throws at 260-0. The next record came in 1977 when Bud Blythe of Alabama threw 268-11.25, a mark that lasted only a year before Bob Roggy of Southern Illinois unleashed a monstrous 290-7.

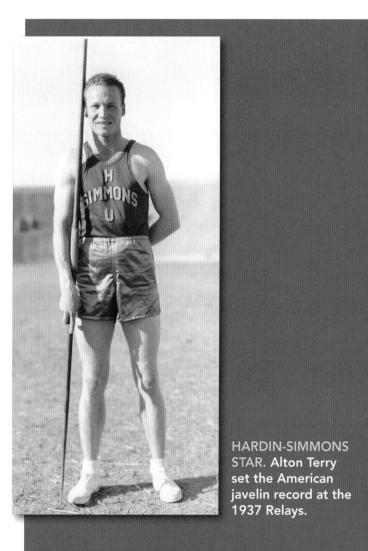

HARDIN-SIMMONS STAR. Alton Terry set the American javelin record at the 1937 Relays.

**INSPECTING THE IMPLEMENT. KU coach Bill Easton (left) helps Jayhawk thrower Bill Alley check out his javelin.**

Roggy's throw has not yet been improved upon at the Relays, but it is a record that needs an asterisk. The javelin had become a dangerous weapon for a couple of reasons. For one, it was simply flying too far. The world record by Uwe Hohn of East Germany was an incredible 343-10. Stadiums were not large enough to safely hold such throws. Secondly, the construction of the javelin allowed for too many flat landings, thus causing the javelin to dangerously skip great distances. It also made judging the event difficult. Therefore, in 1986, the governing body (the IAAF Technical Committee) moved the center of gravity four centimeters forward and blunted the tip to make it less aerodynamic. This caused the point to come down earlier, thus reducing the flight about 10 percent and causing the javelin to stick in the ground rather than skim the surface. The women's javelin was similarly redesigned in 1999.

Because of the redesigned javelin, throws more than 250 feet were less frequent. Only Ed Kaminski, who won four consecutive titles between 1991-1994 and again in 1996, and the aforementioned Russell were able to do so. Kaminski's best throw in that span was 251-4 and Russell has the current record of 268-11.

Women did not start throwing the javelin at the Relays until 1978. The first throw over 160 feet came in 1981 from Dana Olson of Houston (160-10). A year later she threw 192-8, a record still in existence after more than 30 years. Since 1982, throws over 170 have been made by Jeanne Villegas of Tennessee (176-6) in 1986, Laverne Eve of the Bahamas (187-9) in 1991, Kim Engle of American Big Guys (173-0) in 1992, Kristen Schultz of Kansas State

HUSKER HURLER. Kayla Wilkinson won the 2008 javelin title at the Relays.

(171-8) in 1996 and Christina Scherwin in 2004 (190-10). Scherwin became an Olympian for Denmark in 2004 and 2008. Kayla Wilkinson of Nebraska threw 174-0 in 2008, and Ali Pistora of Kansas State threw 170-11 in 2011.

In the boys javelin, between 1958 and 1986, the year of the restricted flight javelin, only five championships out of 29 were won with throws of less than 200 feet. Throws of over 220 were registered by Kansas high schoolers Bob Obee of Wyandotte, Bud Blythe of Uniontown, Frank Perbeck of Manhattan and Dana Hazen of Washburn Rural. The farthest throw of all was by Donnie McKinnis of Lyons, who threw 231-8 in 1980. After 1986, throws of 210 or more were made by Darby Roberts of Hill City, Darrin Kurtz of Baldwin, Darrin File of Beloit, Matt Schwandt of Manhattan, Iain Trimble of Tecumseh-Shawnee Heights, Matt Byers of Wichita East and Macauley Garton of Mill Valley.

High school girls did not begin throwing the javelin at the Relays until 1987. Two-time winner and future college and professional basketball player Kendra Wecker of Marysville, Kan., threw 166-7 in 2001 to set the current record. Others who threw more than 150 feet were Kansans Kim Engel of Hays, Greta Semsroth of Independence, Carrie Stewart of Olathe South, Carrie Buckley of DeSoto, Ashleigh Keats of Salina Central, Roxi Grizzle of Tonganoxie, and Elizabeth Herrs of St. George, plus Hope Harris of Clinton, Mo. Grizzle's throw of 163-11 in 2008 was closest to Wecker's.

# HAMMER THROW

Based on recent history, few would suspect that the United States once dominated the hammer throw on the world stage. The hammer was first contested in the Olympics in 1900 and the USA swept the first three places that year and in the two Olympiads that followed. The United States did not miss a gold medal for the first six Olympiads, and from 1900-1948,

Americans won 18 medals in the event. Only gold medalist Harold Connelly in 1956 and silver medalist Lance Deal in 1996 have medaled since.

The hammer throw from 1960 on has been dominated by international athletes. That dominance is evident in the results of the Kansas Relays hammer competition. The men's hammer was first thrown at the Relays in 1968. Bill Penny, a two-time winner for KU, had the longest throw of the first eight years at 195-5 in 1971.

Penny's record was broken by Great Britain Olympian Robert Weir, who attended SMU. Weir's throw was 222-8 in 1982, a record broken a year later by Yuri Tamm, a member of the Soviet contingent in 1983 (see Chapter 7). His throw of 244-2 is still the Relays record. He was the bronze medalist in both Moscow in 1980 and Seoul in 1988, with the Soviet boycott of the 1984 Los Angeles Games making it impossible for him to add another medal in between.

HAMMERIN' 'HAWK. Bill Penny was a two-time KU Relays champion.

Irish Olympian Roman Linsheid, competing for St. John's (N.Y.) in 1995, had the fifth-best throw in Relays history at 224-9. A year later, Mattias Borman of Colorado State had a significant throw of 216-0. Russell added to his javelin achievements with Relays hammer titles in 2000 (210-8) and

NICK'S FLICKS. Nick Welihozkiy was a three-time champion in the Relays hammer throw.

LETTING GO. Egor Agafonov nabbed two hammer wins at the Relays while throwing for the Jayhawks.

2002 (206-5). In between, three-time Olympian Yuriy Syedikh of the Soviet Union won with a heave of 204-5. Syedikh was past his prime. He had been the gold medalist in Montreal in 1976 and Moscow in 1980. His last Olympic competition had been a silver-medal effort in Seoul in 1988, so his Relays victory came 13 years after that appearance.

The only three-time winner in the event was ex-Stanford thrower Nick Welihozkiy with a longest throw of 222-8 in 2006. Egor Agafonov, a Russian competing for KU, was a two-time champion in 2008 and 2009 with a best of 227-5. Michael Mai, competing for the U.S. Army, had the second-best throw in Relays history in 2009, a throw of 234-11. Steffen Nerdal of Memphis had the third best with a 229-03 toss in 2010.

Women did not start throwing the hammer in the Olympics until Sydney in 2000, but they started throwing at KU in 1996, the same year that the hammer and the women's steeplechase were conducted in the Olympic Trials in Atlanta on an exhibition basis. The first three finishers in those Trials were considered Olympians. Katie Panek of Wichita State finished third in those Trials after winning the first contested hammer throw for women at KU with a 182-3 toss. Laci Heller of Kansas State was a winner in both 2005 and 2006, with a best toss of 197-4.

The first throw over 200 (203-2) came in 2007 and belonged to Zlata Tarasova, a Russian competing for KU. Two-time winners Loren Groves of Kansas State (2008, 2010) and Chandra Andrews, ex-Wichita State, (2009, 2011) both exceeded the 200-foot mark. Alena Krechyk, a Jayhawk by way of Belarus, broke Tarasova's record in 2012 by throwing 216-8. In 2013, Krechyk threw 220-11, but had to settle for fourth behind two-time Olympian Amber Campbell (228-6), who competed collegiately for Coastal Carolina. Also ahead of Krechyk were two former Southern Illinois throwers competing for the New York Athletic Club, Geneva McCall (227-4) and Gwen Berry (221-0).

**EASTERN IMPORTS.** Russian Zlata Tarasova, shown here in 2009 (left), held the hammer throw record at the KU Relays until Alena Krechyk of Belarus bested that mark in 2012. Both were Jayhawks when they set their marks.

Coach Bob Timmons briefly introduced the hammer throw for high school boys in 1973-1975 and again in 1979, but there was never much interest from the prep coaches. Their reasoning was that until it became an event at the state meet, they would not spend valuable practice time in an already short season. Others cited the cost since most high schools did not have the space or finances for a hammer cage. The best throw in the four-year experiment was Marty Weis of Salina (Kan.) South at 150-2.

# Throwers Who Competed in the Kansas Relays and Olympics

| Men | | | | |
|---|---|---|---|---|
| Name | School/Country (if not USA) | Olympics (Year) | Event | Result |
| *John Kuck | Kansas State Teachers College (Emporia State) | Amsterdam (1928) | Shot | Gold |
| Parry O'Brien | USC | Helsinki (1952) | Shot | Gold |
| | | Melbourne (1956) | Shot | Gold |
| | | Rome (1960) | Shot | Silver |
| | | Tokyo (1964) | Shot | Did not medal |
| Al Oerter | Kansas | Melbourne (1952) | Discus | Gold |
| | | Rome (1960) | Discus | Gold |
| | | Tokyo (1964) | Discus | Gold |
| | | Mexico City (1968) | Discus | Gold |
| *Bill Nieder | Kansas | Melbourne (1956) | Shot | Silver |
| | | Rome (1960) | Shot | Gold |
| Randy Matson | Texas A&M | Tokyo (1964) | Shot | Silver |
| | | Mexico City (1968) | Shot | Gold |
| Yuriy Syedikh | USSR | Montreal (1976) | Hammer | Gold |
| | | Moscow (1980) | Hammer | Gold |
| | | Seoul (1988) | Hammer | Silver |
| Adam Nelson | Dartmouth | Sydney (2000) | Shot | Silver |
| | | Athens (2004) | Shot | Gold |
| | | Beijing (2008) | Shot | Did not medal |
| Jeremy Campbell | Central Oklahoma | Beijing (2008) | Paralympic discus | Gold |
| | | London (2012) | Paralympic discus | Gold |
| Fortune Gordien | Minnesota | London (1948) | Discus | Bronze |
| | | Helsinki (1952) | Discus | Did not medal |
| | | Melbourne (1956) | Discus | Silver |
| Darrow Hooper | Texas A&M | Helsinki (1952) | Shot | Silver |
| George Woods | Southern Illinois | Mexico City (1968) | Shot | Silver |
| | | Munich (1972) | Shot | Silver |
| | | Montreal (1976) | Shot | Did not medal |
| Mike Carter | Southern Methodist | Los Angeles (1984) | Shot | Silver |

> continued

> continued

## Men

| Name | School/Country (if not USA) | Olympics (Year) | Event | Result |
|------|------------------------------|------------------|-------|--------|
| Christian Cantwell | Missouri | Beijing (2008)<br>London (2012) | Shot<br>Shot | Silver<br>Did not medal |
| Gene Oberst | Notre Dame | Paris (1924) | Javelin | Bronze |
| Sam Francis | Nebraska | Berlin (1936) | Shot | Bronze |
| Dick Cochran | Missouri | Rome (1960) | Discus | Bronze |
| John Powell | American River (Calif.) JC/San Jose State | Munich (1972)<br>Montreal (1976)<br>Moscow (1980)<br>Los Angeles (1984) | Discus<br>Discus<br>Discus<br>Discus | Did not medal<br>Bronze<br>U.S. Boycott<br>Bronze |
| Yuri Tamm | USSR<br><br>Estonia | Moscow (1980)<br>Seoul (1988)<br>Barcelona (1992)<br>Atlanta (1996) | Hammer<br>Hammer<br>Hammer<br>Hammer | Bronze<br>Bronze<br>Did not medal<br>Did not medal |
| Reese Hoffa | Georgia | Athens (2004)<br>Beijing (2008)<br>London (2012) | Shot<br>Shot<br>Shot | Did not medal<br>Did not medal<br>Bronze |
| Milton Angier | Illinois | Antwerp (1920) | Javelin | Did not medal |
| Allen Terry | Hardin-Simmons | Berlin (1936) | Javelin | Did not medal |
| Mike Lindsay | Oklahoma/Great Britain | Rome (1960) | Shot | Did not medal |
| Terry Beucher | Kansas | Rome (1960) | Javelin | Did not medal |
| Bill Alley | Kansas | Rome (1960) | Javelin | Did not medal |
| Elmer Hackney | Kansas State | Tokyo (1964) | Shot | Did not medal |
| Al Feuerbach | Emporia State | Munich (1972)<br>Montreal (1976) | Shot<br>Shot | Did not medal<br>Did not medal |
| Sam Colson | Kansas | Montreal (1976) | Javelin | Did not medal |
| Art Burns | Colorado | Los Angeles (1984) | Discus | Did not medal |
| Robert Weir | Great Britain | Los Angeles (1984) | Hammer | Did not medal |
| Roman Linscheid | St. Johns (N.Y.)/Ireland | Atlanta (1996) | Hammer | Did not medal |

| Men | | | | |
|---|---|---|---|---|
| Name | School/Country (if not USA) | Olympics (Year) | Event | Result |
| Andy Bloom | Wake Forest | Sydney (2000) | Shot | Did not medal |
| Nedzad Mulabegovic | Purdue/Croatia | Athens (2004)<br>Beijing (2008) | Shot<br>Shot | Did not medal<br>Did not medal |
| Scott Russell | Kansas/Canada | Beijing (2008) | Javelin | Did not medal |
| Vikas Gowda | North Carolina/India | Beijing (2008)<br>London (2012) | Discus<br>Discus | Did not medal<br>Did not medal |
| Justin Rodhe | Mt. Union (Ohio)/Canada | London (2012) | Shot | Did not medal |
| Dorian Scott | Florida State/Jamaica | London (2012) | Shot | Did not medal |
| Ryan Whiting | Arizona State | London (2012) | Shot | Did not medal |
| Women | | | | |
| Laura Desnoo | San Diego State | Los Angeles (1984) | Discus | Did not medal |
| Penny Neer | Michigan | Barcelona (1992) | Discus | Did not medal |
| Katie Panek | Wichita State | Atlanta (1996) | Hammer | Qualified at the Olympic Trials, but event was not contested at the Olympics. |
| Laverne Eve | LSU/Bahamas | Atlanta (1996)<br>Sydney (2000)<br>Athens (2004) | Javelin | Did not medal<br>Did not medal<br>Did not medal |
| Dace Ruskule | Nebraska/Latvia | Athens (2004) | Discus | Did not medal |
| Christina Scherwin | Denmark | Athens (2004)<br>Beijing (2008) | Javelin<br>Javelin | Did not medal<br>Did not medal |
| Amber Campbell | Coastal Carolina | Beijing (2008)<br>London (2012) | Hammer<br>Hammer | Did not medal<br>Did not medal |
| Gia Lewis-Smallwood | Illinios | London (2012) | Discus | Did not medal |
| Amanda Bingson | UNLV | London (2012) | Hammer | Did not medal |

[1]Women did not compete at the Relays until 1975 in the shot, 1978 in the discus and javelin, and 1996 in the hammer.

* Denotes that athlete competed at KU Relays while in high school.

# 13

## 'The Greatest Athletes'
### Multi-Event Stars

"I remember this like it was yesterday and it's been 27 years since I stepped on that track. The bell on Chapel [Campanile] Hill goes off at 9 a.m. Right after it stops ringing, the starter says, 'Come to your marks' and the decathlon begins."

--Phil Mulkey, 1993

Liz Roehrig of Minnesota high jumps during her record-setting heptathlon performance in 2008. She returned in 2012 and won the crown again.

In June 1932, three men from Lawrence, Kan., swept the first three spots in the decathlon Olympic Trials to punch their tickets to the 1932 Olympics in Los Angeles. Of the three decathletes, Wilson "Buster" Charles represented Haskell Institute, while "Jarring Jim" Bausch and Clyde Coffman were Kansas Jayhawks. Joining them would be Glenn Cunningham, slated to run the 1500 meters, and freestyle wrestler Peter J. Mehringer, thus giving the then tiny town of Lawrence five Olympians. Bausch and Mehringer won gold, and Cunningham brought back silver.

On Aug. 5, 1932, the Olympic decathlon began. At the end of the first day, Charles was leading the competition while Bausch was hanging on to fifth. With his customary Bausch bravado, he promised his fellow athletes in the Olympic village that night that he "would not only win the decathlon . . . but break the world record too." To be sure, the events of the second day were in his favor, but they also were for the heavily favored Finn, Akilles Jarvinen, who currently occupied third. Despite placing sixth in the hurdles, the first event of the second day, Bausch moved into third with Jarvinen moving into second. Bausch then won the next three events – the discus, pole vault and javelin. He and teammate Coffman tied for first in the pole vault at 13 feet, 1 ½ inches, an impressive height for a man weighing roughly 210 pounds. The height he and Coffman cleared would have placed fifth as individual competitors.

The real clincher, however, came in the javelin when Bausch defeated Jarvinen by nearly two feet in the Finn's best event. By the time the 1500-meter run was scheduled, Bausch had assembled 7,900 points and all he had to do was finish the race, which he did, plodding around the track in the pedestrian time of 5:17 and finishing next to last. Still, it was his personal best and allowed him to score 8,462.235 points, which, as he had predicted, broke the world record of 8,255.475 that Jarvinen had set two years earlier in Viipuri, Finland. The success of Bausch in the field events prompted a restructuring of the decathlon scoring tables to put more emphasis on running events. Under the restructured tables, Jarvinen would

JARRING JIM. Olympic gold medalist Jim Bausch was one of Kansas' greatest all-around athletes.

OLYMPIC TOWN. Clyde Coffman was one of three Lawrence decathletes who competed in the 1932 Olympics, along with 1500-meter runner Glenn Cunningham and wrestler Peter J. Mehringer.

have won, both in Los Angeles and in Amsterdam in 1928, where he had also placed second. In world-record terms, the adjusted tables would have had Jarvinen ahead of Bausch, 6,865 to 6,736.

As one might expect, a predictable debate ensued about who was the greatest athlete, Jim Thorpe or Bausch. Thorpe was Olympic decathlon champion in 1912 and both were multi-sport athletes. Bausch was a stand-out football, basketball and track athlete at both Wichita University and

KU. The controversial move from Wichita to KU and the interesting life after track for the brash Kansan is beyond the scope of this book, but "The Return of Jarring Jim," an article prompted by Bausch's visit to campus in 1939, was written for the KU Department of History by Mark D. Hersey. It is informative about this colorful personality. Bausch had an interesting high school career. He attended Garden Plain High School and starred in football, basketball and track. His junior year he attended Cathedral Academy, now called Wichita Kapaun, to play on one of the state's best football teams. Strangely enough, he competed for Wichita East in track, where he won the shot put and placed second in the discus and pole vault to lead East to the 1926 state championship.

Memorial Stadium has a Ring of Honor at the top of the north horseshoe listing the names of 16 of KU's greatest football players. Even though Bausch won the James E. Sullivan Award as the nation's most outstanding amateur athlete in 1932 and was inducted into the College Football Hall of Fame in 1954, he is not honored there. In 1979, his selection into the National Track and Field Hall of Fame made him one of a select few who have been enshrined into the halls of fame of multiple sports. Unfortunately, his death in 1974 prevented him from enjoying the recognition.

The winner of the Olympic decathlon is respectfully called "The World's Greatest Athlete." Thirteen men who competed in the Kansas Relays aspired to that prestigious title. Three managed to attain it. Emerson Norton of Kansas won silver in Paris in 1924. Since the first Relays decathlon did not take place until 1928, Norton never competed in the decathlon at the Relays, but showed his considerable talents by placing third in the pole vault and fourth in the broad jump in 1923.

Five of the first seven Relays decathlon winners became Olympians. In 1928, Tom Churchill of Oklahoma competed in the Relays as well as at the Amsterdam Olympics. He followed that up with another Relays championship in 1929. In the Relays decathlons leading up to the 1932 Olympics, Charles won in 1930 while Bausch narrowly defeated him, 7,846 to 7,744,

in 1931. Bausch repeated his victory the following year. His point total of 8,022 in the 1932 Relays would not be surpassed for 42 years until Bruce Jenner of Graceland (Iowa) College did so with a total of 8,240 in 1974. Jenner won gold in Montreal in 1976.

Between the records set by Bausch and Jenner, 1935 winner Coffman and three other Olympians would compete at KU in the decathlon. Glenn Morris of Colorado State won the Relays in 1936 and later won gold in Berlin the same year. At the Relays, Morris' victory came at the expense of Coffman and Chicago's Jay Berwanger, who had become the first recipient of the Heisman Trophy the previous fall. Phil Mulkey of Wyoming, at only 5 feet, 10 inches and 165 pounds, won his first Relays title in 1956,

**PRE-WHEATIES. Before Olympic gold, cereal boxes and Kardashians, Bruce Jenner broke a 42-year-old KU Relays decathlon record while at Graceland College.**

## Wilt and KU Track

While decathlons and heptathlons are dedicated to multi-event athletes, the most famous University of Kansas athlete was truly a multi-*sport* star. Wilt Chamberlain will forever be known first and foremost as a basketball player, but he also competed on the Jayhawk track and field team (it's not hard to figure out who is standing to the left of discus legend Al Oerter in the 1957 team photo). He never competed in the decathlon, but he did show his skills in a variety of events at Memorial Stadium, including high jump, long jump and even the shot put.

① ② ③

④

⑤

followed by five straight wins in 1958-1962. Dave Edstrom from Abilene Christian, who was a teammate of Mulkey's in the 1960 Rome Olympics, broke Mulkey's string of victories in 1963 by a margin of 7,423 to 7,316, but Mulkey managed back-to-back Relays championships in 1965 and 1966 for a total of eight Relays watches.

Other noteworthy decathlon performers between Bausch and Jenner were two-time winners Dick Kearns of Colorado, E. Lee Todd competing unattached, Jim McConnell of Nebraska and Jim Podoley of Central Michigan. In 1982, Gary Kinder from Mississippi was Relays champion and later represented the United States in the 1988 Seoul Olympics. In 1983, nine years after Jenner had established his record of 8,240, Grigory Degtyarev of the USSR scored 8,252 points to set a new record which was not broken until Kansas State's Steve Fritz scored 8,380 in 1997. Fritz won three consecutive titles between 1991 and 1993 and was fourth in the Atlanta Olympics decathlon in 1996. Despite never competing in the decathlon at the Relays, Tom Pappas of Tennessee was a decathlete for the US Olympic team in 2000, 2004 and 2008. Tyrell Ross of Nebraska narrowly defeated Pappas in the 110-meter hurdles at KU in 2008. Darius Draudvila also did not compete in the decathlon at the Relays, but did run the 110-meter hurdles and long jump for Kansas State in both 2004 and 2005. He competed in the decathlon for Lithuania in the 2012 London Games.

**VICTORIOUS.** Grigory Degtyarev of the Soviet Union set a Relays decathlon record in 1983 that stood for 14 years.

# Mulkey's record-setting return

On April 14, 1993, 60-year-old decathlete Phil Mulkey appeared in Lawrence for the expressed purpose of breaking the master's decathlon record for the 60-64 age group. Even though it was early in the season and he could have chosen any other meet to make the attempt, he chose the Kansas Relays for nostalgic reasons.

His quote that opens this chapter, taken from Gary Bedore's April 11 *Lawrence Journal-World* column prior to his record attempt, clearly illustrates his affinity for the venue. He went on to say, "I have to try it at Kansas because of a lifetime of memories."

He had competed in the Relays 11 times and was crowned champion in eight of those years. Despite rain and cold weather in 1993, he scored 8,155 to break the record of 7,990 points set by Boo Morconi in 1982. Mulkey, who was competing on an exhibition basis, scored higher than official winner Steve Fritz, who totaled 7,868. However, in master's competition, multi-events use an age-graded result applied against

Phil Mulkey owned the KU Relays decathlon in the 1950s and '60s, then came back in 1993 for an encore.

the standard scoring table. His M60 record was decertified after the World Masters Association changed the implement specifications, but it remains the best mark.

**MULTI-EVENT JAYHAWK.**
Candace (Mason) Dunback excelled in the heptathlon throughout her KU career. Now, the open event bears her name: the Candace Mason Heptathlon.

**A LEAP FROM LAWRENCE TO ATHENS.** Shelia Burrell was a two-time long jump champ at the KU Relays and an Olympic heptathlete three years later.

The women's heptathlon became a Relays event in 1981. Marlene Harmon, who had competed for Cal State Northridge, won with a point total of 5,704. That record stood until 2008 when Liz Roehrig of Minnesota bested it with the current record of 5,740 points. She won again in 2012. Lisa Wright of Barton County (Kan.) Community College won in 1995 and 1996. Candace Mason of Kansas, for whom the event is now named, won in 1997. No Relays heptathlon champion has qualified for the Olympic Games, but Kansas State athlete Austra Skujyte qualified for four Olympics in the heptathlon and won silver in Athens in 2004 while competing for Lithuania. Though she did not compete in the heptathlon at the Relays, she did win the shot in 2004, 2005, 2006 and 2008; and the long jump in 2004 and 2005. Another Olympic heptathlete who did not compete in the event at KU was Kym Carter. While in high school at Wichita East, she won the girls high jump in both 1981 and 1982, jumping 6 feet, 2 inches as a senior to set a record that still stands. Likewise Shelia Burrell, formerly of UCLA, did not compete in the heptathlon at the Relays, but she did win the long jump in both 2000 and 2001. She placed fourth in the 2004 Athens Olympics in the heptathlon.

# Multi-Sport Athletes Who Competed at the Kansas Relays and Olympics

| Name | School/Country (if not USA) | Olympics (Year) | Result |
|------|------|------|------|
| **Decathlon (Men)** | | | |
| *Jim Bausch | Wichita Univ./Kansas | Los Angeles (1932) | Gold |
| Glenn Morris | Colorado State | Berlin (1936) | Gold |
| Bruce Jenner | Graceland (Iowa) | Montreal (1976) | Gold |
| Jeremy Campbell | Central Oklahoma | Beijing (2008) Paralympic Pentathlon | Gold |
| Emerson Norton | Kansas | Paris (1924) | Silver |
| Tom Churchill | Oklahoma | Amsterdam (1928) | Did not medal |
| Buster Charles | Haskell | Los Angeles (1932) | Did not medal |
| Clyde Coffman | Kansas | Los Angeles (1932) | Did not medal |
| Dave Edstrom | Abilene Christian | Rome (1960) | Did not medal |
| Phil Mulkey | Memphis State/ Wyoming | Rome (1960) | Did not medal |
| Gary Kinder | Mississippi/New Mexico | Seoul (1988) | Did not medal |
| *Steve Fritz | Kansas State | Atlanta (1996) | Did not medal |
| Kip Janvrin | Simpson (Iowa) College | Sydney (2000) | Did not medal |
| Tom Pappas | Tennessee | Sydney (2000) Athens (2004) Beijing (2008) | Did not medal Did not medal Did not medal |
| Darius Draudvila | Kansas State/Lithuania | London (2012) | Did not medal |
| **Heptathlon (Women)** | | | |
| Austra Skujyte | Kansas State/Lithuania | Sydney (2000) Athens (2004) Beijing (2008) London (2012) | Did not medal Silver Did not medal Did not medal |
| *Kym Carter | Houston/Louisiana State | Barcelona (1992) | Did not medal |
| Shelia Burrell | UCLA | Sydney (2000) Athens (2004) | Did not medal Did not medal |

*Denotes that athlete competed at the KU Relays in high school.

# PART IV

The nine-lane track at the new Rock Chalk Park was laid in late 2013. It is the latest innovation to make its mark on the Kansas Relays.

# INNOVATION

The Kansas Relays, storied though it is, has faced many challenges to its existence through the years. Whether because of Mother Nature, war, budget challenges, facility renovations or a changing society, the meet has been on the ropes more than its fair share of times (Chapter 14). But innovative solutions and imaginative leadership have always carried the day to get the Relays through these crises. The creation of the Gold Zone (Chapter 15) provided spectators with a concentrated collection of talent as good as could be found anywhere in the world. Moving two events to the streets of downtown Lawrence (Chapter 16) generated a fan-friendly party atmosphere that is now one of the highlights of Relays week. As Memorial Stadium passes the baton to Rock Chalk Park in 2014 (Chapter 17), the hallowed heartland tradition is poised to be on solid footing for the foreseeable future. But we're not in the homestretch yet. Not by a long shot. There are still thousands more athletes, millions more moments, and still-unknown creative innovations prepared to keep Dr. Outland's singular dream alive.

# 14

## Relays on the Ropes
### Challenges to the Tradition

"Staging the contemporary Kansas Relays in a football stadium is a little like holding the Henley Regatta in the Atlantic Ocean."

--Chuck Woodling, *Lawrence Journal-World* writer, in April 20, 1998 article, "Will Relays return in '99?"

WE'RE EXPERIENCING
A LITTLE DELAY

LAPS IN RACE   :00.00   LAP NUMBER
1              QUARTER   1
TIME OUTS LEFT           TIME OUTS LEFT
DOWN                     BALL ON
University State Bank   The Performance Company

HERSHBERGER
TRACK

The Kansas Relays are catlike in their ability to rebound from near death. From the opening gun, the Relays have fought for life. Financial woes and facilities, or lack thereof, were at the heart of most of the early problems. In the inaugural event in 1923, sponsorships to help defray the cost of expensive awards put a bandage on the immediate problem of attracting contestants. Marketing ploys such as rodeos and inviting Tarahumara runners filled the seats. In the early 1930s, KU Olympians such as Jim Bausch, Clyde Coffman and Glenn Cunningham, along with Iowa hurdler George Sales, provided plenty of star power, but the expenditure of depression dollars to produce a track meet that people couldn't afford to attend seemed wasteful to many.

As Forrest C. "Phog" Allen, director of athletics at the time, said, "It wasn't easy from the start."

A newspaper article may have saved the Relays. Chancellor E. H. Chandler happened to be in Philadelphia while the Relays were in progress. While picking up a morning paper, he read in big, bold headlines, "Illinois Breaks World Record at Kansas Relays." He had never seen Kansas in that big a headline from that far away before.

"That sold him," Allen said. "When he came back, he told me about it, and said the Relays were here to stay."

Having survived the depression years, the next great threat to the continuation of the Relays was the onset of World War II. In the latter 1930s and early 1940s, crowds in the vicinity of 10,000 to 12,000 were treated to outstanding performances. In 1935, Iowa set world records in both the 440-yard relay (40.5) and 880-yard relay (1:25.2). In 1936, with Archie San Romani on the anchor, Kansas State Teachers College (now Emporia State) established a world record in the distance medley relay (10:12.7). Olympians like San Romani, Cunningham, Sam Francis (shot put) and Glenn Morris (decathlon), were just a few of the outstanding athletes to make their mark on the Relays record book. Strong relay teams, particularly from

Indiana, Texas, Kansas State, North Texas State and Missouri challenged the Jayhawks in record-breaking relay events.

The bombing of Pearl Harbor on Dec. 7, 1941 signaled the end of this age of excellence. The Relays in 1942, while still competitive, were relegated to nearly a Big Six event as travel was limited because of the escalating war effort. Track and field seemed a frivolous exercise in the midst of war, and the Relays were cancelled in 1943, 1944 and 1945. This put the continuation of the Relays in jeopardy after the war. Luckily, when the Relays returned in 1946, marks were respectable. Diminutive Harrison Dillard of Baldwin-Wallace (Ohio) made his first Relays appearance. Miserable weather in 1947 reduced crowd numbers, but nearly 10,000 fans showed up for the subsequent 1948 Relays and were treated to two world records, Michigan's Charles Fonville in the shot (58-00.38) and Dillard in the 120-yard high hurdles (13.6). The Relays were once again on solid footing.

RELAYS REVIVAL. The performances of shot putter Charles Fonville (left) of Michigan and hurdler Harrison Dillard of Baldwin-Wallace gave the post-war Relays a major boost in 1948.

Under the direction of coaches Bill Easton (1948-1965) and Bob Timmons (1966-1988), the Relays flourished in the '50s, '60s and early '70s. KU track teams were powerful and made their presence felt as the central jewel in the Texas-Kansas-Drake Triple Crown series. Only the long-established Penn Relays could claim to be in the same class in terms of quality and participation numbers. However, trouble was lurking on the horizon.

Competing meets such as the Ohio Relays were beginning to siphon off talent, including several of the Big Ten schools. Inadequate finances were making the acquisition of elite talent difficult. In April 1962 came a threat from within. The KU Athletic Board announced it was considering adding 7,200 to the seating capacity of Memorial Stadium by tearing out the track and lowering the field. A new track with a seating capacity of 2,500 was to be built near Allen Fieldhouse on what Allen called "The Great Windy Plains." Under the plan, track athletes would use the fieldhouse for dressing facilities, thus providing two basketball locker rooms instead of accommodations for 1,000 under Memorial Stadium. Allen, in a blistering denunciation of the idea, said it would kill the Relays.

"This whole idea, from start to finish, is so ridiculous it's amusing," Allen said in an April 29, 1962, *Kansas City Star* column by Dick Wade. "But when you realize it's made seriously, a tragedy takes shape. They want to dig a cold, deep grave for the relays, and kick Bill Easton's teeth out in the process."

The commentary surrounded a large two-column cartoon head of Allen, mouth wide open, teeth bared, yelling so loud that bystanders' hats come off and clocktower bricks come loose from their foundation. Allen, the venerated "Founder of the Relays," was just getting warmed up. Wade, calling Allen "that battle-scarred old soldier of the Kaw," let him continue: "You can

RAIN, RAIN, GO AWAY ... Leonard Selig was a measurer at the long jump pit during the 1986 Relays, but the rain forced him and others into an impromptu grounds crew. Towels were laid down near the jumpers' runway and needed to be wrung out often.

be sure of this," Allen said. "When they tear out the stadium track, the relays are as dead as the cadavers in the formaldehyde tanks in the medical department's dissecting room."

Obviously, Allen, aided by a lack of available financing, carried the day. The track survived for more than a half century past Allen's tirade, and has managed to be the last one in the Big 12 Conference to remain encircling the football field.

After the 1969 Relays, Bob Hentzen got straight to the point writing about the 44th edition of the KU Relays in his *Topeka Daily Capital* sports column: "It is possible this morning that you are reading about the last Kansas Relays." Thursday events had to be moved to Haskell Institute across town because of rain and the previous year saw some events postponed. KU, with its outmoded, six-lane, poor-draining track could not hope to compete with the all-weather tracks that were springing up around the country.

The only way out of this dilemma was money, about $200,000 worth. The University had been producing a modest profit during Jim Ryun's collegiate years, roughly $45,000 from the previous three years. But Ryun, whose anchor mile of 3:57.6 had helped KU produce a world record in the distance medley relay in 1969, was a senior and could not be counted on to compete in future Relays. The athletic department simply didn't have the funds because they were in debt to the tune of about one million dollars due to the expansion of the stadium and the construction of new offices and facilities at Allen Fieldhouse. The 45th Relays were indeed in jeopardy.

Rain at the Relays, about 1½ inches of it, made its appearance for the fifth consecutive year in 1970. But unlike the previous four years, it was not nearly as much of a dilemma. The cavalry had arrived in the form of Wichita businessman Jim Hershberger, who donated $125,000 to build the eight-lane Tartan track that now bears his name. "It's hard to put into words what it's meant to us," Timmons said, "and what it will mean in the

future." It's reasonable to believe that, in the immediate future at least, the Relays were saved from extinction.

Ryun, temporarily retired and working as a photographer for the school newspaper, said that on the old track on a rainy day, "You could splash around in the mud, fall and drop the baton and it wouldn't matter. On this track, you're still expected to run a good time." Olympic sprinter John Carlos did just that by running a 9.3 100 meters in a hard rain. Hershberger himself ran the master's mile in 4:54.0, finishing third behind KU alumnus Jan Howell and running

**ON THE RIGHT TRACK. KU** alumnus Jim Hershberger (left) donated the money to resurface the Memorial Stadium track prior to the 1970 Relays, ensuring that even on rainy days such as this one, the races could continue. Note the "Hershberger Track" sign below the scoreboard.

journalist Hal Higdon. Despite Hershberger not winning the race, Hentzen wrote in his April 19, 1970 column, "…he (Hershberger) gets my vote as the meet's outstanding athlete. There wouldn't have been one without him."

Another crisis in the Relays saga came in the form of rain, hail, wind and tornado warnings in 1974. First-year athletic director Clyde Walker called it "a great spectacle," but only about 6,500 spectators braved the conditions, and many of those were cut-rate student tickets. The result, despite the elimination of some frills like the post-meet buffet for coaches and the media, was a loss of nearly $5,000. Walker declared that the meet would see its 50th anniversary in 1975, but the future was clouded after that. There simply were problems beyond the university's control. For one, it was not feasible to sell advance tickets as Drake could do in a smaller stadium (approximately 18,000) because in a 52,000 seat stadium people could wait until meet day to decide whether or not

NEITHER RAIN, NOR SLEET … KU Relays meet timers, like these from 1980, have always been counted on to do their jobs, no matter what the fickle northeast Kansas weather brings in a given year.

to attend. For example, Drake, despite miserable weather, had sold out a week in advance at $6.50 a ticket.

Also, the emergence of the professional track circuit eliminated many of the elite athletes, including fan favorite Ryun, from consideration because the archaic Amateur Athletic Union would not allow professionals to compete with amateurs. If the weather was bad – as it had been for the last two

**BOLD DECISION. Bob Timmons endured many wet Relays in his 23 years as Jayhawk coach, but one of his best decisions was to farm out the 1978 meet to five different locations when Memorial Stadium renovations threatened to cancel it altogether.**

years – it was difficult to attract the 20,000 spectators that Timmons estimated it would take to break even. Still, the Relays persisted through the mid-1970s, perhaps aided by the interest in track and field that an Olympic year like 1976 usually generates, plus a larger than expected crowd due to the Vietnam protest in 1972 (see Chapter 6).

The next challenge to the Relays occurred in 1978. Because of a $1.8 million renovation project, the KU Relays were to be canceled. Though Walker said the Relays would return in 1979, many were skeptical. One fear was that some other school would jump in to fill the void. After about a week of being resigned to the reality of no Relays in 1978, Timmons came up with a novel idea to hold the meet at five different sites. Twenty-seven universities went to Oklahoma University in Norman where Coach J. D. Martin was in charge. Coach Phil Delavan oversaw 21 college and 18 women's teams at Emporia State. Twenty-one junior colleges went to Haskell Institute in Lawrence, Kan., with Coach Jerry Tuckwin. And 151 boys and girls high school teams went to Shawnee Mission Northwest in Kansas City, Kan., under the directorship of Tom Trigg. The marathon was held as normal and directed by Gene Burnett in Lawrence.

In addition to the great cooperation from the above coaches, two students should be credited for their role in the success of this daring adventure. Richard Konzem, future KU assistant athletic director, was the track equipment manager responsible for boxing up the equipment that was needed at the various sites. Liz (MacGregor) Phillips was a tri-chair of the

Kansas Relays student committee. She later became the coordinator of KU's emergency services for the campus police. She had been on the Relays committee since her freshman year and, with Barb Glick, was one of only two women members. "It was important to me because it was tradition," Phillips said. With that attitude, she worked tirelessly behind the scenes to help save the meet. Showing a sense of humor, Timmons quipped about the less than ideal circumstances of a fragmented Relays in 1978, "Before, the Big Guy up yonder had only one spot to rain on. He's gonna really be busy this year."

The dispersal of the event to five locations created some fallout beyond losing some equipment due to the renovation. Quite a few quality teams were lost to competing events. For example, Baylor, Missouri and Nebraska went to the University of Texas-El Paso's meet, perhaps in part to find more favorable weather. Others left because the Relays format did not allow schools to bring entire teams. Also, the $30,000 budget presented the quantity-vs.-quality dilemma. Should the money be used to bring in a lot of competitors or a few elite ones? Wes Santee was afraid that the meet was in danger of being turned "into an intramural meet." That didn't happen in 1979 despite the addition of many new events. There was still plenty of star power, including New Mexico's Kipsubai Koskei, whose record setting 3000 meters in 13:40.35 earned him the Most Outstanding Performer award.

The early 1980s were no less impressive. World-class athletes such as Renaldo Nehemiah, Houston McTear, Mike Carter, Cliff Wiley, Al Oerter, Merlene Ottey, Pinkie Suggs, Mike Lehmann and a contingent from the Philadelphia Pioneer Track Club proved that the Relays could still bring in top-notch talent. A coup of major proportions occurred in 1983 as the appearance of Soviet athletes generated interest and attendance for the Relays (see Chapter 7). Another boon to the Relays came that year with the infusion of approximately $65,000 by corporate and private sponsors. Corporate entities included Nike, Hallmark Inc. and Mutual Benefit Life

Insurance Co. Athletes United for Peace contributed financially to bringing in the Russians. Among the individual sponsors was Hershberger, who was co-sponsoring the Relays for the third consecutive year. The practice of individual and corporate sponsorship continues to be a valuable source of revenue today.

SPRING DISPLAY. The addition of a large video screen to the scoreboard in 2000 enhanced the fans' experience and provided sponsors with more space to show their involvement, one of many improvements to Memorial Stadium through the years.

For a variety of reasons, the latter 1980s and early 1990s were dark days for the continuation of the Relays. A perfect storm of declining budgets, difficulty in attracting athletes and a general apathy put the meet in jeopardy. The April 20, 1973, issue of *The University Daily Kansan* devoted two special editions totaling 24 pages to the final weekend of that year's Kansas Relays, but the 1991 *Kansan* published only one 10-inch story to promote it. The journalism students were unable to sell ads for a special edition. The Relays, which generally made money except for rainy days, seldom saw a profit after its shutdown for stadium renovation in 1978. From a high of 32,000 that saw Jim Ryun run in 1972 during a Vietnam protest (see Chapter 6), crowds continued to decline and rarely, except for the Russian invasion in 1983, exceeded 8,000.

The declining revenue from ticket sales, coupled with declining college track budgets across the nation, made the acquisition of elite athletes difficult, especially since the elites were asking for more in appearance fees. Also, the quality of Kansas track teams had declined a bit. "When we had the biggest crowds is when we had the strongest track teams," said Bob Frederick, athletic director at the time. KU coach Gary Schwartz suggested that, "There are just more things to be into now than track and field." The fact that the professional track circuit had failed and that other major events like the Millrose Games in New York were on shaky ground supported that opinion.

The last three chapters of this book close out Part IV, which, along with this chapter, is fittingly titled "Innovation". The late 1990s brought great performances but few crowds, plus more stadium renovations that put the Relays in jeopardy for the 21st century. But new ideas invigorated the meet, and according to the Kansas Track and Field Media Guide for 2012-13, 93,500 track and field fans have passed through the gates of Memorial Stadium in the past six years. The Relays are definitely alive and well as the transition to a new home at Rock Chalk Park is underway.

# Thumbnail History of Kansas Relays' Facilities

| | |
|---|---|
| 1922 | On Nov. 11, Memorial Stadium was formally dedicated prior to the KU-Nebraska game. Seating capacity was 22,000. (Although formally dedicated on Armistice Day in 1922, the first game had been played the year prior, Oct. 29, 1921, a 21-7 KU victory over the Kansas Aggies.) |
| 1925 | The east and west sections were extended to the south. |
| 1927 | The north bowl of the horseshoe stadium was completed, thereby increasing capacity to 35,000. |
| 1960 | A new cinder track was installed. |
| 1963 | A new press box was added and the west stands were expanded 26 rows, making the new capacity 44,900. |
| 1965 | The east stands were expanded and the capacity grew to 51,500. |
| 1970 | The natural-grass surface and six-lane cinder track is replaced with artificial turf and an eight-lane Tartan track and jump runways, thanks to a large donation by Jim Hershberger. |
| 1978 | A $1.8 million renovation included repairing concrete, replacing seats, adding new dressing rooms, additions to the press box and a new artificial turf. |
| 1984 | Hershberger donated an additional $190,000, half of which went toward a new pro-turf surface. |
| 1985 | Glenn Martin, former Jayhawk horizontal jumps standout, donated $30,000 for the construction of the horizontal jumping pits that now bear his name. |
| 1987 | The old south end zone bleachers were removed. |
| 1990 | A new Astroturf field was installed. |
| 1992 | Bleachers were temporarily added in the south end zone. |
| 1997 | Four standards of permanent lights were added. |
| 1999 | A two-year $26 million renovation was completed. Included were infrastructure repairs, a new concourse with improved concession stands and restrooms, a new locker room, improved press box facilities and a new video board. |
| 2000 | A new AstroPlay surface replaced the old AstroTurf. |
| | A large video board in the south curve was installed and allowed for the showing of replays, information, and the showing of events from outside the stadium. |
| | The pole vault was moved from next to the track to the center of the infield. |
| 2003 | The throwing area northeast of the stadium was redesigned and regraded. |
| 2008 | The name Kivisto Field was added to Memorial Stadium. |
| 2014 | The 87th edition of the Kansas Relays is scheduled to debut at Rock Chalk Park. |

# 15

# In the Gold Zone
## Creating the Elite Meet

"The Gold Zone is the next evolution of the Kansas Relays. This finite collection of events, stacked with world-class fields and household names like Maurice [Greene] and Stacy [Dragila], will be the best three hours of track and field Memorial Stadium has ever witnessed."

--Kansas Relays meet director Tim Weaver
prior to Gold Zone I, 2005

John Capel (pointing) holds off Maurice Greene (third from right) and a star-studded 100-meter field during Gold Zone I in 2005.

217

The Kansas Relays, despite a consistent supply of elite athletes, quality performances and even corporate sponsorship, was effectively on life support during the 1990s. It was an extraordinary meet that few people attended. For example, in 1995 Pat Manson and Scott Huffman both cleared 18 feet, 6 ½ inches in a gripping pole vault dual. Garden City (Kan.) High School senior Jason Archibald had a record 7-foot, 3-inch leap in the high jump, and Maurice Greene ran a relay carry. Only about 4,000 saw it. Attendance in 1996 with Columbia Health Care as a corporate sponsor was even more embarrassing. On a day when the weather was as good as it gets for April in Kansas, a small crowd estimated at only 3,500 saw this sampling of stellar showings:

- Stacy Dragila set an American record of 13 feet, 6 ½ inches in the women's pole vault.
- Michael Cox broke the four-minute barrier in the mile.
- Melvin Lister set Relays records in both the long and triple jumps.
- Greene won the 100-meter dash.
- Wanita Dykstra, Kansas State athlete and Canadian Olympian, won the women's high jump at 6 feet, ½ inch.
- Huffman, the American record-holder in the pole vault at 19-7, had gathered together an outstanding field of eight vaulters, seven of whom had personal bests over 18 feet.
- Seven KU Olympians were to be honored: Wes Santee, Bill Alley, Billy Mills, Kent Floerke, Jim Ryun, Cliff Wiley and Al Oerter (who was unable to attend).

In 1997, coach Gary Schwartz assembled a 400-meter hurdle field of Olympians and NCAA champions, eight milers who had run sub-four, and local favorites Steve Fritz in the decathlon and Ed Broxterman in the high jump. In all, 18 former Olympians from five different countries were entered. Still, even with the price of admission as low as five dollars for adults and three dollars for students for two days of competition, the estimated attendance was only 6,000. Then came the postponement of the Relays for stadium renovation in 1998 and 1999. Is it any wonder that many predicted that the Relays would not happen in the 21st century?

Assurances came from Schwartz, athletic director Bob Frederick, and associate athletic director and Relays event coordinator Paul Buskirk that the Relays would be held in 2000, and they were. "I don't want to be the coach that was in the job when the Kansas Relays ceased to function," Schwartz said. The question, given the apathy in the 1990s toward track and field in general was, "How would they be received?"

IDEA MAN. Tim Weaver (foreground) is shown here at a 2006 press conference during Gold Zone II with his former coach, Stanley Redwine. Weaver rejuvenated the Relays when it was at a low point.

In what proved to be a wise decision, Tim Weaver was chosen as event coordinator for the resumption of the Relays. Weaver was passionate about the Relays and had experiences in the track world that would serve him well in his new role. He was a graduate of Bishop Miege High School in Overland Park, Kan., and a sprinter and hurdler for KU coach Stanley Redwine when Redwine was coach at Tulsa University. Weaver graduated from Tulsa in 1995 with degrees in English and Education. He earned a Master of Arts in English from KU, served at the university as an instructor of rhetoric and literature, and was a student assistant in the track and field program.

Weaver was a man of ideas and energy. One of his first actions was to reconvene the Greater Relays Committee to gather still more ideas. This committee was made up of former athletes, officials, starters, current and former coaches, announcers, volunteers, students, sponsors and office staff. All were individuals who wanted the Relays restored to their former grandeur. The student committee, which had dwindled to barely a handful, was expanded and reinvigorated. Also, 2000 was an Olympic year and elite athletes were eager to perform. Through hustle and connections, Weaver was able to bring 27 present or future Olympians to the competition, not the least of which was Greene, the "world's fastest man" at the time and a local favorite from Kansas City, Kan. That, plus a realization of how much the Relays were missed by the community and fans in general created a buzz that the Relays had not experienced in years. Downtown merchants were eager to see the survival of the Relays. Lawrence fourth-graders were wooed with T-shirts and Relays buttons. The only published account listed the attendance in 2000 at around 12,000, but many suspected the true number was twice that. It was clear that the Relays were again appreciated, which gave hope that the momentum could be sustained in the years to come.

The years 2001-2003 continued to showcase numerous elite athletes, but attendance faltered in part because of miserable weather conditions. In 2002 the Friday crowd of 8,000 was the largest since 1983, but only about 1,000 were in the stands when the rain hit Saturday. The 75th-anniversary meet in 2003 had to be cancelled at 4:15 p.m. on Saturday because of lightning strikes and heavy rain. Thirty-nine running events and seven field events were called off, including all the invitational running events that were scheduled to feature 22 Olympians and four world-record holders. It was a crushing disappointment to 8,000 fans, numerous athletes, and above all, Weaver.

Mother Nature relented in 2004 and many records were broken, but attendance was not one of them. Still, Weaver remained optimistic. "I haven't given up hope for our meet or for the sport in the States in general," Weaver said at the time. With that attitude he began to look for solutions, and the idea of The Gold Zone came to fruition. It became the antidote to the problems that created apathy in the first place. The idea of the Gold

Zone was to condense the most popular field events and races into a three-hour schedule on Saturday afternoon, a "meet within a meet." The reasoning was that most major athletic events don't last more than three hours. By condensing the elite athletes into that window of time, it would still be possible to retain the numerous events that suit the needs of so many athletes, high schoolers and collegians alike. For example, the 2004 Relays offered 30 field events and 108 running events (some being preliminaries with multiple heats) over 2½ days. It featured over 5,000 athletes and 620 teams, with 1,274 medals to be awarded. Only the most avid track fan would be there for the duration.

With the Gold Zone format in place, the next step was to execute the plan, which necessitated funding and acquisition of

**LOCAL FAVORITE.** Maurice Greene, who had been coming to the Relays as a high school sprinter from Kansas City, acknowledges the cheers after his relay carry in Gold Zone I in 2005.

elite athletes. Weaver found a funding ally in newly hired athletic director Lew Perkins, who was impressed with his first viewing of the Relays the previous spring. It helped that Perkins had himself been a shot putter and also had some exposure to the Penn Relays in the early 1980s when he was associate director of athletics at the University of Pennsylvania. As Weaver tells it, "I can still recall Lew's voice saying, I want more people in the stands." Perkins, with the philosophy that you have to spend money to make money, approved the funding to secure commitments from some of the biggest names in track and field. The hope was to attract 20-25,000 fans over the course of three days.

Having been given the go-ahead, Weaver set about securing the athletes he hoped would fill Memorial Stadium. His job was made easier by the fact that he had served as head manager for the men's U.S. national team for the 2003 World Indoor Championships in Birmingham, England, and the World Outdoor Championships in Paris. He also assisted the U.S. Olympic team headed to Athens in 2004, so contacts with the stars were in place. When the dust had cleared, the Relays roster for 2005 included more than 30 Olympians and an additional 40-plus athletes with resumés that included championships at the world, U.S., National Collegiate Athletic Association and National Junior College Athletic Association levels. These names, plus an aggressive marketing campaign, attracted 24,619 fans to Memorial Stadium, the third-largest crowd on record and reason enough for an encore presentation in 2006: Gold Zone II.

Gold Zone II did not disappoint. Fifteen Olympic or world champions and 33 Olympians were among nearly 110 pro athletes who competed. The second-largest crowd in Relays history, 26,211, was treated to outstanding performances. One of the most-anticipated events was the 400-meter invitational relay, with Justin Gatlin's Sprint Capitol squad in a match race with Greene's HSI (Hudson Smith International) team. Gatlin's team won in 38.16 seconds, the fastest in the world in 2006. Relays favorite Bershawn "Batman" Jackson ran 48.34 in the 400-meter hurdles, the third-best time in the world that year, and Allyson Felix broke the Relays record by running the 100 meters in 11.04.

**MUST-SEE RELAY.** Justin Gatlin speeds toward the finish ahead of Maurice Greene (right) and the rest of the pack. Gatlin's Sprint Capitol team ran the fastest 400 relay time in the world in their 2006 Relays appearance.

In August of 2006, Weaver resigned as Relays meet director to go into private business, taking with him the far-reaching national and international connections that had contributed to the success of the Gold Zone concept. The glitter of the Gold Zone, despite producing two of the three largest crowds in Relays history, was about to lose some of its luster. Among the reasons for its demise was the constant specter of inclement weather, which could impact the crowd numbers and result in a huge financial loss the way a farmer would tally a crop loss.

Perhaps more importantly, through no fault of KU Relays officials or administration, the ugly side of professional sports produced guilt by association. In August, Gatlin, the 2004 Olympic gold medalist and co-world record holder, drew an eight-year ban, later reduced to four, because of a positive drug test at the Relays. Furthermore, Gatlin's coach Trevor Graham, who was linked to the BALCO steroids scandal, had also mentored 2005 headliners Tim Montgomery and Marion Jones, also under suspicion for using performance-enhancing drugs. Graham had steered several pro athletes to the Relays. In May 2008, he received a felony conviction for lying to federal investigators about his relationship with a steroids dealer and was sentenced to a year of house arrest. The U.S. Olympic Committee barred him from all training sites.

Given the circumstances, it was determined that the Relays should take a different direction with less emphasis on professionals. "We're working to bring back the college division," said Milan Donley, newly appointed meet director.

STAR POWER. The biggest names in track and field, such as Marion Jones (above) in 2005 and Justin Gatlin in 2006, ensured big crowds during Gold Zones I and II.

# Meet Record-Breaking Performances During The Gold Zone

| Name | Team | Event | Mark |
|------|------|-------|------|
| **2005** | | | |
| Dominique Arnold | Nike | Men's 110 hurdles | 13.33 |
| Bershawn Jackson | Nike | Men's 400 hurdles | 48.67 |
| Muna Lee | Nike | Women's 100 | 11.10 |
| **2006** | | | |
| Bershawn Jackson | Nike | Men's 400 hurdles | 48.34 |
| Christian Cantwell | Nike | Men's shot put | 70-3.75 |
| Dwight Thomas, Rodney Martin, Shawn Crawford, Justin Gatlin | Sprint Capitol | Men's 4x100 relay | 38.16 |
| Allyson Felix | adidas | Women's 100 | 11.04 |
| Mary Danner | Nike | Women's 400 | 51.66 |
| LaShinda Demus | Nike | Women's 100 hurdles | 12.93 |

# 16

# Party on Eighth Street
## The Downtown Experiment

"Downtown, things'll be great when you're
Downtown, no finer place for sure
Downtown, everything's waiting for you
Downtown."

-- Lyrics from "Downtown," recorded by Petula Clark

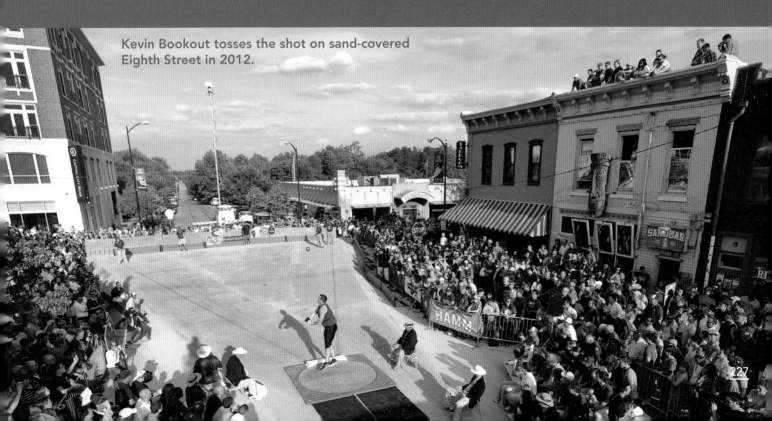

Kevin Bookout tosses the shot on sand-covered
Eighth Street in 2012.

With the departure of Tim Weaver, Milan Donley was appointed to fill the void as Kansas Relays meet director. His first Relays, following a distinguished coaching career, would be the 2007 edition. Among the career highlights for the Beulah, Colo., native and Southern Colorado trackster:

- A Master of Arts in Education from Adams State (Colo.) College in 1983, where he was a graduate assistant for the legendary Dr. Joe Vigil from 1981-84.

- He was head coach for the Adams State women's program in 1984-85 and coached them to the NAIA Indoor national championship.

- He was an assistant (mainly coaching sprints, jumps and multi-events) at some of the finest track and field programs in the country, including Southwest Texas State, the University of California at Berkeley, the University of Illinois and the University of Arkansas.

- From 1995-2000 he became the head coach for track and field and cross country at East Tennessee State, receiving three Southern Conference coach of the year awards.

- He was chosen Midwest Region assistant coach of the year after joining coach Stanley Redwine's KU staff as horizontal jumps coach in 2001, a position he held until becoming the Relays meet director.

- Donley coached numerous All-Americans, four Olympic team members, two U.S. champions and two American record holders, including Olympian Sheila Hudson, a six-time NCAA champion in the long jump and triple jump. He also coached his future wife Julie Jenkins, an 800-meter runner, in the 1992 Olympic Games in Barcelona.

With a resumé this varied, Donley was a logical choice to continue the momentum generated by the spectacular meets since the turn of the 21st century. He was well respected among elite athletes and had extensive coaching experience in the collegiate ranks, a perfect blend for the new direction the Relays were taking. NCAA Div. I schools had been trickling away from the Relays for a variety of reasons ranging from weather concerns to the desire for more traditional meets instead of the relays format. The more traditional meets, like the McDonald Invitational at Arkansas, allowed coaches to take full squads. Perhaps more importantly, they provided the open events necessary to achieve NCAA qualifying marks in what would usually be better weather conditions. The challenge for Donley was to restore the college division to its former level while keeping the fans happy with fewer elites after they had been spoiled by legions of professionals performing in prior years.

Ironically, the disillusioned fans, seeing some of their heroes implicated in the performance-enhancing drug scandals, were perhaps ready to move in this direction anyway. "We wanted to bring in some teams that would make the

**RELAYS FAN.** Hurdling superstar Bershawn "Batman" Jackson has never been shy about stating how much he enjoys the KU Relays.

collegiate meet better," Donley said. "But we're not going to turn our back on the elite division. We've got to find a blending here that we feel works well for the university, our community and our fans." Given the resources at his disposal, he met this difficult task about as well as anyone could hope for. He upgraded the collegiate division and still managed to attract elite athletes like Olympic sprinters Allyson Felix and Muna Lee, as well as 400-meter hurdler Bershawn "Batman" Jackson. As a regular at the Relays, Jackson endeared himself to the fans with comments like, "It's my goal to be a fan favorite, I love to compete here." His time of 48.75 was the fastest in the world in 2007 and the fourth of seven Relays titles.

Attendance was listed at 10,421 in 2007. The heptathlon and decathlon were reinstated after a three-year absence. The success of the Relays continued in 2008 with world-class athletes like Wallace Spearman, Chris Cantwell and of course, Batman, among others. The high school division, always a strength of the Relays even when the collegiate portion was struggling, continued to grow in quantity and quality. High school athletes from 10 states, some as far away as Wyoming and Texas, were providing high schoolers in the Midwest with the best competition they would see in an entire season. It was a unique opportunity that allowed small-school athletes an opportunity to compete against large-school athletes, and 13,500 fans enjoyed the competition.

The Relays in 2009 and 2010 were equally impressive and well attended. There were many outstanding performances from high school and collegiate runners as well as professional athletes, such as 1500-meter runner Alan Webb and sprinters such as Ivory Williams and two-time Olympic gold medalist Veronica Campbell-Brown.

The parade of stars continued in 2011:

- Canadian Olympian and KU alumnus Scott Russell threw the javelin 268 feet, 11 inches to better his own record.
- "Batman" was back for his sixth Relays watch.

**DOUBLE OLYMPIAN.** Veronica Campbell-Brown won the 200 meters at KU in 2010 and 2011. Here, after her win in 2010, she signed autographs.

- Olympic sprinter Lauryn Williams ran the year's second-fastest 100.

- KU freshman and future gold-medal Olympian Diamond Dixon was voted Most Outstanding Female Athlete for her school-record effort in the 400 meters and 4x400 relay.

- The Most Outstanding Male performance came from Blake Leeper, a double-leg amputee who ran an astounding 11.32 in a special Paralympic 100-meter dash.

**IVORY BLUR.** Ivory Williams, shown here in the lead in 2012, has been one of a parade of elite athletes at the Relays in recent years.

Perhaps the most memorable events in 2011 were the hosting of elite shot put and long jump events in a downtown setting for the first time in American history, though similar events had been held in Zurich, Switzerland, and Stockholm, Sweden. Donley, anxious to attract the casual track fan as well as other new fans, thought that an event in a unique setting and lasting 60 to 90 minutes, might serve his purpose. Conversations with Cantwell, a veteran of such events on the European circuit, confirmed the popularity of these events overseas. Lawrence city officials embraced the decision to go ahead with the experiment. The event was made possible by a generous donation of 490 yards of limestone shake by Hamm's Quarry.

According to a 2011 *Lawrence Journal-World* article by Chad Lawhorn, city crews worked about six hours on Wednesday to survey the area, distribute the limestone, level it, pack it down and ready the venue for the evening competition. City crews started removing the dirt at 4:30 a.m. Thursday,

**SPEED ON BLADES. Blake Leeper earned Most Outstanding Male for his 100-meter run in 2011.**

and by 6:30 a.m. assistant public works director Mark Thiel said everything was back to normal at the Eighth and New Hampshire intersection. For its efforts in getting the area ready for the competition and cleaning up thereafter, the city became the beneficiary of the limestone for future use around town, particularly to maintain running and biking trails along the Kansas River levee.

Tom Keegan, sportswriter for the *Journal-World*, wrote to entice fans to a truly unique track and field event: "Soon, the air on Eighth Street between Mass and New Hampshire will be thick with testosterone. Loud music. Men ripping their shirts off and unleashing primal screams of passion." After building the suspense, Keegan clarified that he wasn't referring to a typical college night downtown, but rather a shot put competition featuring several of the world's best. Indeed, it was a Wednesday night in Lawrence. Had the event been held at the McCook throwing complex on campus, only a handful would have vacated the stands to watch these marvelous athletes hurl a 16-pound iron ball nearly the length of a basketball court. Instead, an estimated 2,500 jubilant fans crowded temporary bleachers and stood several tiers deep on Eighth Street to witness this unique experiment.

The shot putters' enthusiasm matched that of the audience. They interacted with the audience in ways you normally don't see at track and field competitions. Loud music, selected by the throwers themselves, blared over the public address system. In a story by Gary Bedore for KUsports.com, he quoted winner Dylan Armstrong as saying, "This is one of the strongest

**TRACK TOWN, HEARTLAND-STYLE.** Shot put venue on the streets of downtown Lawrence, April 20, 2011.

events in the world now in track and field. We had a great group of guys here. We are friends. We push each other hard. The crowd was great. I couldn't have done it without the fans. I hope this is an annual event."

"It's really unique to see that kind of crowd gathered for just one event in track and field," third-place finisher Adam Nelson said. "I think Lawrence did a fantastic job hosting it." Mary Cox, president of Downtown Lawrence, Inc. and an owner of Shark's Surf Shop, was hoping for a repeat performance in 2012 because the downtown merchants seemed to have a good time. Tom Wilson, owner of Teller's Restaurant just down the street said, "It looks like our Wednesday sales got a boost of 30 to 40 percent, and they didn't break any of my windows. That was my biggest concern."

**FINGER TOSS.** Dylan Armstrong used all his strength to win the 2011 downtown shot put crown.

The following evening, on Eighth Street between Vermont and Massachusetts streets, about 500 fans, despite cold and the threat of rain, gathered to watch a long jump competition, unique not only because of its location, but also by the fact that measurements were taken from the jumper's take-off point rather than the usual eight-inch take-off board. This helped to compensate for a slightly shorter runway. The enthusiastic crowd clapped rhythmically to urge the jumpers, and they responded. Eric Babb, a KU graduate in 2007 and a math instructor on campus, pleased his cheering section by jumping 25 feet 2 ½ inches on his first attempt. That mark led the competition until Nicholas Gordon, a Nebraska senior from Jamaica, equaled it

A SCREAMING GOOD TIME. Adam Nelson was third in 2011 and fourth in 2012 (shown here) in his visits to downtown Lawrence.

on his last jump. Gordon was declared the winner because he had the second longest jump. Both men were pleased with the response of the large number of fans in attendance. "It was a big motivator having all these friends here," Babb said.

Based on the athletes' positive response, the size and exuberance of the crowds, and the endorsements of the downtown merchants, the downtown experiments were continued in 2012 with great success. At the shot put venue, an estimated crowd of 3,500 – including the Jayhawk mascot – sat on temporary bleachers in close proximity to these world-class athletes.

The throwers seemed to enjoy the attention and graciously interacted with the crowd, signing many autographs after the competition. In a change from 2011, the downtown long jump was contested by women instead of men. Despite a light drizzle, Janay DeLoach's jump of 21-8.25 was impressive, and she quickly became a fan favorite. "The fans are closer to you and they get to really see what it is like up close and personal," she said. "I like to put on a little bit of a show, so I liked it."

Given the success of the first two years, quality fields were lined up for the 2013 downtown competitions. However, downtown didn't happen. Given the threat of severe thunderstorms, Donley and city officials decided to move both the shot put on Wednesday and the long jump on Thursday to a venue that would ensure safety for both athletes and fans. The choice was the livestock arena at the Douglas County fairgrounds. In an interview with Keegan, Donley put a positive spin on the change by declaring, "If people enjoyed watching those guys throw, it will be just as exciting.

SANDY STREET. Despite forbidding clouds, diehard fans came out to watch the long jumpers in 2012.

INDOORS AND OUT. Janay DeLoach won outdoors on Eighth Street in 2012 (left) and again in 2013 as Janay DeLoach-Soukup when forced indoors to the livestock arena because of weather.

It actually could be louder in there if people show up and support them." People did show up in person, and many more witnessed the events on Metro Sports TV in the Lawrence area and on ESPN3 nationwide. It appears that the downtown experiment is on its way to becoming a downtown tradition.

**CELEBRATING INDOORS.**
Athletes and fans didn't let the move into the livestock arena (top) be a downer in 2013. Fans of shot putter Kurt Roberts let their allegiance be known (center). The real show-stopper was Reese Hoffa, who lasted much longer than a cloud of smoke (middle right). Although he didn't defend his 2012 title, he celebrated his runner-up finish with a cartwheel (bottom right) and also defeated KU basketball player Kevin Young in a Rubik's cube dual (middle left). Hoffa has a personal best of solving the 3-D puzzle in 38 seconds.

239

# Downtown Results, 2011-2013

| Place | Name | Affiliation | Mark |
|-------|------|-------------|------|
| **2011 Men's Shot Put** | | | |
| 1 | Dylan Armstrong | Nike | 70-7 |
| 2 | Reese Hoffa | NYAC | 69-3.5 |
| 3 | Adam Nelson | Saucony | 68-5.25 |
| 4 | Cory Martin | Nike | 67-11.25 |
| 5 | Ryan Whiting | Nike | 67-10.75 |
| 6 | Dorian Scott | Nike | 66-0.5 |
| 7 | Noah Bryant | Unattached | 65-10.75 |
| 8 | Dan Taylor | Nike | 62-7 |
| **2011 Men's Long Jump** | | | |
| 1 | Nicholas Gordon | Nebraska | 25-2.5 |
| 2 | Eric Babb | Unattached | 25-2.5 |
| 3 | Ja'Rod Tolbert | Nike | 24-10.75 |
| 4 | Fabian Florent | Unattached | 24-3.5 |
| 5 | Eric Fattig | Unattached | 23-11.5 |
| 6 | Eric Bertelsen | Unattached | 23-10.5 |
| **2012 Men's Shot Put** | | | |
| 1 | Reese Hoffa | NYAC | 71-3.5 |
| 2 | Christian Cantwell | Nike | 71-2.5 |
| 3 | Justin Rodhe | Nike | 69-3 |
| 4 | Adam Nelson | Saucony | 68-2.5 |
| 5 | Ryan Whiting | Nike | 67-8.5 |
| 6 | Dan Taylor | Nike | 66-4 |
| 7 | Cory Martin | Nike | 66-2.25 |
| 8 | Nedzad Mulabegović | Nike | 65-7.75 |
| 9 | Kevin Bookout | Unattached | 63-11.5 |
| 10 | Dylan Armstrong | Nike | Foul |

| Place | Name | Affiliation | Mark |
|---|---|---|---|
| | **2012 Women's Long Jump**[1] | | |
| 1 | Janay DeLoach | Nike | 21-8.25 |
| 2 | Tori Polk | Unattached | 21-1.25 |
| 3 | Brianna Glenn | Unattached | 20-10.75 |
| 4 | Rose Richmond | Unattached | 20-10.5 |
| 5 | Bettie Wade | Nike | 20-2.5 |
| 6 | Amber Bledsoe | Unattached | 20-1.5 |
| 7 | Crystal Manning | Unattached | 19-7.5 |
| 8 | Natasha Coleman | Unattached | 19-6.25 |
| | **2013 Men's Shot Put** | | |
| 1 | Ryan Whiting | Nike | 71-0.25 |
| 2 | Reese Hoffa | NYAC | 70-10.25 |
| 3 | Justin Rodhe | California | 69-3.5 |
| 4 | Cory Martin | Nike | 66-8 |
| 5 | Nedzad Mulabegovic´ | Croatia | 64-8.75 |
| 6 | Joe Kovacs | Unattached | 63-11.5 |
| 7 | Kurt Roberts | Nike | 63-4.5 |
| 8 | Christian Cantwell | Nike | 59-10 |
| | **2013 Women's Long Jump**[1] | | |
| 1 | Janay DeLoach-Soukup | Nike | 22-4.5 |
| 2 | Tori Bowie | California | 21-9 |
| 3 | Jimoh Funmi | Neosho County (Kan.) Community College | 21-2.25 |
| 4 | Jessie Gains | Unattached | 21-2.25 |
| 5 | Arantxa King | Bermuda | 20-4.25 |
| 6 | Jovana Jarrett | Puma | 19-10 |
| 7 | Bettie Wade | Nike | 19-8 |

[1] A take-off board was used.

# 17

# A New Home
## The Move to Rock Chalk Park

*"All changes, even the most longed for, have their melancholy; for what we leave behind us is a part of ourselves; we must die to one life before we can enter another."*

Anatole France, French writer

The Rock Chalk Park track facility, as of Dec. 22, 2013, months before its planned debut as the site of the KU Relays.

Memorial Stadium on the campus of the University of Kansas was dedicated on Nov. 11, 1922. When the Kansas Relays take place in April 2014, she will be 91 years old going on 92. She has aged well, growing from a seating capacity of 22,000 to 51,500. Because of several face lifts, most notably in 1998 and 1999, she now shines brightly as she nestles in the Mt. Oread Valley. The press box high above the west stands has become a comfortable place for announcers to speak and scribes to compose spellbinding stories of prodigious athletic feats or dismal disappointments. A massive video board spews impressive amounts of information, even to the point of recalling precisely what was, through the power of replay.

One would think it the perfect place to hold an athletic competition. In fact, it has been. Though not as heralded as the iconic Allen Fieldhouse across campus, Memorial Stadium has been witness to phenomenal feats by local athletes and from those around the world. All the while it has also served the needs of thousands of performers who did not fit into the category of "elites." Yet, in April 2014, she will stand like an empty locust husk, void of cheering fans, blaring PA systems and starting pistol shots. Instead, the national anthem will usher in a new era as the track and field stars of today run, jump and throw in a new venue 5½ miles to the west on the Kansas prairie. If you ask why, you will not be the first to pose the question. Forrest C. "Phog" Allen, who insisted that a track be built around the football field in the first place, asked it in 1962, stating vehemently in a *Kansas City Star* article that moving the Relays out of Memorial Stadium would kill them.

In 1962, it might have, for the projected new track and field facility was to have seating for only 2,500. But times have changed. There was a time when football, basketball and track were part of the same university sports entity. Relays visionary Dr. John Outland was a football player and coach. Dr. James Naismith, the inventor of basketball, served as head track coach for six years between 1901 and 1906. Allen, universally known for his impact on basketball, was a prime mover in the establishment and continuation of the Kansas Relays. Innovative football coach Bill Hargiss, who led KU on the gridiron, served as head track coach from 1933 to 1943. Two- and three-sport athletes like Jim Bausch, Wilt Chamberlain, Gale Sayers, Nolan Cromwell, Karl Salb and Tyke Peacock made major contributions to the Relays and Kansas track and field, as well as to the other nationally recognized KU sports in which they competed. The reality is that multi-sport athletes at NCAA Div. I schools are as rare nowadays as mechanical stopwatches. Each sports program, though part of the greater university athletic community, exists pretty much independently from the others.

**LAYING THE GROUNDWORK.**
The Rock Chalk Park track gets a smooth surface on Sept. 19, 2013.

Since 1922, Kansas track and field has shared a facility with football. Given the fabulous legacy carved out by KU, the track program has unquestionably earned its own venue. As stated in the 2012-13 Kansas Track & Field Media Guide, "Since its inception, the Kansas track & field program has been home to legendary coaches, conference titles and Olympic champions. The program has captured six NCAA team national championships, 60 league crowns, 71 individual national champions and groomed over 400 All-Americans. The program's roots also extend internationally, as Kansas has developed 27 Olympians, 10 medalists and five gold medalists."

To this array of talent from the host school, coaches from other collegiate programs in the Midwest and beyond brought their finest athletes to do battle with KU and one another. Domestic and foreign professionals battled for watches and prestige in a never-ending display of excellence. Wide-eyed high schoolers got their first exhilarating taste of what it was like to compete in a

MEMORIES. The Kansas Relays has its own display as part of the Booth Family Museum connected to Allen Fieldhouse that chronicles the deep Jayhawk athletic tradition. Until 2014, those Relays memories were made at Memorial Stadium. Rock Chalk Park will now be the site where new memories are made.

large-scale sporting arena. It was an insult to track and field that in many of those years, meager crowds made the 50,000 seat stadium seem cavernous. Rock Chalk Park, with seating in the range of 10,000, will be a case where less is more. It will be rare when the new stadium is not filled to capacity on Relays day; and with the closer proximity to the action, the drama generated by track and field competition will be even more palpable and exciting.

By all accounts, the quality of the new track will put Rock Chalk Park in rarified air. The International Association of Athletics Federations (IAAF), track and field's international governing body, gave the track surface a Class I certification on Feb. 26, 2014 -- only the fifth such track in the United States and one of only 105 in the entire world. The Class I designation allows KU to go after not just regional meets but national ones. Elite athletes will almost certainly be excited to compete on a surface that gives them an opportunity to run fast times.

**ON THE OPEN PRAIRIE.** An endless horizon extends beyond the construction work at Rock Chalk Park in August 2013. The new track-only facility will not require the track and field program to share space with the football team.

Moving to a new location does not presage the demise of the Relays. The spirit of its founders and the visionaries who nurtured it through 86 years have laid a solid foundation, strong enough to bear the weight of countless more Kansas Relays. We can hope that 86 years from now in the year 2100, the Relays will begin life in its third century.

Dr. John Outland threw a stone into the track and field waters in 1923. The resulting ripples have been felt around the world as fans, coaches and competitors take their memories with them to savor and reflect upon wherever they go. No stadium could contain the forcefulness of those ripples, because they transcend physical boundaries. The Kansas Relays has not reached its exalted status because of where it occurred, but rather because of what it represents: a tradition of excellence and accomplishment, a symbol of what is good about sports and competition. Thus it is that the Kansas Relays, a track and field tradition in the heartland, is alive, well and growing.

*TO BE CONTINUED ...*

# Appendix A
# Most Outstanding Performers

Dominique Arnold, 2005 Most Outstanding Male Performer

1948: Harrison Dillard, Baldwin-Wallace
1949: Bob Walters, Texas
1950: Bill Carroll, Oklahoma
1951: Don Cooper, Nebraska
1952: Wes Santee, Kansas
1953: Darrow Hooper, Texas A&M
1954: Wes Santee, Kansas
1955: Dean Smith, Texas
1956: Bobby Whilden, Texas
1957: Billy Tidwell, Emporia
1958: Eddie Southern, Texas
1959: Charlie Tidwell, Kansas
1960: Cliff Cushman, Kansas
1961: Bill Kemp, Baylor
1962: Ray Saddler, Texas Southern
1963: Jim Miller, Colorado
1964: Robin Lingle, Missouri
1965: Clarence Robinson, New Mexico
1966: Jim Ryun, Kansas
1967: Jim Ryun, Kansas
1968: Jim Murphy, Air Force
1969: Jim Ryun, Kansas
1970: Larbi Oukada, Fort Hays
1971: Jim Ryun, ex-Kansas
1972: Jim Bolding, Oklahoma State
1973: Mike Boit, Eastern New Mexico
1974: Phillip Ndoo, Eastern New Mexico
1975: Charlton Ehizuelen, Illinois
1976: Nolan Cromwell, Kansas

1977: **Clifford Wiley, Kansas**
1978: Gregg Byram, Oklahoma
1979: Kipsubai Koskei, New Mexico
1980: Jocelyn Bentley, Highland Park
Joe Dial, Marlow (Okla.) HS
1981: Merlene Ottey, Nebraska
**Clifford Wiley, DC International**
1982: Merlene Ottey, Nebraska
Tyke Peacock, Kansas
1983: Merlene Ottey, Nebraska
Doug Hedrick, Shawnee Mission East
1984: Nawal El Moutawakol, Iowa State
Scott Lofquist, unattached
1985: Michelle Macey, Kansas State
Joe Dial, unattached
1986: Pinkie Suggs, unattached
Kenny Harrison, Kansas State
1987: LaTonya Sheffield, San Diego TC
Joe Dial, unattached
1988: Leah Kirklan, John Marshall HS
Scott Huffman, Kansas
1989: Kim Kilpatrick, Kansas State
Felicia Allen, Missouri
Amy Rodehaver, Jenks HS
Mark Dailey, Eastern Michigan
1990: Angie Miller, Kansas State
Kevin Little, Drake

| | |
|---|---|
| 1991: | Beverly McDonald, Barton County CC<br>Marlon Cannon, Barton County CC |
| 1992: | Inez Turner, Barton County CC<br>Michael Cox, Kansas |
| 1993: | Inez Turner, Barton County CC<br>Winston Tidwell, Topeka West HS |
| 1994: | Natasha Shafer, Kansas<br>David Oaks, Oklahoma |
| 1995: | Dawn Steele-Slavens, Kansas<br>Michael Cox, Kansas |
| 1996: | Stacy Dragila, unattached<br>Michael Cox, Kansas |
| 1997: | Amy Wiseman, Lee's Summit HS<br>Kevin Toth, unattached |
| 2000: | Andrea Branson, Kansas<br>Walter Davis, Barton County CC |
| 2001: | Aleen Bailey, Barton County CC<br>Robert Howard, unattached |
| 2002: | **Christian Cantwell, Missouri** |

Trecia Smith, Jamaica

| | |
|---|---|
| 2003: | Drew Moreno, St. Thomas Aquinas<br>Andrea Dutoit, unattached |
| 2004: | Nathan Leeper, Nike<br>Austra Skujyte, unattached<br>Julius Jiles, KC Central<br>Sarah Stevens, Fort Collins |

| | |
|---|---|
| 2005: | Dominique Arnold, Nike<br>**Muna Lee, Nike** |

Jared Huske, Highland Park
Rachel Talbert, Wichita Home School

| | |
|---|---|
| 2006: | Daniel Maina, Cowley County CC<br>**Allyson Felix, adidas** |
| 2007: | Ashley Usery,<br>McCluer-So.<br>Berkeley<br>Trina Cox, Pacers/<br>Brooks |
| 2008: | Bershawn Jackson,<br>Nike<br>Emily Sisson, Millard<br>North (Neb.) |
| 2009: | James White,<br>Grandview (Mo.)<br>Emily Sisson, Parkway Central (Mo.) |
| 2010: | Ivory Williams, Nike<br>Tiffani McWilliams, Pembroke HS |
| 2011: | Blake Leeper, unattached<br>Diamond Dixon, Kansas |
| 2012: | Bershawn Jackson, Nike<br>Ali Cash, Shawnee Mission West |
| 2013 | Michael Tinsley, unattached<br>Alexa Harmon-Thomas,<br>Lawrence (Kan.)-Free State |

# Appendix B
# Meet Referees

| | | | |
|---|---|---|---|
| 1923 | Louis C. Mederia III, Penn | 1947 | John Jacobs, Oklahoma |
| 1924 | Dr. John Outland, Kansas, Penn | 1948 | Frank Potts, Colorado |
| 1925 | Knute Rockne, Notre Dame | 1949 | Ward Haylett, Kansas State |
| 1926 | Fielding Yost, Michigan | 1950 | Dr. Garfield Weede, Kansas State Teachers College of Pittsburg (Pittsburg State) |
| 1927 | Harry Gill, Illinois | | |
| 1928 | Tom Jones, Wisconsin | 1951 | Ralph Higgins, Oklahoma A&M |
| 1929 | Major John L. Griffith, Big Ten Commissioner | | |
| 1930 | Avery Brundage, AAU President | | |
| 1931 | Ossie Sloem, Drake | | |
| 1932 | Amos Alonzo Stagg, Chicago | | |
| 1933 | Henry Schulte, Nebraska | | |
| 1934 | George Bresnahan, Iowa | | |
| 1935 | Clyde Littlefield, Texas | | |
| 1936 | C.N. Metcalf, Iowa State | | |
| 1937 | Henry Schulte, Nebraska | | |
| 1938 | Major John L. Griffith, Big Ten Commissioner | | |
| 1939 | Frank Hill, Northwestern | | |
| 1940 | Jim Kelly, Minnesota | | |
| 1941 | Tom Jones, Wisconsin | | |
| 1942 | Glenn Cunningham, Cornell College | | |
| 1946 | George Bresnahan, Iowa | | |

The next generation of track fans watches a race at the 2010 KU Relays.

| 1952 | Ed Weir, Nebraska |
|------|-------------------|
| 1953 | Tom Botts, Missouri |
| 1954 | E.A. Thomas, KSHSAA Commissioner |
| 1955 | J.H. "Cap" Shelton, Howard-Payne |
| 1956 | Frank Anderson, Texas A&M |
| 1957 | Jim Kelly, Minnesota |
| 1958 | Karl Schlademan, Michigan State |
| 1960 | Volney Ashford, Missouri Valley |
| 1961 | Ward Haylett, Kansas State |
| 1962 | Oliver Jackson, Abilene Christian |
| 1963 | Pop Noah, North Texas State |
| 1964 | Johnny Morris, Houston |
| 1965 | Clyde Littlefield, Texas (retired) |
| 1966 | Fritz Snodgrass, Wichita State |

**1967** **Univ:** Bob Karnes, Drake
**College:** Stan Wright, Texas Southern
**HS:** Orlis Cox, Ottawa

**1968** **Univ:** Frank Potts, Colorado
**College:** Bruce Drummond, Oklahoma Bapist
**HS:** Elton Brown, Hoisington

**1969** **Univ:** Emmett Brunson, Rice
**College:** Alex Francis, Fort Hays State
**HS:** Francis Swaim, Wyandotte
**Honorary** Referee: Bill Easton

**1970** **Univ:** Lew Hartzog, Southern Illinois
**College:** G.W. "Doc" Weede, Pittsburg State
**HS:** Herschel Betts, Oberlin

**1971** **Univ:** DeLoss Dodds, Kansas State
**College:** Dwight T. Reed, Lincoln
**HS:** J.D. Edmiston, Wichita East

**1972** **Univ:** Frank Sevigne, Nebraska
**College:** Ray Vaughn, Oklahoma Christian
**Women's:** Dr. John Davis, Topeka
**JC:** Nelson Sorem, Hutchinson CC
**HS:** Jack Hague, Great Bend

**1973** **Univ:** Tom Botts, Missouri
**College:** L.D. Welden, Graceland
**JC:** H.E. Llewellyn, Haskell Institute
**HS:** Merlin Gish, Shawnee Mission North

**1974** **Univ:** Cleburne Price, Texas
**College:** David Suenram, Pittsburg State
**JC:** Bill Miller, Florissant Valley
**HS:** Don Bliss, Topeka

**1975** **Univ:** Francis Cretzmeyer, Iowa
**College:** Phil Delavan, Emporia State
**JC:** Glen Stone, Eastern Oklahoma State
**HS:** Verlyn Schmidt, Shawnee Mission East

**1976** **Univ:** Herm Wilson, Wichita State
**College:** Joe Vigil, Adams State
**JC:** Dale Meadors, Garden City

KU Relays pole vault, April 20, 2012.

Women's: Barry Anderson, Kansas State
HS: Ray Graham, Wichita West
Honorary Referee: Elwyn Dees

1977  Men's Univ: Mel Bradt, Bowling Green State
Men's College: Fred Beile, Doane College
JC: Terry Masterson, Hutchinson CC
HS: Joe Schrag, Topeka West
Women's: Chris Murray, Iowa State

1978  Univ.: Bill Carroll, Oklahoma
College: Ken Gardner, NE Missouri State
JC: Lew Llewllyn, Haskell Indian JC
HS: Don Kornhaus, Ottawa

1979  Univ.: Guy Kochel, Arkansas State
College: Lloyd Cardwell, Sr., Nebraska-Omaha
JC: Roger Bowen, Meramec CC
HS: Wendell Goldsmith, WaKeeney
Women's: Dorothy Doolittle, Missouri

1980  Univ.: Bill McClure, LSU
College: Jim Pilkington, C. Missouri State
JC: Orland Aldridge, Garden City CC
HS: Clyde Strimple, Wyandotte
Women's: Pete Kron, Oklahoma

1981  Men's Univ/Open: Mike Ross, Kansas State
Men's College: Ted Lloyd, Harding Univ.
Men's JC: Jerry Tuckwin, Haskell Indian JC
Women's: Bill Tidwell, Emporia State
HS: Karl Englund, Shawnee Mission East

1982  Women's Univ.: Gary Pepin, Nebraska
Men's Univ: Gary Wieneke, Illinois
Girls HS: Steve Sublett, Lawrence
Boys HS: Van Rose, Shawnee Mission NW

1983  Women's Univ.: John Kornelson, Wichita State
Men's Univ: Jack Harvey, Michigan
Girls HS: Dixie Barb, Topeka-Highland Park
Boys HS: Marvin Estes, Wichita-Kapaun
  Mt. Carmel

1984  Men's Univ: Bob Ehrhart, Drake
Women's Univ.: Gordon Fox, Colorado
Girls HS: Bill Congleton, Manhattan
Boys HS: Clardy Vinson, Topeka

1985  Men's Univ: John Coughlan, Illinois State
Women's Univ.: Ron Renko, Iowa State
Girls HS: Bill Van Hecke, Bishop Miege
Boys HS: Doug Smith, Salina Central

1986  Men's Univ: Bill Bergan, Iowa State
Women's Univ.: Steve Miller, Kansas State
Girls HS: Dick Reamon, Lawrence
Boys HS: Harry McDonald, Blue Valley

1987  Men's Univ: Dennis Shaver, Barton County CC
Women's Univ.: Joyce Morton, Illinois State
Girls HS: Bob Camien, Topeka-Seaman
Boys HS: Garrett Wheaton, Lyons
Honorary Referee: Al Oerter

1988  Men's Univ: Frank Zubovich, Ohio State
Women's Univ.: Rick McGuire, Missouri
Girls HS: Bob Schmoekel, Junction City
Boys HS: Sparky Patterson, Topeka-Hayden

1989  Men's Univ: Steve Kueffer, Lawrence
Women's Univ.: John Capriotti, Kansas State
Girls HS: Mike Naster, Shawnee Mission South
Boys HS: Bob Whitehead, Blue Valley North

1990  Men's Univ: Bob Parks, Eastern Michigan
Women's Univ.: Dave Burgess, Johnson County CC
Girls HS: Carl Owczarzak, Shawnee Mission West
Boys HS: Bill Freeman, Lawrence
Honorary Referee: Ralph Vernacchia

1991  Men's Univ: Paul Parent, Central State (Ohio)
Women's Univ.: Jerry Hassard, Iowa
Girls HS: Bob Karr, Emporia
Boys HS: David Bertholf, Wyandotte

1992  Men's Univ: Jim Krob, Fort Hays State
Women's Univ.: Lee Ann Shaddox,
  Northern Iowa
Boys HS: Bill Young, Leavenworth
Girls HS: Earl Ventura, Paola

1993  Men's Univ: Dwight T. Reed, Lincoln University
Women's Univ.: Jay Flanagan, Arkansas State
Girls HS: Steve Sell, Wichita East
Boys HS: Mike Nash, Tecumseh-Shawnee Heights
  Heights

1994  Men's Univ: Richard Clark,
  Southwest Missouri St.
Women's Univ.: Harry Kitchener Cloud CC
Girls HS: John McGinnis, Jenks
Boys HS: Don Morgan, Manhattan

1995    **Men's Univ:** Chris "Bucky" Bucknam, N. Iowa
**Women's Univ.:** Russ Jewett, Pittsburg State
**Girls HS:** Clark Hay, Shawnee Mission West
**Boys HS:** Roger Matheson, Kearney

1996    **Men's Univ:** Bill Cornell, Southern Illinois
**Women's Univ.:** Al Hobson, Nike Central
**Boys HS:** Larry Barnhart, Newton
**Girls HS:** Tamra Strano, Leavenworth

1997    **Men's Univ:** Al Cantello, Navy
**Women's Univ.:** Doug Max, Colorado State
**Boys HS:** Mark Lamb, Wichita North
**Girls HS:** Gene McClain, N. Kansas City

2000    **Men's Univ:** John Kornelson, Wichita State
**Women's Univ.:** Rick McGuire, Missouri
**Boys HS:** Mike Wallace, Olathe East
**Girls HS:** Van Rose, Shawnee Mission Northwest

2001    **Men's Univ:** Bill Thornton, St. Olafs
**Women's Univ.:** Cliff Rovelto, Kansas State
**Boys HS:** Ken Russell, Abilene
**Girls HS:** Kathy Strecker, Topeka-Hayden

2002    **Men's Univ:** Joe Dial, Oral Roberts
**Women's Univ.:** Ron Boyce, SW Missouri State
**Boys HS:** Jerry Skakal, Lawrence
**Girls HS:** Claudia Welch, Topeka-Seaman

2003    **Men's Univ:** Steve Lynn, Iowa State
**Women's Univ.:** Kirk Hunter, Butler County CC
**Boys HS:** Mark Hanson, Blue Valley West
**Girls HS:** Martha O'Rourke, Jenks

2004    **Men's Univ:** Dick Weis, Oklahoma State
**Women's Univ.:** Theo Hamilton, UMKC
**Boys HS:** Mike Cooper, Shawnee Mission Northwest
**Girls HS:** Richard Ebel, Paola HS

2005    **Men's Univ:** Dave Harris, Emporia State
**Women's Univ.:** Ted Schmitz, Cloud County CC

**Boys HS:** Rich Ludwig, Gardner-Edgerton
**Girls HS:** John Lewis, Topeka West

2006    **Men's Referee:** Steve Rainbolt, Wichita State
**Women's Referee:** Pat Becher, Hutchinson CC
**Boys Referee:** Joe Amos, Blue Valley North
**Girls Referee:** Randy Wells, Emporia

Pole vaulter Jordan Scott's hair, 2011.

2007    **HS:** Karl Englund
**Univ:** David Ramsey

2008    **Collegiate/Open:** David Ramsey
**HS:** Karl Englund
**Multi-Events:** Mark Schwarm

2009    **Running Events:** Patricia Hanna
**Field Events:** John Kornelson
**Multi-Events:** Mark Schwarm

2010    **Running Events:** Patricia Hanna
**Field Events:** Tom Doyle
**Multi-Events:** Mark Schwarm

2011    **Running Events:** Patricia Hanna
**Field Events:** John Kornelson
**Multi-Events:** Patrick Pretty

2012    **Running Events:** Pat Becher
**Field Events:** John Kornelson
**Multi-Events:** Patrick Pretty

2013    **Running** Events: Del Hessel, Colorado State
**Field** Events: Dick Railsback
**Multi-Events:** Patrick Pretty

# Appendix C
# Meet Starters

These are the starters for the collegiate portion of the meet. When the high schools merged with the colleges, starters did both. The following narrative information about select starters is gleaned in large measure from Kansas Relays programs. There have been many competent starters over the years. Those featured are noteworthy for their many years of service or because they have an interesting connection to the Relays.

**1923   John L. Griffith.** The starter for the first Kansas Relays in 1923, Griffith was inducted into the Track and Field Hall of Fame as an administrator in 1979. He is credited with founding the Drake Relays in 1910.  The initial Drake meet consisted of three universities and three high schools and took place in a blizzard.  Within five years only the Penn Relays and the Olympics were considered to be larger meets.

**1924-1937   John C. Grover.** Starter for 14 years, "Jack" Grover, a Kansas City, Mo., attorney, was known throughout the Missouri Valley territory as dean of sports officials.

**1937   Gwinn Henry**

**1938, 1940-41   Clyde Littlefield.**  A Relays starter for three years, Littlefield was the track coach at the University of Texas for 41 years. He is credited with being a co-founder of the Texas Relays (1925) with athletic director Theo Bellmont. He was inducted into the Track and Field Hall of Fame in 1981.

**1938-1942   A. E. Talbot**

**1939, 1946-1950   H. E. Schemmer**

**1942   Karl A. Schlademan.** The  Relays' collegiate starter in 1942, Schlademan was KU head track and field coach when the Relays started in 1923. He started the Relays' high school meets from 1923-26. Schlademan coached the Jayhawks to the first of 60 conference championships during his seven-year tenure and has been inducted into several Halls of Fame: Drake Relays, Michigan University, Washington State University, US Track & Field, and Cross Country Coaches.

**1951-1956   Bill Hargiss.** The Relays' collegiate starter for six years, Hargiss coached both football and track at KU after successful coaching stints at College of Emporia and Kansas State Normal Teachers College in Emporia. He coached four world record holders (John Kuck, Glenn Cunningham, Jim Bausch and Clyde Coffman). He also coached Olympic champion wrestler John Mehringer in football. While track coach at KU, he routinely started the high school portion of the Relays before starting the collegiate portion during the 1950s.

**1956-1967   Ed Higgenbotham.** Higgenbotham served as assistant starter for Bill Hargiss for one year and Les Duke for nine years.

**1957-1967   Les Duke.** The veteran Midlands athletic director, track coach and track official started the Kansas Relays 11 times. He guided Grinnell to three Missouri Valley track crowns from 1927-1947, and was athletic director there from 1940-1947. Duke graduated from Grinnell in 1925 and served as Dean of Men there from 1948-1952 before resigning to enter private business. Duke also served one term on the NCAA Track and Field rules committee.

**1966-1967   Herman Wilson**

**1968-1981   Dick Ernst.** Ernst was head starter at the Relays for 13 years. A graduate of Michigan State, Ernst started over 30 national championships, including the NAIA Indoor and Outdoor, the USTFF Outdoor and NCAA Division I, II and III Outdoors. He also started the Drake Relays, the Big 8 Indoor and Outdoor, the Missouri Valley Indoor and Outdoor, the Central Collegiate Championships and the Mid-American Conference championships.

**1968-1971   Tom Thorne**

**1972-1973, 1977   Guy Barnes**

**1974-1975, 2003   Kelly Rankin**

**1977, 1979-1995   Jerry Reichart.** A track starter for over 30 years, Reichert started the NAIA Championships for 18 years as well as Big 8 and National Junior College Championships. He was a starter for the 1992 Big 8 Indoor. A favorite among high school coaches, Reichart started eight indoor and 23 Kansas State Outdoor Championships.

**1978**   Relays not on campus

**1979-1997, 2000-2010   John Deardorff.** A veteran starter for over 30 years, Deardorff became a permanent fixture at the Relays until his retirement in 2010. He has worked numerous prestigious events like the AIWA National Championships and USA-TFA competitions. Deardorff has started at the Drake Relays, the Missouri Valley Conference, the Big 8 Conference and Kansas State High School Championships. In 1992, he was a starter at the Big 8 Indoors as well as the NCAA Cross Country Championship in Lawrence.

**1998-1999**   No Relays held.

**1988-1997, 2000-2001   Mark Schwarm.** A former track athlete at Kansas State, Mark was a starter for the 12 KU Relays between 1988 and 2001. He has started Big 8 cross country, indoor and outdoor championships, and the AAU, National Junior College, and Missouri Valley Conference championships.

**1991-1997, 2000-2013   John Brandt.** Brandt came to KU in 1971 following a track career and graduate study at Iowa University, as well as a faculty position at the University of Florida. At Florida he was a head timer and starter for the Florida Relays. Brandt has fulfilled a similar role at KU. In 1998 he was a starter for the NCAA Cross Country Championships.

**1997, 2000, 2002-2006, 2009-2013   Larry Able.** A USA Track and Field-certified official from Lenexa, Kan., Able has been a starter for KU programs since 1996. He has started NJCAA National Indoors, Big 12 Indoor and Outdoor Championships, NCAA Division II Outdoor Nationals, and NCAA Division I and II National Cross Country Championships.

**2001**   Bill Thornton

**2002, 2006**   Pat McRoberts

**2003**   Jim Muck

**2004, 2008, 2013**   Victor Everett

**2005**   Brad Clark

**2007**   Ken Graber

**2007, 2010-2013**   Harold Cribbs

**2009**   Doug Reynolds

**2011-2013**   Rich Ludwig

# Appendix D

# Kansas Relays Hall of Fame

1 **John Outland,** inducted 2006
2 **Wayne Osness,** inducted 2007
3 **Charlie Greene,** inducted 2006
4 **Ed Elbel,** inducted 2005
5 **Bill Easton,** inducted 2004 (left)
   **Cliff Cushman,** inducted 2005 (right)
6 **Merlene Ottey,** inducted 2005
7 **Harrison Dillard,** inducted 2008
8 **Joe Dial,** inducted 2007
9 **Forrest C. "Phog" Allen,** inducted 2007
10 **Karl Salb,** inducted 2006
11 **Bill Alley,** inducted 2005
12 **Jim Hershberger,** inducted 2005
13 **Charlie Tidwell,** inducted 2005
14 **Phil Mulkey,** inducted 2005
15 **Jim Ryun,** inducted 2004
16 **Bill Nieder,** inducted 2005 (left)
   **Al Oerter,** inducted 2004 (right)

17 **Bob Timmons,** inducted 2004
18 **Joe Schrag,** inducted 2007
19 **Billy Mills,** inducted 2004
20 **Glenn Cunningham,** inducted 2004
21 **Kenny Harrison,** inducted 2008
22 **Pinkie Suggs,** inducted 2006
23 **Michael Cox,** inducted 2008
24 **Wes Santee,** inducted 2004

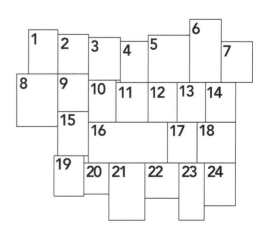

# Appendix E

# World Records Set at the Kansas Relays

Intercollegiate and American records set at the Kansas Relays are too numerous to mention. The following list consists of world records set at the meet.

Allison Mayfield, 2012 KU Relays high jump.

**1925:** Kansas ran 42.0 in the 440-yard relay. The team was composed of George Powers, Tin Luke Wongwai, Howard Rooney and Ray Fisher.

Illinois ran 1:27.0 in the 880-yard relay. The team was composed of Schoch, Yarnell, Hughes, and Evans.

**1926:** Roland Locke of Nebraska ran 9.6 for 100 yards. The record was disallowed because of a tailwind.

**1927:** Notre Dame tied the world record in the 440-yard relay in 41.6.

José Torres ran the 50.6 miles from Kansas City to Memorial Stadium in Lawrence, Kan., in 6 hours, 46 minutes, 41 seconds to better the record by over an hour that had been set in 1882.

Lola Cuzarare ran 30.6 miles from Topeka to Lawrence in 5 hours, 37 minutes, and 45 seconds.

**1930:** Illinois tied the world record by running 41.0 in the 440 relay. The team was composed of Useman, Dickenson, Cave and Paterson.

**1932:** Ex-Kansas University athlete Jim Bausch scored 7,842 points in the decathlon.

**1934:** Kansas State ran 1:01.7 in the 480-yard shuttle hurdle relay.

**1935:** Iowa ran 40.5 in the 440-yard relay and 1:25.2 in the 880-yard relay. Both teams were composed of Dooley, Briggs, Nelson, and Owen.

**1936:** Emporia State ran 10.12 7 in the distance medley relay. Archie San Romani anchored.

**1948:** Charles Fonville of Michigan threw the shot 58 feet, 3/8 of an inch.

Harrison Dillard of Baldwin-Wallace ran the 120-yard high hurdles in 13.6.

**1954:** Texas ran 40.3 for the 440-yard relay. The team consisted of Dean Smith, Jerry Prewit, Al Frieden and Charlie Thomas.

**1956:** Texas ran 40.1 in the 440-yard relay. The team consisted of George Schneider, Jerry Prewit, Bobby Whilden and Frank Daugherty. While considered a world record at the time, it was eventually ratified as a new American record only.

**1957:** Texas ran 39.9 for the 440-yard relay. The team was composed of Wally Wilson, Eddie Southern, Hollis Gainey and Bobby Whilden.

**1968:** Charlie Greene of Nebraska tied the world record by running 10.0 for 100 meters.

**1969:** Kansas ran 9:33.0 in the distance medley relay. The team consisted of Jim Niehouse (880), Randy Julian (440), Thorn Bigley (1320) and Jim Ryun (mile).

**1993:** Phil Mulkey set the world master's decathlon record for the 60-64 age group by scoring 8,155 points.

**2012:** The Kansas Relays, according to the World Record Academy, set the world record for the largest nacho serving. The **4,689-pound nacho plate** bettered the previous Guinness world record by 90 pounds. It was over 80 feet long, two feet wide, and 10 inches deep.

# Appendix F:

# Year-by-Year Summaries

T hese capsule looks at each year the Relays have been held, from 1923 to 2013, were provided courtesy of the University of Kansas Sports Information Department.

Cory Martin and shadow, 2011 downtown shot put.

## 1923

Kansas dominated its first Relays in Memorial Stadium, sweeping the 440 and 880-yard relays, finishing second in the mile baton event and third in the two-mile relay. Merwin Graham and Tom Poor chipped in with individual victories for the Jayhawks, Graham winning the broad jump at 22-1.50 and Poor skimming over 6-0.25 in the high jump. Lester Edwin of Kansas State won his first of two 100-yard dash crowns in 10.1 on a sloppy track while Earle McKown, Emporia State's great pole vaulter, was gathering the first of his three straight titles at 12-9. Illinois' Milton Angier, then the American record holder in the javelin, bagged his specialty with a cast of 193-5. Frazier, Baylor's national AAU hurdles king, finished fourth in the 120-yard highs, which Harold Crawford of Iowa took in 15.5. Almost every event was run in steady rain.

## 1924

Little Occidental College came out of California to make one of the most wholesale sweeps in Kansas Relays history. Coach Joe Pipal's gang slammed all four baton events in the college class: the 880, mile, two mile, and distance medley, and invaded the University division for a triumph in the quarter mile. All four of its wins in the college class went for records, snapping marks made in the first relays. The Californians toured the half in 1:31.5, the mile in 3:23.3, the two mile in 8:12.0 and the medley in 7:48.0.

## 1925

The 1925 Relays was one of the most eventful on record. Kansas and Illinois smashed world records in the 440 and 880-yard relays. Earle McKown of Emporia State pole vaulted to a new intercollegiate record of 13-2.88 and Herb Schwarze of Wisconsin fired the shot 49-10.13 to establish a Relays mark which stood for eight years. The Jayhawk quarter mile quartet of George Powers, Tin Luke Wongwai, Howard Rooney and Ray Fisher hung up 42 seconds flat for their effort. Illinois blazed to 1:27 with Schoch, Yarnell, Hughes and Evans to win the 880. The remainder of the University baton marks went by the boards also. Grinnell shattered the mile at 3:20.4, Iowa State became the first team to dip below eight minutes in the two mile at 7:56.2 and Oregon State lowered the four mile standard to 18:07.8. Ed Weir, the Nebraska track and football great, smashed the 120-yard high hurdles mark with a 15 seconds flat performance. Harold Crawford of Iowa had won the first two meets in 15.5 seconds. Another Cornhusker, Roland Locke, equaled the 100-yard dash mark in 10 seconds flat.

## 1926

Big John Kuck, the Wilson, Kan., behemoth, and Roland Locke, Nebraska's famed sprinter, shared honors at the fourth Relays. The massive Emporia Teachers' weightman won the shot at 49-2.50 and set a javelin mark that survived for 11 years with a heave of 206-6.25. Kuck, who was coached by Bill Hargiss, later a KU track and football tutor, went on to win the shot put at the 1928 Olympics with a pitch over 52 feet. Locke equaled the world record for the 100-yard dash with a steaming 9.6, but it was disallowed because of the wind. Frank Potts, former Colorado track coach, then an Oklahoma pole vaulter, tied for first in that event with Wirsig of Nebraska and Carter of Kansas State at 12-11.88. Occidental ran off with the half mile title in the College class relays.

## 1927

Notre Dame equaled the world record for the quarter-mile relay in a blazing 41.6 seconds, a mark that stood as a Kansas Relays record for three years. Iowa took the half mile baton event in 1:28.3 when Kansas, which finished in front, was disqualified. The Hawkeyes also won the mile in 3:20.1, a tenth of a second off the record they had set the previous season. Melvin Whitlock came all the way from Oregon State to win the javelin throw and his distance of 190-3 was the lowest on record up to that time.

## 1928

Jack Elder, Notre Dame's famous halfback, won the 100-yard dash in 10 seconds flat. Kansas won the quarter-mile relay in 42 seconds and Missouri broke through for its first baton triumph by waltzing to an 8:03 triumph in the two-mile event. Oklahoma won the newly-inaugurated distance medley in 10:37.2. Hippo Howell of the Sooners set a new discus record with a fling of 141-9. Tom Churchill, also of OU, won the first Relays decathlon with a total of 7,385 points.

## 1929

Tom Churchill, Oklahoma's great all-around athlete, returned to snare his second-successive decathlon crown, defeating the talented Oneida, Wilson

"Buster" Charles of Haskell, by 24 points with a score of 7,422. Charles led until the last event in an afternoon of heavy rain. Despite the downpour, two records went down. George Otterness of Minnesota and Tom Warne, Northwestern, climbed over 13-4.75 to share the pole vault title while Daniel Beattie of Colorado State broke Howell's discus standard with a throw of 146-9.5. Jack Elder, who was destined to beat Army the following fall with his storied interception of a Chris Cagle pass, won his second 100-yard dash medal in 9.8. Leas of Indiana whipped KU's distance star Poco Frazier in the 3,000 meters after trailing the Jayhawker until the final 220 yards.

## 1930

Cy Lealand, TCU's famous speed king, smoked to a Kansas Relays record of 9.4 in the 100-yard dash, whipping such noted figures as Claude Bracey of Rice and Michigan's Eddie Tolan.

Tolan, who later won the 100 and 200 meters for the United States in the 1932 Olympics, anchored the Wolverines to a win in the 880-yard relay at 1:26.7, a tenth of a second above the record. His teammates were Seymour, Smith and Campbell. Illinois set a new Relays record of 41-flat in the quarter-mile relay, a figure which also tied the world mark for that distance. Useman, Dickenson, Cave and Paterson were the Illini runners. Indiana snapped the four mile record at 18:03.4 with Brocksmith, Kemp, Leas and Clophorn while Marquette was establishing a new standard for the distance medley at 10:28.7 with Moyan, Sweeney, P.

Walter and J. Walter. Lee Sentman, a lean hurdler from Illinois, won his second 120-yard high hurdles crown, the first man to accomplish the feat since Crawford's opening two victories. Hugh Rhea, Nebraska tackle, bested a field of other renowned footballers in the shot put at 48-6. KU's Jim Bausch placed second and Clarence Munn of Minnesota was fourth. Kansas' Mutt Thornhil shattered the discus record for the third consecutive year when he unfurled a throw of 153-7.25.

## 1931

Six records went by the boards in one of the top Kansas Relays of all-time. Jim Bausch, Kansas' brawny track performer, led the parade when he set a new Relays and American mark in the decathlon at 7,846 points, surpassing the old record set by Ken Doherty in 1929. Lee Sentman won his third 110-meter high hurdles championship for Illinois to become the first man in the history of the Mt. Oread Games to accomplish the feat. He beat such talented performers as Iowa State's Bob Hager and George Saling of Iowa in a time of 14.6 seconds. Saling won the Olympic title in the 120-yard high hurdles the following year. Ed Gordon, Iowa's great broad jumper, established a new mark with a leap of 25-4.38. Illinois set a four mile relay standard that stood at 17:37.8 for 12 years. Kansas set a new record for the 880-yard baton whirl at 1:26.5, clipping a tenth of a second off Nebraska's 1926 time. Clyde Coffman, another of the Jayhawkers' fine all-around stars, interrupted his efforts in the pole vault to run the first leg of that race as well as the 440 relay. He then tied for first in the vault with Lennington of Illinois at 13-6. His teammates were Ralph Sickel, George Jones and Joe Klaner for the short race; Sickel, Bernie Gridley and Klaner for the record breaker. Swift of Washington State won the 100-yard dash beating such top-flighters as Peyton Glass of Oklahoma A&M and Sickel and Lee of Nebraska. Frank Purma, an Ellsworth, Kan., boy, won the discus throw for Illinois at 139-6.5. Glenn Dawson of Oklahoma won the 3,000 meters at 8:53.5. The crowd observed a moment of silence for Knute Rockne, killed in a plane crash near Emporia just a month before the Relays. The great Notre Dame coach had refereed the 1925 Relays.

## 1932

Dr. Garfield Weede's Pittsburg State team ran off with most of the honors in the 10th Relays, sweeping the four college class relay events. The Gorillas won the 880 in 1:28.7, the mile in 3:23.9, the two mile in 8:07.4 and the distance medley in 10:43.5. Hal Thompson of Minnesota blazed to a 9.7 win in the 100m dash, whipping Kansas' Joe Klaner, who finished second. Iowa's George Saling clipped another Jayhawker, Ray Flick, in the 120-yard high hurdles in 14.7. KU's Glenn Cunningham won the first 1,500 meters easily in 4:02.5. Jayhawker Mutt Thornhill returned as discus king on a pitch of 139-6.25. Rain kept all records safe.

## 1933

Four new relay records were hoisted in the 11th Mt. Oread Olympics. Minnesota's foursome of Kilborn, LaRogue, Koblauch and Scheifley won the 480-yard shuttle hurdles in 1:02.3. Indiana set a splendid mark of 3:17.2 in the mile with Carroll, Christiansen, Kennicott and Hellmich while Kansas State rewrote the distance medley in 10:27.4 with Costello, Darnell, McNeal and Landon. Pittsburg State established a new college mile relay mark which stood at 3:17.3 for 13 years. Emporia State snapped the old two mile college standard at 7:50.5. KU's Ed Hall bested Peyton Glass of the Oklahoma Aggies in the 100-yard dash in 10 seconds flat. The Jayhawkers' Glenn Cunningham registered his second 1,500 meters win, beating Oklahoma's Glenn Dawson in 3:53.7.

## 1934

Kansas State's hurdling corps of Doug Russell, Oren Stoner, Larry Schmutz and Joe Knappenberger set a new world record in the 480-yard shuttle in the 12th Kansas Relays with a

time of 1:01.7. B.M. Erwin, a hefty Texas A&M weightman, smashed the nine-year-old standard in the shot put with a toss of 50-3.50. Kansas' Elwyn Dees, who bagged the NCAA title the next year, was only an inch and a half behind. Erwin also won the discus throw at 141-3. Glenn Cunningham downed his most persistent rival, Penn's Gene Venzke, by 20 yards with a fine 4:12.7 performance in the special mile run. Ray Sears, Butler's NCAA two-mile king, grabbed the 1,500 meters in 3:57.5. Sam Allen, Oklahoma Baptist's brilliant hurdler, won his first of three 120-yard Relays' crowns in 14.6, equaling the record established by Illinois' Lee Sentman and Iowa's George Saling. Durwood Crooms, Emporia State's halfback, upset KU's Ed Hall in the 100-yard dash with a 9.8 performance.

## 1935

Eight records went by the boards in this Relays to make it one of the best in the history of the Jayhawker Games. Iowa showed the way by snapping meet marks in the 440 and 880-yard relays in 40.5 and 1:25.2, respectively. Both performances also set world records, the quarter by three-tenths of a second, the half by six-tenths. The same foursome wrote both the marks – Dooley, Briggs, Nelson and Owen. Texas and Kansas State also set records which stood for 12 years, the Longhorns galloping home in 3:16.1 for the mile and the Wildcats notching 7:45.7 for the two mile. Texas' quartet was Austin,

Gruneisen, Edwards and Harvey Wallender. State's foursome featured Nixon, Eberhardt, Dill and O'Reilly. Indiana added the fifth baton record, negotiating the distance medley in 10:21.2. Oklahoma Baptist's Sam Allen hung up a new 120-yard high hurdles figure in 14.5 to snap a three-way hold on the old record of 14.6. J.C. Petty, the bulky Rice discus pegger, hit a new record in his specialty with a fling of 154 feet, thus wiping out the five-year standard hung up by Kansas' Mutt Thornhill. Jayhawker Elwyn Dees completed the day's records, smashing the shot put mark with a flip of 51-3.38. He won the NCAA title two months later. Oklahoma's Glenn Dawson handed Glenn Cunningham his first defeat of the season by winning the special mile in 4:17.4. Clyde Coffman of Kansas took the decathlon crown.

## 1936

Ten thousand fans turned out to watch the greatest Kansas Relays decathlon performance in history as Glenn Morris, wearing the spangles of the Denver AC, established a new American record with 7,576 points to whip Clyde Coffman of Kansas (7,136) and Jay Berwanger, Chicago's great athlete and the first-ever Heisman Trophy winner after the previous fall's football season (6,774). Emporia State set the day's only other record when its distance medley team rambled home in a world-record time of 10:12.7. Archie San Romani, a member of the United States Olympic 1,500 meter team that year, anchored this effort with a 4:12 mile. The Hornets' second team also won the college class in this event at 10:40.3. Indiana's Tommy Deckard set a record in the steeplechase at 9:30.4.

## 1937

Alton Terry, an iron-armed javelin thrower from Hardin-Simmons turned in the day's most startling performance when he flung the iron-tipped wand 229-2.5 to set a new Kansas Relays and American record. Terry's feat smashed an 11-year mark established by Emporia State's mighty John Kuck of 206-6.25 in 1925. Sam Francis, Nebraska's All-American shot putter and fullback, southpawed a record of 51-6 in the event to wipe out Elwyn Dees' figure of 51-3.38 set two years before. Francis also took the discus at 144-3.75. He had placed third in the Olympic shot put in Berlin the previous summer. Archie San Romani, greatest distance runner in Emporia Teachers history, clipped Glenn Cunningham in the special mile with a nifty 4:14.1 performance before 10,000 fans. Cunningham had finished second to New Zealand's Jack Lovelock in the Olympic 1,500 meters the summer before. Jack Vickery of Texas and Tom Stevens of Pittsburg State combined to elevate the high jump mark to 6-6.375. Dick Kearns of Colorado won the decathlon at 6,484, a figure far below Morris' record of the previous spring which he established on his way to the Olympic championship. Indiana scored the greatest sweep the University division baton events ever have seen by capturing the 880, mile, two mile, distance medley and mile team race.

## 1938

Under sullen skies, 10,000 fans sat to watch another wholesale record slaughtering as eight marks went down the drain in the 16th Kansas Relays. Texas' Beefus Bryan, Freddy Wolcott of Rice and Gil Cruter of Colorado hung up marks in the pole vault, 120-yard high hurdles and high jump, respectively, while five baton records were toppled. Bryan cleared 13-11.75 to fracture an eight-year mark held by Northwestern's Tom Warne. Wolcott clipped three-tenths of a second off Sam Allen's timber figure at 14.2 and Cruter twisted over 6-7.56 for a high jump standard that had stood 10 years. Wolcott also placed third in the 100 which went to Clyde Jeffrey of Riverside California JC. Rice set a new sprint medley mark of 3:27.4. Oklahoma A&M lowered the 480-yard shuttle hurdles figure to 1:01.6. Riverside JC snapped the College class 880 standard at 1:26.7. Conners' Aggies broke the junior college sprint medley at 3:22.3. Archie San Romani beat a fancy mile field including Glenn Cunningham, Don Lash and Gene Venzke in 4:13.

## 1939

Glenn Cunningham came back to win the special mile run in 4:29.2, beating Wisconsin's Chuck Fenske in the last 220 yards before 12,000 fans. Three records were broken with Beefus Bryan of Texas upping his own pole vault mark to 14-2 and Elmer Hackney of Kansas State hitting 52-1.50 in the shot put. North Texas State, with Blaine and Wayne Rideout showing the way, cut more than 17 seconds from the College distance medley figure to win in 10:06.9. John Munski of Missouri, who was to win the NCAA mile championship the next summer, paced the Tigers to a distance medley triumph with a 4:12 anchor mile. Rice's Freddy Wolcott, who equaled the world record a year later, gathered his second 120-yard high hurdles title with a fine 14.3 performance. Mozelle Ellerbe, two-time NCAA century champ from Tuskegee, won that crown, inching out Michigan State's Wilbur Greere in the last eight yards at 9.5. E. Lee Todd won the decathlon on 6,557 points.

## 1940

Twelve thousand Kansas Relays fans watched Glenn Cunningham bow out of the Mt. Oread picture by running last in the special mile that now has come to bear his name for the meet each year. Glenn's farewell was a sad one as North Texas State's Blaine Rideout won in a record time of 4:10.1, one of the finest mile performances in the nation that year. Oklahoma's quartet of Bill Lyda, Orv Mattews, George Koettel and Ray Gahan set a new sprint medley record of 3:25.3. Individual highlights found Boyce Gatewood of Texas winning the 120-yard high hurdles in 14.4, Myron Piker of Northwestern edging out Nebraska's Gene Littler in the 100 in 9.8, K-State's Elmer Hackney reaping his third-straight shot put title at 49-5.63 and "Giant" Jack Hughes of Texas beating Minnesota's Bob Fitch in the discus throw at 153-3.50.

## 1941

Stellar performers from Billy Hayes' Indiana team smashed two records at the 19th Kansas Relays. Archie Harris, the great discus pegger, shattered the old platter mark by more than 17 feet when he unfurled a heave of 171-6.75. Anchored by their NCAA 880-yard champion, Campbell Kane, the Hoosiers swept the sprint medley title in 3:25.2 to shave a tenth of a second off Oklahoma's 1940 time. Kane came through with a 1:51.1 burst on the anchor leg. Missouri's John Munski won the special mile in 4:13.4. Carlton Terry of Texas scampered the 100 in 9.4, but was not allowed as a record-tying mark because of a stiff tailwind.

## 1942

With World War II already beginning to squeeze the sports world, the 20th Relays were almost a Big Six affair. Missouri romped off with the 440 and 880-yard relays with such aces as Owen Joggerst, Joe Shu and Don Walters doubling in both races. The times were 41.7 and 1:27.8, respectively. Oklahoma came back to take its old favorite, the sprint medley, in 3:27.1 with the great Bill Lyda furnishing the anchor lap. He also anchored the winning distance medley quartet.

## 1943, 1944, 1945

World War II caused the cancellation of the collegiate portion of the Kansas Relays.

## 1946

The first post-war Kansas Relays got off to a steady start which saw respectable performances all along the line although every record survived. Harrison Dillard, one of the greatest hurdlers of all time, won his first of two 120-yard high hurdles crowns in 14.2. This never reached the Relays records books as the Baldwin-Wallace flash was aided by a seven-mph tailwind. Bill Make of Drake won the Glenn Cunningham mile in 4:24.2, beating Hal Moore of Kansas by 100 yards. Jayhawker Tom Scofield added the Kansas Relays high jump title to his Texas Relays crown at 6-7.88. Baylor smoked to a win in the 440 yard relay at 41.0 with Jim Isaacs, Jim McGilberry, Stoney Cotton and Bill Martineson romping home ahead of Texas. Missouri nabbed the 880 relay when Bob Crowson, the Big Six sprint champ, outraced Earl Collins, Texas' NCAA 220 king, on the anchor leg.

## 1947

Torrential rain and cold in Kansas Relays history reduced the 22nd Relays to a whisper. There were no records broken but Fortune Gordien of Minnesota turned in a splendid performance when he sailed the discus 154-4 and put the shot 51-7 out of a muddy ring. Allen Lawyer sloshed to a surprise win over Texas teammate Charlie Parker in the 100-yard dash, winning in a time of 9.7. Baylor's Bill Martineson was disqualified for two false starts, thus eliminating a much heralded duel before it could start. Colorado's broad jumping specialist, Jack McEwen, won the first post-war decathlon, nosing out Kansas' All-American basketballer, Charlie Black, 6,333-6,284. Texas swept the 440- and 880-yard sprints with Lawyer and Parker joining forces on both occasions. Little Jerry Thompson anchored the Steers home first in the distance medley. Six men tied for first place in the rain-drenched pole vault at 11-6. KU's Tom Scofield and Bonte Kinder of Nebraska divided high jump honors at 6-1, finishing the event on the Jayhawk indoor track under the east wing of the stadium.

## 1948

The 23rd Relays hit a post-war peak before 10,000 fans. Two world records were broken, the shot put by Michigan's Charles Fonville at 58-0.38 and the 120-yard high hurdles by Harrison Dillard at 13.6. Fonville's pitch was almost a foot beyond the old world mark of 57-1 set by LSU's Jack Torrance in 1934 and five and a half feet farther than Elmer Hackney's Kansas Relays figure. Dillard had to be fast to whip Arkansas' Clyde Scott, also one of the nation's best timber toppers. The Baldwin-Wallace phenom shaved one tenth of a second off the accepted world mark held jointly by Georgia's Spec Towns and Fred Wolcott of Rice. Four other records went by the wayside in 1948. Anchored by Don Gehrmann, who bagged the NCAA 1,500 meter title two months afterward, Wisconsin set a new two mile relay mark at 7:44.7, clipping a full second off Kansas State's 12-year standard. Gehrmann's teammates were Jenson, Kamner and Whipple. Dave Bolen, a terrific quarter-miler from Colorado, moved into the 400-meter hurdles to score a close victory over Missouri's Dick Ault in a record time of 53.0. Oklahoma's Herman Nelson had held the old mark of 55.4 since 1936. East Texas State raced to a new sprint medley mark in the college class, a foursome of Valls, Salinas, Colorado and Mercado scampering home

in 3:31 to cut 16 seconds off the old record established by Abilene Christian the previous spring. The Texas Aggies accounted for the sixth new mark when they smashed a 12-year-old standard of 3:16.1 in the mile relay which Texas etched on the books in 1935. Coach Frank Anderson's Cadets turned in a 3:15.6 performance to add the Kansas crown to their Texas Relays title. The following week they added Drake to the conquest to complete the Midwestern Grand Slam. Don Cordon, E.G. Bilderback, Ray Holbrook and Art Harnden filled out the team.

## 1949

Don Gehrmann, Wisconsin's Olympic miler, and Bob Walters, a virtual unknown from Texas, were the individual standouts of the fourth post-war Kansas Relays. Gehrmann outlegged another distance ace, Texas grad Jerry Thompson, in the record-equaling time of 4:10.1, in the Glenn Cunningham Mile. Walters elevated the high jump record to 6-8.19. Gehrmann's effort matched that of Blaine Rideout of North Texas State in 1941. Walter's performance wiped out Gil Cruter's 10-year-old standard of 6-7.56. The Longhorn junior wasn't picked to win, much less establish a new Relays standard. Other sterling individual performances were flashed by Herb Hoskins of Kansas State, who negotiated the broad jump at 24-9, the second longest leap on the Relays books at that time. Denver's Jerome Biffle won the 100 in 9.8, picked up second in the broad jump and a tie for third in the high jump. Oklahoma A&M whipped Kansas for the two-mile relay title in the day's best race, with Harold Tarrant out-blazing the Jayhawkers' terrific Pat Bowers in the anchor leg by four yards. Both teams smashed Wisconsin's one-year-old record with the Cowpokes going on the books in 7:41.0. However, the Jayhawks leapt into the limelight for the first time since Cunningham's heyday by toppling Missouri for the four-mile crown and scoring an individual first with sophomore Jack Greenwood in the hurdles. Nebraska's Jim McConnell won the decathlon with 6,698 points, 30 more than former national champ Bill Terwilliger.

## 1950

Eight new records marked the Silver Anniversary of the Kansas Relays as competing squads shot to their highest post-war peak in rewriting the books on a warm, windy day. Voted most outstanding was the feat of Oklahoma's Bill Carroll, who sprang 14-5 in the pole vault to smash an 11-year-old mark held by Beefus Bryan of Texas at 14-2. The host Jayhawkers took a hand in the baton division record splintering when Cliff Abel, Herb Semper, Pat Bowers and Bob Karnes erased a 12-year-old standard in the four-mile relay. Bill Easton's foursome ran a 17:34.2 to wipe out the old 17:37.8 mark held by Illinois. Given a fat lead, Michigan's Don McEwen bested Wisconsin's Don Gehrmann in the anchor lap of the distance medley to pace the Wolverines to a new

mark of 10:09.7. So swift was the pace in the college mile relay that three teams: Abilene Christian, Los Angeles City College and Oklahoma Baptist all smashed the old standard of 3:17.3. The winners' time was 3:16.8. Rice fractured the University figure for the same event in 3:15.0 with Tom Cox hurtling an unofficial 46.8 in the anchor leg. North Texas State pared seven-tenths of a second off the College half-mile relay mark in 1:26.0. Compton Junior College whizzed 3:27.1 in the college sprint medley for another record. Gehrmann won the featured Glenn Cunningham Mile in 4:16.4, whipping Javier Montes of Texas Western by 15 yards. Nebraska's Jim McConnell paced a fine decathlon field with 7,120 points to gather his second consecutive title. Brayton Norton, Santa Ana JC sophomore, was second with 7,083 points.

## 1951

Nebraska's Don Cooper kicked a hole in the dripping gray sky above the 26th Kansas Relays to join the charmed circle of pole vaulters when he sailed 15-0.13 to erect a new national collegiate record. However, the mark lasted only two hours before Don Laz of Illinois sailed 15-1 in a triangular meet at Los Angeles after hearing the news of Cooper's effort. Cooper thus joined Cornelius Warmerdam, Laz, and Bob Richards, also of Illinois, at the magic 15-foot level. He also became the first collegian to manage the height outdoors. His feat overshadowed a photo finish in the Glenn Cunningham Mile which saw Fred Wilt, the GI from Indiana,

suddenly open a 15-yard lead over Wisconsin-ex Don Gehrmann, as they headed into the backstretch of the gun lap, and then barely outlast the lean Badger at the tape. Oklahoma dominated the Relays by capturing the 440, two mile and mile events. Kansas won the distance medley and four-mile. Texas A&M's brawny Darrow Hooper was the meet's only double winner when he captured the shot in 51-8 and the discus at 145-5. He was only the third sophomore in history to win a Relays shot title and went on to top the NCAA. Ken Stearns, the 6-6 Baker basketball center, placed the Orangemen in the individual winner's circle for the first time in meet history when he won the high jump at 6-4.63. Jack Greenwood of Kansas and Thane Baker of Kansas State added individual championships for the Big Seven when they won the 120-yard high hurdles and 100-yard dash, respectively.

## 1952

With Wes Santee, its fabulous sophomore distance ace earning the Most Outstanding Performer accolade, Kansas was one of the four record-breakers and three double-winners in the 27th Jayhawker Games. The "Ashland Flyer" earned the honor by anchoring the winning four-mile relay quartet in 4:11.6 and spinning a 3:02.0 three-quarters carry for the distance medley champions. With Lloyd Koby, Art Dalzell and Herb Semper running ahead of Santee, Bill Easton's crew set a new Relays mark of 17:18.3 in the four-mile, just 2.2 seconds off the national collegiate standard. Oklahoma and Texas joined KU in the double-winner's circle; a Sooner foursome of Harry Lee, Quanah Cox, Chuck Coleman and J.W. Mashburn smoked to a new mark of 3:14.8 in the mile relay, nipping Texas A&M at the wire to reverse a decision at the Texas Games which saw OU disqualified after finishing ahead of their Southwest Conference rivals. John Jacobs' troupe also successfully defended its two-mile title. The Longhorns bagged the 440 and 880-yard relays, equaling a long-standing record of 1:25.2 in the latter race. This figure was spun by a quartet of Dean Smith, Carl Mayer, Jim Brownhill and Charles Thomas, thus matching the standard which Iowa's 1935 team had held alone for 17 years. Lee Yoder, Arkansas hurdler, and Jim Gerhardt, Texas graduate student, set the other records. Yoder beat KU's Bob DeVinney, later to become NCAA champion and record holder, in the 400-meter hurdles, in 52.2 seconds. Gerhardt, a former Rice athlete, leaped 47-2 in the hop-step-jump, erasing the 46-9 record set in 1936. Texas A&M's Darrow Hooper became the first man in Relays history to win the shot put-discus double for the second successive year with respective casts of 53-9 and 152-8.25. Ted Wheeler, a towering Iowa sophomore, upset Javier Montes in the 1,500 meters in 3:54.4. Thane Baker of Kansas State reversed a Texas Relays' defeat by beating Dean Smith in a 9.5 century.

## 1953

Forty-five degree temperatures and gusty winds kept all records safe in the 28th running of the Kansas Relays. Nebraska's Glenn Beerline would have

toppled the triple jump mark had it not been for the friendly tailwind; he bounded 48-4, more than a foot beyond the existing record mark. John Bennett of Marquette scored the Hill Toppers' first Relays victory in a standard event when he leaped 25-4 in the broad jump, just an eighth-inch short of Ed Gordon's 22-year-old record. He upset a fine field including Texas A&M's Bobby Ragsdale and Neville Price, Oklahoma's Big Seven champion. Bennett and Ragsdale went on to finish 1-2 in the NCAA a couple of months later. Oklahoma's Bruce "Bulldog" Drummond scored another upset when he outlasted Rick Ferguson, Iowa's 1953 NCAA two-mile champion, and Sture Landqvist of Oklahoma A&M, with a 4:15.1 effort in the Glenn Cunningham Mile. He came back to anchor the Sooners to the distance medley title. Darrow Hooper, Texas A&M's streamlined muscleman, won the Most Outstanding Performer accolade when he completed the first Relays twin triple crown with victories in the shot put (55-3) and discus throw (163-2). Kansas State's great Olympic sprinter, Thane Baker, fired the Wildcats to their first baton in years since 1936 when he anchored home their 880 team in 1:26.4 with a closing surge of 20.1. He also brought the mile relay foursome home in second with a 46.7 anchoring time, and became the first man in history to claim three consecutive 100-yard dash titles when he ran 10.0.

## 1954

Kansas' Wes Santee churned the second-swiftest mile to date in American history to win the Glenn Cunningham Mile feature of the 29th

Relays, with a smoking 4:03.1. Challenged early by Bjorn Bogerud of Oklahoma A&M, Bruce Drummond, an Oklahoma grad, and Drake's Ray McConnell, Santee pulled out after the second quarter and reduced the race to a question of whether or not he would reach the four-minute mile, which was to be turned in two months later by England's Roger Bannister. As good as he was, Santee had to share the spotlight with Texas' torrid sprint foursome of Dean Smith, Jerry Prewit, Al Frieden and Charlie Thomas, who ran two-tenths below the world record at 40.3 in the quarter-mile relay. The same crew also swept the 880 in 1:25.5, while Smith, Frieden and Thomas placed 1-2-3 in the 100. Two Southern Methodist relay teams wore the Mustangs' name in the blue-ribbon circle for the first time. A combination of Ad Bartek, Al Bartek, David Waver and Don Morton edged past Iowa, Missouri and Texas A&M in a four-team blanket finish to win the mile relay in 3:15.8, only the fourth time in history the winner has dipped under 3:16. Morton, Ad Bartek, Tommy Armstrong and Weaver captured the sprint medley from strong Notre Dame and Oklahoma A&M in 3:26.6. Three other records were set before the record crowd of 16,000. Abilene Christian's quartet of George Adrian, Burl McCoy, Don Conder and Leon Lepard pressed four-tenths off the College mile relay standard at 3:16.2. Iowa's Rich Ferguson brought down the 3,000-meter steeplechase mark of 9:20.4. Central Michigan's Jim Podoley outlasted a slim five-man decathlon field on 6,128 points. Two young Kansans, Leon Wells and Don Sneegas, won surprise individual titles; Wells tied for first in the high jump with Texas' Bob Billings. TCU's Wes Ritchey missed a triple in the latter event when he fell to fourth place.

## 1955

Oklahoma A&M marched in the 30th Kansas Relays, sweeping three baton events en route to establishing two of the meet's five records. Ralph Higgins' Cowpokes tore more than three seconds off Oklahoma's three-year-old mile mark with a scorching 3:11.6 and lowered another Sooner record in the sprint medley with a flight of 3:22.8. A quartet of Jackie Hayes, Fred Schermerhorn, Bill Heard and J.W. Mashburn got the first mark. Mashburn, Hayes, Marion, Muncrief and Heard nailed the sprint medley. A combination of Heri Geller, Bjorn Bogerud, Sture Landqvist and Fred Eckhoff added the four-mile. Kansas broke through this surge by winning the distance medley while Texas was flying to triumphs in the 440, 880 and two-mile. The Longhorns' Dean Smith earned the meet's Most Outstanding Performer award with blazing speed in the two sprint triumphs and a wind-blown 100-yard dash victory of 9.4. North Texas State notched the only College class record in the sprint medley and tied the mile. An Eagle combine of Mike Hegler, Boyd Dollar, Dean Renfro and Paul Patterson ran 3:24.2 in the former event to prune almost three seconds off Compton Junior College's old 3:27.1 standard which had existed since 1949. Patterson barely stood off Emporia State's Billy Tidwell in the anchor lap. Jimmie Weaver and Jimmie Huffman ran ahead of Dollar and Patterson to tie the 3:16.2 mile mark established just a year earlier by Abilene Christian. Central Michigan veteran Jim Podolev and Kansas freshman Kent Floerke accounted for the only individual records. The former eclipsed his own one-year-old decathlon total of 6,128 by accumulating 6,340 to win over a good 11-man field, which included Oklahoma A&M's Eddie Ray Roberts and Michigan State's Joe Savoldi. Floerke smashed the old 47-2 hop-step-jump mark four times with a 49-0.50 leap on his final trial. Running in rain, hail and wind, Wes Santee could do no better than 4:11.4 in the Glenn Cunningham Mile. He beat Ted Wheeler, a former Iowa Hawkeye, by 25 yards. Two other freshmen joined Floerke in upset victories: KU's Bob Nicholson kept Iowa's Rich Ferguson from his third-straight 3,000-meter steeplechase title, while Gene O'Connor nipped varsity teammate Ray Russell in the 400-meter hurdles.

## 1956

Texas' blazing foursome of George Schneider, Jerry Prewitt, Bobby Whilden and Frank Daugherty bettered the world 440-yard relay record (it eventually was ratified as a new American mark only) at 40.1 to headline the 31st Relays. This clocking lopped two-tenths off the ancient Relays figure established by Iowa in 1935 and tied by the 1952 Texas quartet. Eight other meet or stadium records were toppled. Baylor gunned down the University 880 standard. Howard Payne, coached by 1955 Relays Referee Cap Shelton, ripped seven seconds off the College two-mile mark. Missouri Valley lowered the Invitational sprint medley to 3:35.0. The decathlon record went down for the fourth-straight year when Wyoming's Phil Mulkey won in a mild surprise. Defending champion Jim Podoley of Central Michigan could not defend due to an injury and thus missed the opportunity to complete a rare triple. Podoley also had won the 10-event grind in 1954. Kansas' Bill Nieder, who became the first collegian to crash 60 feet just a week earlier, added more than a foot to Charles Fonville's old world record of 58-00.25 and set a Relays shot put record at 59-7.88. Competing on an exhibition basis, world record holder Parry O'Brien fired 60-02.50. This pair was to finish 1-2 in the Melbourne Olympics in November. Kansas State's Gene O'Connor pared three-tenths off the 400-meter hurdles record, down to 52. Arkansas' Lee Yoder had held the old mark since 1952. Compton College's Charles Dumas, later to become the world's first seven-footer, set a new stadium high jump mark at 6-8.75. Of equal brilliance was Whilden's 9.4 in the 100, giving him half-share of the record, which TCU's Cy Leland had held since 1930. Baylor's 880 quartet of Bobby Herod, Clyde Hart, Ray Vickery and halfback Del Shofner, which had run 40.2 behind Texas in the quarter, scorched 1:24.6 to lop six-tenths off the previous record. Allen Tipps, Louie Hays, Don Sheppard and Les Fambrough motored Howard Payne's new two-mile mark. Abilene Christian recorded the old mark in 1940 with a time of 7:28.4. A ninth record was disallowed when Iowa was disqualified in the University two mile. The Hawkeyes had run 7:40.5, a half-second below Oklahoma A&M's 1952 mark. Texas was declared the winner in 7:41.1. Fifteen thousand spectators saw the show.

## 1957

Another smoking sprint foursome from Texas – Wally Wilson, Eddie Southern, Hollis Gainey and Bobby Whilden – wrote a new world 440 relay record of 39.9 to feature the 32nd running of the Kansas Relays. The Longhorns thus lowered their listed world mark of 40.2 and the pending 40.1 erected the previous year. The Steers also upset host Kansas in the 880 with a new record of 10:04.2 in the distance medley. Eleven other meet records also were discarded. Kansas became the first college team in history to dip below 17:00 in the four-mile relay, clocking a new intercollegiate time of 16:57.8. Jerry McNeal's 4:12.7 anchor leg carried the team. With Rom Skutka doubling back from the four-mile, the Jayhawkers also set a new two-mile standard of 7:32.3. They completed the day by setting a school record in the mile (3:12.6), besting Colorado, North Texas, and upsetting Texas in a four-team blanket finish. Kiowa senior Billy Tidwell pulled Emporia State to college-class marks in the sprint medley (3:22.6) and mile (3:15.1) to earn the Most Outstanding Athlete award. Upsets were the motif in the individual events at the 1957 Relays. Missouri's Charlie Batch unwound the swiftest 120-high hurdles flight in conference history, 14.1, to upset Southern in that race. Kansas freshman Cliff Cushman dethroned Kansas State's Gene O'Conner in the 400-meter intermediates with a new mark of 51.9. It was Cushman's first effort in this event. Col-

orado's Ken Yob, a 230-footer, fell to New Mexico's Buster Quist in the javelin throw. Yob's teammate, sophomore Jesse Undlin, skied 14-0 in the pole vault to surpass a field of veterans. Bill Nieder, just a year out of KU, fired the longest heave in the world for 1957, 62-2, to whip Olympic champion Parry O'Brien in a shot put exhibition of post-grad giants.

## 1958

Sixteen thousand fans watched the first two-day meet in Relays history as the old high school extravaganza was integrated into the University-College field. Oklahoma won the greatest sprint medley relay in track history to lead a parade of two new intercollegiate records and 10 meet marks in the 33rd Kansas Relays. Drawing an unofficial 1:48 cleanup leg from sophomore Gail Hodgson, the Sooners blazed 3:19.5 to cut down the 3:20.2 intercollegiate listing posted by Wes Santee-anchored Kansas in 1954 and California's pending 3:19.8, unwrapped two weeks earlier at Texas. Gary Parr, Johnny Pellow and Deem Govems ran ahead of the smooth South African. This foursome had to perform well in order to edge Houston (3:19.6), Oklahoma State (3:19.7) and Nebraska (3:20.0), all of which cut under the listed intercollegiate mark. No less electrifying was Texas' 3:09.1 mile relay burst, which brought down California's ancient intercollegiate figure of 3:09.4 (1941) as

well as the 3:11.6 meet standard erected by Oklahoma State in 1955. Eddie Southern clocked in an unofficial 44.6 anchor leg, after firing the Longhorns to the 440 title as well. Wally Wilson, Drew Dunlap and Jim Holt ran ahead of Southern in the mile. The fans got to see Hodgson warm-up for Saturday's sprint medley with a 4:07.4 anchor carry in the distance medley on Friday as the Sooners churned 9:50.8 to beat arch-rival Texas by 13 yards and rip 13 seconds off the Longhorns' one-year-old meet record. Another South African sophomore, Ernst Kleynhans, clocked a 3:02 three-quarters ahead of Hodgson. Hi Gernert and Bob Ringo completed an all-sophomore contingent ahead of him. Drawing 1:50.0 in the third carry from Dave Lean and 1:48.8 in the cleanup from Willie Atterberry, Michigan State wheeled to a new meet two-mile record of 7:24.8 to beat Kansas and lift the Jayhawkers' year-old record of 7:32.3. Staked to a six-yard lead on the field by Orlando Hazley's leadoff burst, Oklahoma State barreled 1:23.5 to destroy Texas' year-old 1:24.2 mark in the 880. Howard Payne ran its third consecutive record, clocking in the college two-mile at 7:39.9. Texas' Bruce Parker finally brought down the 229-2.50 javelin record (an American and intercollegiate mark by Hardin-Simmons' Alton Terry in 1937) with 232-8. John Macy, from Houston, clocked 9:12.5 for a steeplechase mark. Kansas State's Gene O'Connor clipped his upsetter of 1957, KU's Cliff Cushman, in a record 51.3 flight of 400-meter hurdles. Oklahoma sophomore Dee Givens dethroned Oklahoma State's Orlando Hazley in a 9.5 century. East Texas State's Buddy McKee upset Nebraska's Keith Gardner at 14.0 in the 120 highs. Phil Mulkey, competing for the Memphis A.C., upped his own decathlon record to 6,544.

273

## 1959

Kansas scored the greatest baton sweep since Indiana's four-title surge of 1936 in the 34th Relays, which were telescoped into one day of action following an unprecedented postponement of Friday's show because of heavy rain. Bill Easton's Jayhawkers upset Texas to bag their first 440 victory since 1931, then added the sprint medley, two-mile and four-mile to its string. They also crowned three individual kings, Ernie Shelby in the broad jump, Bill Alley in the javelin and Charlie Tidwell in the 100 meters. Tidwell was named the meet's Most Outstanding Athlete for his 9.9 century victory plus anchoring the 440 and spinning the third leg of the sprint medley. Alley authored a new record with a heave of 254-9 off the slippery turf, appending 22 feet to the year-old mark of Texas' Bruce Parker, who finished third trying to defend his crown. Two Houston aces, John Macy and Jack Smyth, plus New Mexico's Dick Howard, joined Alley in individual record-smashing. Macy toured the two-mile in 8:59.2 to bring down the year-old standard of 9:06.9 erected by teammate Jerry Smartt. Smyth added three inches to his own triple jump mark at 50-1. Howard ripped more than a second off Gene O'Conner's 51.3 400-meter hurdles record at 50.1. He joined Tidwell, Shelby and Alley as NCAA champions two months later in Lincoln. Carrying the colors of the Memphis Olympic club, Phil Mulkey became the first man in Relays history to bag three decathlon titles, winning on a total of 6,302 points. A Central Michigan foursome of Ken Blalock, Bob Waters, Dick Anspach and Dave Myers set the only new baton mark, flying 3:14.7 in the college mile. One final event, the broad jump, was completed Friday before a second downpour forced postponement of the opening day's program until Saturday. Despite the rain and mud, Shelby grazed Ed Gordon's ancient 25-4.375 record (for Iowa in 1931) at 25-3.25.

## 1960

Gusty wind and a new track, still too soft for good running, preserved every record save one in the 35th Kansas Relays. East Texas State's Jim Baird gunned down the oldest mark in the books, Ed Gordon's 25-4.375 broad jump from 1931, with a 25-5.25 span in Friday's opening action. Even then, he nipped Emporia State's Noel Certain by only a fourth of an inch. All were jumping in front of a gusty wind, but referee Volney Ashford ruled the new mark would count. East Texas also tied two College class marks, the 440 and 880, and added the sprint medley to become the first team in this division to bag three baton titles since 1933. Sid Garton, barely beaten by KU's defending champion Charles Tidwell in the 100, anchored a 41.4 burst in the quarter and a 1:26.0 in the half. He also ran the second 220 leg on the sprint medley foursome. Tidwell smoked 9.4 in the century, but excessive wind kept him from sharing the meet record. Former Kansas NCAA champion Bill Nieder, competing for the Presidio as a first lieutenant, set a new stadium shot put mark of 63-10.25, after hitting a prodigious 66-1.25 in warmups. The most exciting race of the day found Jayhawk sophomore Bill Dotson holding off a last-second lunge by his high school rival, Archie San Romani, Jr., Wichita freshman, to win the 1,500 in 4:00.4. Colorado's 190-lb. fullback, Ted Woods, later to become an NCAA 400-meter champion, reeled in 10 yards of a Cliff Cushman lead to bring the Buffaloes home a yard ahead of Kansas in the best baton match of the day. Houston's Bobby Weise handed Missouri's defending NCAA discus champion, Dick Cochran, his first defeat by a collegian in two years, 169-4.50 to 164-0.50. Sixteen thousand witnessed the two-day show.

## 1961

Baylor's Southwest conference champions unwound their greatest onslaught in Kansas Relays history, capturing six clear-cut championships and tying for a seventh to dominate the 36th Mt. Oread Games. John Fry opened his assault Friday by bagging the Bears' first individual title in meet annuals with a 170-7.50 discus cast. Bill Kemp and Bob Mellgren added wins in the 100 and steeplechase while Eddie Curtis shared the high jump crown. Kemp also anchored winning Bear combines in the 440 and 880 relays. Lone Star state teams dominated elsewhere too. Texas Southern flashed to record bursts of 41.0 and 1:24.2

in the College 440 and 880 relays. Houston spun the nation's fastest four-mile of the young season, 17:02.3. North Texas State blazed a record 9:49.3, fastest time of the year to date, to win the University distance medley. Dick Menchaca swept the Eagles from fourth place into a 12-yard lead with a 2:59.9 three-quarters carry and John Cooper wired-in a 4:07.1 cleanup mile to whip Missouri, Kansas and Houston. A Saturday crowd of 13,500 watched Drake win its first baton title since 1947, sweeping from far back to edge Kansas in the two-mile by three yards on 7:30.00, equaling the nation's best mark to date. Emporia State fled to a new college mile record of 3:12.2. Howard Payne bagged its sixth successive College two-mile championship on a record 7:32.00. John Kelly, the former Stanford great, pushed the triple jump record out to 50-3 as ex-Kansas ace, Kent Floerke, fouled a 50-9 on his final leap. Phil Mulkey won his fifth decathlon crown on a record 7,268. Jim Grelle, a former Oregon great, defeated Ermie Cunliffe by 20 yards to win the Glenn Cunningham Mile in 4:07.4. The heralded pole vault dual between Oklahoma's J.D. Martin and Oklahoma State's sophomore sensation, George Davies, failed to reach the predicted 15-0, as they split the blue ribbon at 14-10.

## 1962

Women made their first appearance in the Relays in a limited number of events this year. Eleven Tigers from Texas Southern scored the greatest divisional sweep in Kansas Relays history, bagging all six baton crowns in the college section and garnishing two of them with records. Coach Stan Wright's invincibles, paced by a lithe freshman, Ray Saldler, boiled a sprint medley record of 3:19.8 and lowered the mile mark to 3:11.6 in Friday's opening session. They returned Saturday to annex the two-mile in 7:43.1, the 440 in 41.3, the 880 in 1:24, the distance medley in 10.09.2 and climaxed with another new mile standard of 3:11.00. They did it with ridiculous ease too, their smallest winning margin measuring 15 yards. Only three teams ever had won as many as four baton hauls in the previous 26 years of Kansas foot-racing. The Tigers' efforts overshadowed all else, but there were many other outstanding performances in a meet lashed by winds which gusted up to 11 miles per hour. McMurry's Bill Miller upset Oklahoma Olympian Anthony Watson with a record 25-6 in the broad jump. Bob Swafford brought Texas Tech its first Kansas gold medal in history when he beat two post-grad aces, Rex Stucker, formerly of Kansas State, and ex-Kansan Cliff Cushman, in the 400-meter hurdles, clocking 52.3. Discus thrower John McGrath reaped Occidental's first individual crown since 1926 when he threw 172-3.75. Rice's Fred Hansen beat the world's first 16-foot pole vaulter, John Uelses, with a record lift of 15-6.25, almost five inches higher than his celebrated opponent. Missouri's Don Smith and Texas' Ray Cunningham added the second leg of eventual Midwest Grand Slams by winning the shot put (57-4.25) and high hurdles (13.9), respectively. With Bill Dostson anchoring in 4:05.2, Kansas gunned down the four-mile relay mark in 16:53.1, beating a new menace, Southern Illinois, by 150 yards with the swiftest time ever by a Big Eight combine. Missouri clipped the Jayhawkers in the two-mile on a record 7:24.2, up to that time the best mark any conference team had unfurled for that event. The Tigers got a 1:50.2 closing half from their 1962 NCAA 440 runner-up, Jim Baker, to hold off Dotson. Jerry McFadden, Greg Pelster and Bill Rawson ran ahead of Baker. Nine thousand watched the 37th Games.

## 1963

Rice's Fred Hansen catapulted the first 16-foot vault in Kansas Relays history to highlight a parade of six records in the 38th Mount Oread Games. The defending champion added a half-foot to his one-year-old mark of 16-6.25 in near-darkness as he battled against the classiest field in Relays history. Fired home by a cleanup 4:06.6 anchoring mile by Tom O'Hara, Chicago Loyola ripped almost 13 seconds off the college distance medley record in 9:54.2. The Tigers had a 50-yard lead going into the anchor lap, but O'Hara chilled Major Adams with his scorching mile to come home 60 lengths in front. Southern also was under the old mark at 10:06.3. TCU high jumper Jackie Upton set a new mark of 6-8.75 while another Southwest conference ace, Rice's Ed Red, was stretching the javelin to 256-1.50. Yul Yost, 32-year-old senior for the host Jayhawkers, kept another Southwestern athlete out of the shot put title when he beat Texas A&M's Danny Roberts, 57.75 to 57-5. Robin Lingle, sitting out the one-year transfer rule after moving from Army to Missouri, clipped Emporia State's Texas Relays champion, John Camien, in 4:04.8 to bag the Glenn Cunningham Mile. Nate Adams brought Purdue its first gold medal of all-time by edging Omaha's "Rocket" Roger Sayers in a 9.6 100. Kansas upset arch-rival Missouri in the University two-mile when Kirk Hagan fired a 1:49.2 cleanup carry into Big Eight indoor champion Greg Pelster. However, the Jayhawkers lost their usual four-mile conquest to an all-Australian lineup from Houston. Lauie Elliott outstepped Tonnie Coane, 4:11.7 to 4:12.6 in the anchor leg to bring the Cougars home four yards on top in 17:11, the fifth-best time in meet history. Nebraska won its first sprint medley title of all-time when Gil Gebo, normally a quarter-miler, unreeled a 1:48.6 anchor carry to hold off a great trio of rival anchormen: Bill Frazier (Iowa), Bill Cornell (Southern Illinois) and Pelster. McMurry's Bill Miller completed the first long jump in history when he bounded 25-2.75 ft. Former Oregon ace Dave Edstrom, later an Air Force Lieutenant at Oxnard, Calif., AFB, upset Phil Mulkey's bid for a sixth-straight decathlon crown when he scored 7,423 points against the latter's 7,316. An opening-day crowd of 3,000 lifted overall attendance to 14,000 as both sessions were favored by balmy, windy weather.

## 1964

The Missouri Tigers, led by miler Robin Lingle, prevented the Southwest Conference team from completely dominating the relay events at the 39th annual Kansas Relays. The Black and Gold from Mizzou took the four-mile relay on Friday in record time of 16:41.6. Lingle raced 4:01 in the anchor

mile and beat Hadley of Kansas in this event after having to make up a 50 yard deficit. The Jayhawkers held the old mark of 16:53.1 with their 1962 team. The Big Eight indoor champs also took a blue ribbon on Saturday with the best time in the two-mile relay. On Saturday, the Southwest Conference copped four of five baton events with SMU taking both the 440 and the 880 yard relays; Texas took the blue ribbon in the distance medley and Rice edged Nebraska in the meet's final event, the mile relay. In all, there were nine meet records shattered and two others tied. During the first day of the Kansas track and field carnival, the Tigers' record-breaking performance and Jim Ryun's 4:11 mile were the top two performances. The Wichita East miler easily shattered Archie San Romani's record by six and a half seconds. Geoff Walker of Houston ran the fastest 5,000 meters ever recorded at the Kansas Relays at 14:36.0 on Friday before 3,000 fans. Even though the weather was far from ideal, Saturday's 9,000 fans and the athletes were able to fare well with the cool 56-degrees as six meet records were surpassed and two others equaled. Texas A&M's Dan Roberts etched a new shot put record with a heave of 60-2.75, which bettered KU's Neider's best effort in 1956 by over six inches. Roberts also won the discus to become only the eighth man in the history of the meet to cop both the shot and the discus the same year. SMU recorded a new standard in the 880 relay with a 1:23.4 clocking led by the Ponies' colorful and talented anchorman, John Roderick. The Texas Longhorns won a KU Relays watch for their performance in the distance medley with a record-breaking time of 9:48, which was 1.3 faster than the previous mark. Hylke van der Wal of the University of Manitoba ran the 3,000 meter steeplechase in record time 8:56.3. Texas Southern's domination of the college division was terminated as Lincoln University of Missouri won as many baton titles as

the Texas Tigers. John Camien's anchor mile aided the Emporia State Hornets in rewriting the College distance medley mark to 9:48.4 as the E-State miler turned in a 4:03.2 time for the final four laps. Even though the host team was frustrated in the relay events, KU Coach Bill Easton had three individual winners. Sophomore sprinter Bob Hanson won the 100 in 9.7, Tyce Smith took first in the high jump at 6-4.25 and Captain Floyd Manning won the pole vault by clearing 15-9.25. Missouri's Robin Lingle was voted the meet's Outstanding Performer by the sports writers and broadcasters, beating out standouts such as Texas A&M shot putter Dan Roberts, SMU sprinter John Roderick, Wichita East miler Jim Ryun and Emporia State miler John Camien.

## 1965

The 40th annual Kansas Relays ended Saturday in a blaze of glory, with 12 new records written into the books for a two-day total of 19. Thanks to almost ideal weather, 14,000 fans were in Memorial Stadium to savor the show. To add to the enjoyment, Big Eight athletes dominated this 40th annual show, which was dedicated to the late Don Pierce, former KU sports publicist. For two days, Big Eight teams won championships in the 880 relay, the distance medley, the 440 relay, the two-mile and four-mile relays. In individual events the Big Eight was first in the high jump, the javelin, the 100 yard dash and the 400-meter hurdles. However, two non-Big Eight athletes stole the show.

Clarence Robinson of New Mexico broad jumped to a record 26-2.50 on Friday and then returned Saturday to write a new mark in the triple jump at 50-6.50. Robinson was voted the meet's top athlete, an honor restricted to College-University performers. The other "show stealer" was Wichita East's fabulous Jim Ryun, who ran 4:04.8 in the Friday open high school mile, then returned Saturday with a 1:47.7 half-mile anchor that gave East a national record in the two-mile relay at 7:42.9. Another double winner was George Scott of Oklahoma City, who won the tough 5,000-meter run on Friday and the Glenn Cunningham Mile on Saturday. Phil Mulkey of Memphis won his seventh decathlon in 11 tries and promptly announced that this would be his final one. Texas A&M giant Randy Matson made his heralded appearance and promptly pushed the shot put record to 65-10.75. He got the record on his fifth throw. Kansas State's Bill Floerke apparently shook the injury bug, firing the javelin 266-5.50 for a record on his final toss of the day. Saturday's crowd was in a holiday mood. It wanted to be entertained, and entertained it was. Floerke's record javelin throw brought the crowd to its feet for a short time, but Ryun's anchor run while East was working for the national record had the fans on their feet for almost half the race. And the record-setting East team got a standing ovation from the throng when it climbed onto the platform for its first place medals. It was one of the finest Relays in modern history. All events were on schedule, there was a minimum of fuss and no complaints were registered, even though some relay teams were disqualified. In the Glenn Cunningham Mile, Kansas freshman Gene McClain was second with a fine 4:10.3, and K-State sophomore Charles Harper was third at 4:10.8. Coach Easton called the work of the two men "excellent." It was fitting that the most thrilling race was saved for last, the University mile relay. Southern Illinois won

in 3:09.3, slightly ahead of second place Nebraska at 3:09.3 and Oklahoma State was third at 3:09.6.

## 1966

The sun never did break through the clouds on the final day of the 41st Kansas Relays, but it made no difference as athletes broke seven records at Memorial Stadium on a soggy track. Among all the records set, no feat was more delightful to the crowd of 15,000 than the 3:55.8 mile run by Kansas' own freshman phenom, Jim Ryun. It was Ryun's second sub-four minute mile in three days and the second fastest time in the world in 1966. Ryun continued to show how fantastic he was when just a few hours later he anchored the winning Frosh-Juco mile relay to victory in 3:15.5 for another Relays record.

## 1967

The 42nd annual Kansas Relays were chock-full of record-breaking performances, but the record that everyone was paying attention to was Jim Ryun's mile. A record crowd of 23,700

was treated to thrill after thrill as 12 total records were broken and four others were tied. There were great performances by individual athletes and by relay teams with Rice's units repeating in three University relays and Texas Southern's flashing speedsters rolling to three college division marks. Steve Herndon of Missouri grabbed a share of the spotlight with a seven-foot high jump, Fred Burton of Wichita with a 16-7 pole vault, Chris McCubbins of Oklahoma State with an 8:46.6 triumph in the 3,000-meter steeplechase, and Jim Hines of Texas Southern, who tied the oldest mark on the books with a 9.4 in the 100 plus running two great anchor carries for the Tigers. Ryun, the slender Kansas sophomore, added two records to his bulging collection as he broke his own Kansas Relays record as well as the national collegiate record.

## 1968

Foul weather put a damper on the 43rd Kansas Relays as puddles were standing all over the track and infield until the last day, when some 20,000 fans poured into Memorial Stadium -- mostly to see Kansas' Jim Ryun. Ryun did not disappoint as he tested a strained hamstring muscle and still pulled off a convincing victory in the 1,500 meters in a good time of 3:42.8. The Ryun victory, however, was only one of many thrills on a day which saw a world record equaled, a race lost because of a miscalculation of where the finish line was, and the sprint duel of a week spoiled by a disqualification. Charlie

Greene, a graduate of Nebraska, equaled the world mark of 10 seconds flat in the 100 meter dash. Jim Hines, one of the eight athletes who also shared that record, was disqualified when he was twice called for false starts. Billy Mills, former Kansas star and Olympic gold medalist, thought that the finish line was at the end of the runway instead of the mid-point of the 10,000 meter run. As a result, his kick was only 25 yards and was not enough to overtake Jim Murphy of Air Force. Chuck Rogers of Colorado cleared 17-0.50 in the pole vault to set a new standard. Other records included Doug Knop of Kansas in the discus, Lennox Burgher of Nebraska in the triple jump and Ryun's 1,500.

## 1969

KU athletes dominated the 44th annual Kansas Relays as the Jayhawks took four relay crowns and seven individual titles while doing the most damage on Saturday. Jim Ryun provided the topper for the great showing as the Jayhawk senior, running in his last Relays in a KU uniform, ran a 3:57.6 mile on the end of KU's distance medley relay, which resulted in a world record time of 9:33.0. Jim Niehouse led off with a 1:50.4 half-mile, Randy Julian cranked out a 47.1 quarter mile and KU's lead was three yards. Thorn Bigley ran a solid 2:57.9 three-quarter leg, but it wasn't good enough as Drake's Gordon Hoffert ran a blistering 2:56.2 to give the Bulldogs the lead. Ryun wasted no time making up the deficit and then some as KU celebrated the world record. Only

Kansas State and Rice broke the Jayhawks' relay domination. Ken Swenson of K-State beat Texas' David Matina as the Wildcats took the two-mile relay. Rice took the mile relay with a fine 3:07.0. Kansas' total of four relays and seven individual winners had never been equaled in the 145-meet history of the Texas Relays-Kansas Relays-Drake Relays circuit. In the shot put ring, Karl Salb led a 1-2-3 finish for Kansas as he heaved it 63-5.50 to beat teammates Steve Wilhelm and Doug Knop. Jon Callen of Wichita East took over the Kansas high school all-time best two-mile record with a 9:03.4. Kansas legend Al Oerter made his way back to the Relays and showed the crowd he could still toss the discus, winning the event with a fling of 189-7.50, much to his own surprise.

## 1970

In the 45th version of the Kansas Relays, the meet took on a whole new look when runners got the chance to race on the Hershberger Track. The new all-weather track, funded by former KU sprinter Jim Hershberger, was expanded to eight lanes. The tartan track could not have come at a better time, and was put to the test under a steady downpour of rain and succeeded as athletes turned in standout performances. Distance running phenom Larbi Oukada of Morocco delighted the crowd and was voted Most Outstanding Performer. Running for Fort Hays State, Oukada won the six-mile run in a record time of 28:45.5. He also anchored Fort Hays to victory in the distance medley and finished third in the 3,000-meter steeple-

plechase. Karl Salb of Kansas needed only one throw - 66 feet, four inches - to break the University division shot put record, but had to settle for second as Olympian Randy Matson heaved the shot 67-9.50. Doug Knop, another Jayhawk Goliath, won his third-straight Relays discus title by sailing the platter 182-5. Missouri's Mel Gray and KU's Phil Reaves staged an exciting dual in the 100-yard dash with Gray coming out the victor.

## 1971

The 46th Kansas Relays were dedicated to Dr. Ed Elbel, who was managing the Relays for the 41st time. Twelve world and national record holders competed in the 1971 Relays, including famous names such as Jim Ryun, Randy Matson, Bruce Jenner, Cliff Branch and Frank Shorter. The Relays were a return to glory as it was the first meet on the Hershberger track without the hindrance of rain showers. The fans came out in bunches to see the return of Ryun, who promptly circled the mile in the fastest time in two and a half years, 3:55.8. Competing in the decathlon, Bruce Jenner bested the field with a point total of 7,330. The shot put was won by Matson competing for the Texas Striders with a toss of 68-3.50. The Mills brothers of Texas A&M led Aggie teammates Steve Barre and Donnie Rogers to record times in the 440 and 880. Mel Gray of Missouri claimed his third-straight 100 title with a time of 9.5. Florida law student Frank Shorter shaved an incredible 30 seconds off the Relays record in winning the three-mile run in 13:08.6.

## 1972

A record crowd of 32,000 came out in 70-degree temperatures to witness the 47th annual Kansas Relays. Although the main attraction was to see the great miler Jim Ryun, there was much more going on at these Relays. Demonstrators and protestors positioned themselves on the hill to sing out against bombing in North Vietnam. Meanwhile on the track, Herb Washington of Michigan opened a string of feature events with a record-breaking 100-yard dash time of 9.2. In the shot put, Al Feuerbach defeated Olympic champion Randy Matson with a record heave of 69-1 to break Matson's record of 68-3.25 set the year before. Kjell Isaksson, the world record-holder in the pole vault, won the open vault with 17-5. With the majority of the fans in attendance to see their home-town hero, Jim Ryun, who didn't disappoint. The Wichita native won the mile in a time of 3:57.1, good enough to please the crowd, but a disappointing performance for his high standards. Additionally, KU sophomore Barry Schur became the first Kansas athlete to clear seven feet in the high jump. His jump of 7-1 set the new Kansas Relays meet record.

## 1973

At the 48th Kansas Relays, Eastern New Mexico's Mike Boit was honored with Most Outstanding Performer accolades after anchoring both the winning sprint medley and distance medley baton teams, as well as the second-place mile relay foursome. Records were set or tied in the 440-yard relay, four-mile relay, 120-yard hurdles, triple jump and discus. Kansas great Wes Santee returned to run the masters 440 and 880-yard runs and finished first with a time of 2:05.7. Phillip Ndoo of Eastern New Mexico dazzled the fans with wins in the 3,000-meter steeplechase and the Julius Marks six-mile run. Al Feuerbach of the Pacific Coast Track Club bested his own Relays record with a 69-2.50 shot put heave. Terry Ziegler toured the marathon in a record time two hours, 15 minutes and 15 seconds. Led by Dave Wottle, Bowling Green University set a Relays record of 16:24.0 in the four-mile relay. Kansas' Terry Porter won the pole vault with a leap of 17-0.

## 1974

Under a downpour of rain and 30 mile per hour winds, the 49th Kansas Relays went on as five meet records were broken. Kenyan Phil Ndoo, who was named Most Outstanding Performer, won three watches as he set a meet record in the six-mile run, followed by titles in the three-mile run and two-mile relay. He went for a fourth win as he tried to defend his title in the 3,000-meter steeplechase, but fell short. Mark Lutz dazzled a world-class laden Open Division 220 field with a brilliant wind-aided 20.3 performance. Lutz was just better than Joe Pouncy of Southern Methodist, Larry Burton of Purdue and Ivory Crockett of the Philadelphia Pioneer Athletic Club. KU's Danny Seay leaped an incredible 26-9 in the long jump in the midst of a heavy downpour. Marshall Smith of Colorado College broke the Relays discus record by over five feet with a throw of 194-11. Rick Wohlhuter won the Glenn Cunningham Mile in 4:08.1, Crockett took home the 100-yard dash title in 9.5 and Bruce Jenner won the decathlon.

## 1975

The 50th annual Kansas Relays marked a year of quantity and quality. Events were added to give something for everyone, but at the same time many top-notch athletes came to Mount Oread for a fine show. World record holders Ivory Crockett, Dave Roberts and Rick Wohlhuter were among the stars in attendance. Wohlhuter won the mile easily. Maxie Parks won the open 440 in 47.3. Kansas State easily worked over the competition in the two-mile relay at 7:28.8. Eastern New Mexico College took the College distance medley baton title for the fourth-straight year. With Nolan Cromwell running the first leg, Kansas won the Chuck Cramer Mile Relay. Charlton Ehizuelen of Illinois won the Most Outstanding Performer award after taking his second-straight triple jump crown and winning the long jump. This year's Relays also marked an expansion of the women's events from two relays in 1974 to two relays and eight individual events in 1975.

## 1976

The 51st Kansas Relays continued to expand as 1976 marked the first year that a full array of women's events were sponsored. Famous runner Rick Wohl-huter, competing for the Chicago Track Club, established a new 1,500 meter record with a swift 3:38.62. For the second-straight year, Kansas' relay team of Nolan Cromwell, Waddell Smith, Jay Wagner and Randy Benson won the mile relay. Cromwell also won the Cliff Cushman 400-meter intermediate hurdles. Arkansas State standout Ed Preston took the top spot in the 100- and 200-meter dashes, establishing the standard in the 100 as it was the first time the event was run. Frank Shorter of the Florida Track Club erased the previous mark in the 5,000-meter run with a blazing 14:17.2. In the 3,000-meter steeplechase, Randy Smith improved the record to 8:33.68. Kansas football legend Nolan Cromwell led a mile relay foursome to the title, as well as picking up Most Outstanding Performer Award.

## 1977

At the rain-drenched 52nd Kansas Relays, Kansas women's graduate assistant track coach Teri Anderson made a big splash by setting an American-best and meet record 16:08.8 in the 5,000-meter run. Records were set in four events the first day alone, as New Mexico freshman Peter Butler captured the 10,000-meter run in 29:10.1. Around 1,000 fans made their way to the discus ring to see former Jayhawk great Al Oerter launch the discus 190-5 feet. KU junior Clifford Wiley sped to two wins in the open 100 and 200 meter dashes, defeating some top competitors, including the defending champion Ed Preston. Kansas great Sheila Calmese won the 100-meter dash in a time of 11.63. Arkansas took home its third straight distance medley relay crown led by anchorman Niall O'Shaughnessy. Bob McLeod of Pittsburg State broke Frank Shorter's 5,000 meter record.

## 1978

The 53rd Kansas Relays was barely the Kansas Relays. In fact, the University and Open Divisions were in Norman, Okla. With renovations being done on Memorial Stadium, the Relays took on numerous sites including Norman, junior college events at Haskell, high school events at Shawnee Mission Northwest and at Emporia State, where the college entrants competed. The only event intact was the marathon, which remained in Lawrence. The Sooners dominated the "Kansas-Oklahoma Relays" as Sooner sophomore William Snoddy grabbed much of the spotlight by winning the 200-meter dash and then anchoring the winning 880-yard relay team. In all, Snoddy took home five championship watches. Bob Roggy of Southern Illinois hurled the javelin 290-7.50, a throw meet officials called the best of the year. The 1978 Relays brought about a refreshing change as high school girls competition was added.

## 1979

Around 40 records were established or broken in the 54th Kansas Relays as many new events were introduced and others were changed to the metric system. Kansas'

relay team of Deon Hogan, Stan Whitaker, Tommy McCall and Lester Mickens took home the championship in the mile relay in a time of 3:07.55. Kansas State's Vince Parette set a new meet record of 54-6.75 in the triple jump. Kipsubai Koskei of New Mexico won the Most Outstanding Performer award. The Shawnee Mission South foursome of Craig Carter, John Breeden, Brent Steiner and Steve Smith took over the high school distance medley relay standard with a time of 10:19.93, a mark that still stands in 2009.

## 1980

The 55th Kansas Relays was billed as one of the strongest fields in several years as world-class athletes such as Renaldo Nehemiah, Houston McTear, James Mallard, Steve Riddick, Ron Livers, Tony Darden, Mike Carter, Mel Lattany and Emmit King were among the competitors. The Philadelphia Pioneer foursome of Riddick, Herman Frazier, Fred Taylor and Darden breezed through the 880-yard relay tour in 1:21.55 to break the U.S. mark. Freshman sensation Michael Carter of Southern Methodist heaved the shot put 62-6.50 inches for the win although he suffered from an upset stomach. 1980 marked the first year that both a male and female Most Outstanding Athlete were named, with Jocelyn Bentley of Highland Park taking home the first women's award.

## 1981

Former Kansas sprinter Cliff Wiley highlighted the 56th Kansas Relays as the KU law student took home the Most Outstanding Performer award after winning the open 100 and 400-meter dashes. Al Oerter lit up the discus ring with a fling of 204-9 to take the top honors in the event named after him. Greg Schaper of Arkansas State won the open high jump in a meet-record 7-3.50, while KU grad Jay Reardon was second at 7-1.75. Dana Olson of Houston took the women's open javelin crown in a Relays record 160-10, while Ernie Billups of the Chicago Track Club also set a meet record winning the masters 800 in 2:00.3. Relay event records were set by Oklahoma in the women's mile relay, sprint medley relay and two-mile relay. The Philadelphia Pioneer Track Club posted several impressive wins, but none were record-setting performances.

## 1982

The 57th Kansas Relays were highlighted by meet outstanding performers Tyke Peacock of Kansas and Merlene Ottey of Nebraska, who won her second-straight Most Outstanding Performer honor. Numerous new marks were set in the throws including Robert Weir of SMU who smashed the hammer throw record by more than 25 feet with a throw of 222-8. Pinkie Suggs of Manhattan High broke her own mark in the girls shot put, extending her throw to 46-11.50. Mike Lehmann of Illinois topped Karl Salb's shot put standard with a heave of 67-2.25. Ottey dominated the 100 and 200-meter dashes, setting new records in both. Joe Dial of Oklahoma State claimed a victory in the pole vault with a jump of 17-0, beating out Kansas' Jeff Buckingham in the process.

## 1983

The 1983 Kansas Relays took on an international flavor as a contingent of 12 athletes from the Soviet Union made a historic visit to Memorial Stadium in the midst of the Cold War. The Relays had never seen an international team of better quality than the Soviets. Several members were ranked in the top-10 of their respective events when they made the trip across the Atlantic. In all, the Soviets won nine events and set seven Relays records, three of which still stand. Among those marks set included 8,252 points in the decathlon by Grigory Degtyarev, breaking the 1974 mark of United States gold medalist Bruce Jenner. The mark stood for 14 years until Steve Fritz broke it in 1997. Fans were also treated to several other record-setting performances from the Soviet athletes, including Svetlana Ulmasova's time of 9:13.50 in the women's

3,000-meter run. Other records that were broken by the Soviet athletes included Janis Bojars in the shot put (68-7.75), Alexander Krupsky in the pole vault (18-4), Nikolai Musyenko in the triple jump (55-9.25), Yuri Tamm in the hammer throw (244-2) and Nadezhda Raldugina in the 1,500-meter run (4:08.94). Each member of the Soviet contingent was given a Relays watch to commemorate their time in Lawrence. 1983 also marked the 20th anniversary of women's track & field at the University of Kansas.

## 1984

International athletes again highlighted the 59th Kansas Relays, but this time it was athletes from countries other than the Soviet Union. Morocco's Nawal El Moutawakel, competing for Iowa State, set a new women's collegiate record of 55.67 in the 400-meter intermediate hurdles. Coming into the Relays, El Moutawakel was already an Olympic qualifier for the Moroccan team. Another Cyclone, Sunday Uti of Nigeria, won the 400-meter dash and anchored the surprising 440-yard winning relay team. K-State's freshman Kenny Harrison leaped 52-1.50 on his first triple jump attempt before pulling out of the competition, but it turned out to be the winning mark. El Moutawakel and Scott Lofquist, the men's discus winner, were named Most Outstanding Performers. Kansas thrower Clint Johnson won the shot put with a heave of 62-5. The Nebraska women's sprint medley foursome demolished the Relays record with a quick time of 1:40.28. In all, five women's records were broken and the women's triple jump was established as a new event. 1984 also marked Olympic gold medal winner Billy Mills' return to the Relays to be inducted into the Kansas Relays Hall of Fame.

## 1985

In the 60th Kansas Relays Joe Dial, competing unattached, and Michelle Maxey of Kansas State were named the Most Outstanding Performers. Dial set two records in the pole vault as he vaulted 18-5 in the preliminaries to break the University record of 18-4.50 set by Steve Stubblefield in 1984. Dial broke the Invitational record in the finals with a vault of 18-8. Maxey won the women's 400-meter dash, anchored Kansas State's winning sprint medley relay team and ran the second leg on the Lady Wildcats' winning 440-yard relay team.

## 1986

The 61st Kansas Relays were led by Kenny Harrison of Kansas State and Pinkie Suggs, formerly of Kansas State. Both were named Most Outstanding Performers. Harrison set a new Relays record in the triple jump, jumping 55-11 to break the old University mark of 55-9.50 by Nikolai Musyenko of the Soviet Union. Suggs established a new mark of 53-8 in the shot, eclipsing the 53-4 standard set by Elaine Sobansky in 1984. Besides Suggs' record-breaking performance, the top-four competitors were all within four feet of each other. Additionally, Harold Hadley set a new Masters' record in the 800-meter run. His time of 1:57.84 broke his previous record of 1:58.61.

## 1987

The 62nd Kansas Relays were highlighted by former Oklahoma State pole vaulter Joe Dial, who earned his third Relays' Most Outstanding Performer award. Dial completed his hat trick after becoming the first high school athlete to win the award (1980), winning the honor as an Oklahoma State competitor (1985) and then finally capping off his Relays career with the award in 1987 as an unattached athlete. Dial smashed the Relays' pole vault record with an eye-popping 19-4.75 vault. In women's action, LaTonya Sheffield of the San Diego Track Club led a baton team to a blazing Kansas Relays record time of 3:36.57 in the mile relay. Nebraska's Renita Robinson's leap of 43-0 in the triple jump shattered the previous women's record of 41-5.25 by over a foot-and-a-half. Kansas legend Al Oerter was also present to be inducted into the Kansas Sports Hall of Fame. Oerter was a four-time Olympic gold medal winner in the discus.

## 1988

In the 63rd Kansas Relays, the show was stolen by high school junior Leah Kirklan of John Marshall (Okla.) High School. Kirklan won the triple jump at 41-1 and long jump at 19-4.50, both Kansas Relays records although the triple jump wound up being disallowed because of wind. Kirklan topped her weekend by anchoring the winning 440-yard relay team. Kirklan's counterparts on the John Marshall boys team set a new record in the 440-yard relay of 42.03. The old record of 42.30 was set in 1985, also by John Marshall. In a very exciting college high jump, Hollis Conway of Southwestern Louisiana and Tom Smith of Illinois State both cleared 7-3.50 with Conway taking the title. William Beasley of Arkansas nationally qualified in the triple jump as he easily won the event with an effort of 54-5. The men's javelin featured four national qualifying performances with Ron Bahm winning the event unattached with a throw of 232-3. KU's Vince Labosky finished second with a throw of 228-11. Scott Huffman of Kansas won the event that would later be named after him, as he took his first Relays title in the pole vault. Huffman's national qualifying effort of 18-00.50 feet was nearly five inches higher than the second place finisher. Long-time Kansas coaching legend Bob Timmons coached his final Kansas Relays for the University of Kansas. Timmons officially retired following the 1988 season.

## 1989

The 64th Kansas Relays saw several record-setting performances. Eastern Michigan's Mark Dailey set the Relays and Memorial Stadium record in the 800 meters and was named the men's Most Outstanding Performer for his efforts. Kansas State's Kim Kilpatrick, Missouri's Felicia Allen and Jenks High School's Amy Rodehaver were all declared the 1989 Relays Most Outstanding Female Performers. In an exciting Invitational pole vault, KU's Pat Manson edged former Jayhawk Scott Huffman with a national qualifying mark of 18-3. Karen Welke and Kimberly Haluscsak of Michigan dominated the women's 5,000-meter run with a one-two finish in the event. Craig Watcke of Kansas won the men's 5,000 with a time of 14:45.31.

## 1990

Drake sprinter Kevin Little and Kansas State All-America thrower Angie Miller took top honors in the 65th Kansas Relays. Little delighted the crowd in the 100 and 200-meter dashes, while Miller flung the discus 163-5 and heaved the shot put 50-10 for two wins. Rachelle Roberts of Iowa floated 4:23.16 in the women's Invitational 1,500-meter run to claim a new Relays record. David Johnston of Lawrence High was a triple winner taking first in the mile run, the two-mile run and as a member of the two-mile relay team. Shanele Stires of Salina Central took first place in the shot put and javelin and third in the discus. Lawrence High School completed a sweep of the meet's four high school relays with wins in the 440, mile, two-mile and distance medley relays.

## 1991

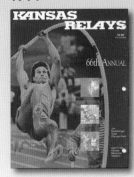

Barton County Community College made a clean sweep of the Most Outstanding Performer awards in 1991 as Marlon Cannon and Beverly McDonald took the honors. Cannon was a four-time winner, taking the titles in the 400-meter dash, sprint medley relay, 440-yard relay and mile relay. McDonald competed in five events, finishing first in four. She helped her team with two individual titles in the 100- and 200-meter dashes, and grabbed relay titles in the 440- and 880-yard relays. She also finished second in the sprint medley relay. McDonald's 200 time of 23.48 was good for a new Relays records. Laverne Eve of the Bahamas set a new standard in the women's javelin, while Penny Neer of the Nike Coast Club set a new mark in the discus. Other records were set in the women's 880-yard relay, boys 800 meters, boys triple jump and women's 100-meter hurdles. The Kansas men's distance medley team of Donnie

Anderson, Kwanza Johnson, Dan Waters and Michael Cox took home a set of champions' watches for their winning effort in a time of 9:50.70. Additionally, the men's four-mile relay team won the prestigious Relays watch on an incredible anchor leg by freshman Michael Cox. The KU women's two-mile relay team outran runner-up Kentucky to win watches of their own. Former KU standout Scott Huffman cleared 18-0 to win the Open pole vault.

## 1992

Kansas sophomore Michael Cox led the Jayhawks to a four-mile relay title and picked up the Most Outstanding Performer honor at the 67th Kansas Relays. Inez Turner of Barton County Community College was named the women's Most Outstanding Performer. She won the 400 in a time of 53.8 and also ran on the winning distance medley and mile relay teams. DeSoto's Carrie Buckley threw a Relays record 156-4 in the javelin while Sheldon Carpenter of Shawnee Mission East sailed a record 7-1.25 in the boys high jump. Heather Burroughs of Kansas City Pembroke Hill won both the two mile and mile. KU's MaryBeth Labosky nationally qualified in the high jump and broke the University of Kansas record in the high jump, leaping 6-1.50. Four athletes in the women's javelin throw nationally qualified in the event. Kim Engle of American Big Guys crushed the competition in the event with a throw of 173 feet. KU's Julia Saul won the 3,000-meter run with a time of 9:36.38. Former Kansas State All-American

Steve Fritz defended his title in the men's decathlon. Fritz, along with runner-up Rick Schwieger, qualified for the Olympic Trials with their performances. Former Kansas Athletic Director Bob Frederick placed 87th in the town and campus 10,000-meter road race. MaryBeth Labosky of Kansas won the women's high jump with a leap of 6-1 while senior Cathy Palacios won the 1,500 meters with a winning time of 4:28.7. Former Jayhawk Pat Manson won the pole vault with a leap of 18-4.

## 1993

The 68th Kansas Relays nearly escaped without a record being broken, but the women's distance medley relay team of Jessica Kluge, Richelle Webb, Karen Harvey and Molly McClimon of Michigan changed that when they set a new standard with a time of 11:32.61. Inez Turner of Barton County Community College won her second consecutive Most Outstanding Performer award. Turner was a winner in the 400-meter dash for the second-straight year. Julia Saul of Kansas won the 10,000-meter run with ease as she paced the field with a time of 35:15.0. Jayhawk high jumper and All-American MaryBeth Labosky broke her own University record in the event with a first-place finish and best jump of 6-1.75. Due to afternoon rains, the Elite Open pole vault was moved inside to Anschutz Pavilion where former Jayhawk Scott Huffman won another Relays title.

## 1994

The 69th edition of the Kansas Relays was a success for Jayhawk fans. KU won both the men's and women's Collegiate team titles, while Natasha Shafer became the first Kansas woman to be named Most Outstanding Performer. Former Arkansas athlete Ed Kaminski won his fourth consecutive Relays javelin crown. He threw 241-2, outdistancing John Corwin of Johnson County Track Club. Kevin Toth won his second-straight shot put title with a toss of 65-4.75. John Bazzoni won his third Kansas Relays pole vaulting championship, clearing 17-4.50. Oklahoma's Kim Roland leaped 19-6.50 on her final long jump attempt for a thrilling victory. Senior Daniela Daggy won the 5,000 in 17:22.31. Barton County's Richard Kosgei won the men's 10,000 in 30:10.3. KU's Cheryl Evers won the women's shot put while her brother, Michael, also performed well, qualifying for the NCAA meet in the decathlon. With a winning time of 10:00.29, the KU men's distance medley relay brought home Relays gold. Additionally, the Jayhawk women won the 400-meter relay. A new twist was thrown into the 1994 Relays with the introduction of the team relay trophy, which is given to the teams who score the most points.

## 1995

Kansas senior distance runner Michael Cox and Kansas junior sprinter Dawn Steele-Slavens swept the Most Outstanding Performer honors for the Jayhawks at the 70th Kansas Relays. Cox's attempt at a sub-four minute mile came up short with a time of 4:00.93, which was still good for first place. The time marked the fourth-best time ever by a Jayhawk miler. He also ran the final leg on the four-mile relay team. Steele-Slavens placed first in the 400-meter hurdles and as a member of the 400-meter relay team. KU also got a win in the high jump when senior Nick Johannsen cleared the bar at 7-1.75. Maurice Greene, who was coming off a 100-meter dash win over Carl Lewis just two weeks earlier at the Texas Relays, ran the final leg for Nike Central in the 400-meter relay. Former Jayhawks Pat Manson and Scott Huffman finished first and second in the Invitational pole vault. The Jayhawk 400-meter relay team of Diamond Williams, LaTanya Holloway, Steele-Slavens and Natasha Shafer edged in-state rival Kansas State to win the event. Johannsen won the Carl Rice High Jump with a provisional mark of 7-1.75. Garden City senior Jason Archibald cleared a meet record 7-3 in the high jump. Emporia senior and KU signee Kevin McGinn was a two-event champion, winning the high school boys mile and anchoring Emporia's winning distance medley relay. KU ended the day with wins in three relay events: the men's distance medley, women's 400-meter relay and the women's two-mile relay.

## 1996

The 71st Kansas Relays added a new chapter to the Relays' history as Columbia Healthcare signed on to become the Kansas Relays' title sponsor. The partnership was formed to attract top-level athletes and in turn larger audiences on an annual basis by creating feature events and higher appearance guarantees. 1996 marked a reunion for some of the greatest athletes in KU history. Returning to the Relays were Billy Mills, Jim Ryun, Bill Alley, Wes Santee, Mark Lutz, Clifford Wiley and Kent Floerke. Each of these athletes were former Olympic competitors. The 1996 Relays also featured a new event as the women's pole vault was held for the first time. Stacy Dragila, the top-ranked vaulter in America, won the event and set the American record by clearing 13-6.50. Her effort earned her the 1996 women's Most Outstanding Performer achievement. Kansas miler Michael Cox picked up his third Relays male Most Outstanding Performer accolade after becoming only the third KU runner to run the mile under four minutes, doing so in a time of 3:59.2. Ed Kaminski of the Nike Track Club won the men's javelin with a toss of 251-4 with KU's Jeff Dieterich finishing as the runner-up. Bill Deering won the Invitational pole vault, clearing 18-10. Maurice Greene won the Invitational 100-meter dash in a time of 10.23. Kevin Toth of Nike was the shot put champion with a throw of 67-0. Kwani Stewart, also of Nike, won the women's 100 meters in 13.28, a Relays record. KU's Dawn Steele-Slavens won the 400-meter hurdles in a time of 1:00.3.

## 1997

The 72nd Kansas Relays was a very successful one, particularly for KU. Not only did the team earn several individual titles, but the men were named University Relays champions. 1997 marked the inaugural running of the women's 3,000-meter steeplechase. The event also saw unattached competitor Kevin Toth, who was named the men's Most Outstanding Performer, shatter the Relays' 24-year-old shot put record. Toth's throw of 71-2.50 made him the 1997 world leader. Steve Fritz, of Accusplit Sports, set a new mark in the Jim Bausch Decathlon with 8,380 points. Octavius Terry, unattached, ran the 400-meter hurdles in a Relays record time of 49.10. In women's action, Renetta Seiler of Kansas State flung the hammer throw a record 195-5 feet.

## 1998, 1999

The Kansas Relays were cancelled due to renovations on Memorial Stadium in 1998 and 1999. A Kansas-only high school event was hosted by Olathe East coach Mike Wallace during these years. As the year 2000 approached, it seemed to most that after 72 editions, the Kansas Relays had awarded its last trophy. Declining interest, shrinking budgets, NCAA qualifying mark-chasing and a general apathy all played a role in these dark years of the Kansas Relays.

## 2000

The 2000 track and field season marked the 73rd running of the Kansas Relays as a field of world-class athletes joined the Relays to bring in the new millennium. The Kansas Relays returned with the excitement and energy that fans had enjoyed from years past. The eventual 2000 Olympic gold medal winner in the 100 meters, Maurice Greene, highlighted the meet when his relay team of Curtis Johnson, Ato Boldon and Brian Howard set a new stadium and Relays record with a blazing time of 38.45 seconds in the 400-meter relay. Kansas' Andrea Branson took home the top spot with a personal-best and record-breaking height of 13-10 in the pole vault. Jayhawk junior Scott Russell took first place in both the hammer throw and javelin. In high school action, Jenks High of Oklahoma shattered the Relays record in the girls distance medley relay with a time of 12:29.29. A crowd of 12,500 came out on a perfect spring afternoon to see the Relays once again in full bloom. Director Tim Weaver made his first attempt to lead the meet and brought 27 present or future Olympians to Memorial Stadium.

## 2001

The 2001 Relays, "An Olympic Return," marked the 74th anniversary of the event, and saw some big names make their way back to their old stomping grounds. Day three of the Relays was a day of record-breaking performances. Eight Kansas Relays records were broken along with a Memorial Stadium record in the women's shot put by Kansas State's Rebekah Green. Other broken records included the men's 110-meter shuttle hurdle relay (Nebraska, 54.02), the girls javelin throw (Kendra Wecker, Marysville, 166-7), the girls 300-meter hurdles (Julie Curtis, Manhattan, 43.26), women's sprint medley relay (SMS, 3:50.74), girls distance medley relay, (Jenks, Okla., 12:29.29) and the girls pole vault (Lindsey Bourne, Joplin, Mo., 11-11.75). Two-time Olympic gold medalist Yuriy Syedikh, the world record holder in the men's hammer throw, won the Kansas Relays with a toss of 204-5 at the age of 45. Olympian Robert Howard won an exciting long jump competition, leaping 26-7 over runner-up Melvin Lister. Howard also won the triple jump competition on his way to earning Male Outstanding Performer honors. Competing unattached in his redshirt season for KU, Charlie Gruber was victorious in the men's mile. KU assistant coach Doug Reynolds won the discus, beating Andy Bloom of Nike. Olympian Nathan Leeper won the high jump at 7-3, and KU's own Brian Blachly won the men's 1,500 meters.

## 2002

The 2002 Kansas Relays marked the 75th anniversary of the event. After a lightning strike and a 90-minute delay due to inclement weather, officials were forced to cancel the final day of action midway through competition after an exciting three and a half days. In total, over 40 events were cancelled because of the rain, including all of the Invitational running events that were scheduled to feature 22 Olympians and four world record holders. Despite being cut short, the Kansas athletes got off to a good start when senior Scott Russell won his second Kansas Relays hammer title with a heave of 206-5. The Jayhawks picked up two first-place finishes on the third day, winning both the women's and men's distance medley races. The team of Brian Blachly, Jabari Wamble, Brandon Hodges and Charlie Gruber teamed for the victory on the men's side with a time of 9:54.88. The women's foursome of Laura Lavoie, Kim Clark, Stacy Keller and Katy Eisenmenger took the title with a time of 11:42.21. Despite the untimely weather, five high school girls Kansas Relays records were broken including the 3,200-meter run, the distance medley, the discus, the 800-meter relay and the 1,600-meter sprint medley relay. The high school boys 800-meter relay record was also broken. In addition, 11 NCAA provisional and three automatic marks were recorded in the three-day event.

## 2003

Kansas State's Rebekah Green, the Kansas Relays shot put record-holder, found success in a different throwing event, adding the 2003 Kansas Relays hammer throw champion to her list of accolades with a first-place throw of 181-6. Records were set in the men's shuttle hurdle relay (Nebraska, 59.10), the boys 800-meter run (Marble Falls' Leonel Manzano, 1:51.54), the boys 400-meter relay (Jenks, 41.60) and the girls 800-meter run (Shawnee Heights' Trisa Nickoley, 2:12.53). Highlighting the women's events was Nike's Trecia Smith, claiming her third-consecutive Kansas Relays women's triple jump title with a distance of 43-7 feet. Despite opening the final day of the 2003 Kansas Relays with heavy showers and lightning that caused a two-hour delay in Memorial Stadium, all but eight events were completed before the storm returned. The rain could not stop record-breaking performances however, as men's shot put competitor Kevin Toth threw a massive 74-4.50, the best throw in the world since 1988 and a new Relays record. Toth's mark was later voided due to a violation of doping rules. The highly anticipated men's Invitational mile title was claimed by former Kansas standout Charlie Gruber with a time of 4:05.21. Premier miler Alan Webb of Nike came in second (4:06.73) and high school standout Adam Perkins came in third (4:10.12).

## 2004

A total of 16 records were broken or tied over three days of outstanding competition at the 77th annual Kansas Relays. The amazing weather and record-breaking performances made way for one of the most exciting weekends the Relays have ever seen. Nathan Leeper and Austra Skujyte were named the Most Outstanding Performers of the meet. Leeper recorded a first-place finish in the men's high jump with a mark of 7-5.75, which stood as the second-best in the world. Skujyte won the women's long jump with a mark of 20-4.25 and took home the shot put title with a throw of 52-1.25. Fort Collins High School senior Sarah Stevens and K.C. Central High School senior Julius Jiles were named Most Outstanding High School Performers of the meet. Stevens set two Kansas Relays records in the shot put and discus with marks of 48-8.25 and 156-6, respectively. Jiles tied the Kansas Relays record in the 300-meter hurdles with a time of 37.42 and won the 110-meter hurdles title with a time of 14.23. Stevens started off the day by setting the Kansas Relays record in the shot put, a record previously held by Kansas State's Pinkie Suggs, who threw the shot 46-11.50 at the 1982 Kansas Relays. Former Jayhawk All-American Leo Bookman won the Invitational 100-meter dash in what would have been a Kansas Relay record time of 10.04, if it were not for too much wind. Shawnee Heights senior Trisa Nickoley won her fourth-straight 800-meter title at the Kansas Relays in a record time of 2:06.76. Nickoley broke her own record of 2:12.53 that was set at the 2003 Kansas Relays. Former KU great Scott Russell recorded a first-place finish for Nike Athletics in the javelin with a throw of 242-08.

## 2005

The third-largest crowd (24,619) enjoyed the 78th edition of the Relays under pristine conditions and witnessed record-setting performances. 2005 introduced the Gold Zone, a three hour window on Saturday that featured some of the top professional track and field athletes in the country, including 30 former Olympians. Fans witnessed the return of local favorite Maurice Greene, the former Olympic 100-meter champion, who placed third in the Goldzone 100-meter dash and took first in the 400-meter relay as part of the HSI team. Also appearing was former Olympian Marion Jones, whose 4x200m relay team won its event but was disqualified due to a late hand-off foul. Former KU greats Amy Linnen and Leo Bookman also returned to the Kansas Relays. Linnen finished second in the women's Invitational pole vault while Bookman captured the men's Invitational 200 meters. Nike's Muna Lee was selected as one of the meet's Most Outstanding Performers after breaking the women's 100 meters record in a blazing time of 11.10. The previous record was held by the legendary Merlene Ottey, who had established the record in 1983.

## 2006

The 79th annual Kansas Relays saw the second-largest crowd in the event's history, as 26,211 fans witnessed the four days of competition. The highlight of the weekend was the Gold Zone II event, featuring professional athletes and Olympians from around the country. In the 400-meter invitational relay, Justin Gatlin's Sprint Capitol squad faced off against the HSI team, anchored by Kansas City native and Olympic champion Maurice Greene. Sprint Capitol won the event in an incredible 38.16 seconds, the fastest time in the world in 2006 and the best in Relays history. In the 400-meter Invitational hurdles, Bershawn "Batman" Jackson finished in 48.34 seconds, which was the third-best time in the world in 2006. On the women's side, Allyson Felix broke the Relays record with a time of 11.04 in the 100.

## 2007

The 80th edition of the Kansas Relays saw spectacular competition – as well as weather – over the four days at Memorial Stadium. Bershawn "Batman" Jackson ran the fastest time in the world in 2007 in the 400-meter hurdles, while a handful of Jayhawks picked up individual victories. Fans were treated to several outstanding performances from athletes competing in the Gold Zone event. Jackson's winning time of 48.75 seconds represented the world's best time in the event by over a second and made him the three-time defending Kansas Relays champion. The competition on Saturday started well for KU as senior Eric Babb jumped 7.85 meters to win the men's College long jump. Kansas continued to be successful throughout the day as sophomores Victoria Howard and Sha'Ray Butler collected victories in the women's 100-meter and 400-meter hurdles, respectively. Egor Agafonov, the 2007 national champion in the indoor weight throw, won the men's hammer throw with a season-best toss of 69.33 meters. Agafonov cruised past the competition, besting the second-place finisher by over 20 feet. On the women's side, Zlata Tarasova set a new Kansas Relays record in the women's hammer throw with a toss of 61.93 meters.

## 2008

Over 13,500 fans enjoyed 11 meet records, a world-leading time and several thrilling performances throughout the four days of the 81st Annual Kansas Relays at Memorial Stadium. Kansas junior Nickesha Anderson broke a 30-year old KU record in taking the 100 meter title in a time of 11.23, eclipsing Sheila Calmese's time of 11.44 from the 1978 Arkansas Relays. Nike's Bershawn Jackson won the Male Most Outstanding Performer award after running the fastest time in the world in the 400-meter hurdles. Jackson won the event for the fourth-consecutive time and fifth time in the last six years with a time of 48.32. Millard North High School (Neb.) sophomore Emily Sisson took the Female Most Outstanding Performer honor with meet records in the girls 1,600-meter run and 3,200-meter run. Her time of 4:51.42 in the 1,600 meters topped a four-year-old mark, while her finish of 10:25.42 was 19 seconds faster than Erin Mortimer's time in 2002. In the Candace Mason Heptathlon, Minnesota junior Liz Roehring broke a 24-year-old record in winning the event. Her score of 5,740 points topped the Kansas Relays record set by Deb Clark of Nebraska in 1984. In the 3,000-meter steeplechase, Lauren Bonds led for the majority of the race and crossed the finish line at 11:02.83 to claim the 2008 Kansas Relays title.

## 2009

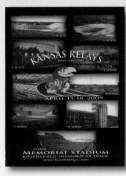

The 82nd edition of the Kansas Relays did not disappoint, as fans again enjoyed four days of superior track and field performances. As the morning drizzle subsided on the final day of competition at the 2009 Kansas Relays, fans witnessed five records broken and saw Emily Sisson of Parkway West High School (St. Louis, Mo.) defend her 1,600-meter title after she successfully defended her 3,200 meter title in a record setting time of 10:31.07. Her repeat titles in 2009 gave her the distinction of being the first high school athlete to win the events representing two different high schools. Sisson also became the first high school girl to win the Most Outstanding Female Performer in back-to-back years. In the boys division, James White of Grandview set the high jump record of 7-03.25 feet, earning Most Outstanding Male Performer accolades. Bonner Springs boys 4x100-meter relay team got to the podium by winning in a Relays record time of 43.53. In the elite field, spectators saw Kansas City native Muna Lee sprint past her competitors to win the women's 200-meter dash. The "race of the day" to the fans' delight was watching Alan Webb run the fifth fastest mile in Kansas Relays history, and the first sub-four minute mile since 1997, as he clocked in at 3:58.90.

# 2010

The 83rd edition of the Kansas Relays was one for the books. Sprinters highlighted the 2010 meet, starting with Nike's Ivory Williams. The sprinter recorded a world-leading 100-meter time of 9.95 seconds Saturday afternoon. Despite enduring two false-start resets, Williams flew out of the blocks on the third go-around and kept pace for the full 100 meters. In addition to running the fastest time in the world at that point in the 2010 season, Williams set a new Kansas Relays record with his blistering 9.95 sprint. He replaced Bredan Christensen in the Relays' record book, who owned the previous record of 10.01, set in 2007. For his stellar efforts in the 100-meter dash, Williams was named the 2010 Kansas

Relays Most Outstanding Male Performer. Two-time Olympic gold medalist Veronica Campbell-Brown etched her name in the Relays' record book as well, sprinting across the 200-meter finish line in 22.32 to best the previous record by more than three tenths of a second. That record was held by Campbell-Brown's 2008 Olympic teammate, Aleen Bailey, since 2001. In addition to the individual Relays' records set on Saturday, Kineke Alexander, Valerie Brown, Shellene Williams and Halimat Ismali (International All Stars) combined for a new meet record-time of 3:35.65 in the women's 4x400-meter relay. In the high school division, Tiffani McReynolds of Pembroke Hill ran the third-fastest prep time in the nation in the 100-meter hurdles, clocking in at 13.73. Her winning time also marked a new Relays' record by nearly two tenths of a second. McReynolds also won the girls 100-meter dash with a time of 11.79. The high school senior was honored as the Most Outstanding Female Performer of the 2010 Relays after capturing two individual titles, one of which was a new meet record.

# 2011

The 84th annual Kansas Relays was a historic occasion as the meet hosted elite shot put and long jump events in a downtown setting for the first time in American history. Nebraska's Nicholas Gordon took the long jump title while Canadian champion Dylan Armstrong won the shot put crown in front of nearly 2,500 fans with a mark of 70-07.25 ft. In the more traditional events,

The Relays saw only two records fall as Andrea Dutoit (Unatt.) set a new top height in the pole vault with a clearance of 14-09 ft. and KU alum and Canadian national record holder Scott Russell smashed his own javelin record with a throw of 268-11 ft. On the high school side Lee's Summit West's girls 4-mile relay team set a new meet record with a time of 21:17.74 en route to claiming their third-consecutive event win. KU's Mason Finley won both the collegiate shot put and discus competitions for the second-straight year. It was another star-studded field on the Jim Hershberger track as Bershawn "Batman" Jackson returned to win his sixth Kansas Relays 400-meter hurdles title, while Olympic sprinter Lauryn Williams ran the second-fastest 100-meters in the U.S. of the year. Blake Leeper, a double-leg amputee, earned the Male Outstanding performer honor for his lightning fast 11.32 in the Paralympic 100-meters. KU freshman Diamond Dixon was named the Outstanding Female Athlete for her school-record performances in the 400 meters and 4x400-meter relay.

# 2012

It was another memorable year at the 85th Relays as just over 14,500 fans inside Memorial Stadium saw Bershawn 'Batman' Jackson reprise his role as one of the top athletes to ever compete at the Kansas Relays. He broke his own 400-meet hurdle record with a world-leading time of 48.20 to claim his seventh KU Relays victory. For the first time in two years, a high schooler was named the Outstanding Female Performer as Shawnee Mission West's Ali Cash earned the distinction after her wins in both the 800-meter and 1,600-meter races. The Relays also hosted the second edition of the elite shot put and long jump events in downtown Lawrence. Reese Hoffa took the trophy in the shot put while Janay DeLoach took the long jump crown. Both Hoffa and DeLoach went on to claim bronze medals at the 2012 London Olympics. In what would be his final competitive appearance at the KU Relays, KU alum and Canadian national record holder Scott Russell won his ninth javelin competition in Lawrence. Twenty-twelve featured another historical moment as fans saw the world record broken for the largest single serving of nachos.

2013

The 2013 Kansas Relays was one of the most memorable on record. Six meet records were either tied or broken. In addition, there were three NCAA or world-leading performances. Michael Tinsley defeated seven-time Relays champion "Batman" Jackson and a star studded field of 400-meter hurdlers by running 48.77, which was the fastest time in the world up to then in 2013. KU's sophomore Michael Stigler was runner-up. For his efforts, Tinsley was selected as the Outstanding Male Athlete. Another race loaded with Olympians and All-Americans was the Glenn Cunningham Mile. Cory Leslie, former All-American at Ohio State, emerged victorious over Leo Manzano, Nick Symmonds and A. J. Acosta, among others. Leslie's time of 3:58.18 marked the 18th time the mile was run under four minutes at the Relays. In a

shorter run, double amputee Blake Leeper took his second Relays victory by running 11.24 in the Paralympic 100-meter dash. The KU men won the mile (3:07.78) and two-mile (7:44.08) relays. In boys competition Papillion-LaVista (Neb.) ran 41.60 to easily win the 400 relay. In women's action, Geneva McCall, the former Southern Illinois national champion, was runner-up in the hammer throw Thursday, winner of the shot put on Friday and discus champion on Saturday with a throw of 177-4. Runner-up in the discus was Jessica Maroszek, KU junior. Former Notre Dame star Mary Saxer pole vaulted 14-9 to tie the Relays record. Former Michigan star Nicole Sifuentes ran 4:14.54 in the 1,500 meters, the fastest time at the Relays since 1983. She won her second race of the day an hour later by running 800 meters in 2:04.17. The KU women won the mile relay by running 3:32.94, the second fastest in Relays history. In girls high school action, Alexa Harmon-Thomas from Free State in Lawrence (Kan.) high jumped 5-8, long jumped 19-4.25, and ran the 100-meter hurdles in 14.30 to become the Outstanding Female Athlete. Lincoln-Way East (Ill.) smashed the previous 400-meter relay record by posting a 47.36.

# About the Author

Joe Schrag is a native of Norwich, Kan., lifelong resident of the Sunflower State and holds a Master of Arts degree in English from the University of Kansas. He has attended every Kansas Relays since 1954 as either an athlete, coach, official or (one year) as a spectator. Schrag is a member of five Halls of Fame including being a 2007 inductee into the Kansas Relays Hall of Fame. Others include the Topeka West High School Athletic Hall of Fame (2003), National High School Athletic Coaches Association Hall of Fame (2005), Kansas State High School Activities Association Hall of Fame (2010) and the Shawnee County Sports Council Hall of Fame (2010). He served as high school meet referee at the KU Relays in 1977. Schrag spent 41 years (1962-2003) at Topeka West High School in Topeka, Kan.,

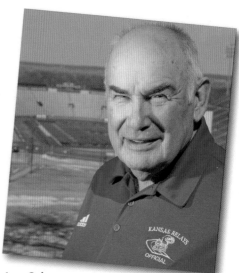

Joe Schrag

serving as coach of track and field and cross country during that entire span. He also taught English and served as athletic director. He sent hundreds of athletes to the Kansas Relays during his years as coach, a career that resulted in eight state championships. A former competitive runner, Schrag completed 37 marathons, including Boston (1972) and New York (1993). He won the Masters age-group titles in Kansas City (1980), Tulsa (1983), Omaha (1985), St. Louis (1988) and Oklahoma City (1989), and was three-time Kansas Collegiate Athletic Conference mile champion while at Bethel College in North Newton. His granddaughters, Zoe and Ava, are always welcome at his rural home south of Topeka, where he resides with his wife Nancy.

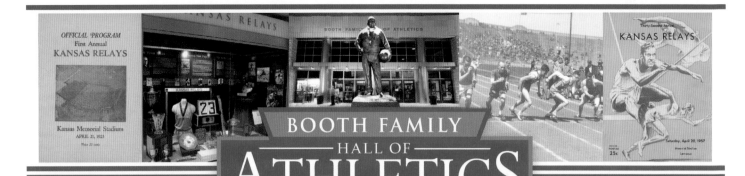

# BOOTH FAMILY
## HALL OF
# ATHLETICS
### KANSAS ATHLETICS

The Booth Family Hall of Athletics honors KU's historic varsity athletics programs, its coaches and student-athletes, past and present.

*COME EXPERIENCE THE HISTORY AND TRADITION OF KANSAS ATHLETICS.*

**LOCATION**
1651 Naismith Drive
Lawrence, KS 66045

**ADMISSION**
FREE to the public.
No food or drinks allowed.

**HOURS OF OPERATION**
Mon.-Sat.: 10 a.m. to 5 p.m.

**TOUR INFO**
All tours are self-guided unless advance reservations are made.

**For more information or to make a reservation:**
785-864-7966
boothhoa@ku.edu